W9-AFU-203

PRIZE STORIES

1996

THE O. HENRY

AWARDS

PRIZE STORIES

1·9·9·6

·THE·

O. HENRY

AWARDS

◆

*Edited and with
an Introduction by*

William Abrahams

DOUBLEDAY

New York London Toronto Sydney Auckland

PUBLISHED BY DOUBLEDAY
a division of Bantam Doubleday Dell Publishing Group, Inc.
1540 Broadway, New York, New York 10036

DOUBLEDAY and the portrayal of an anchor with a dolphin
are trademarks of Doubleday,
a division of Bantam Doubleday Dell Publishing Group, Inc.

Library of Congress Cataloging-in-Publication Data
Prize stories. 1947–
New York, N.Y., Doubleday.
v. 22 cm.
Annual.
The O. Henry awards.
None published 1952–53.
Continues: O. Henry memorial award prize stories.
1. Short stories, American—Collected works.
PZ1.011   813′.01′08—dc19   21-9372
                                            MARC-S

ISBN: 0-385-48130-6
ISBN: 0-385-48182-9 (pbk.)

April 1996

1   3   5   7   9   10   8   6   4   2

First Edition

CONTENTS

PUBLISHER'S NOTE

This volume is the seventy-sixth in the O. Henry Memorial Award series, and the thirtieth to be edited by William Abrahams.

*   *   *

In 1918, the Society of Arts and Sciences met to vote upon a monument to the master of the short story: O. Henry. They decided that this memorial should be in the form of two prizes for the best short stories published by American authors in American magazines during the year 1919. From this beginning, the memorial developed into an annual anthology of outstanding short stories by American authors, published, with the exception of the years 1952 and 1953, by Doubleday.

Blanche Colton Williams, one of the founders of the awards, was editor from 1919 to 1932; Harry Hansen from 1933 to 1940; Herschel Brickell from 1941 to 1951. The annual collection did not appear in 1952 and 1953, when the continuity of the series was interrupted by the death of Herschel Brickell. Paul Engle was editor from 1954 to 1959, with Hanson Martin coeditor in the years 1954 to 1960; Mary Stegner in 1960; Richard Poirier from 1961 to 1966, with assistance from and coeditorship with William Abrahams from 1964 to 1966. William Abrahams became editor of the series in 1967.

In 1970, Doubleday published under Mr. Abrahams's editorship *Fifty Years of the American Short Story*, and in 1981, *Prize Stories of the Seventies*. Both are collections of stories selected from this series.

The stories chosen for this volume were published in the period from the summer of 1994 to the summer of 1995. A list of the magazines consulted appears at the back of the book. The choice of stories and selection of prizewinners are exclusively the responsibility of the editor. Biographical material is based on information provided by the contributors and obtained from standard works of reference.

INTRODUCTION

For thirty years I have enjoyed the privilege and challenge of choosing the stories for this annual collection—from *Prize Stories 1967* to *Prize Stories 1996*. Since the Introduction I am writing now is in effect a farewell, I hasten to add that this decision is entirely my own, as has also been true from first to last of the choice of stories and selection of prizewinners. In that respect, and in many others, Doubleday, the publisher of the O. Henry Awards from their inception, has been exemplary—a model of tact, congeniality, and encouragement—and I am happy to acknowledge this.

For the 1996 volume I have chosen twenty stories from among the approximately one thousand that were eligible—stories by American authors published in magazines in the twelve-month period from summer 1994 to summer 1995. The winnowing and sifting procedure reduced the number of plausible candidates dramatically. Perhaps one hundred stories remained to be reread and reconsidered. Then, another winnowing—and several worthy stories were reluctantly let go. Ultimately, I settled on the final twenty, making a collection about which I am prepared to say: This is one of the very best.

I have been describing here the procedure I followed for thirty years. Now, some totals that have resulted from it. In the collections from 1967 to 1996 there are 580 stories, chosen from a total of 30,000 published in magazines of varying quality, circulation, and standards, over the thirty-year period. Thirty thousand written and published stories is an impressive number. But what of all the stories that were written and not published? There is no way to be certain, but by extrapolating, I can guess they numbered in the hundreds of thousands; and I would further guess that among them were stories that should have been published but were not.

It would seem inarguable that there are writers who find some sort of fulfillment in writing stories, whether or not what they write is offered or accepted for publication. After all, the impulse to tell stories is universal and historical. In that sense are we not all of us storytellers throughout our lives? As in: "What's the story?" or "Do I have a story for you!" in the nonstop et cetera of daily life, or the exchanges of correspondence (and the rising tide of electronic mail that Ralph Lombreglia draws upon for his story of 1999 that concludes this collection).

The stories I look for originate in that universal impulse, but in the writing, quite mysteriously, are transformed and brought alive on the page. Such stories are uncommon, measured against the general production—say twenty out of a thousand, as in the present collection. At the least, each has its own thumbprint, its own voice, its own individual identity. Collected, they stand independent of each other, even as they unite to exemplify the continuing diversity and vitality of the American short story.

I want to express my thanks to all the authors whose work I have chosen over the years, and whose names will be found in the complete chronological list at the end of this volume. At Doubleday, special thanks to Samuel S. Vaughan, whose idea it was that I should become editor of the series; to Sally Arteseros for her support through many collections in the 1970s and 1980s, and in the 1990s to Arabella Meyer. In California, thanks to William Merz.

—William Abrahams

Stephen King

THE MAN IN THE BLACK SUIT

I am now a very old man and this is something that happened to me when I was very young—only nine years old. It was 1914, the summer after my brother, Dan, died in the west field and not long before America got into the First World War. I've never told anyone about what happened at the fork in the stream that day, and I never will. I've decided to write it down, though, in this book, which I will leave on the table beside my bed. I can't write long, because my hands shake so these days and I have next to no strength, but I don't think it will take long.

Later, someone may find what I have written. That seems likely to me, as it is pretty much human nature to look in a book marked "Diary" after its owner has passed along. So, yes—my words will probably be read. A better question is whether anyone will believe them. Almost certainly not, but that doesn't matter. It's not belief I'm interested in but freedom. Writing can give that, I've found. For twenty years I wrote a column called "Long Ago and Far Away" for the Castle Rock *Call*, and I know that sometimes it works that way—what you write down sometimes leaves you forever, like old photographs left in the bright sun, fading to nothing but white.

I pray for that sort of release.

A man in his eighties should be well past the terrors of childhood, but as my infirmities slowly creep up on me, like waves licking closer and closer to some indifferently built castle of sand, that terrible face grows clearer and clearer in my mind's eye. It glows like a dark star in the constellations of my childhood. What I might have done yesterday, who I might have seen here in my room at the nursing home, what I might have said to them or they to me—those things are gone, but the face of the man in the black suit grows ever clearer, ever closer, and I remember every word he said. I don't want to think of him but I can't help it, and sometimes at night my old heart beats so hard and so fast I think it will tear itself right clear of my chest. So I uncap my fountain pen and force my trembling old hand to write this pointless anecdote in the diary one of my great-grandchildren—I can't remember her name for sure, at least not right now, but I know it starts with an "S"—gave to me last Christmas, and which I have never written in until now. Now I will write in it. I will write the story of how I met the man in the black suit on the bank of Castle Stream one afternoon in the summer of 1914.

The town of Motton was a different world in those days—more different than I could ever tell you. That was a world without airplanes droning overhead, a world almost without cars and trucks, a world where the skies were not cut into lanes and slices by overhead power lines. There was not a single paved road in the whole town, and the business district consisted of nothing but Corson's General Store, Thut's Livery & Hardware, the Methodist church at Christ's Corner, the school, the town hall, and half a mile down from there, Harry's Restaurant, which my mother called, with unfailing disdain, "the liquor house."

Mostly, though, the difference was in how people lived—how *apart* they were. I'm not sure people born after the middle of the century could quite credit that, although they might say they could, to be polite to old folks like me. There were no phones in western Maine back then, for one thing. The first one wouldn't be installed for another five years, and by the time there was a phone in our house, I was nineteen and going to college at the University of Maine in Orono.

But that is only the roof of the thing. There was no doctor closer than Casco, and there were no more than a dozen houses in what you would call town. There were no neighborhoods (I'm not even sure we knew the word, although we had a verb—"neighboring"—that described church functions and barn dances), and open fields were the exception rather than the rule. Out of town the houses were farms that stood far apart from each other, and from December until the middle of March we mostly hunkered down in the little pockets of stove warmth we called families. We hunkered and listened to the wind in the chimney and hoped no one would get sick or break a leg or get a headful of bad ideas, like the farmer over in Castle Rock who had chopped up his wife and kids three winters before and then said in court that the ghosts made him do it. In those days before the Great War, most of Motton was woods and bog—dark long places full of moose and mosquitoes, snakes and secrets. In those days there were ghosts everywhere.

This thing I'm telling about happened on a Saturday. My father gave me a whole list of chores to do, including some that would have been Dan's, if he'd still been alive. He was my only brother, and he'd died of a bee sting. A year had gone by, and still my mother wouldn't hear that. She said it was something else, *had* to have been, that no one ever died of being stung by a bee. When Mama Sweet, the oldest lady in the Methodist Ladies' Aid, tried to tell her—at the church supper the previous winter, this was—that the same thing had happened to her favorite uncle back in '73, my mother clapped her hands over her ears, got up, and walked out of the church basement. She'd never been back since, and nothing my father could say to her would change her mind. She claimed she was done with church, and that if she ever had to see Helen Robichaud again (that was Mama Sweet's real name) she would slap her eyes out. She wouldn't be able to help herself, she said.

That day Dad wanted me to lug wood for the cookstove, weed the beans and the cukes, pitch hay out of the loft, get two jugs of water to put in the cold pantry, and scrape as much old paint off the cellar bulkhead as I could. Then, he said, I could go fishing, if I didn't mind going by myself—he had to go over and see Bill Eversham about some cows. I said I sure didn't mind going by myself, and my dad smiled as if that didn't surprise him so very much. He'd given me a bamboo pole the week before—not because it was my birthday or anything but just because he liked to give me things sometimes—and I was wild to try it in Castle Stream, which was by far the troutiest brook I'd ever fished.

"But don't you go too far in the woods," he told me. "Not beyond where the water splits."

"No, sir."

"Promise me."

"Yessir, I promise."

"Now promise your mother."

We were standing on the back stoop; I had been bound for the springhouse with the water jugs when my dad stopped me. Now he turned me around to face my mother, who was standing at the marble counter in a flood of strong morning sunshine falling through the double windows over the sink. There was a curl of hair lying across the side of her forehead and touching her eyebrow—you see how well I remember it all? The bright light turned that little curl to filaments of gold and made me want to run to her and put my arms around her. In that instant I saw her as a woman, saw her as my father must have seen her. She was wearing a housedress with little red roses all over it, I remember, and she was kneading bread. Candy Bill, our little black Scottie dog, was standing alertly beside her feet, looking up, waiting for anything that might drop. My mother was looking at me.

"I promise," I said.

She smiled, but it was the worried kind of smile she always seemed to make since my father brought Dan back from the west field in his arms. My father had come sobbing and bare-chested. He had taken off his shirt and draped it over Dan's face, which had swelled and turned color. *My boy!* he had been crying. *Oh, look at my boy! Jesus, look at my boy!* I remember that as if it were yesterday. It was the only time I ever heard my dad take the Saviour's name in vain.

"What do you promise, Gary?" she asked.

"Promise not to go no further than where the stream forks, Ma'am."

"Any further."

"Any."

She gave me a patient look, saying nothing as her hands went on working in the dough, which now had a smooth, silky look.

"I promise not to go any further than where the stream forks, Ma'am."

"Thank you, Gary," she said. "And try to remember that grammar is for the world as well as for school."

"Yes, Ma'am."

Candy Bill followed me as I did my chores, and sat between my feet as I bolted my lunch, looking up at me with the same attentiveness he had shown my mother while she was kneading her bread, but when I got my new bamboo pole and my old, splintery creel and started out of the dooryard, he stopped and only stood in the dust by an old roll of snow fence, watching. I called him but he wouldn't come. He yapped a time or two, as if telling me to come back, but that was all.

"Stay, then," I said, trying to sound as if I didn't care. I did, though, at least a little. Candy Bill *always* went fishing with me.

My mother came to the door and looked out at me with her left hand held up to shade her eyes. I can see her that way still, and it's like looking at a photograph of someone who later became unhappy, or died suddenly. "You mind your dad now, Gary!"

"Yes, Ma'am, I will."

She waved. I waved, too. Then I turned my back on her and walked away.

The sun beat down on my neck, hard and hot, for the first quarter-mile or so, but then I entered the woods, where double shadow fell over the road and it was cool and fir-smelling and you could hear the wind hissing through the deep, needled groves. I walked with my pole on my shoulder the way boys did back then, holding my creel in my other hand like a valise or a salesman's sample case. About two miles into the woods along a road that was really nothing but a double rut with a

grassy strip growing up the center hump, I began to hear the
hurried, eager gossip of Castle Stream. I thought of trout with
bright speckled backs and pure-white bellies, and my heart
went up in my chest.

The stream flowed under a little wooden bridge, and the
banks leading down to the water were steep and brushy. I
worked my way down carefully, holding on where I could and
digging my heels in. I went down out of summer and back into
mid-spring, or so it felt. The cool rose gently off the water, and
there was a green smell like moss. When I got to the edge of
the water I only stood there for a little while, breathing deep of
that mossy smell and watching the dragonflies circle and the
skitterbugs skate. Then, further down, I saw a trout leap at a
butterfly—a good big brookie, maybe fourteen inches long—
and remembered I hadn't come here just to sightsee.

I walked along the bank, following the current, and wet my
line for the first time, with the bridge still in sight upstream.
Something jerked the tip of my pole down once or twice and
ate half my worm, but whatever it was was too sly for my
nine-year-old hands—or maybe just not hungry enough to be
careless—so I quit that place.

I stopped at two or three other places before I got to the
place where Castle Stream forks, going southwest into Castle
Rock and southeast into Kashwakamak Township, and at one
of them I caught the biggest trout I have ever caught in my life,
a beauty that measured nineteen inches from tip to tail on the
little ruler I kept in my creel. That was a monster of a brook
trout, even for those days.

If I had accepted this as gift enough for one day and gone
back, I would not be writing now (and this is going to turn out
longer than I thought it would, I see that already), but I didn't.
Instead I saw to my catch right then and there as my father had
shown me—cleaning it, placing it on dry grass at the bottom of
the creel, then laying damp grass on top of it—and went on. I
did not, at age nine, think that catching a nineteen-inch brook
trout was particularly remarkable, although I do remember being amazed that my line had not broken when I, netless as well
as artless, had hauled it out and swung it toward me in a
clumsy tail-flapping arc.

Ten minutes later, I came to the place where the stream split in those days (it is long gone now; there is a settlement of duplex homes where Castle Stream once went its course, and a district grammar school as well, and if there is a stream it goes in darkness), dividing around a huge gray rock nearly the size of our outhouse. There was a pleasant flat space here, grassy and soft, overlooking what my dad and I called South Branch. I squatted on my heels, dropped my line into the water, and almost immediately snagged a fine rainbow trout. He wasn't the size of my brookie—only a foot or so—but a good fish, just the same. I had it cleaned out before the gills had stopped flexing, stored it in my creel, and dropped my line back into the water.

This time there was no immediate bite, so I leaned back, looking up at the blue stripe of sky I could see along the stream's course. Clouds floated by, west to east, and I tried to think what they looked like. I saw a unicorn, then a rooster, then a dog that looked like Candy Bill. I was looking for the next one when I drowsed off.

Or maybe slept. I don't know for sure. All I know is that a tug on my line so strong it almost pulled the bamboo pole out of my hand was what brought me back into the afternoon. I sat up, clutched the pole, and suddenly became aware that something was sitting on the tip of my nose. I crossed my eyes and saw a bee. My heart seemed to fall dead in my chest, and for a horrible second I was sure I was going to wet my pants.

The tug on my line came again, stronger this time, but although I maintained my grip on the end of the pole so it wouldn't be pulled into the stream and perhaps carried away (I think I even had the presence of mind to snub the line with my forefinger), I made no effort to pull in my catch. All my horrified attention was fixed on the fat black-and-yellow thing that was using my nose as a rest stop.

I slowly poked out my lower lip and blew upward. The bee ruffled a little but kept its place. I blew again and it ruffled again—but this time it also seemed to shift impatiently, and I didn't dare blow anymore, for fear it would lose its temper completely and give me a shot. It was too close for me to focus on what it was doing, but it was easy to imagine it ramming its

stinger into one of my nostrils and shooting its poison up
toward my eyes. And my brain.

A terrible idea came to me: that this was the very bee that
had killed my brother. I knew it wasn't true, and not only
because honeybees probably didn't live longer than a single
year (except maybe for the queens; about them I was not so
sure). It couldn't be true, because honeybees died when they
stung, and even at nine I knew it. Their stingers were barbed,
and when they tried to fly away after doing the deed, they tore
themselves apart. Still, the idea stayed. This was a special bee,
a devil-bee, and it had come back to finish the other of Albion
and Loretta's two boys.

And here is something else: I had been stung by bees before,
and although the stings had swelled more than is perhaps
usual (I can't really say for sure), I had never died of them.
That was only for my brother, a terrible trap that had been laid
for him in his very making—a trap that I had somehow escaped. But as I crossed my eyes until they hurt, in an effort to
focus on the bee, logic did not exist. It was the *bee* that existed,
only that—the bee that had killed my brother, killed him so
cruelly that my father had slipped down the straps of his overalls so he could take off his shirt and cover Dan's swollen,
engorged face. Even in the depths of his grief he had done that,
because he didn't want his wife to see what had become of her
firstborn. Now the bee had returned, and now it would kill me.
I would die in convulsions on the bank, flopping just as a
brookie flops after you take the hook out of its mouth.

As I sat there trembling on the edge of panic—ready to bolt
to my feet and then bolt anywhere—there came a report from
behind me. It was as sharp and peremptory as a pistol shot,
but I knew it wasn't a pistol shot; it was someone clapping his
hands. One single clap. At that moment, the bee tumbled off
my nose and fell into my lap. It lay there on my pants with its
legs sticking up and its stinger a threatless black thread against
the old scuffed brown of the corduroy. It was dead as a door-
nail, I saw that at once. At the same moment, the pole gave
another tug—the hardest yet—and I almost lost it again.

I grabbed it with both hands and gave it a big stupid yank
that would have made my father clutch his head with both

hands, if he had been there to see. A rainbow trout, a good bit larger than either of the ones I had already caught, rose out of the water in a wet flash, spraying fine drops of water from its tail—it looked like one of those fishing pictures they used to put on the covers of men's magazines like *True* and *Man's Adventure* back in the forties and fifties. At that moment hauling in a big one was about the last thing on my mind, however, and when the line snapped and the fish fell back into the stream, I barely noticed. I looked over my shoulder to see who had clapped. A man was standing above me, at the edge of the trees. His face was very long and pale. His black hair was combed tight against his skull and parted with rigorous care on the left side of his narrow head. He was very tall. He was wearing a black three-piece suit, and I knew right away that he was not a human being, because his eyes were the orangey red of flames in a woodstove. I don't mean just the irises, because he *had* no irises, and no pupils, and certainly no whites. His eyes were completely orange—an orange that shifted and flickered. And it's really too late not to say exactly what I mean, isn't it? He was on fire inside, and his eyes were like the little isinglass portholes you sometimes see in stove doors.

My bladder let go, and the scuffed brown the dead bee was lying on went a darker brown. I was hardly aware of what had happened, and I couldn't take my eyes off the man standing on top of the bank and looking down at me—the man who had apparently walked out of thirty miles of trackless western Maine woods in a fine black suit and narrow shoes of gleaming leather. I could see the watch chain looped across his vest glittering in the summer sunshine. There was not so much as a single pine needle on him. And he was smiling at me.

"Why, it's a fisherboy!" he cried in a mellow, pleasing voice. "Imagine that! Are we well met, fisherboy?"

"Hello, sir," I said. The voice that came out of me did not tremble, but it didn't sound like my voice, either. It sounded older. Like Dan's voice, maybe. Or my father's, even. And all I could think was that maybe he would let me go if I pretended not to see what he was. If I pretended I didn't see there were flames glowing and dancing where his eyes should have been.

"I've saved you a nasty sting, perhaps," he said, and then,

to my horror, he came down the bank to where I sat with a dead bee in my wet lap and a bamboo fishing pole in my nerveless hands. His slick-soled city shoes should have slipped on the low, grassy weeds dressing the steep bank, but they didn't; nor did they leave tracks, I saw. Where his feet had touched—or seemed to touch—there was not a single broken twig, crushed leaf, or trampled shoe-shape.

Even before he reached me, I recognized the aroma baking up from the skin under the suit—the smell of burned matches. The smell of sulfur. The man in the black suit was the Devil. He had walked out of the deep woods between Motton and Kashwakamak, and now he was standing here beside me. From the corner of one eye I could see a hand as pale as the hand of a store-window dummy. The fingers were hideously long.

He hunkered beside me on his hams, his knees popping just as the knees of any normal man might, but when he moved his hands so they dangled between his knees, I saw that each of those long fingers ended in not a fingernail but a long yellow claw.

"You didn't answer my question, fisherboy," he said in his mellow voice. It was, now that I think of it, like the voice of one of those radio announcers on the big-band shows years later, the ones that would sell Geritol and Serutan and Ovaltine and Dr. Grabow pipes. "Are we well met?"

"Please don't hurt me," I whispered, in a voice so low I could barely hear it. I was more afraid than I could ever write down, more afraid than I want to remember. But I do. I do. It never crossed my mind to hope I was having a dream, although it might have, I suppose, if I had been older. But I was nine, and I knew the truth when it squatted down beside me. I knew a hawk from a handsaw, as my father would have said. The man who had come out of the woods on that Saturday afternoon in midsummer was the Devil, and inside the empty holes of his eyes his brains were burning.

"Oh, do I smell something?" he asked, as if he hadn't heard me, although I knew he had. "Do I smell something . . . wet?"

He leaned toward me with his nose stuck out, like someone

who means to smell a flower. And I noticed an awful thing; as the shadow of his head travelled over the bank, the grass beneath it turned yellow and died. He lowered his head toward my pants and sniffed. His glaring eyes half closed, as if he had inhaled some sublime aroma and wanted to concentrate on nothing but that.

"Oh, bad!" he cried. "Lovely-bad!" And then he chanted: "Opal! Diamond! Sapphire! Jade! I smell Gary's lemonade!" He threw himself on his back in the little flat place and laughed.

I thought about running, but my legs seemed two counties away from my brain. I wasn't crying, though; I had wet my pants, but I wasn't crying. I was too scared to cry. I suddenly knew that I was going to die, and probably painfully, but the worst of it was that that might not be the worst of it. The worst might come later. *After* I was dead.

He sat up suddenly, the smell of burnt matches fluffing out from his suit and making me feel gaggy in my throat. He looked at me solemnly from his narrow white face and burning eyes, but there was a sense of laughter about him, too. There was always that sense of laughter about him.

"Sad news, fisherboy," he said. "I've come with sad news."

I could only look at him—the black suit, the fine black shoes, the long white fingers that ended not in nails but in talons.

"Your mother is dead."

"No!" I cried. I thought of her making bread, of the curl lying across her forehead and just touching her eyebrow, of her standing there in the strong morning sunlight, and the terror swept over me again, but not for myself this time. Then I thought of how she'd looked when I set off with my fishing pole, standing in the kitchen doorway with her hand shading her eyes, and how she had looked to me in that moment like a photograph of someone you expected to see again but never did. "No, you lie!" I screamed.

He smiled—the sadly patient smile of a man who has often been accused falsely. "I'm afraid not," he said. "It was the same thing that happened to your brother, Gary. It was a bee."

"No, that's not true," I said, and now I *did* begin to cry.

"She's old, she's thirty-five—if a bee sting could kill her the way it did Danny she would have died a long time ago, and you're a lying bastard!"

I had called the Devil a lying bastard. I was aware of this, but the entire front of my mind was taken up by the enormity of what he'd said. My mother dead? He might as well have told me that the moon had fallen on Vermont. But I believed him. On some level I believed him completely, as we always believe, on some level, the worst thing our hearts can imagine.

"I understand your grief, little fisherboy, but that particular argument just doesn't hold water, I'm afraid." He spoke in a tone of bogus comfort that was horrible, maddening, without remorse or pity. "A man can go his whole life without seeing a mockingbird, you know, but does that mean mockingbirds don't exist? Your mother—"

A fish jumped below us. The man in the black suit frowned, then pointed a finger at it. The trout convulsed in the air, its body bending so strenuously that for a split second it appeared to be snapping at its own tail, and when it fell back into Castle Stream it was floating lifelessly. It struck the big gray rock where the waters divided, spun around twice in the whirlpool eddy that formed there, and then floated away in the direction of Castle Rock. Meanwhile, the terrible stranger turned his burning eyes on me again, his thin lips pulled back from tiny rows of sharp teeth in a cannibal smile.

"Your mother simply went through her entire life without being stung by a bee," he said. "But then—less than an hour ago, actually—one flew in through the kitchen window while she was taking the bread out of the oven and putting it on the counter to cool."

I raised my hands and clapped them over my ears. He pursed his lips as if to whistle and blew at me gently. It was only a little breath, but the stench was foul beyond belief— clogged sewers, outhouses that have never known a single sprinkle of lime, dead chickens after a flood.

My hands fell away from the sides of my face.

"Good," he said. "You need to hear this, Gary; you need to hear this, my little fisherboy. It was your mother who passed that fatal weakness on to your brother. You got some of it, but you also got a protection from your father that poor Dan somehow missed." He pursed his lips again, only this time he made a cruelly comic little *tsk-tsk* sound instead of blowing his nasty breath at me. "So although I don't like to speak ill of the dead, it's almost a case of poetic justice, isn't it? After all, she killed your brother Dan as surely as if she had put a gun to his head and pulled the trigger."

"No," I whispered. "No, it isn't true."

"I assure you it is," he said. "The bee flew in the window and lit on her neck. She slapped at it before she even knew what she was doing—*you* were wiser than that, weren't you, Gary?—and the bee stung her. She felt her throat start to close up at once. That's what happens, you know, to people who can't tolerate bee venom. Their throats close and they drown in the open air. That's why Dan's face was so swollen and purple. That's why your father covered it with his shirt."

I stared at him, now incapable of speech. Tears streamed down my cheeks. I didn't want to believe him, and knew from my church schooling that the Devil is the father of lies, but I *did* believe him just the same.

"She made the most wonderfully awful noises," the man in the black suit said reflectively, "and she scratched her face quite badly, I'm afraid. Her eyes bulged out like a frog's eyes. She wept." He paused, then added: "She wept as she died, isn't that sweet? And here's the most beautiful thing of all. After she was dead, after she had been lying on the floor for fifteen minutes or so with no sound but the stove ticking and with that little thread of a bee stinger still poking out of the side of her neck—so small, so small—do you know what Candy Bill did? That little rascal licked away her tears. First on one side, and then on the other."

He looked out at the stream for a moment, his face sad and thoughtful. Then he turned back to me and his expression of bereavement disappeared like a dream. His face was as slack and as avid as the face of a corpse that has died hungry. His eyes blazed. I could see his sharp little teeth between his pale lips.

"I'm starving," he said abruptly. "I'm going to kill you and eat your guts, little fisherboy. What do you think about that?"

No, I tried to say, *please no*, but no sound came out. He meant to do it, I saw. He really meant to do it.

"I'm just so *hungry*," he said, both petulant and teasing. "And you won't want to live without your precious mommy, anyhow, take my word for it. Because your father's the sort of man who'll have to have some warm hole to stick it in, believe me, and if you're the only one available, you're the one who'll have to serve. I'll save you all that discomfort and unpleasantness. Also, you'll go to Heaven, think of that. Murdered souls *always* go to Heaven. So we'll both be serving God this afternoon, Gary. Isn't that nice?"

He reached for me again with his long, pale hands, and without thinking what I was doing, I flipped open the top of my creel, pawed all the way down to the bottom, and brought out the monster brookie I'd caught earlier—the one I should have been satisfied with. I held it out to him blindly, my fingers in the red slit of its belly, from which I had removed its insides as the man in the black suit had threatened to remove mine. The fish's glazed eye stared dreamily at me, the gold ring around the black center reminding me of my mother's wedding ring. And in that moment I saw her lying in her coffin with the sun shining off the wedding band and knew it was true—she had been stung by a bee, she had drowned in the warm, bread-smelling kitchen air, and Candy Bill had licked her dying tears from her swollen cheeks.

"Big fish!" the man in the black suit cried in a guttural, greedy voice. "Oh, *biiig fiiish!*"

He snatched it away from me and crammed it into a mouth that opened wider than any human mouth ever could. Many years later, when I was sixty-five (I know it was sixty-five, because that was the summer I retired from teaching), I went to the aquarium in Boston and finally saw a shark. The mouth of the man in the black suit was like that shark's mouth when it opened, only his gullet was blazing orange, the same color as his eyes, and I felt heat bake out of it and into my face, the way you feel a sudden wave of heat come pushing out of a fireplace when a dry piece of wood catches alight. And I didn't imagine that heat, either—I know I didn't—because just before he slid the head of my nineteen-inch brook trout between his gaping jaws, I saw the scales along the sides of the fish rise up and begin to curl like bits of paper floating over an open incinerator.

He slid the fish in like a man in a travelling show swallow-ing a sword. He didn't chew, and his blazing eyes bulged out, as if in effort. The fish went in and went in, his throat bulged as it slid down his gullet, and now he began to cry tears of his own—except his tears were blood, scarlet and thick.

I think it was the sight of those bloody tears that gave me my body back. I don't know why that should have been, but I think it was. I bolted to my feet like a Jack released from its box, turned with my bamboo pole still in one hand, and fled up the bank, bending over and tearing tough bunches of weeds out with my free hand in an effort to get up the slope more quickly.

He made a strangled, furious noise—the sound of any man with his mouth too full—and I looked back just as I got to the top. He was coming after me, the back of his suit coat flapping and his thin gold watch chain flashing and winking in the sun. The tail of the fish was still protruding from his mouth and I could smell the rest of it, roasting in the oven of his throat.

He reached for me, groping with his talons, and I fled along the top of the bank. After a hundred yards or so I found my voice and went to screaming—screaming in fear, of course, but also screaming in grief for my beautiful dead mother.

He was coming after me. I could hear snapping branches and whipping bushes, but I didn't look back again. I lowered my head, slitted my eyes against the bushes and low-hanging branches along the stream's bank, and ran as fast as I could. And at every step I expected to feel his hands descending on my shoulders, pulling me back into a final burning hug.

That didn't happen. Some unknown length of time later—it couldn't have been longer than five or ten minutes, I suppose, but it seemed like forever—I saw the bridge through layerings of leaves and firs. Still screaming, but breathlessly now, sound-ing like a teakettle that has almost boiled dry, I reached this second, steeper bank and charged up.

Halfway to the top, I slipped to my knees, looked over my shoulder, and saw the man in the black suit almost at my heels, his white face pulled into a convulsion of fury and greed. His cheeks were splattered with his bloody tears and his shark's mouth hung open like a hinge.

"*Fisherboy!*" he snarled, and started up the bank after me, grasping at my foot with one long hand. I tore free, turned, and threw my fishing pole at him. He batted it down easily, but it tangled his feet up somehow and he went to his knees. I didn't wait to see any more; I turned and bolted to the top of the slope. I almost slipped at the very top, but managed to grab one of the support struts running beneath the bridge and save myself.

"You can't get away, fisherboy!" he cried from behind me. He sounded furious, but he also sounded as if he were laughing. "It takes more than a mouthful of trout to fill *me* up!"

"Leave me alone!" I screamed back at him. I grabbed the bridge's railing and threw myself over it in a clumsy somersault, filling my hands with splinters and bumping my head so hard on the boards when I came down that I saw stars. I rolled over on my belly and began crawling. I lurched to my feet just before I got to the end of the bridge, stumbled once, found my rhythm, and then began to run. I ran as only nine-year-old boys can run, which is like the wind. It felt as if my feet only touched the ground with every third or fourth stride, and, for all I know, that may be true. I ran straight up the right-hand wheel rut in the road, ran until my temples pounded and my eyes pulsed in their sockets, ran until I had a hot stitch in my left side from the bottom of my ribs to my armpit, ran until I could taste blood and something like metal shavings in the back of my throat. When I couldn't run anymore I stumbled to a stop and looked back over my shoulder, puffing and blowing like a wind-broken horse. I was convinced I would see him standing right there behind me in his natty black suit, the watch chain a glittering loop across his vest and not a hair out of place.

But he was gone. The road stretching back toward Castle Stream between the darkly massed pines and spruces was empty. And yet I sensed him somewhere near in those woods, watching me with his grassfire eyes, smelling of burned matches and roasted fish.

I turned and began walking as fast as I could, limping a little—I'd pulled muscles in both legs, and when I got out of bed the next morning I was so sore I could barely walk. I kept looking over my shoulder, needing again and again to verify that the road behind me was still empty. It was each time I looked, but those backward glances seemed to increase my fear rather than lessen it. The firs looked darker, massier, and I kept imagining what lay behind the trees that marched beside the road—long, tangled corridors of forest, leg-breaking deadfalls, ravines where anything might live. Until that Saturday in 1914, I had thought that bears were the worst thing the forest could hold.

A mile or so farther up the road, just beyond the place where it came out of the woods and joined the Geegan Flat Road, I saw my father walking toward me and whistling "The Old Oaken Bucket." He was carrying his own rod, the one with the fancy spinning reel from Monkey Ward. In his other hand he had his creel, the one with the ribbon my mother had woven through the handle back when Dan was still alive. "Dedicated to Jesus" that ribbon said. I had been walking, but when I saw him I started to run again, screaming *Dad! Dad! Dad!* at the top of my lungs and staggering from side to side on my tired, sprung legs like a drunken sailor. The expression of surprise on his face when he recognized me might have been comical under other circumstances. He dropped his rod and creel into the road without so much as a downward glance at them and ran to me. It was the fastest I ever saw my dad run in his life; when we came together it was a wonder the impact didn't knock us both senseless, and I struck my face on his belt buckle hard enough to start a little nosebleed. I didn't notice that until later, though. Right then I only reached out my arms and clutched him as hard as I could. I held on and rubbed my hot face back and forth against his belly, covering his old blue workshirt with blood and tears and snot.

"Gary, what is it? What happened? Are you all right?"

"Ma's dead!" I sobbed. "I met a man in the woods and he told me! Ma's dead! She got stung by a bee and it swelled her all up just like what happened to Dan, and she's dead! She's on the kitchen floor and Candy Bill . . . licked the t-t-tears . . . off her . . . off her . . ."

Face was the last word I had to say, but by then my chest was hitching so bad I couldn't get it out. My own tears were flowing again, and my dad's startled, frightened face had blurred into three overlapping images. I began to howl—not like a little kid who's skinned his knee but like a dog that's seen something bad by moonlight—and my father pressed my head against his hard flat stomach again. I slipped out from under his hand, though, and looked back over my shoulder. I wanted to make sure the man in the black suit wasn't coming. There was no sign of him; the road winding back into the woods was completely empty. I promised myself I would never go back down that road again, not ever, no matter what, and I suppose now that God's greatest blessing to His creatures below is that they can't see the future. It might have broken my mind if I had known I *would* be going back down that road, and not two hours later. For that moment, though, I was only relieved to see we were still alone. Then I thought of my mother—my beautiful dead mother—and laid my face back against my father's stomach and bawled some more.

"Gary, listen to me," he said a moment or two later. I went on bawling. He gave me a little longer to do that, then reached down and lifted my chin so he could look down into my face and I could look up into his. "Your mom's fine," he said.

I could only look at him with tears streaming down my cheeks. I didn't believe him.

"I don't know who told you different, or what kind of dirty dog would want to put a scare like that into a little boy, but I swear to God your mother's fine."

"But . . . but he said . . ."

"I don't care *what* he said. I got back from Eversham's earlier than I expected—he doesn't want to sell any cows, it's all just talk—and decided I had time to catch up with you. I got my pole and my creel and your mother made us a couple of jelly fold-overs. Her new bread. Still warm. So she was fine half an hour ago, Gary, and there's nobody knows any different that's come from this direction, I guarantee you. Not in just half an hour's time." He looked over my shoulder. "Who was this man? And where was he? I'm going to find him and thrash him within an inch of his life."

I thought a thousand things in just two seconds—that's what it seemed like, anyway—but the last thing I thought was the most powerful: if my Dad met up with the man in the black suit, I didn't think my Dad would be the one to do the thrashing. Or the walking away.

I kept remembering those long white fingers, and the talons at the ends of them.

"Gary?"

"I don't know that I remember," I said.

"Were you where the stream splits? The big rock?"

I could never lie to my father when he asked a direct question—not to save his life or mine. "Yes, but don't go down there." I seized his arm with both hands and tugged it hard. "Please don't. He was a scary man." Inspiration struck like an illuminating lightning bolt. "I think he had a gun."

He looked at me thoughtfully. "Maybe there wasn't a man," he said, lifting his voice a little on the last word and turning it into something that was almost but not quite a question. "Maybe you fell asleep while you were fishing, son, and had a bad dream. Like the ones you had about Danny last winter."

I *had* had a lot of bad dreams about Dan last winter, dreams where I would open the door to our closet or to the dark, fruity interior of the cider shed and see him standing there and looking at me out of his purple strangulated face; from many of these dreams I had awakened screaming, and awakened my parents as well. I had fallen asleep on the bank of the stream for a little while, too—dozed off, anyway—but I hadn't dreamed, and I was sure I had awakened just before the man in the black suit clapped the bee dead, sending it tumbling off my nose and into my lap. I hadn't dreamed him the way I had dreamed Dan, I was quite sure of that, although my meeting with him had already attained a dreamlike quality in my mind, as I suppose supernatural occurrences always must. But if my Dad thought that the man had only existed in my own head, that might be better. Better for him.

"It might have been, I guess," I said.

"Well, we ought to go back and find your rod and your creel."

He actually started in that direction, and I had to tug frantically at his arm to stop him again and turn him back toward me.

"Later," I said. "Please, Dad? I want to see Mother. I've got to see her with my own eyes."

He thought that over, then nodded. "Yes, I suppose you do. We'll go home first, and get your rod and creel later."

So we walked back to the farm together, my father with his fish pole propped on his shoulder just like one of my friends, me carrying his creel, both of us eating folded-over slices of my mother's bread smeared with black-currant jam.

"Did you catch anything?" he asked as we came in sight of the barn.

"Yes, sir," I said. "A rainbow. Pretty good-sized." *And a brookie that was a lot bigger,* I thought but didn't say.

"That's all? Nothing else?"

"After I caught it I fell asleep." This was not really an answer but not really a lie, either.

"Lucky you didn't lose your pole. You didn't, did you, Gary?"

"No, sir," I said, very reluctantly. Lying about that would do no good even if I'd been able to think up a whopper—not if he was set on going back to get my creel anyway, and I could see by his face that he was.

Up ahead, Candy Bill came racing out of the back door, barking his shrill bark and wagging his whole rear end back and forth the way Scotties do when they're excited. I couldn't wait any longer. I broke away from my father and ran to the house, still lugging his creel and still convinced, in my heart of hearts, that I was going to find my mother dead on the kitchen floor with her face swollen and purple, as Dan's had been when my father carried him in from the west field, crying and calling the name of Jesus.

But she was standing at the counter, just as well and fine as when I had left her, humming a song as she shelled peas into a bowl. She looked around at me, first in surprise and then in fright as she took in my wide eyes and pale cheeks.

"Gary, what is it? What's the matter?"

I didn't answer, only ran to her and covered her with kisses. At some point my father came in and said, "Don't worry, Lo— he's all right. He just had one of his bad dreams, down there by the brook."

"Pray God it's the last of them," she said, and hugged me

tighter while Candy Bill danced around our feet, barking his shrill bark.

"You don't have to come with me if you don't want to, Gary," my father said, although he had already made it clear that he thought I should—that I should go back, that I should face my fear, as I suppose folks would say nowadays. That's very well for fearful things that are make-believe, but two hours hadn't done much to change my conviction that the man in the black suit had been real. I wouldn't be able to convince my father of that, though. I don't think there was a nine-year-old who ever lived would have been able to convince his father he'd seen the Devil walking out of the woods in a black suit.

"I'll come," I said. I had come out of the house to join him before he left, mustering all my courage to get my feet moving, and now we were standing by the chopping block in the side yard, not far from the woodpile.

"What you got behind your back?" he asked.

I brought it out slowly. I would go with him, and I would hope the man in the black suit with the arrow-straight part down the left side of his head was gone. But if he wasn't, I wanted to be prepared. As prepared as I could be, anyway. I had the family Bible in the hand I had brought out from behind my back. I'd set out just to bring my New Testament, which I had won for memorizing the most psalms in the Thursday-night Youth Fellowship competition (I managed eight, although most of them except the Twenty-third had floated out of my mind in a week's time), but the little red Testament didn't seem like enough when you were maybe going to face the Devil himself, not even when the words of Jesus were marked out in red ink.

My father looked at the old Bible, swollen with family documents and pictures, and I thought he'd tell me to put it back, but he didn't. A look of mixed grief and sympathy crossed his face, and he nodded. "All right," he said. "does your mother know you took that?"

"No, sir."

He nodded again. "Then we'll hope she doesn't spot it gone before we get back. Come on. And don't drop it."

.   .   .

Half an hour or so later, the two of us stood on the bank at the place where Castle Stream forked, and at the flat place where I'd had my encounter with the man with the red-orange eyes. I had my bamboo rod in my hand—I'd picked it up below the bridge—and my creel lay down below, on the flat place. Its wicker top was flipped back. We stood looking down, my father and I, for a long time, and neither of us said anything.

Opal! Diamond! Sapphire! Jade! I smell Gary's lemonade! That had been his unpleasant little poem, and once he had recited it, he had thrown himself on his back, laughing like a child who has just discovered he has enough courage to say bathroom words like shit or piss. The flat place down there was as green and lush as any place in Maine that the sun can get to in early July. Except where the stranger had lain. There the grass was dead and yellow in the shape of a man.

I was holding our lumpy old family Bible straight out in front of me with both thumbs pressing so hard on the cover that they were white. It was the way Mama Sweet's husband, Norville, held a willow fork when he was trying to dowse somebody a well.

"Stay here," my father said at last, and skidded sideways down the bank, digging his shoes into the rich soft soil and holding his arms out for balance. I stood where I was, holding the Bible stiffly out at the ends of my arms, my heart thumping. I don't know if I had a sense of being watched that time or not; I was too scared to have a sense of anything, except for a sense of wanting to be far away from that place and those woods.

My dad bent down, sniffed at where the grass was dead, and grimaced. I knew what he was smelling: something like burnt matches. Then he grabbed my creel and came on back up the bank, hurrying. He snagged one fast look over his shoulder to make sure nothing was coming along behind. Nothing was. When he handed me the creel, the lid was still hanging back on its cunning little leather hinges. I looked inside and saw nothing but two handfuls of grass.

"Thought you said you caught a rainbow," my father said, "but maybe you dreamed that, too."

Something in his voice stung me. "No, sir," I said. "I caught one."

"Well, it sure as hell didn't flop out, not if it was gutted and cleaned. And you wouldn't put a catch into your fisherbox without doing that, would you, Gary? I taught you better than that."

"Yes, sir, you did, but—"

"So if you didn't dream catching it and if it was dead in the box, something must have come along and eaten it," my father said, and then he grabbed another quick glance over his shoulder, eyes wide, as if he had heard something move in the woods. I wasn't exactly surprised to see drops of sweat standing out on his forehead like big clear jewels. "Come on," he said. "Let's get the hell out of here."

I was for that, and we went back along the bank to the bridge, walking quick without speaking. When we got there, my dad dropped to one knee and examined the place where we'd found my rod. There was another patch of dead grass there, and the lady's slipper was all brown and curled in on itself, as if a blast of heat had charred it. I looked in my empty creel again. "He must have gone back and eaten my other fish, too," I said.

My father looked up at me. "*Other* fish!"

"Yes, sir. I didn't tell you, but I caught a brookie, too. A big one. He was awful hungry, that fella." I wanted to say more, and the words trembled just behind my lips, but in the end I didn't.

We climbed up to the bridge and helped each other over the railing. My father took my creel, looked into it, then went to the railing and threw it over. I came up beside him in time to see it splash down and float away like a boat, riding lower and lower in the stream as the water poured in between the wicker weavings.

"It smelled bad," my father said, but he didn't look at me when he said it, and his voice sounded oddly defensive. It was the only time I ever heard him speak just that way.

"Yes, sir."

"We'll tell your mother we couldn't find it. If she asks. If she doesn't ask, we won't tell her anything."

"No, sir, we won't."

And she didn't and we didn't, and that's the way it was.

· · ·

That day in the woods is eighty years gone, and for many of the years in between I have never even thought of it—not awake, at least. Like any other man or woman who ever lived, I can't say about my dreams, not for sure. But now I'm old, and I dream awake, it seems. My infirmities have crept up like waves that will soon take a child's abandoned sand castle, and my memories have also crept up, making me think of some old rhyme that went, in part, "Just leave them alone / And they'll come home / Wagging their tails behind them." I remember meals I ate, games I played, girls I kissed in the school cloak-room when we played post office, boys I chummed with, the first drink I ever took, the first cigarette I ever smoked (corn-shuck behind Dicky Hamner's pig shed, and I threw up). Yet of all the memories the one of the man in the black suit is the strongest, and glows with its own spectral, haunted light. He was real, he was the Devil, and that day I was either his errand or his luck. I feel more and more strongly that escaping him was my luck—*just* luck, and not the intercession of the God I have worshipped and sung hymns to all my life.

As I lie here in my nursing-home room, and in the ruined sand castle that is my body, I tell myself that I need not fear the Devil—that I have lived a good, kindly life, and I need not fear the Devil. Sometimes I remind myself that it was I, not my father, who finally coaxed my mother back to church later on that summer. In the dark, however, these thoughts have no power to ease or comfort. In the dark comes a voice that whis-pers that the nine-year-old fisherboy I was had done nothing for which he might legitimately fear the Devil, either, and yet the Devil came—to him. And in the dark I sometimes hear that voice drop even lower, into ranges that are inhuman. *Big fish!* it whispers in tones of hushed greed, and all the truths of the moral world fall to ruin before its hunger.

Akhil Sharma

IF YOU SING LIKE THAT
FOR ME

Late one June afternoon, seven months after my wedding, I woke from a short, deep sleep in love with my husband. I did not know then, lying in bed and looking out the window at the line of gray clouds, that my love would last only a few hours and that I would never again care for Rajinder with the same urgency—never again in the five homes we would share and through the two daughters and one son we would also share, though unevenly and with great bitterness. I did not know this then, suddenly awake and only twenty-six, with a husband not much older, nor did I know that the memory of the coming hours would periodically overwhelm me throughout my life.

We were living in a small flat on the roof of a three-story house in Defense Colony, in New Delhi. Rajinder had signed the lease a week before our wedding. Two days after we married, he took me to the flat. I had thought I would be frightened entering my new home for the first time, but I was not. I felt very still that morning, watching Rajinder in his gray sweater bend over and open the padlock. Although it was cold, I wore only a pink silk sari and blouse, because I knew that my thick eyebrows, broad nose, and thin lips made me homely, and to win his love I must try especially hard to be appealing, even though I did not want to be.

The sun filled the living room through a window that took up half a wall and looked out onto the concrete roof. Rajinder went in first, holding the heavy brass padlock in his right hand. In the center of the room was a low plywood table with a thistle broom on top, and in a corner three plastic folding chairs lay collapsed on the floor. I followed a few steps behind Rajinder. The room was a white rectangle. Looking at it, I felt nothing. I saw the table and broom, the window grille with its drooping iron flowers, the dust in which we left our footprints, and I thought I should be feeling something—some anxiety, or fear, or curiosity. Perhaps even joy.

"We can put the TV there," Rajinder said softly, standing before the window and pointing to the right corner of the living room. He was slightly overweight and wore sweaters that were a bit large for him. They made him appear humble, a small man aware of his smallness. The thick black frames of his glasses, his old-fashioned moustache, as thin as a scratch, and the fading hairline created an impression of thoughtfulness. "The sofa before the window." At that moment, and often that day, I would think of myself with his smallness forever, bearing his children, going where he went, having to open always to his touch, and whatever I was looking at would begin to waver, and I would want to run. Run down the curving dark stairs, fast, fast, through the colony's narrow streets, with my sandals loud and alone, until I got to the bus stand and the 52 came, and then at the ice factory I would change to the 10, and finally I would climb the wooden steps to my parents' flat and the door would be open and no one would have noticed that I had gone with some small man.

I followed Rajinder into the bedroom, and the terror was gone, an open door now shut, and again I felt nothing, as if I were marble inside. The two rooms were exactly alike, except the bedroom was empty. "And there, the bed," Rajinder said, placing it with a slight wave of his hand against the wall across from the window. He spoke slowly and firmly, as if he were describing what was already there. "The fridge we can put right there," at the foot of the bed. Both were part of my dowry. Whenever he looked at me, I either said yes or nodded my head in agreement. We went outside and he showed me the kitchen and the bathroom, which were connected to the flat but could be entered only through doors opening onto the roof.

From the roof, a little after eleven, I watched Rajinder drive away on his scooter. He was going to my parents' flat in the Old Vegetable Market, where my dowry and our wedding gifts were stored. I had nothing to do while he was gone, so I wandered in and out of the flat and around the roof. Defense Colony was composed of rows of pale two- or three-story buildings. A small park, edged with eucalyptus trees, was behind our house.

Rajinder returned two hours later with his elder brother, Ashok, and a yellow van. It took three trips to bring the TV, the sofa, the fridge, the mixer, the steel plates, and my clothes. Each time they left, I wanted them never to return. Whenever they pulled up outside, Ashok pressed the horn, which played "Jingle Bells." I was frightened by Ashok, because, with his handlebar moustache and muscular forearms, he reminded me of my father's brothers, who, my mother claimed, beat their wives. Listening to his curses drift out of the stairwell each time he bumped against a wall while maneuvering the sofa, TV, and fridge up the stairs, I felt ashamed, as if he were cursing the dowry and, through it, me.

On the first trip they brought back two suitcases that my mother had packed with my clothes. I was cold, and when they left, I changed in the bedroom. My hands were trembling by then, and each time I swallowed, I felt a sharp pain in my throat that made my eyes water. Standing there in the room gray with dust, the light like cold, clear water, I felt sad and lonely and excited at being naked in an empty room in a place where no one knew me. I put on a sylvar kamij, but even completely covered by the big shirt and pants, I was cold. I added a sweater and socks, but the cold had slipped under my skin and lingered beneath my fingernails.

Rajinder did not appear to notice I had changed. I swept the rooms while the men were gone, and stacked the kitchen shelves with the steel plates, saucers, and spoons that had come as gifts. Rajinder and Ashok brought all the gifts except

the bed, which was too big for them. It was raised to the roof
by pulleys the next day. They were able to bring up the mattress, though, and the sight of it made me happy, for I knew I
would fall asleep easily and that another eight hours would
pass.

We did not eat lunch, but in the evening I made rotis and
lentils on a kerosene stove. The kitchen had no lightbulb, and I
had only the stove's blue flame to see by. The icy wind swirled
around my feet. Nearly thirty years later I can still remember
that wind. I could eat only one roti, while Rajinder and Ashok
had six each. We sat in the living room, and they spoke loudly
of their family's farm, gasoline prices, politics in Haryana, and
Indira Gandhi's government. I spoke once, saying that I liked
Indira Gandhi, and Ashok said that was because I was a Delhi
woman who wanted to see women in power. My throat hurt
and I felt as if I were breathing steam.

Ashok left after dinner, and Rajinder and I were truly alone
for the first time since our marriage. Our voices were so respectful, we might have been in mourning. He took me silently
in the bedroom, on the mattress beneath the window with the
full moon peering in. When it was over and Rajinder was
sleeping, I lifted myself on an elbow to look at him. I felt somehow that I could look at him more easily while he was asleep. I
would not be nervous, trying to hide my scrutiny, and if the
panic came, I could just hold on until it passed. I thought that
if I could see him properly just once, I would no longer be
frightened; I would know what kind of a man he was and
what the future held. But the narrow mouth and the stiff,
straight way he slept, with his arms folded across his chest,
said one thing, and the long, dark eyelashes denied it. I stared
at him until he started flickering, and then I closed my eyes.

Three months earlier, when our parents introduced us, I did
not think we would marry. The neutrality of Rajinder's features, across the restaurant table from me, reassured me that
we would not meet after that dinner. It was not that I expected
to marry someone particularly handsome. I was neither pretty
nor talented, and my family was not rich. But I could not imagine spending my life with someone so anonymous. If asked, I

would have been unable to tell what kind of man I wanted to marry, whether he should be handsome and funny. I was not even certain I wanted to marry, though at times I thought marriage would make me less lonely. What I wanted was to be with someone who could make me different, someone other than the person I was.

Rajinder did not appear to be such a man, and although the fact that we were meeting meant that our families approved of each other, I still felt safe. Twice before, my parents had sat on either side of me as I met men found through the matrimonial section of the Sunday *Times of India*. One received a job offer in Bombay, and Ma and Pitaji did not want to send me that far away with someone they could not be sure of. The other, who was very handsome and drove a motorcycle, had lied about his income. I was glad that he had lied, for what could such a handsome man find in me?

Those two introductions were also held in Vikrant, a two-story dosa restaurant across from the Amba cinema. I liked Vikrant, for I thought the place's obvious cheapness would be held against us. The evening that Rajinder and I met, Vikrant was crowded with people waiting for the six-to-nine show. We sat down and an adolescent waiter swept bits of sambhar and dosa from the table onto the floor. Footsteps upstairs caused flecks of blue paint to drift down.

As the dinner began, Rajinder's mother, a small, round woman with a pockmarked face, spoke of her sorrow that Rajinder's father had not lived to see his two sons reach manhood. Ashok, sitting on one side of Rajinder, nodded slowly and solemnly at this. Rajinder gave no indication of what he thought. After a moment of silence Pitaji, obese and bald, tilted slightly forward and said, "It's all in the stars. What can a man do?" The waiter returned with five glasses of water, his fingers dipped to the second joint in the water. Rajinder and I were supposed to speak, but I was nervous, despite my certainty that we would not marry, and could think of nothing to say. We did not open our mouths until we ordered our dosas. Pitaji, worried that we would spend the meal in silence, asked Rajinder, "Other than work, how do you like to spend your time?" Then, to impress Rajinder with his sophistication, he added in English, "What hobbies you have?" The door to the kitchen, a few tables from us, was open, and I saw a cow standing near a skillet.

"I like to read the newspaper. In college I played badminton," Rajinder answered in English. His voice was respectful, and he smoothed each word with his tongue before letting go.

"Anita sometimes reads the newspapers," Ma said, and then became quiet at the absurdity of her words.

The food came and we ate quickly and mostly in silence, though all of us made sure to leave a bit on the plate to show how full we were.

Rajinder's mother talked the most during the meal. She told us that Rajinder had always been favored over his elder brother—a beautiful, hardworking boy who obeyed his mother like God Ram—and how Rajinder had paid her back by being the first in the family to leave the farm in Bursa to attend college, where he got a master's, and by becoming a bank officer. To get to work from Bursa he had to commute two and a half hours every day. This was very strenuous, she said, and Rajinder had long ago reached the age for marriage, so he wished to set up a household in the city. "We want a city girl," his mother said loudly, as if boasting of her modernity. "With an education but a strong respect for tradition."

"Asha, Anita's younger sister, is finishing her Ph.D. in molecular biology and might be going to America in a year, for further studies," Ma said slowly, almost accidentally. She was a short, dark woman, so thin that her skin hung loose. "Two of my brothers are doctors; so is one sister. And I have one brother who is an engineer. I wanted Anita to be a doctor, but she was lazy and did not study." My mother and I loved each other, but sometimes something inside her would slip, and she would attack me, and she was so clever and I loved her so much that all I could do was feel helpless.

Dinner ended and I still had not spoken. When Rajinder said he did not want any dessert, I asked, "Do you like movies?" It was the only question I could think of, and I had felt pressured by Pitaji's stares.

"A little," Rajinder said seriously. After a pause he asked, "And you, do you like movies?"

"Yes," I said, and then, to be daring and to assert my personality, I added, "very much."

Two days after that Pitaji asked me if I would mind marrying Rajinder, and because I could not think of any reason not to, I said all right. Still, I did not think we would marry. Something would come up. His family might decide that my B.A. and B.Ed. were not enough, or Rajinder might suddenly announce that he was in love with his typist.

The engagement occurred a month later, and although I was not allowed to attend the ceremony, Asha was, and she described everything. Rajinder sat cross-legged before the pandit and the holy fire. Pitaji's pants were too tight for him to fold his legs, and he had to keep a foot on either side of the fire. Ashok and his mother were on either side of Rajinder. The small pink room was crowded with Rajinder's aunts and uncles. The uncles, Asha said, were unshaven and smelled faintly of manure. The pandit chanted in Sanskrit and at certain points motioned for Pitaji to tie a red thread around Rajinder's right wrist and to place a packet of one hundred five-rupee bills in his lap.

Only then, as Asha, grinning, described the ceremony, did I realize that I would actually marry Rajinder. I was shocked. I seemed to be standing outside myself, a stranger, looking at two women, Anita and Asha, sitting on a brown sofa in a wide, bright room. We were two women, both of whom would cry if slapped, laugh if tickled. But one was doing her Ph.D. and possibly going to America, and the other, her elder sister, who was slow in school, was now going to marry and have children and grow old. Why will she go to America and I stay here? I wanted to demand of someone, anyone. Why, when Pitaji took us out of school, saying what good was education for girls, did Asha, then only in third grade, go and re-enroll herself, while I waited for Pitaji to change his mind? I felt so sad I could not even hate Asha for her thoughtlessness.

As the days until the wedding evaporated, I had difficulty sleeping, and sometimes everything was lost in a sudden brightness. Often I woke at night and thought the engagement was a dream. Ma and Pitaji mentioned the marriage only in

connection with the shopping involved. Once, Asha asked
what I was feeling about the marriage, and I said, "What do
you care?"

When I placed the necklace of marigolds around Rajinder's
neck, to seal our marriage, I brushed my hand against his neck
to confirm the reality of his presence. The pandit recited Sanskrit verses, occasionally pouring clarified butter into the holy
fire, which we had just circled seven times. It is done, I
thought. I am married now. I felt no different. I was wearing a
bright-red silk sari and could smell the sourness of new cloth.
People were surrounding us, many people. Movie songs blared
over the loudspeakers. On the ground was a red-and-black-
striped carpet. The tent above us had the same stripes. Rajinder
draped a garland around my neck, and everyone began cheering. Their voices smothered the rumble of the night's traffic
passing on the road outside the alley.

Although the celebration lasted another six hours, ending at
about one in the morning, I did not remember most of it until
many years later. I did not remember the two red thrones on
which we sat and received the congratulations of women in
pretty silk saris and men wearing handsome pants and shirts. I
know about the cold only because of the photos showing vapor
coming from people's mouths as they spoke. I still do not remember what I thought as I sat there. For nearly eight years I
did not remember Ashok and his mother, Ma, Pitaji, and Asha
getting in the car with us to go to the temple hostel where the
people from Rajinder's side were housed. Nor did I remember
walking through the long halls, with moisture on the once
white walls, and seeing in rooms, long and wide, people sleeping on cots, mattresses without frames, blankets folded twice
before being laid down. I did not remember all this until one
evening eight years later, while wandering through Kamla
Nagar market searching for a dress for Asha's first daughter. I
was standing on the sidewalk looking at a stall display of hair
bands and thinking of Asha's husband, a tall, yellow-haired
American with a soft, open face, who I felt had made Asha
happier and gentler. And then I began crying. People brushed
past, trying to ignore me. I was so alone. I was thirty-three
years old and so alone that I wanted to sit down on the sidewalk until someone came and picked me up.

I did remember Rajinder's opening the blue door to the room where we would spend our wedding night. Before we entered, we separated for a moment. Rajinder touched his mother's feet with his right hand and then touched his forehead with that hand. His mother embraced him. I did the same with each of my parents. As Ma held me, she whispered, "Earlier your father got drunk like the pig he is." Then Pitaji put his arms around me and said, "I love you," in English.

The English was what made me cry, even though everyone thought it was the grief of parting. The words reminded me of how Pitaji came home drunk after work once or twice a month and Ma, thin arms folded across her chest, stood in the doorway of his bedroom and watched him fumbling to undress. When I was young, he held me in his lap those nights, his arm tight around my waist, and spoke into my ear in English, as if to prove that he was sober. He would say, "No one loves me. You love me, don't you, my little sun-ripened mango? I try to be good. I work all day, but no one loves me." As he spoke, he rocked in place. He would be watching Ma to make sure she heard. Gradually his voice would become husky. He would cry slowly, gently, and when the tears began to come, he would let me go and continue rocking, lost gratefully in his own sadness. Sometimes he turned out the lights and cried silently in the dark for a half hour or more. Then he locked the door to his room and slept.

Those nights Ma offered dinner without speaking. Later she told her own story. But she did not cry, and although Ma knew how to let her voice falter as if the pain were too much to speak of, and her face crumpled with sorrow, I was more impressed by Pitaji's tears. Ma's story included some beautiful lines. Lines like "In higher secondary a teacher said, In seven years all the cells in our body change. So when Baby died, I thought, It will be all right. In seven years none of me will have touched Baby." Other lines were as fine, but this was Asha's favorite. It might have been what first interested her in microbiology. Ma would not eat dinner, but she sat with us on the floor and, leaning forward, told us how she had loved Pitaji once, but after Baby got sick and she kept sending telegrams to Beri for Pitaji to come home and he did not, she did not send a telegram about Baby's death. "What could he do," she would say,

looking at the floor, "although he always cries so hand-
somely?" I was dazzled by her words—calling his tears handsome—in comparison with which Pitaji's ramblings appeared
inept. But the grief of the tears seemed irrefutable. And because Ma loved Asha more than she did me, I was less compassionate toward her. When Pitaji awoke and asked for water to
dissolve the herbs and medicines that he took to make himself
vomit, I obeyed readily. When Pitaji spoke of love on my wedding night, the soft, wet vowels of his vomiting were what I
remembered.

Rajinder closed and bolted the door. A double bed was in
the center of the room, and near it a small table with a jug of
water and two glasses. The room had yellow walls and smelled
faintly of mildew. I stopped crying and suddenly felt very
calm. I stood in the center of the room, a fold of the sari covering my head and falling before my eyes. I thought, I will just
say this has been a terrible mistake. Rajinder lifted the sari's
fold and, looking into my eyes, said he was very pleased to
marry me. He was wearing a white silk kurta with tiny flowers
embroidered around the neck and gold studs for buttons. He
led me to the bed with his hand on my elbow and with a light
squeeze let me know he wanted me to sit. He took off the loose
shirt and suddenly looked small. *No, wait. I must tell you,* I said.
His stomach drooped. What an ugly man, I thought. *No. Wait,* I
said. He did not hear or I did not say. Louder. *You are a very
nice man, I am sure.* The hard bed with the white sheet dotted
with rose petals. The hands that undid the blouse and were
disappointed by my small breasts. The ceiling was so far away.
The moisture between my legs like breath on glass. Rajinder
put his kurta back on and poured himself some water and then
thought to offer me some.

Sleep was there, cool and dark, as soon as I closed my eyes.
But around eight in the morning, when Rajinder shook me
awake, I was exhausted. The door to our room was open, and I
saw one of Rajinder's cousins, a fat, hairy man with a towel
around his waist, walk past to the bathroom. He looked in and
smiled broadly, and I felt ashamed. I was glad I had gotten up
at some point in the night and wrapped the sari on again. I had
not felt cold, but I had wanted to be completely covered.

Rajinder, Ashok, their mother, and I had breakfast in our

room. We sat around the small table and ate rice and yogurt. I wanted to sleep. I wanted to tell them to go away, to stop talking about who had come last night and brought what, and who had not but might still be expected to send a gift—tell them they were boring, foolish people. Ashok and his mother spoke, while Rajinder just nodded. Their words were indistinct, as if coming from across a wide room, and I felt I was dreaming them. I wanted to close my eyes and rest my head on the table. "You eat like a bird," Rajinder's mother said, looking at me and smiling.

After breakfast we visited a widowed aunt of Rajinder's who had been unable to attend the wedding because of arthritis. She lived in a two-room flat covered with posters of gods and smelling of mothballs and old sweat. As she spoke of how carpenters and cobblers were moving in from the villages and passing themselves off as upper-castes, she drooled from the corners of her mouth. I was silent, except for when she asked me about my education and what dishes I liked to cook. As we left, she said, "A thousand years. A thousand children," and pressed fifty-one rupees into Rajinder's hands.

Then there was the long bus ride to Bursa. The roads were so bad that I kept being jolted awake, and my sleep became so fractured that I dreamed of the bus ride and being awakened. And in the village I saw grimy hens peering into the well, and women for whom I posed demurely in the courtyard. They sat in a circle around me and murmured compliments. My head and eyes were covered as they had been the night before, and as I stared at the floor, I fell asleep. I woke an hour later to their praise of my modesty. That night, in the dark room at the rear of the house, I was awakened by Rajinder's digging between my legs, and although he tried to be gentle, I just wished it over. His face, flat and distorted, was above me, and his hands raised my nipples cruelly, resentful of being cheated, even though I never heard anger in Rajinder's voice. He was always polite. Even in bed he was formal. "Could you get on all fours, please?"

So heavy and still did I feel on the first night in our new rooftop home, watching Rajinder sleep on the moonlight-soaked mattress, that I wanted the earth and sky to stop turning and

for it always to be night. I did not want dawn to come and the
day's activities to start again. I did not want to have to think
and react to the world. I fell asleep then, only to wake in panic
an hour later at the thought of the obscure life I would lead
with Rajinder. Think slowly, I told myself, looking at Rajinder
asleep with an arm thrown over his eyes. Slowly. I remembered the year between my B.A. and my B.Ed., when, through
influence, I got a job as a typist in a candle factory. For nearly a
month, upon reaching home after work, I wanted to cry, for I
was terrified at the idea of giving up eight hours a day, a third
of my life, to typing letters concerning supplies of wax. And
then one day I noticed that I no longer felt afraid. I had learned
to stop thinking. I floated above the days.

In the morning I had a fever, and the stillness it brought
with it spread into the coming days. It hardened around me, so
that I did not feel as if I were the one making love or cooking
dinner or going home to see Ma and Pitaji and behaving there
as I always had. No one guessed it was not me. Nothing could
break through the stillness, not even Rajinder's learning to ca-
ress me before parting my legs, or my growing to know all the
turns of the colony's alleys, and the shopkeepers calling me by
name.

Winter turned into spring, and the trees in the park swelled
green. Rajinder was thoughtful and generous. Traveling for
conferences to Baroda, Madras, Jaipur, Bangalore, he always
brought back saris or other gifts. The week I had malaria, he
came home every lunch hour and cooked gruel for me. On my
twenty-sixth birthday he took me to the Taj Mahal, and arranged to have my family hidden in the flat when we returned
in the evening. What a good man, I thought then, watching
him standing proudly in a corner. What a good man, I thought,
and was frightened, for that was not enough. I knew I needed
something else, but I did not know what. Being his wife was
not so bad. He did not make me do anything I did not want to,
except make love, and even that was sometimes pleasant. I did
not mind his being in the flat, and being alone is difficult.
When he was away on his trips, I did not miss him, and he, I
think, did not miss me, for he never mentioned it.

Summer came, and hot winds swept up from the Rajasthani deserts. The old cows that wander unattended on Delhi's streets began to die. The corpses lay untouched for a week sometimes; their tongues swelled and, cracking open the jaw, stuck out absurdly.

The heat was like a high-pitched buzzing that formed a film between flesh and bone, so that my skin felt thick and rubbery and I wished that I could just peel it off. I woke at four every morning to have an hour when breathing air would not be like inhaling liquid. By five the eastern edge of the sky was too bright to look at, even though the sun had yet to appear. I bathed both before and after breakfast and again after doing laundry but before lunch. As June progressed, and the very air seemed to whine under the heat's stress, I stopped eating lunch. Around two, before taking my nap, I would pour a few mugs of water on my head. I liked to lie on the bed imagining that the monsoon had come. Sometimes this made me sad, for the smell of wet earth and the sound of the rain have always made me feel as if I have been waiting for someone all my life and that person has not yet come. I dreamed often of living near the sea, in a house with a sloping red roof and bright-blue window frames, and woke happy, hearing water on sand.

And so the summer passed, slowly and vengefully, until the last week of June, when the *Times of India* began its countdown to the monsoon, and I awoke one afternoon in love with my husband.

I had returned home that day after spending two weeks with my parents. Pitaji had had a mild heart attack, and I took turns with Ma and Asha being with him in Safdarjung Hospital. The heart attack was no surprise, for Pitaji had become so fat that even his largest shirts had to be worn unbuttoned. So when I opened the door late one night and saw Asha with her fist up, ready to start banging again, I did not have to be told that Pitaji had woken screaming that his heart was breaking.

While I hurried a sari and blouse into a plastic bag, Asha leaned against a wall of our bedroom, drinking water. It was three. Rajinder, in his undershirt and pajama pants, sat on the bed's edge and stared at the floor. I felt no fear, perhaps because Asha had said the heart attack was not so bad, or perhaps because I just did not care. The rushing and the banging on doors appeared to be the properly melodramatic behavior when one's father might be dying.

An auto-rickshaw was waiting for us downstairs, triangular, small, with plasticized cloth covering its frame. It seemed like a vehicle for desperate people. Before getting in, I looked up and saw Rajinder. He was leaning against the railing. The moon was yellow and uneven behind him. I waved and he waved back. Such formalities, I thought, and then we were off, racing through dark, abandoned streets.

"Ma's fine. He screamed so loud," Asha said. She is a few inches taller than I am, and although she, too, is not pretty, she uses makeup that gives angles to her round face. Asha sat slightly turned on the seat so that she could face me. "A thousand times we told him, Lose weight," she said, shaking her head impatiently. "When the doctor gave him that diet, he said, 'Is that before or after breakfast?' " She paused and added in a tight whisper, "He's laughing now."

I felt lonely sitting there while the city was silent and dark and we talked of our father without concern. "He wants to die," I said softly. I enjoyed saying such serious words. "He is so unhappy. I think our hopes are made when we are young, and we can never adjust them to the real world. He was nearly national champion in wrestling, and for the past thirty-seven years he has been examining government schools to see that they have the right PE equipment. He loves eating, and that is as fine a way to die as any."

"If he wants to die, wonderful; I don't like him. But why is he making it difficult for us?"

Her directness shocked me and made me feel that my sentimentality was dishonest. The night air was still bitter from the evening traffic. "He is a good man," I said unsteadily.

"The way he treated us all. Ma is like a slave."

"They are just not good together. It's no one's fault."

"How can it be no one's fault?"

"His father was an alcoholic."

"How long can you use your parents as an excuse?"

I did not respond at first, for I thought Asha might be saying this because I had always used Ma and Pitaji to explain away my failures. Then I said, "Look how good he is compared with his brothers. He must have had something good inside that let him be gentler than them. We should love him for that part alone."

"That's what he is relying on. It's a big world. A lot of people are worth loving. Why love someone mediocre?"

Broken glass was in the hallways of the hospital, and someone had urinated in the elevator. When we came into the yellow room that Pitaji shared with five other men, he was asleep. His face looked like a shiny brown stone. He was on the bed nearest the window. Ma sat at the foot of his bed, her back to us, looking out at the fading night.

"He will be all right," I said.

Turning toward us, Ma said, "When he goes, he wants to make sure we all hurt." She was crying. "I thought I did not love him, but you can't live this long with a person and not love just a bit. He knew that. When they were bringing him here, he said, 'See what you've done, demoness.' "

Asha took Ma away, still crying. I spent the rest of the night dozing in a chair next to his bed.

We fell into a pattern. Ma usually came in the morning, around eight, and I replaced her, hours later. Asha would take my place at three and stay until six, and then Ma's brother or his sons would stay until Ma returned.

I had thought I would be afraid of being in the hospital, but it was very peaceful. Pitaji slept most of the day and night because of the medicines, waking up every now and then to ask for water and quickly falling asleep again. A nice boy named Rajeeve, who also was staying with his father, told me funny stories about his family. At night Asha and I slept on adjacent cots on the roof. Before she went to bed, she read five pages of an English dictionary. She had been accepted into a postdoctoral program in America. She did not brag about it as I would have. Like Ma, Asha worked very hard, as if that were the only way to live and one needn't talk about it, and as if, like Ma, she assumed that we are all equally fortunate. But sometimes Asha would shout a word at me—"Alluvial!"—and then look at me as if she was waiting for a response. Once,

Rajinder came to drop off some clothes, but I was away. I did not see him or talk with him for the two weeks.

Sometimes Pitaji could not sleep and he would tell me stories of his father, a schoolteacher, who would take Pitaji with him to the saloon, so that someone would be there to guide him home when he was drunk. Pitaji was eight or nine then. His mother beat him for accompanying Dadaji, but Pitaji, his breath sounding as if it were coming through a wet cloth, said that he was afraid Dadaji would be made fun of if he walked home alone. Pitaji told the story quietly, as if he were talking about someone else, and as soon as he finished, he changed the subject. I could not tell whether Pitaji was being modest or was manipulating me by pretending modesty.

He slept most of the day, and I sat beside him, listening to his little green transistor radio. The June sun filled half the sky, and the groundskeeper walked around the courtyard of the hospital in wide circles with a water bag as large as a man's body slung over one shoulder. He was sprinkling water to keep the dust settled. Sometimes I hummed along to Lata Mangeshkar or Mohammed Rafi singing that grief is no letter to be passed around to whoever wants to read.

There were afternoons when Pitaji became restless and whispered conspiratorially that he had always loved me most. Watching his face, puffy from the drugs, his nose broad and covered with blackheads, as he said again that Ma did not talk to him or that Asha was indifferent to his suffering, I felt exhausted. When he complained to Asha, "Your mother doesn't talk to me," she answered, "Maybe you aren't interesting."

Once, four or five days before we took him home, as he was complaining, I got up from the chair and went to look out the window. Beyond the courtyard was a string of yellow-and-black auto-rickshaws waiting under eucalyptus trees. I wanted desperately for Asha to come, so that I could leave, and bathe, and lie down to dream of a house with a red-tiled roof near the sea. "You must forgive me," Pitaji said as I looked out the window. I was surprised, for I could not remember his ever apologizing. "I sometimes forget that I will die soon and so act like a man who has many years left." I felt frightened, for I suddenly wanted to love him but could not trust him enough.

From then until we went home, Pitaji spoke little. Once, I forgot to bring his lunch from home and he did not complain, whereas before he would have screamed and tried to make me feel guilty. A few times he began crying to himself for no reason, and when I asked why, he did not answer.

Around eleven the day Pitaji was released, an ambulance carried Ma, Pitaji, and me to the Old Vegetable Market. Two orderlies, muscular men in white uniforms, carried him on a stretcher up three flights of stairs into the flat. The flat had four rooms and was part of a circle of dilapidated buildings that shared a courtyard. Fourteen or fifteen people turned out to watch Pitaji's return. Some of the very old women, sitting on cots in the courtyard, asked who Pitaji was, although he had lived there for twenty years. A few children climbed into the ambulance and played with the horn until they were chased out.

The orderlies laid Pitaji on the cot in his bedroom and left. The room was small and dark, smelling faintly of the kerosene with which the bookshelves were treated every other week to prevent termites. Traveling had tired him, and he fell asleep quickly. He woke as I was about to leave. Ma and I were speaking in whispers outside his bedroom.

"I am used to his screaming," Ma said. "He won't get any greasy food here. But once he can walk . . ."

"He seems to have changed."

"Right now he's afraid. Give him a few days and he'll return to normal. People can't change, even if they want to."

"What are you saying about me?" Pitaji tried to call out, but his voice was like wind on dry grass.

"You want something?" Ma asked.

"Water."

As I started toward the fridge, Ma said, "Nothing cold." The clay pot held only enough for one glass. I knelt beside the cot and helped Pitaji rise to a forty-five-degree angle. His heaviness and the weakness of his body moved me. Like a baby holding a bottle, Pitaji held the glass with both hands and made sucking noises as he drank. I lowered him when his shoulder muscles slackened. His eyes were red, and they moved about the room slowly. I wondered whether I could safely love him if I did not reveal my feelings.

"More?" he asked.

"Only fridge water," I said. Ma was clattering in the kitchen. "I am going home."

"Rajinder is good?" He looked at the ceiling while speaking.

"Yes," I said. A handkerchief of light covered his face, and faint blue veins, like delicate, almost translucent roots, showed through the skin of his forehead. "The results for his exam came," I told him. "He will be promoted. He was second in Delhi." Pitaji closed his eyes. "Are you hurting?" I asked.

"I feel tired."

I, too, felt tired. I did not know what to do with my new love or whether it would last. "That will pass, the doctor said. Why don't you sleep?"

"I don't want to," he said loudly, and my love drew back.

"I must go," I said, but made no move to.

"Forgive me," he said, and again I was surprised. "I am not worried usually, but I get frightened sometimes. Sometimes I dream that the heaviness is dirt. What an awful thing to be a Muslim or a Christian." He spoke slowly, and I felt my love returning. "Once, I dreamed of Baby's ghost."

"Oh."

"He was eight or nine and did not recognize me. He did not look like me. I was surprised, because he was my son and I had always expected him to look like me."

I felt exhausted. Something about the story was both awkward and polished, which indicated deceit. But Pitaji never lied completely, and the tiring part was not knowing. "God will forgive you," I said. But why should he? I thought. Why do people always think hurting others is all right, as long as they hurt themselves as well?

"Your mother has not."

I placed my hand on his, knowing that I was already in the trap. "Shhh."

"At your birthday, when she sang, I said, 'If you sing like that for me every day, I will love you forever.' "

"She loves you. She worries about you."

"That's not the same. When I tell Asha this, she tells me I'm sentimental. Ratha loved me once. But she cannot forgive.

What happened so long ago, she cannot forgive." He was blinking rapidly, preparing to cry. "But that is a lie. She does not love me because," and he began crying without making a sound, "I did not love her for so long."

"Shhh. She loves you. She was just saying 'Oh, I love him so. I hope he gets better, for I love him so.'"

"Ratha could have loved me a little. She could have loved me twenty for my eleven." He was sobbing.

"Shhh. Shhh. Shhh." I wanted to run away, far away, and be someone else.

The sleep that afternoon was like falling. I lay down, closed my eyes, and plummeted. I woke as suddenly, without any half memories of dreams, into a silence that meant that the power was gone, and the ceiling fan was still, and the fridge was slowly warming.

It was cool, I noticed, unsurprised by the monsoon's approach—for I was in love. The window curtains stirred, revealing TV antennas and distant gray clouds and a few sparrows wheeling in the air. The sheet lay bunched at my feet. I felt gigantic. My legs stretched thousands of miles; my head rested in the Himalayas and my breath brought the world rain. If I stood up, I would scrape against the sky. But I was small and compact and distilled, too. I am in love, I thought, and a raspy voice echoed the words in my head, causing me to panic and lose my sense of omnipotence for a moment. I will love Rajinder slowly and carefully and cunningly, I thought, and suddenly felt peaceful again, as if I were a lake and the world could only form ripples on my surface, while the calm beneath continued in solitude. Time seemed endless, and I would surely have the minutes and seconds needed to plan a method of preserving this love, like the feeling in your stomach when you are in a car going swiftly down a hill. Don't worry, I thought, and I no longer did. My mind obeyed me limply, as if a terrible exhaustion had worn away all rebellion.

I got up and swung my legs off the bed. I was surprised that my love was not disturbed by my physical movements. I walked out onto the roof. The wind ruffled the treetops and small, gray clouds slid across the cool, pale sky. On the street eight or nine young boys played cricket. The school year had just started, and the children played desperately, as if they must run faster, leap higher, to recapture the hours spent indoors.

Tell me your stories, I would ask him. Pour them into me, so that I know everything you have ever loved or been scared of or laughed at. But thinking this, I became uneasy and feared that when I actually saw him, my love would fade and I would find my tongue thick and unresponsive. What should I say? I woke this afternoon in love with you. I love you too, he would answer. No, no, you see, I really love you. I love you so much that I think anything is possible, that I will live forever. Oh, he would say, and I would feel my love rush out of me.

I must say nothing at first, I decided. Slowly I will win his love. I will spoil him, and he will fall in love with me. And as long as he loves me, I will be able to love him. I will love him like a camera that closes at too much light and opens at too little, so his blemishes will never mar my love.

I watched the cricket game to the end. I felt very happy standing there, as if I had just discovered some profound secret. When the children dispersed, around five, I knew Rajinder would be home soon.

I bathed and changed into new clothes. I stood before the small mirror in the armoire as I dressed. Uneven brown areoles, a flat stomach, the veins in my feet like pen marks. Will this be enough? I wondered. Once he loves me, I told myself. I lifted my arms and tried to smell the plantlike odor of my perspiration. I wore a bright-red cotton sari. What will I say first? *Namastay*—how was your day? With the informal "you." How was your day? The words felt strange, for I had never before used the informal with him. I had, as a show of modesty, never even used his name, except on the night before my wedding, when I said it over and over to myself to see how it felt—like nothing. Now when I said "Rajinder," the three syllables had too many edges, and again I doubted that he would love me. "Rajinder, Rajinder," I said rapidly several times, until it no longer felt strange. He will love me because to do otherwise would be too lonely, because I will love him so. I heard a scooter stopping outside the building and knew that he had come home.

My stomach was small and hard as I walked onto the roof. The dark clouds made it appear as if it were seven instead of five-thirty. I saw him roll the scooter into the courtyard and I felt happy. He parked the scooter and took off his gray helmet. He combed his hair carefully to hide the growing bald spot. The deliberateness of the way he tucked the comb into his back pocket overwhelmed me with tenderness. We will love each other gently and carefully, I thought.

I waited for him to rise out of the stairwell. The wind made my petticoat, drying on the clothesline, go *clap, clap*. I was smiling rigidly. How was your day? How *was* your day? Was your day good? Don't be so afraid, I told myself. What does it matter how you say hello? Tomorrow will come, and the day after, and the day after that.

His steps sounded like a shuffle. Leather rubbing against stone. Something forlorn and steady in the sound made me feel as if I were twenty years older and this were a game I should stop or I might get hurt. Rajinder, Rajinder, Rajinder, how are you?

First the head: oval, high forehead, handsome eyebrows. Then the not so broad but not so narrow shoulders. The top two buttons of the cream shirt were opened, revealing an undershirt and some hair. The two weeks had not changed him, yet seeing him, I felt as if he were somehow different, denser.

"How was your day?" I asked him, while he was still in the stairwell.

"All right," he said, stepping onto the balcony. He smiled, and I felt happy. His helmet was in his left hand and he had a plastic bag of mangoes in his right. "When did you get home?" The "you" was informal, and I felt a surge of relief. He will not resist, I thought.

"A little after three."

I followed him into the bedroom. He placed the helmet on the windowsill and the mangoes in the refrigerator. His careful way of folding the plastic bag before placing it in the basket on top of the refrigerator moved me. "Your father is fine?" I did not say anything.

Rajinder walked to the sink on the outside bathroom wall. I stood in the bedroom doorway and watched him wash his hands and face with soap. Before putting the chunk of soap down, he rinsed it of foam, and only then did he pour water on himself. He used a thin washcloth hanging on a nearby hook for drying.

"Yes," I said.

"What did the doctor say?" he asked, turning toward me.

He is like a black diamond, I thought.

She said, I love you. "She said he must lose weight and watch what he eats. Nothing fattening. That he should rest at first and then start exercising. Walking would be best."

I watched Rajinder hang his shirt by the collar tips on the clothesline, and suddenly felt sad at the rigorous attention to detail necessary to preserve love. Perhaps love is different in other countries, I thought, where the climate is cooler, where a woman can say her husband's name, where the power does not go out every day, where not every clerk demands a bribe. That must be a different type of love, I thought, where one can be careless.

"It will rain tonight," he said, looking at the sky.

The eucalyptus trees shook their heads side to side. "The rain always makes me feel as if I am waiting for someone," I said, and then regretted saying it, for Rajinder was not paying attention, and perhaps it could have been said better. "Why don't you sit on the balcony, and I will make sherbet to drink?"

He took a chair and the newspaper with him. The fridge water was warm, and I felt sad again at the need for constant vigilance. I made the drink and gave him his glass. I placed mine on the floor and went to get a chair. A fruit seller passed by, calling out in a reedy voice, "Sweet, sweet mangoes. Sweeter than first love." On the roof directly across, a boy seven or eight years old was trying to fly a large purple kite. I sat down beside Rajinder and waited for him to look up so that I could interrupt his reading. When Rajinder looked away from the paper to take a sip of sherbet, I asked, "Did you fly kites?"

"A little," he answered, looking at the boy. "Ashok bought some with the money he earned, and he would let me fly them sometimes." The fact that his father had died when he was young made me hopeful, for I thought that one must suffer and be lonely before one can love.

"Do you like Ashok?"

"He is my brother," he answered, shrugging and looking at the newspaper. He took a sip of the sherbet. I felt hurt, as if he had reprimanded me.

I waited until seven for the power to return; then I gave up and started to prepare dinner in the dark. I sat beside Rajinder until then. I felt happy and excited and frightened being beside him. We spoke about Asha's going to America, though Rajinder did not want to talk about this. Rajinder had been the most educated member of his and my family and resented the idea that Asha would soon assume that position.

As I cooked in the kitchen, Rajinder sat on the balcony and listened to the radio. "This is Akashwani," the announcer said, and then music like horses racing played whenever a new program was about to start. It was very hot in the kitchen, and every now and then I stepped onto the roof to look at the curve of Rajinder's neck and confirm that the tenderness was still there.

We ate in the living room. Rajinder chewed slowly and was mostly silent. Once he complimented me on my cooking. "What are you thinking?" I asked. He appeared not to have heard. Tell me! Tell me! Tell me! I thought, and was shocked by the urgency I felt.

A candle on the television made pillars of shadows rise and collapse on the walls. I searched for something to start a conversation with. "Pitaji began crying when I left."

"You could have stayed a few more days," he said.

"I did not want to." I thought of adding, "I missed you," but that would have been a lie, and I would have felt embarrassed saying it, when he had not missed me.

Rajinder mixed black pepper with his yogurt. "Did you tell him you would visit soon?"

"No. I think he was crying because he was lonely."

"He should have more courage." Rajinder did not like Pitaji, thought him weak-willed, although Rajinder had never told me that. He knew Pitaji drank, but Rajinder never referred to this, for which I was grateful. "He is old and must remember that shadows creep into one's heart at his age." The shutter of a bedroom window began slamming, and I got up to latch it shut.

I washed the dishes while Rajinder bathed. When he came

out, dressed in his white kurta pajamas, with his hair slicked back, I was standing near the railing at the roof's edge, looking out beyond the darkness of our neighborhood at a distant ribbon of light. I was tired from the nervousness I had been feeling all evening. Rajinder came up behind me and asked, "Won't you bathe?" I suddenly doubted my ability to guard my love. Bathe so we can have sex. His words were too deliberately full of the unsaid, and so felt vulgar. I wondered if I had the courage to say no and realized I didn't. What kind of love can we have? I thought.

I said, "In a little while. Comedy hour is about to start." We sat down on our chairs with the radio between us and listened to Maurya's whiny voice. This week he had gotten involved with criminals who wanted to go to jail to collect the reward on themselves. The canned laughter gusted from several flats. When the music of the racing horses marked the close of the show, I felt hopeful again, and thought Rajinder looked very handsome in his kurta pajamas.

I bathed carefully, pouring mug after mug of cold water over myself until my fingertips were wrinkled and my nipples erect. The candlelight made the bathroom orange and my skin copper. I washed my pubis carefully to make sure no smell remained from urinating. Rubbing myself dry, I became aroused. I wore the red sari again, with a new blouse, and no bra, so that my nipples would show.

I came and stood beside Rajinder, my arm brushing against his kurta sleeve. Every now and then a raindrop fell, and I wondered if I were imagining it. On balconies and roofs all around us I could see the dim figures of men, women, and children waiting for the first rain. "You look pretty," he said. Somewhere Lata Mangeshkar sang with a static-induced huskiness. The street was silent. Even the children were hushed. As the wind picked up, Rajinder said, "Let's close the windows."

The wind coursed along the floor, upsetting newspapers and climbing the walls to swing on curtains. A candle stood on the refrigerator. As I leaned over to pull a window shut, Rajinder pressed against me and cupped my right breast. I felt a shock of desire pass through me. As I walked around the rooms shutting windows, he touched my buttocks, pubis, stomach.

When the last window was closed, I waited for a moment before turning around, because I knew he wanted me to turn around quickly. He pulled me close, with his hands on my buttocks. I took his tongue in my mouth. We kissed like this for a long time.

The rain began falling, and we heard a roar from the people on the roofs nearby. "The clothes," Rajinder said, and pulled away.

We ran out. We could barely see each other. Lightning bursts would illuminate an eye, an arm, some teeth, and then darkness would come again. We jerked the clothes off and let the pins fall to the ground. We deliberately brushed roughly against each other. The raindrops were like thorns, and we began laughing. Rajinder's shirt had wrapped itself around and around the clothesline. Wiping his face, he knocked his glasses off. As I saw him crouch and fumble around helplessly for them, I felt such tenderness that I knew I would never love him as much as I did at that moment. "The wind in the trees," I cried out, "it sounds like the sea."

We slowly wandered back inside, kissing all the while. He entered me like a sigh. He suckled on me and moved back and forth and side to side, and I felt myself growing warm and loose. He sucked on my nipples and held my waist with both hands. We made love gently at first, but as we both neared climax, Rajinder began stabbing me with his penis and I came in waves so strong that I felt myself vanishing. When Rajinder sank on top of me, I kept saying, "I love you. I love you."

"I love you too," he answered. Outside, the rain came in sheets and the thunder was like explosions in caverns.

The candle had gone out while we made love, and Rajinder got up to light it. He drank some water and then lay down beside me. I wanted some water too, but did not want to say anything that would make him feel bad about his thoughtlessness. "I'll be getting promoted soon. Minaji loves me," Rajinder said. I rolled onto my side to look at him. He had his arms folded across his chest. "Yesterday he said, 'Come, Rajinderji, let us go write your confidential report.' " I put my hand on his stomach, and Rajinder said, "Don't," and pushed it away. "I said, 'Oh, I don't know whether that would be good, sir.' He laughed and patted me on the back. What a nincompoop. If it weren't for the quotas, he would never be manager." Rajinder chuckled. "I'll be the youngest bank manager in Delhi." I felt cold and tugged a sheet over our legs. "In college I had a schedule for where I wanted to be by the time I was thirty. By twenty-two I became an officer; soon I'll be a manager. I wanted a car, and we'll have that in a year. I wanted a wife, and I have that."

"You are so smart."

"Some people in college were smarter. But I knew exactly what I wanted. A life is like a house. One has to plan carefully where all the furniture will go."

"Did you plan me as your wife?" I asked, smiling.

"No. I had wanted at least an M.A., and someone who worked, but Mummy didn't approve of a daughter-in-law who worked. I was willing to change my requirements. Because I believe in moderation, I was successful. Everything in its place. And pay for everything. Other people got caught up in love and friendship. I've always felt that these things only became a big deal because of the movies."

"What do you mean? You love me and your mother, don't you?"

"There are so many people in the world that it is hard not to think that there are others you could love more."

Seeing the shock on my face, he quickly added, "Of course I love you. I just try not to be too emotional about it." The candle's shadows on the wall were like the wavery bands formed by light reflected off water. "We might even be able to get a foreign car."

The second time he took me that night, it was from behind. He pressed down heavily on my back and grabbed my breasts.

I woke at four or five. The rain scratched against the windows and a light like blue milk shone along the edges of the door. I was cold and tried to wrap myself in the sheet, but it was not large enough.

William Hoffman

STONES

The liver-and-white pointers, Zack and Rattler, ranged wide across lespedeza which rasped Chip's leather-faced hunting britches. His father still allowed him only eight shells—the bobwhite limit in Virginia. Chip had to account for each one fired, and if he averaged more than two per bird his father acted as if he'd bitten into an unripe persimmon.

The father's counting of shells had been part of Chip's training to make him bring the walnut stock to his cheek and level his eyes along the entire length of the L. C. Smith's sixteen-gauge side-by-side. He frequently carried home meat on a bird-for-shell average, pleasing his father who kidded him by asking, "You ain't shooting them on the ground?"

This was November 20th, the first day of the new season, and the dogs dropped on point midway across the field. Before Chip reached them, he saw the new fence—three strands of barb wire stapled to freshly cut cedar posts. Red soil had been tamped around the base of each post, and on every other one a *No Trespassing* sign had been tacked.

Zack and Rattler were stanch. Their tails spiked upward, and the bird scent was so strong their bodies trembled. Chip, the L. C. Smith held high, stepped forward between them.

The covey erupted right at the fence line and swung left. He dropped a bird that flew high and then a sleeper. He watched the covey glide down among distant pines. The two birds had fallen on the other side of the fence. The dogs waited for his command to fetch. He sent them across.

Zack found the sleeper. He retrieved it, his mouth working feathers, but his teeth never punctured flesh. Chip took it from him, smoothed the feathers of the cock bird wetted by Zack's saliva, and stuck it in the game pouch of his canvas vest. He'd already drawn two more No. 8s from loops of the vest and thumbed them into the shotgun's chambers.

Rattler hadn't found the second bird. Zack joined in to work the lespedeza. The bobwhite had been winged and was running. Chip stood at the fence. He read the name written at the bottom of posted sign: A. I. Benjamin.

Still the dogs didn't find the bird. Chip looked toward the house. This property was called the Gatlin Place. Once it'd been a tobacco plantation of three thousand acres mostly given to the growing of dark-fired tobacco. Julius Temple Gatlin, the patriarch whose portrait hung in the courthouse, had raised a troop to ride with Jeb Stuart and died a judge at ninety-six while sitting on the bench trying a horse-thieving case.

Over the years portions had been sold off or leased out by Gatlin women. Georgia Pacific had bought a section for saw timber that ran all the way down to the Hidden River. The house had been abandoned. Wisteria and briars grew to riot in the family cemetery and box bushes of what'd once been a formal garden.

The dogs again jerked on point. Chip'd never be able to whistle them off. He could fire the L. C. Smith, which might cause them to break, yet the bird would most likely be left dead. He felt anger that anybody had fenced in part of his prime hunting territory.

He pushed down the middle strand of barb wire and ducked through. The dogs pointed into a honeysuckle patch, heads down, their eyes bugged. Chip stepped in boldly. He kicked his boot through honeysuckle. Still no bird. "Hie on!" he commanded.

Rattler bolted forward and came up with the bird. It'd been hit by one pellet through the breast and able to run a distance before dying. Chip allowed the dogs to mouth it, the reward for good work. He made over them, and as he fitted the bird in his game pouch, he heard the shout.

Hurrying across the field from the direction of the house came a man wearing a dark unbuttoned overcoat and gray fedora. Closer, Chip saw he was black. He had on a gray suit, vest and shiny black shoes not meant for lespedeza. Beggar lice stuck to his pants legs and the bottom of the overcoat.

"What's your name?" he demanded. He was bulky, but not soft. He had a round pitted face. He wore gloves, not the work kind, but brown tender leather.

"John Kincaid," Chip said. "I shot the birds on the other side of the fence and just couldn't leave them."

"Give them to me," the man said. His eyes were more dark purple than black.

"They didn't come from this side," Chip said.

"You picked them up off my land," the man said. "Give them to me or we discuss it with the game warden."

Discussing it with game warden didn't sound like Howell County talk. Chip knew the general district judge, a hunter himself who taught Sunday School at the Olive Branch Methodist Church and was likely to be understanding of a trespassing case. When the man held out a gloved hand, Chip hesitated, then drew the birds from his pouch and tossed them on the ground.

"That's where they come from on your side of the fence," he said. As he bowed back through the fence, something struck his back. The nigger had thrown the birds at him.

"Mister, you're pretty brave doing that to a man holding a gun," Chip said.

"Man you call yourself?" he asked and laughed. "One razor blade would last you your lifetime up to now. Don't cross my fence ever again."

For an instant Chip felt hot and the gun wanting to lift. At least fan the nigger and make him dance in his city clothes. But that was dumb. He eased his thumb off the safety and spat before whistling in the dogs. When he glanced behind him, the nigger had the birds and was walking up toward the house.

· · ·

He didn't tell his father the whole thing. His father was a switchman for Norfolk-Southern. He had a temper. He broke dogs hard, laying into them with a leather strap he carried hooked to his belt if they failed to honor points or chewed a bird. At the dinner table Chip did mention the fence.

His mother heard something in his voice. When the father went to the weekly fire meeting, she asked what'd happened.

"Just let it alone," she said when Chip finished telling her. She was a small, wiry woman who worked at the shoe factory. "You got plenty of other hunting territory."

The father found out about Mr. A. I. Benjamin by asking around at the fire meeting. Abram Isaac Benjamin had bought the house through a Lynchburg real estate agent. Benjamin was from New York. That was enough to blacken him in Howell County no matter about his skin color.

"What's he fixing to do with the Gatlin Place?" the old men and ne'er-do-wells loafing in the shade of Tobaccoton's courthouse elms asked. Rumor was he meant to cut off and sell lots. What would happen to land values if he brought down a bunch of uppity niggers? Maybe they'd be a heathenistic religious cult.

Despite what Chip's mother told him, he sure didn't mean to allow Mr. A. I. Benjamin to keep him off that part of the land this side of the fence. He wouldn't shoot birds over it, but he'd take anything he could get right up to the line.

On a January Saturday, the last week of the season, he drove his Dad's '77 rattling Ford 150 longbody pickup out to the field. The weather was warm and windy, not right for good scenting. Worn down, Zack and Rattler went about finding birds in a trifling fashion.

As Chip directed them along the fence line, a cry came on the wind. If a cry. He listened. Maybe what he'd heard was a piece of loose roofing tin screeching on an old outbuilding.

He again heard it. He drew the shells from his gun before crossing the barbed wire. He ordered the dogs to heel and walked toward the house—a sprawling frame dwelling with four brick chimneys and verandas upstairs and down. A building permit had been nailed to a white oak. The Gatlin place must've been grand, but wind had peeled off the paint, slates were missing from the roof, and the empty windows seemed to stare out like blind eyes.

The voice was loud, coming from inside the house. Chip climbed the rickety steps to the front porch and shouted a hello through the open door.

"Up here!" the voice answered. "Come up here!"

Chip entered the front hall. Plaster had fallen in chunks. There was a large round hole in the ceiling where a light or chandelier must've hung. Broken glass lay on the floor, and mantels had been torn from fireplaces. Dry hay bales were stacked in what'd once probably been a dining room or parlor.

He looked up the curved staircase. The window on the landing was gone. He ordered the dogs to stay and started up. The steps felt shaky. The soles of his boots crunched glass. On the second floor he looked down a hallway to more fallen plaster. Dirt daubers had built nests on exposed lathing. All light fixtures had been ripped out, and twisted wires dangled.

"Here!" the voice called.

Chip looked into what had likely been a bedroom. Strips of faded rose wallpaper curled to the floor. Mr. A. I. Benjamin lay among a pile of bricks. Part of a chimney had fallen in on him.

He wore bib overalls, a leather jacket and was floured by mortar dust.

"Can't move the leg," he said, his eyes clenched.

Chip started to tell him *too damn bad, go to hell,* and might've left, but thought of his mother. She was chairlady of the Women of the Church down at Olive Branch Methodist. He leaned his L. C. Smith against the door frame, tested the floor as he moved forward, and checked the gap in the chimney to be sure no more of it was coming down. He began lifting bricks off Mr. A. I. Benjamin, who sweated and was biting back pain. When Chip got him uncovered, Mr. A. I. Benjamin's leg was bent funny. He dragged himself across the floor and vomited.

"Can you drive me to a doctor?" he whispered, hunched and panting.

"I'd pick up a runover hound," Chip said and helped him stand. Benjamin leaned his stinking weight on Chip. As they

worked down the steps, grains of plaster fell. Mr. A. I. Benjamin tried to swallow his hurting, but moaning got out.

His car, a black Mercedes, was parked behind the house. It
was a clean recent model, an SEL 420. Chip didn't know of
another in all of Howell County. Even the doctors, lawyers and
bankers drove Caddys and Lincolns.

"Just help me lie across the back seat," Mr. A. I. Benjamin
said.

"Sure going to mess up your car," Chip said. "Need to take
the dogs part way, too."

Chip had never driven a Mercedes before. Might never
again. He ordered Zack and Rattler up front on seats that
creaked like fine saddle leather. He stopped at the pickup and
put the dogs in the box pen he and his daddy had built to carry
on the truck's bed during hunting season.

Mr. Benjamin fainted once or twice as Chip drove him out
the rutted lane from the Gatlin Place. Chip left him at the
Emergency Entrance of the Tobaccoton Community Hospital.
The attendants lifted him onto a wheeled litter. He had his
wallet in hand and tried to pay Chip with a twenty-dollar bill.

Chip turned his back and hitched a ride to the pickup. An
afternoon's hunting shot to hell.

When he got home from school Tuesday, his mother had set
a letter for him on the kitchen table. It was handwritten in neat
script. "James Lee Kincaid, Jr., has permission to hunt on all
my property wheresoever located." It was signed A. I. Benjamin.

After school was out in June, Chip searched for a job. He usually measured tobacco for the Dept. of Agriculture, but Henry
Boggs, a college boy, beat him to it. As with everything, the
choice involved politics. Henry's father was a cousin of Lawrence Hicks, the Commonwealth's Attorney.

"I'll never vote for that sonofabitch again," Chip's father
said. He threw a clod of plowed garden dirt at the mother's
calico cat. All bird hunters hated cats.

Chip stopped by Southside Hardware & Appliance hoping
to get hired as a clerk. Mr. A. I. Benjamin must've overheard
Chip talking to Gates Hamlett, the owner. Mr. Asshole Idiot

Benjamin waited outside the store. He again wore a gray suit and vest. The Mercedes was parked at the curb.

"You want work?" he asked. He had a limp.

"Not from you," Chip said and started away.

"You won't take even six dollars an hour from a nigger?" Mr. A. I. Benjamin asked.

Six dollars an hour was two dollars and sixty-five cents above minimum wage. Chip craved a red '84 TransAm, a clean, one-owner, low-mileage model he could get for two hundred down and twenty-four monthly payments.

"Doing what?" he asked.

"I assume you can use a hammer and saw," Mr. A. I. Benjamin said.

Chip didn't like him any more than that first day. Benjamin talked fancy, and the corners of his mouth turned down. Chip could use a hammer and saw. His daddy had taught him. He had saved the down payment for the TransAm, and six dollars an hour steady work might keep him in wheels. What he didn't have was the prospect of a job anywhere else. And every day he feared the TransAm would be sold off the lot down at Dixie Auto.

He drove the pickup to the Gatlin Place at nine o'clock Monday morning. Benjamin had cleared the wild growth around the house. He worked tearing slate off the roof. His Mercedes was parked by a cabin in the rear that most likely had once been a kitchen. Mortar crumbled between the bricks. Chip climbed the swaying aluminum ladder.

"Be here by eight," Benjamin said. He wore the bib overalls as well as a straw hat and hightop clodhoppers. "Get more done while it's cooler. Help yourself to a wrecking bar."

Chip pried and busted slate from the roof. The day was already hot. He took off his shirt and looked down along the wild greening fields he'd hunted. He thought of shots he'd made. Out west of the house was the old Gatlin cemetery surrounded by an iron fence that had tangles of honeysuckle and cow vine growing among the pickets. The old ladies in the Gatlin family had used to send in a servant to keep the cemetery mowed. Maybe they were all dead.

Chip worked without a break, at first extra careful of the

roof, but the oak trusses felt solid, no give. Most slates too were unbroken. He wondered why Benjamin meant to take them all off when a patching job might do.

"You need to put on another roof?" he asked.

"This one's served its time," Benjamin said without turning.

They both dripped sweat and slapped green flies. Benjamin laid planks across exposed trusses to stand on. Slates cracked and shattered in the yard.

"I could use a drink of water," Chip said, wiping sweat.

"You going to last even a day?" Benjamin asked, and this time pivoted to look at Chip out of those purplish eyes. Drops of sweat had lodged in pits of his face. "There's a dipper at the well."

Chip climbed down the ladder. The well behind the house had been newly oiled, and the tin dipper hung from the hook. When he pumped the iron handle, water bubbled up cool. He didn't use the dipper. Instead he got a good flow going and cupped his palms under the stream. As he rose to swallow, he saw Benjamin watching from the roof.

Chip climbed back up, and they worked without talking. Benjamin didn't seem to need water. Chip thought Benjamin didn't mean to stop for lunch either, but he finally laid down his wrecking bar.

"You bring food?" he asked.

"I got me a baloney sandwich and a Sun Drop," Chip said.

"Should've guessed," Benjamin said.

They climbed down the ladder. Benjamin limped to the well and as he drank looked over the dipper at Chip. He rinsed it before crossing to the old kitchen.

Chip sat on the pickup's tailgate to eat his sandwich. He'd parked in the shade of a hackberry. He listened to a hawk's cry and the fuss it caused among crows in the pine woods. They chased after the hawk, dived at him, but that redtail flew on like crows weren't worth bothering about.

He'd hardly swallowed the last bite of his sandwich before Benjamin was again up the ladder to the roof. Not fifteen minutes had gone by since they climbed down. Why not just get in the damn pickup and drive off? Chip asked himself. He didn't want to be working for any kind of nigger in the first place and especially a mean sonofabitching one.

But Benjamin owed him wages for what he'd already done, and Chip pictured the TransAm glittering on the lot down at Dixie Auto. He climbed the ladder. He went at it hard, using the wrecking bar. He'd not ask again for water. He'd show a New York fancy nigger what a country boy could do.

The sun reflected off slates. His hands became slippery on the iron bar. He was in shape. He played football for the Howell County High Rebels. But he felt himself giving out. He kept glancing at the sun to determine the time.

The heat caused the air to wiggle, and locusts tuned up, their chirring throbbing across the steamy fields. Because the wrecking bar was so slick in Chip's fingers, he almost banged his foot. Flies sucked blood from his bare back. It had to be past five o'clock. They hadn't finished the roof, but it was sure God time to give it up for the day.

Still Benjamin didn't quit. Chip felt dizzy as he looked at the ground. He steadied himself by reaching to a chimney. He started to say he had an appointment and needed to leave. Yet that meant the black bastard'd whipped him.

They bared the roof down to the trusses. There was just the platform of planks to stand on. Benjamin indicated Chip was to go first down the ladder. Chip threw the wrecking bar to the ground. He'd just about given out of strength.

Benjamin drew his pocket watch and crossed to the kitchen. When he came back, he held six new ten-dollar bills.

"Will you take my money this time?" he asked and smiled with only about half his mouth.

Chip told himself he'd be goddam if he'd work for Benjamin again, but throughout the night he kept seeing that TransAm scratching out to the blue yonder. He drove to the Gatlin Place the next morning at eight. Benjamin was swinging a sledge against a chimney. He looked at his gold pocket watch like he believed Chip might be late.

He put Chip to work removing trusses, which some carpenter during olden times had numbered in sequence using deeply chiseled Roman numerals. Why was Benjamin taking the trusses out? They were so sound Chip had to grunt like a hog to saw them free. "Don't you want to save them?" Chip asked.

"Just drop them right into the house," Benjamin said.

At lunch Chip again walked out to eat on the pickup's tailgate. Benjamin came around the house and sat with his back against the hackberry. He pushed up the brim of his straw hat. He held a sandwich made of white bread and a slab of rat cheese.

"Those trusses looked all right to me," Chip said. "You could use 'em again."

"You a contractor?" Benjamin asked, his chewing steady.

"No," Chip said. "Are you?"

"I'm employed by a firm named Lilly," Benjamin said.

"You all sell lilies and flowers?" Chip asked.

"Eli Lilly," Benjamin said and smiled for once with both sides of his mouth. "Yes, we peddle genetic flowers that in their design and bloom are marvels of intricate beauty. You know what genetics is?"

"Something about genes," Chip said.

"You are correct," Benjamin said and laughed so hard he hocked up an oyster of ugly dark stuff. "Something about genes."

"Then what you doing here rebuilding a house?" Chip asked.

"I'm on sabbatical," he said. "I enjoy working with my hands."

Chip didn't ask what a sabbatical was, and that afternoon they tore down the last trusses. They also sledged a chimney to the second-floor level. Again Benjamin paid Chip with new bills for the time he'd put in.

The rest of the week Chip worked at prizing loose the house's pine siding. A few boards had dried and warped, but most could be used after scraping and repainting. Benjamin told him to throw them all, good or bad, on top of the trusses.

When Chip got himself a drink at the pump, he saw the foot end of a cot in the old kitchen and a clothesline that Benjamin had strung up. He had to be cooking, too, because he stayed away from town where he spoke as few words as possible. The gleaming Mercedes looked out of place parked beside the swayback building with its rusty roof and scaling mortar.

Friday after work Chip hurried to Tobaccoton and put the

first payment down on the TransAm. Oh, she was sweet wheels, and the engine sang his song. He picked up Alice Anne, who had blond hair and was head cheerleader at Lee-Jackson. They ate corndogs at the Tastee Freez before going to the drive-in movie early so everybody'd see the car.

Buster Wesley didn't like Chip being with Alice Anne. He drove an '87 Thunderbird and pulled up alongside to ask how Chip liked rolling on nigger wheels. Chip hit him through the window, and they punched each other around till they got thrown out.

"I've a mind to make you take that car back," Chip's mother said when she saw his torn shirt and bruised face. He'd tried to keep them hidden.

"Boys got to fight over girls," his daddy said. "It's in the blood. And he whipped Buster."

"I'd like to whip the both of you," she said and banged a pan in the sink.

Sunday afternoon Chip took Alice Anne down to Hidden River, and they fished off the bank. As they drove back at dusk with a mess of blue cats in a pail, he wondered what Benjamin did with himself of an evening. He drove in slow along the cedar-darkened lane to the Gatlin Place. Alice Anne saw Benjamin first. He was walking in the field east of the house, stopping, and jabbing a pole or pipe into the ground.

"He fetching salad?" Alice Anne asked. She wore pink shorts, a yellow shirt, and was rosy from river sun.

"Salad's all seed in this heat," Chip said.

They watched. Benjamin moved in a pattern by taking two steps, pausing, and jabbing the pole or pipe before moving on. As darkness settled, they saw only the white of his shirt.

"I got it," Chip said. "He's searching for oil."

"It's spooky," she said. "Let's hightail it out of here."

When Chip drove to work Monday, Benjamin had finished knocking down a second chimney and started on another. He lowered the eight-pound sledge and wiped sweat which he flung aside. He gleamed like a greased skillet.

"Mule kick you?" he asked, breathing hard.

"Hardly a mule left in the county," Chip said. "Everything's tractor now."

"Didn't realize tractors had fists," Benjamin said.

He put Chip to work tearing down the second-story framing. Clothes hung on the line at the old kitchen. A black kettle sat on bricks of a makeshift fireplace. From the kettle stuck a stick. Chip first figured Benjamin must've been cooking himself a stew. Then he guessed Benjamin had been boiling his clothes to wash them the way darkies used to do.

When they quit at lunch, Benjamin dug a plastic fork into a can of Vienna sausage and produced apples for himself and Chip. Among tangles of wisteria Benjamin had found a stunted tree. The apples were shrunken, hard and bitter. Chip took just one bite, but Benjamin finished his.

"Imagine a tree still bearing any kind of fruit on this place," Benjamin said.

Chip looked out toward the west where purplish rain clouds formed up. He'd been thinking about the work they'd done. Benjamin stood from the hackberry.

"If I didn't know better, I'd say you weren't rebuilding the house but tearing it down," Chip said.

"You're real smart for a redneck boy got kicked by a mule," Benjamin said.

"Why not just burn it?" Chip asked. "Save a lot of effort."

"I told you I enjoy working with my hands," Benjamin said.

"You find yourself any oil?" Chip asked.

Benjamin stopped in mid stride to stare, and that pitted face hardened like asphalt setting. He slowly crushed the empty Vienna can and turned away without answering.

They again worked late. When Chip left, he remembered he'd forgotten his thermos. He'd been bringing his own water. Night was gathering, and he left the pickup's engine running. As he walked toward the house, he glimpsed Benjamin out in the field behind the old kitchen. He was leaning his weight on the pole or pipe, his head bowed as if praying out there in the dark. He must've sensed Chip 'cause he turned and stood straight. Chip got the thermos and left.

He told his mother about it. She'd kept dinner for him. She too was tired from the stitching machine at the shoe factory but sat with him. She set her elbows on the table and rested her face on her cupped palms.

"I been thinking about it," she said. "He's got to have some connection with the Gatlin Place."

"Benjamin's a Jew name and no Jew ever lived out there," his father said. He'd come from picking roasting ears in the backyard garden. Barefooted, he wore beltless Levis and an undershirt. Corn pollen stuck to sweat along his arms.

"It's a Biblical name," his mother said. "Lots of them took or were given names from the Bible."

"Maybe so," his father said, washing his hands at the sink. "They had to get names somewhere."

"What happened to them?" Chip asked.

"Who?" his father asked and turned from the sink where he shucked ears of Silver Queen. The clean white kernels glistened.

"Those that got names," Chip said. "Must've been a bunch way back when to work all that tobacco."

"Many surely lived and died out there," his mother said, nodding.

"Hell, who knows or cares now?" his father said.

By late August they'd torn the house down, all of it, and filled the basement with what they'd pitched in. Benjamin paid Willie Hendrick to flatbed in his dozer, cover everything with soil, and level the house plot off. He limed, fertilized, and seeded the area with Kentucky 31 fescue.

"You want me back for anything?" Chip asked. He'd been paid exactly, as always with new bills.

"Keep the grass cut," Benjamin said. "I'll send a monthly check. Bring a mower. I'll add a dollar an hour for that."

That's the last Chip saw of Mr. Benjamin. For a while after he left, there was bad talk around about his doings. Crazy, some said. The sheriff should've stopped it. Except for Julius' courthouse portrait, no trace remained of what the Gatlins had meant to Howell County.

When Chip lifted the mower from the pickup, he found Benjamin had razed the old kitchen and outbuildings, too. He also discovered what he first believed was a gravestone planted at the center of the grassed-over plot. Burying a house? If it was a grave marker, it had no writing on it. He thought maybe there could be a single letter and ran a finger into the grainy dip. Nope, it was just a flat upright brown fieldstone, lopsided, speckled with mica.

For two years Chip cut grass and received checks from a New York bank. By that time he'd gotten himself hired at Virginia Power. The third spring the checks stopped coming, and a Lynchburg agent pounded a For Sale sign in the ground near the head of the lane.

Chip still hunted the fields, with his own dogs now that he was married to Alice Anne and worked steady. Wind had long since blown loose the posted signs along the fence, and the barb wire sagged and had gaps.

Buck and Snapper pointed a covey among ragged box bushes of the old formal garden. Briars, honeysuckle and creeper were claiming everything back. Because of the wild growth Chip could barely see the upright stone or Gatlin cemetery.

Crossing behind the house past where the well pump had been, he kicked up among weeds the dipper he'd never drunk from. Its handle was bent, the dented tin cup almost rusted through. He tossed it to the ground and glanced once more at snaking tangles of wisteria vines hanging from the ancient white oaks spaced around the overgrown house plot.

He called to the dogs but kept looking back till the pines in a bend of the field blocked his view. He felt an urge to retrieve the dipper and carry it home with him. What the hell for? Might hold a story but no cooling water to quench any man's thirst. He hitched up his britches. He meant to find another covey before dark.

T. M. McNally

SKIN DEEP

When my mom asks me what will make me feel better, I tell her nothing. Then I tell her it is merely sunburn, only a matter of time before it goes away. But my mom is not a practical woman. She believes in the power of dreams, and higher consciousness. She believes she can take away the pain, even if she's pretty certain she does not want to.

George, her boyfriend, tells her she should throw me out. George is an indefinitely-suspended-without-pay fireman; he used to work out at Rural Metro and drive a lime-green truck. The entire summer George has been busy watching out for brushfires, and I have spent the entire day at the river. My boss and his cousin and their girlfriends—we took the day off and went out to the river and floated down the stream. It's best to avoid the weekends, and it will probably be the last time I ever go. Before, we went often, but in three days I'll be moving to Massachusetts. Rick & Brad say Massachusetts is a nice place, even if there's not much work. Rick & Brad are like family, and Landscapers, and have their own business. A long time ago, my dad did Rick a favor, because there wasn't much work here, either. My mom, even if she never does any, says work is where you make it. Like this summer—I am a Landscaper. At

the river we smoked a couple of joints, to celebrate, and I
didn't feel the sun at all.

The water was clear and cold. At one place, there were kids
with long hair and wispy beards leaping from a cliff. There
must have been a couple hundred altogether. Probably I
shouldn't have taken off my top. We found a quiet inlet, and
Brad went off somewhere to fight with his girlfriend, who reminds him of his wife, Cheryl, who sells hardware and sneakers at the Smittys. The tops of my legs and ankles are in pretty
bad shape, too. As a landscaper, you spend a lot of time out in
the sun, though usually I have more clothes on—a pair of
shorts, boots and a tank. Also there isn't all that water reflect-
ing.

We picked up our beer cans, so it's not as if we caused a lot
of damage. Recycling, says my mom, is an important thing to
do. *Can do,* she says. We also count on it, the cans, for groceries.
Basically my mom believes my life's important, which sounds
nicer than it is, and which explains why she's so upset. No,
disappointed, because if you are upset, you cannot be in control
of your own *destiny.* My mom is standing over my sleeping
bag, because we sold the bed two garage sales ago; she is passing me the lotion, sipping her nectarine and guava juice, and
now she says, "Lacy, I choose to be angry. You have shown
bad judgment. You have choosed to behave badly."

"Chosen, Mom. It was hot."

"You know exactly what I mean. What's wrong with the
backyard!"

That's where George hangs out, especially when I'm out
there too, but I don't say this: her positive energy is by afternoon usually pretty well depleted. Mostly she's upset because
maybe some paparazzi took my picture. She worries someday
one will show up in the newspaper, at the grocery store, after
I've become famous. She says, no longer upset, because she's
taken a couple deep breaths, and a big hit from her nectarine
and guava, "You got to be careful. You got to be very, very
careful."

"Mom, I'm not going to be famous."

"Oh yes you are," she says, shutting the door. Now she is
heading down the hall, using the walls, one foot and then an-

other, which is what she always does. Then she calls back, happily, "You better believe it, too!"

I have decided I no longer want to be bad. If I am bad, I will not do well in college, in Massachusetts, and if I do not do well in Massachusetts, then I will have to come back here and spend the rest of my life dealing coke or selling hardware in a supermarket. My dad is bad, which is why he's in Florence—the Big House, we call it. *Oh, he's staying for a while in the Big House.* It makes my mom feel rich, saying that, as if we actually had a dozen, and George doesn't seem to mind. Actually, my dad will be there for another six to ten years, depending on the quality of his good behavior. Before my mom changed her name, she used to visit twice a year, because she still loved him. Mr. Y, my father's lawyer, says just because I never went to class doesn't mean I have to turn out bad. Mr. Y helped me find a college, his alma mater, which wouldn't mind the fact of all my bad grades. It's in a small town in Massachusetts: I've seen pictures. There's a library, and dormitories, and a gymnasium named after Mr. Y's dead brother, because his dead brother was almost a famous person once.

Mr. Y wrote the college and said I needed a lot of room to grow. Since he did help my dad, pro bono, he knows we don't have any money left. Landscaping, I'm making close to six dollars an hour, though my mom collects all the checks. My mom worries about the calluses on my hands and feet, the damage from all the sun; she says you start with small steps and practice making bigger ones—steps, in order to build a fine career. My friend, Mitchell, whose parents think he is terminally confused, says I'm merely acting out. Mitchell goes to a shrink once a week because his parents don't want him to be so confused. His parents don't know my dad is staying in the Big House. Mitchell says when people don't like their parents, or their life, they often feel bad.

"Hey," he says. "I brought you your mail."

He's standing beside the disco ball we stole from high school. We send my mail to Mitchell's house, because my mother says she wants me to go to Broadway, which really means she doesn't want me to leave home. First, I'm supposed to take acting classes at the community college, in order to learn nearby. My admissions counselor, from Massachusetts, who doesn't know that I have lied to her . . . she says she's looking forward to meeting me. In the letter she says my essay was charming, particularly the part about my dad. She says, *A chop shop? Your family owns a restaurant?* She says, *Your uncle,* meaning Mr. Y, *has requested that all bills be sent to him.* Then she says I'll be on *Close Advising* throughout the first year and we can't wait to meet you, et cetera.

Three days, and I'll be gone, and still I haven't told my mom or George. Truth is, I don't even want to be a lawyer. Mr. Y said for the application I shouldn't write too much about my family. I don't feel bad because my dad is such a loser; I feel bad because, secretly, I think that I still like him. Of course, I don't want to grow to *be* like him. Last month, before she stopped talking entirely to Dad, my mom decided she was going to be a Broadway agent. She says this way she will be able to lay the groundwork for my career. Her card says "PBA—Pretty Bird Associates," and on the phone she tells people her degrees, plural, are in Marketing and Dance and Agentry. She says Neil Simon has asked specifically for her assistance.

As in Cats? Never mind.

Before she stopped visiting my dad and changed her name and became an agent, she decided to build a fortune out of laundry soap. You know, Amway. This is when her degrees, plural, were in Economics and Dance and Consumer Distribution. She bought three thousand dollars' worth of soap, using her sister's Visa, and told me to stack it all up inside the garage. She even bought special shelves that came without enough screws. Later we'd move into a warehouse downtown. We already had all the different flavors, though: soap for whites, soap for colors, soap for fine washables and furs. We even had soap for cars, and shoe polishes and extra-deep stain removers. Mostly she figured she'd have the business expanding into Mexico by the time Dad came home from Florence. My dad has a lot of connections in Tijuana.

Once I rode my bike to Florence, to say good-bye, because I knew my mom wasn't going to drive me. Between Chandler and the prison it's all Indian reservation—about forty miles' worth. At first I thought I was going to be dehydrated, for lack of water, and then I finally got there and had to park my bike. My legs were wobbly and you could see the razor wire, gleaming in the sunlight.

Mitchell says to me now, looking at my letter from Massachusetts, reading, "So how's the sunburn?"

"Okay," I say, wincing. I lower the sheet, and there I am, all pink and swollen and sharp. When skin burns, at least you know it isn't dead yet. "Rick & Brad gave me the day off. To recover."

Mitchell puts the letter back in place, in the envelope, and gives off a low whistle, meaning he understands.

I've never had a lot, certainly not as much as I could have, which I've always been glad for overall. I reach for the lotion, with aloe vera, because I like the way it smells. We have cases of this stuff in the garage.

Mitchell says, "You're going to see the Mobster tomorrow?"

Mr. Y isn't really a Mobster: he's actually much bigger and very famous. "For lunch," I say. "We're finishing a job in Paradise Valley."

"Cool," says Mitchell, nodding, looking at his feet.

"It's still really hot," I say, touching my skin.

"You're just a little burned," he says, looking up. "You'll get over it."

Because my mom doesn't want her life to be meaningless, she's decided mine has to become really important, which means if I don't become famous, preferably on Broadway, then she won't be able to feel successful. Everything she does is all for me. All the vitamins she takes, all the clothes she buys for George, all the magazines she reads before she gets her hair done. My mom says when an important man, like a director, takes special interest in an unimportant girl, then the unimportant girl should smile a lot and not make any waves.

"Hi," I say, waving to Mr. Y. He is standing by his black car, with the chauffeur inside, looking right at me. Rick & Brad said I could borrow the truck, and I have tossed my boots and socks in back. Now I'm wearing thongs, though you can see dirt between my toes. Because it's summer, and hot, Mr. Y is wearing dark glasses and a bola tie.

"Lacy," he says, nodding.

We go into Henry's, which is a bar; there's an autographed picture of Mr. Y behind the cash register. *To Henry*, it says. In the picture he is wearing his dark glasses. There's also a picture of Bob Crane, who used to act at the Windmill Dinner Theater, before he was shot. Bob Crane was a Hollywood actor before he went to the Windmill; I don't think he did too well on Broadway. He did play Hogan, on "Hogan's Heroes." When the cops found his body, he was naked, and his motel room was full of video tapes.

At the bar, Mr. Y says *Howdy, Hank. She's with me.* Then he asks me if I'd like a beer or a ginger ale.

I take a Coke with lemon, and he orders a gin straight up, with a side of orange juice. We sit at a table in the corner, and he says, "Would you like a sandwich? You're all skin and bones, Lacy."

"No, thank you," I say, smiling. "I have to get back to work."

"Ah," he says, nodding. "Work."

"Work."

"You still haven't spoken with your mother yet? About Massachusetts?"

"I'm supposed to go to SCC and live with her, and then she's going to be my agent and send me to New York."

Mr. Y nods, sadly, because he has met my mother.

"If I tell her," I say, "she'll keep my money."

"Your dad?"

"He says I shouldn't tell her."

Mr. Y looks at his drink, lifts it, and polishes it off. The bar is dark and musty, so it's not as if anybody is going to notice.

"I have to tell you something," he says.

"Okay."

"You have to listen. Carefully," he says. "You have to listen to what is never said. People, people who . . ." He looks at Henry, who is a bartender, and nods. "Your dad did me a favor once."

"Okay."

I look at his glass, and then his eyes. They are sad eyes, the kind you tell yourself you will remember, though still you don't until it's long over.

"Lacy," he says, patting my hand. "You can do anything you want. Anything."

"Anything?"

"If you want it," he says, pulling back. "You need some lunch."

"No, really."

"We're supposed to be having lunch. Henry," he calls. "A sandwich. Something with sprouts." Mr. Y looks at me and says, "I'll eat half, okay?"

"Okay."

"Yes, indeed, okay. You get some sun lately?"

"I don't want to go to Broadway. Is that what you mean?"

"It's a start. Some people get a family," he says, holding out his hands. "My father built that school's library. The land came from my great-great-grandfather."

"Uh huh."

"Dairy. A dairy farm. It's a small school, but it's like family. We take care of our own."

"I see what you mean," I say, not seeing anything in particular. Because I don't know where to put my hands, and because Mr. Y doesn't seem to notice, I decide to sit on them. Actually, they feel really hard.

"Family takes you in. Family lets you go. All you have to do is let it."

Now he slides me a manila envelope across the table, around my Coke. The envelope is thin, and inside there's a check for seven hundred and fifty dollars and a plane ticket. Truth is, I was expecting only the ticket.

"You're going to need some winter clothes," he says. "And a coat. Some tweedy dresses."

"But—"

"No buts, Lacy. When you get to New England, open up an account. There's no need to tell your mom about that, either."

My hands are in the way again, and I don't know what to do with them. "She doesn't even know I'm leaving."

"Family," he says, nodding. "Don't forget to write."

Once my mom went on a retreat for Surviving Lovers of Criminals, in Sedona, where she met George and changed her name to Blue Feather. Since then, she calls my dad her X and no longer visits him. Mr. Y said he wanted to help my dad because he knew more than we did, though he also says nobody needs to know a thing about him helping—not his name, certainly not his reasoning. As I understand it, Mr. Y is a director, but not of plays. Instead he directs the state government. He directs the flow of traffic across Nogales. He directs the general direction of a lot of recent foreign investment.

I know a lot more now than I used to. I know that when Don Boles stepped into his car in 1976, he never expected it to explode. The cops *say* they don't know who bombed the car, but it's not as if a journalist who goes digging into private matters shouldn't be a little cautious. I don't want to be a journalist, but I do know how to read the papers. Bob Crane stopped making "Hogan's Heroes" and slept with teenagers and videotaped them and died in a motel in Scottsdale with the TV on. As for this summer, the news has been full of brushfires, and George, my mom's unemployed fireman, has been kept fairly busy keeping up.

It was a wet spring. The grass grew, and now it only takes a spark, or a flung cigarette—there's combustion in the air. After I leave Mr. Y, I go back to the job site, because I still have a job to do. On the street there's a truck unloading three and a half tons of granite with the crew all standing nearby. The granite is yellow—Glitter Gold, they call it—and now Rick & Brad are firing up the Bobcat.

"You're tardy!" Rick calls, who is driving.

"Sorry."

"One shot," Brad says, flinging his cigarette. "We finish this off in one shot."

The Mexicans are nodding, because Rick & Brad always buy the beer at the end of a job. There are three of them altogether—Ramón, Manuel, and Joe. Scuzz Bucket, who is an ex-con from New York, is picking at a new tattoo. Then there's me.

Because it's my last day, I want to do a nice job. The Mexicans line up the wheelbarrows, three of them real tight, and Rick drops the first load. The barrows fill up, full, granite pouring over the sides, and then Rick does a little wheelie with the Bobcat, and Brad yells, *Go! Let's fucking go!* and the Mexicans are haulin' ass, and now I've got my square point. It takes a while to get the feel, the way you tilt the wrist, flipping it just so. If you do it right, the granite floats out in a fan. Mostly, it's all in the shoulders and legs, then the wrist. Meanwhile, I'm on point, with Scuzz Bucket and Brad, and the granite keeps coming, and this is something I know I'm pretty good at. Not that I want to turn it into a career, but even so, it's nice to know the way groundcover works. It's nice to hold a shovel in your hands and know you know exactly what you're doing with it. It's nice to know the guys don't mind your noticing the way they stumble, lifting the wheelbarrows, one after another. Because it's hot and brutal, and mostly what I'm thinking about is college, and carrying around my books in Massachusetts, where there's going to be a lot of ice and snow. Maybe I'll hang out in the library and read a lot and become whatever it is I'm supposed to be. Mostly, I don't want to be related to my parents, even if my dad says he understands, and now I'm thinking about the sun, the way it lights up all the dust, and the heat, and the way I'm not even tired. I'm thinking about the shovel in my hands and the way the sun feels so good and hot and the way I know I'm going to miss it.

We are the downwardly mobile. The only thing we still own for sure is our house, but the property taxes keep going up, and sooner or later my mom is going to sell the house, too. She's already borrowed on my life insurance policy. Every two months, she holds another garage sale. There's hardly any furniture left at all and my mom says she still needs my paycheck to jump-start the business. She means the Agent Business, not the Soap Business. She still owes her sister three thousand for all the laundry soap in the garage. Sometimes she goes to special seminars: "How to Think Right and Live," "Vitamins for Success and Beauty." We have two phone lines, a post office box, and a fax machine, but we do not have a couch. Once my mom went to Canada to learn how to write screenplays. At night, when George is home, I hear them in the living room.

My dad, before he moved into the Big House, owned a body shop. When the last recession came, people stopped getting their cars fixed, so he turned it into a chop shop. There were still some real customers, but mostly he was into felony and fraud and stolen vehicles. Then he started stealing people's cars—not *real* stealing. Some guy can't make his car payment, he makes an arrangement with my dad: leaves a couple hundred under the floor mat, and my dad steals the car for him. He chops up the parts, mixes them up, does a quick paint job, and ditches the car in Tijuana or Las Vegas. Thing is, my dad stole the wrong car. He stole the mayor's.

Actually, the car belonged to his wife, and the mayor was up for reelection. My dad knew something was wrong when he couldn't find a check under the floor mat. The parking garage had a video camera. At the door, when the cops came, they were nice and didn't use any handcuffs. My dad had stolen a lot of cars, even one belonging to a cop, who still was grateful. Of course, I didn't know my dad was a crook. I thought he liked to go fishing. You know, in Mexico. I thought he liked his weekends off since things seemed so busy at the shop. The last thing he said to my mom as a free man was, "Do not sell the house."

Apparently, he had put it in her name a long time ago, just in case. Later a group of federal agents with ties came over and tore the place apart—the kitchen, the laundry room. They went through my underwear drawer and my CD collection and the crawl space. Afterward, they came up with close to fourteen thousand in cash, and my mom said it was hers. She'd been skimming off the groceries. To save for Christmas, she said.

"It's supposed to be a surprise!"

She did a pretty good job, screaming and crying. Then there were people from Chicago and Denver and L.A. who came in to testify. My dad, at the trial, said he was sorry and wore a conservative suit. Mr. Y put his best junior partner on the case, which helped a little, but it was still big news. Before, the biggest news was Don Boles, who blew up, and then Bob Crane, shot while diddling with himself while watching his home movies, and then my dad went to prison for stealing the car that just happened to belong to the wife of the mayor who was tough on crime. After, the wife didn't want it back, because it was dirty, and then they took my dad out of the courtroom and Mom started taking a correspondence course in real estate. Mostly, I remember the newspeople, saying they've put another bad man behind bars. Bad, they said. The streets are safer now.

I was about to turn nine. The police called it a sting operation. Sometimes, when I used to visit my dad, I'd bring him cigarettes and magazines.

At nine, George fires up the VCR—*Buns of Steel*—and I ride my bike over to Mitchell's and change my clothes there. Then we get in his car and drive through Central. Then we go other places. We go to the Incognito Lounge, and other places, because certain types of bars are better than others. The music is fast and people don't pinch you on the ass and everybody dances altogether. I like to dance, but I don't want to go to Broadway. Before, when my family was normal, and happy, I was on "Star Search." I made it to the semifinals and wore a green and red costume and then I lost to an acrobatic family from Scandinavia. There were more of them, smiling, than there were of me. Ed McMahon had the shakes, and forgot my name introducing me, and had to check his cue card: this is the only time I've ever been to California. We drove there in a van my dad was customizing for a dealer, who said he didn't mind as long as we disconnected the speedometer cable. My dad said he was considering buying one for Mom, for all the shopping, and because of the way it looked so neat.

At one place, Mitchell and I get some drinks. He's flirting with a boy in purple. Before, Mitchell and I used to date, and we'd go out cruising, like this, and then sometimes we'd practice. Once, I got him off, in the car, and he started crying. He said he didn't know what was wrong. Of course, nothing was *wrong*, just different.

"You won't like me anymore," he said.

There was sperm all over my sweatshirt and wrist, and he was ashamed, and I held him and said it was okay. I said he was my friend and he said he was, and then we started laughing. Him first, because it seemed so stupid. We were in his little car and the windows were all fogged up, and before, the only thing I ever worried about keeping secret was the fact that I had lost to a bunch of Scandinavian people on "Star Search" when I was eight years old, and then the fact that my father was a crook, but I had never thought about having to keep a secret for my friend. Because it wasn't a secret for me. It was a secret for him, and not for anybody else, and it made me feel responsible and important.

"This just makes it easier," I said.

"I know," he said, wiping his eyes. "I know."

Then we went out dancing. Usually he told me about his dates—"encounters," he said. I never had many all by myself, mostly because I wasn't sure just what I wanted. One guy at school dumped me for a cheerleader, which was okay. She had pretty, long hair and green eyes. Then she dumped him for somebody else, and I started hanging out with Mitchell. A few times I slept with Brad, last June, when he was fighting with his wife. He was drunk most of the time and tired from working all day in the sun. I also knew his girlfriend, and she was sweet and didn't know as much as I did, especially about Brad. But Mitchell is the only person I think that I have ever loved, and even if it isn't ever going to work, sometimes I used to hope that we'd get married. A long time from now, of course. After I went to college.

"Hey, Lace," he says to me, holding out his hand.

We are in a club in Tempe, by the university. Mostly it's full of college students and married men. On the ceiling is a disco ball just like the one we stole from high school, and I'm trying really hard to stand still and not think about my future. Mostly I feel wrong inside and scared. Inside Mitchell's palm are two tiny pills.

"Ritalin," he says. "Very clean."

I pop the speed, because I want it, and he says, "Hey, what's wrong?"

"Happy tears," I say.

"In Massachusetts," he says. "You think maybe I can visit?"

"First I have to get there."

"Jesus, Lace. You're halfway home."

"I want to dance," I say, taking his hand. "Not alone."

It was Mitchell's idea to steal the disco ball. "For your room," he said. "It will look nice."

When I rode my bike to visit my dad, at the Big House, I knew it was important. Two guards frisked me, slowly, and then they went through my backpack. I was tired and hot and had to drink a lot of water, and then they sent me into the room, the special room for certain convicts, the one with all the Plexiglas and telephones. My dad had lost more weight, and then I slid him the cigarettes and magazines—a *Penthouse* and two Victoria's Secret catalogs and the *Sports Illustrated* swimsuit issue.

"Thanks," he said.

My dad, wearing all that blue, looked different. Before he was a crook, he'd wear jeans or army pants on weekends, sometimes a jacket when we went out to dinner, but now he just looked like everybody else behind the Plexiglas. He could have been a murderer or drug czar.

"It's okay."

"You look pale," he said.

"I rode my bike. It's a long way."

"Blue Feather," he said, folding his hands. "How's Blue—"

"She doesn't know. George lost his job. He wants her to sell the house."

"She's going to, isn't she."

It wasn't really a question, which he must have realized. A man came into the room and sat beside my dad's booth. He was young and had a toothpick in his mouth, and he sat there quietly, looking at the phone.

"Dad," I said. "I want to go to college, and Mr.—"

"I know. I know." He couldn't light a cigarette, because of the No Smoking laws. He packed one on the counter and said, "Don't tell your mom."

"She's going to have to find out. She's going—"

"Lacy, your mother is a sweet woman. She is sweet. But you do not have to grow up to be like her."

"She's become an agent. For actors."

"Go to Massachusetts," my dad said. "Say hey to Rick & Brad."

After a while we didn't have much to say. He asked me if I had any dates. He asked me if George ever hit me. Then he said, leafing through one of the catalogs, "Any questions?"

"No," I said. "No, wait. In the army . . ."

"Yes?"

"What did you do in the army, Dad?"

He puffed on his cigarette, as if it were lit, and said, "A lot of things, Lace. I used to do a lot of things."

He left first, as usual. When he got up to go, he waved to me. The man sitting beside him nodded politely, then he turned to me, as if I were his girlfriend or wife. The man was sitting behind the Plexiglas, and then he stood up, slid over to the place where my father had been, and tucked his body into the booth. Meanwhile, my dad waved and stepped through an iron doorway, the magazines in his hand, and then the man in the booth reached into his pants. He was already hard, as if he were about to build something with a hammer and a board: his arm was full of knots. Then he undid his fly, stroked himself once, twice, and came all over the tabletop. He stood looking at me, then reached for the phone, as if he had something more to say, and I went out into the lobby and cried for half an hour. I called up Mitchell, collect, and asked him to come pick me up. I took my bike and walked it to the edge of the highway and sat on a rock. There were visitors driving by, going back to Phoenix. A couple of people stopped to ask if I was okay, and eventually Mitchell showed up, and we took off my front wheel and put the bike inside his car and then we drove home.

"How's your dad?" Mitchell said, driving home.

"I don't know."

We left Tempe near 2:00 A.M., driving, listening to the stereo. Mitchell talked a lot about what he was going to do in college, in California. He talked about the way he was going to miss his shrink, and me, and then he wondered what we'd be like if we hadn't known each other.

"You know," he said, driving, "if we'd lived in different places."

"You mean if we were different people," I said.

"Yeah," he said. "If we were different people."

It made me feel dizzy, thinking that way, because it was impossible. Altogether I just knew I did not want to be bad, and after a while we ended up near Carefree. We were driving fast and then we saw the smoke, and the light from the smoke, rising into the sky.

There were a few cars pulled over to the side of the road,

and you could see the entire field, glowing. The fire was in a huge field behind a subdivision, and there was a man with a pickup truck, full of shovels and picks, and there were lots of people in their pajamas. We each grabbed a shovel and started work on the fire while two people with garden hoses sprayed their rooftops. After a while the fire department came, with even bigger hoses, and Mitchell and I kept digging at the fire. I taught him to use the wrist, not his back, to spread the dirt over the flames because you kill a fire by covering it with what it burns—by giving it precisely what it needs—and you could see us, maybe fifty or sixty by the end, shoveling and shoveling. The fire was loud, roaring, like the ocean or an animal, or a natural disaster, and sometimes I'd feel it burning my eyebrows and the skin on my hands. You'd never think something so pretty could be so hot or dangerous, and the air was full of smoke, and it was hot, too, but somehow never hot enough to kill us. It wasn't going to kill us, at least this time, because we were so many, even if it was past curfew, and because there weren't any trees big enough to burn: just leftover grass from an unusually wet spring. And then I realized my father must have thought the same things: breaking the law, stealing a car here, maybe wiring another there—he must have known a lot about demolition. He must have known why Don Boles had gone up in flames, and even if he didn't do it—even if my father did not kill the most important journalist in all of Phoenix—I knew then that he could have. I knew that he could have done what anybody told him to: there was a lot of heat nearby and the world was becoming dangerous and my father was a crook. My father was a crook and I was doing a lot of speed and eventually the flames began to fall away. The sky darkened, and after a while I could barely see what I was doing, and when we were all done, after all the fire trucks but one had gone away, a man said thank you as he shook my hand. He was standing in his pajamas and cowboy boots beside the pickup truck full of shovels and picks. His pajamas were streaked with dirt, and now he was shaking Mitchell's hand, and Mitchell said, "Hey. It's cool."

"We could have lost everything," the man said. "Everything."

· · ·

My dad never did come clean. Before the cops came, he told me once he thought his was the kind of life best kept in the dark. Then he said, looking down at me, "You know, the kind nobody ever knows too much about. Behind the scenes, Lace."

This was before I was bad. Usually, when my dad came home from work, we watched "Hogan's Heroes" while my mom made dinner. My mom had decided to be a chef then; her degrees, plural, were in Home Economics, Dance, and French Cuisine. Now it had been years since she turned on the stove. When Mitchell dropped me off at home, he said for me to take my time.

I went inside while Mitchell stayed in the driveway, the engine running. Inside, my mom and George were asleep on the living room floor, where the sofa should have been, the TV all full of snow, and I decided I wasn't going to take much. The sun was rising, and you could hear a couple of birds, chirping. On the answering machine was a message for Ms. Blue Feather from a man named Thunder Storm. I poured myself a soda and went into my room to pack.

I took my hiking boots and dictionary and sleeping bag. I took two sweaters, most of my underwear, two pairs of jeans, and a skirt. I took three pens, an engraved mechanical pencil, my best eraser, and a picture of my dad and me. In it we are standing beside the borrowed van somewhere on the highway to California; I am wearing my dance outfit, and his arm is around me, and you can tell he's happy even if I lost. Then I went into the bathroom and I packed my shampoo and tooth-brush and a small box of concentrated laundry detergent for fine washables. I didn't leave a note, the way I had planned, mostly because I figured someday it would be easier to call and explain from far away.

I looked into the mirror and checked my hair. My eyes were tired and burnt, from all the speed. There were smudge marks on my cheeks, from the fire, and all that ash, and my hair smelled like wood smoke, and then I turned and saw my mom, standing there.

"Going somewhere?" she said.

The knapsack was packed, behind the door. She looked cross, not yet in control of her destiny, and I knew she'd spend the rest of the day with George in the living room until he finally woke up. Maybe she'd get Mr. Thunder Storm on TV, and I knew I could have told her the truth. I also knew I could have lied. Instead I turned back to the sink and ran some water to rinse my eyes.

"Work," I said.

"When do you get paid?"

"Today. I'll pick up my check today."

She folded her arms and leaned into the doorway. I could see her in the mirror, staring, and then she said, "George and I have decided to sell the house. Last night."

The water felt cool and good. It was something I liked, water. I rinsed again and then reached for a towel. It was the same towel that had been hanging there for weeks.

"Do you have anything to say?"

"It's your house," I said.

Now she reached for the aloe vera, sitting on a ledge, and handed it to me. "For your sunburn," she said, turning. "Don't be late."

"One more thing," said Mr. Y.

I was in the parking lot, lacing up my boots, and I looked up at him—all fine clothes and dark glasses. The sun was behind him, so I had to squint, and I could feel my sunburn, and the way sometimes your skin begins to itch.

"It's okay," I said, standing. I walked over to him, stood on my toes, and kissed him in the parking lot.

I did it gently, the way you do when you are really grateful.

"No," he said, wiping his mouth. He used the back of his hand. Then he held me by the arms, and I leaned into him, nudging him, and he said again, "No."

"It's okay," I said. "I understand."

"No, Lacy. You do not."

The truth is, I felt mostly confused. I held up my arms and said, "One more thing? Things that are never said?"

He laughed now, but gently, in order not to hurt my feelings. He laughed and then he said, putting his arm around me, "The thing about family, real family . . . The thing about family, Lace, is that there are no conditions. No strings. No payback whatsoever."

"You don't want anything?"

"You are always free to change your mind."

"My mind," I said.

"Yes, Lacy. It's okay to change your mind. A boyfriend, a job. Where you go to school. You don't have to be a lawyer and you are always free to change your mind."

Then he kissed me, on the top of the head, and led me to Rick & Brad's truck. When I slid in, he shut the door for me, and then he said, "It doesn't mean anything if you know you didn't have a choice."

"Like my dad."

"Your dad didn't have much of a choice. At least not in the end. But you do."

"Okay," I said.

"All you have to do is try hard," he said, nodding.

Then I said thanks, and tried not to feel stupid and embarrassed, and he reached through the window and squeezed my shoulder. I was holding onto the steering wheel of Rick & Brad's truck, and Mr. Y turned away, looking for his car, and his chauffeur, and then he said, "One more thing."

"Okay," I said. "One more thing."

"You cannot disappoint me. Remember that."

I took the aloe vera, too. Later that morning when I stepped into the driveway, the sun was rising in the east, where it was supposed to. I stood in front of my mother's house, which she would soon sell, and held everything I was going to take with me in my arms. It didn't seem like a lot then, standing in the yard: there was a saguaro and a couple of bottle trees, and you could see where the weeds were coming through the ground-cover. You could see my friend Mitchell, sitting in his small car, waiting. Then I remembered one more thing and ran inside the house for my disco ball. In the car, I asked Mitchell to keep it safe, in case my mother tried to sell it. We sat in the car for a moment and then he asked me if there was anyplace else I had to go. First we went to Rick & Brad's, where I picked up my last paycheck and we all went out for breakfast. We told them about the fire, out past Rawhide, and they said I could have a job with them, anytime, even Mitchell if he ever felt like it, and then they told me to say hey to my dad and they went off to work, and Mitchell took me home to his house. His parents were at work, and we went swimming in his pool, and then we took a shower and a nap. In the shower, my hair was still full of smoke, it would take days to wash out completely, and now there was also some chlorine, and then I put a lot of lotion on my legs and my shoulders and chest, and Mitchell got out my plane ticket, to check the time, and I fell asleep wrapped up in a towel on his parents' sofa. I don't remember what I dreamed about, but I do remember feeling Mitchell nearby. I remember him rubbing lotion onto my back, rubbing it deep into my skin, deep circles that make you feel lost, the kind going deep into the center of your spine, and I remember that feeling I had just before he sat on the edge and kissed me on the cheek in order to wake me up. I remember I felt loved, and cold from all the air-conditioning, and very, very scared.

"It's time," he said.

I'd never left home before. And I hoped a little part of me was dying. I hoped it wouldn't be a big part, just the part I'd like to forget: the part about my mother, asking me to cook for George; the part about my dad, and the things he must have done; or my mom, a pencil in her ear, explaining the difference between a lover and a husband, a job and a career, a woman and a man. A man is taught to love himself, and a woman must be taught to love him back, or else she will be lonely, because my mom believed in the healing power of the womb and positive thinking, because my mom believed I could be a star on Broadway, even when I didn't want to be one. In college, and after, people would ask me about my family, and I would say my father was a former assistant to the governor, before he retired, and I would say my mother was involved with theater, though I wasn't certain just exactly where she was living now, or with whom. I would say, *Yes, yes, it was a good place to grow up,* particularly when pressed for details I didn't want to give, and I would talk about what it was like, sometimes, going down the river in July, or the smell of mesquite when the rains came in December, the orange blossoms in May, and then the long ride through summer all over again. I'd talk about the heat and the way it rose up off the surface like a sunburn. I'd talk about my friend Mitchell, who wrote me often for the first year, and the pools we used to swim in. I never did mention Mr. Y, because that was part of the bargain, and he continued to pay all my bills: he offered to send me on to graduate school, though by then I didn't need his help. Twice he visited me in Massachusetts, and we went out to dinner, and he asked me questions about my classes. Once he told me my father had died; he didn't tell me his throat had been slit, in the showers, and that there were no longer any suspects. He didn't tell me there was any more to know because by now I suppose he knew I understood that. And even then there were still new parts forming, especially then, because everything then was still enormous and wide open: my past, and what I was going to do with my life, and how I was going to live with what I'd done, and whom I was going to love, as opposed to sleep with, or have dinner with, in order to have someday my own family. I never heard from Rick & Brad again, which often feels wrong, because they were tall and reminded me of uncles, and because after a while I forgot entirely I had ever slept with Brad a couple of times when he was angry with his wife, or she him, because I now know this is precisely the way memory works: you remember what you need to know in order only to remember more. And what you forget is what you never did become. Mostly I remember being seventeen and driving to the airport with my friend, Mitchell Hemly. He parked the car in the garage, and then we walked into the airport full of carpet. All around us there were people going places, and then Mitchell bought me some peanuts, for the long flight ahead, and he took me to the gate because we didn't have any bags to check. At the gate I put my arms around him and didn't cry, and he said, *It's okay, Lace,* and I said, beginning to cry, *I am not going to change my mind,* and he said, *Don't forget to write.* And then some lady in a blue uniform told me it was time to get on board, so I walked onto the plane and found my place, beside a window, and never did come home again.

Alison Baker

CONVOCATION

On Thursdays Judith had her daughter, who had often threatened to commit suicide if Judith failed to love her sufficiently.

"You can't possibly understand my life," Rain said at about 2:00 every Thursday afternoon. "You just want to control me. You *want* me to die."

Judith would sigh and try not to look at her watch. The van came at 4:30 to carry Rain back to the halfway house, leaving Judith free to wash her hair and spend the evening decompressing in front of the television, so she could go back to her own life on Friday.

"I never thought life would turn out like this," she said to Dickie every Friday morning over coffee at the Village Inn. "I really didn't expect it. Did you? Did you ever have any idea?"

"None," Dickie said. "I thought my mother would be hale and hearty into her nineties, and then die in her sleep." Instead, Dickie's mother, old Mrs. Partee, was bedridden, suspicious, and vague, just alert enough to weep when Dickie showed up late for his daily visit.

"I'm about at my wit's end," Judith said. She poured herself more coffee from the never-empty pot and sat stirring sugar into it. "I'm damned if I do take care of her and damned if I don't."

"You're worse off than I am," Dickie said. "At least my mother's statistically likely to die before I do. I may have some time to myself before I gork out."

It was some satisfaction to know that Dickie thought her situation was worse than his, but it also made Judith feel guilty. "It's not that I don't love her," she said.

"I know," Dickie said, smiling.

Dickie Partee was a hairdresser who was four feet eight inches tall. He was said to have a remarkable way with wayward hair, but Judith had never gone to him. They had met after sitting through one meeting of a support group together; in the parking lot afterwards each heard the other heave a tremendous sigh of relief, and they burst into laughter and went out for a drink. Now they had a routine—two hours a week over coffee, and no holds barred when it came to mothers or daughters.

Judith had sometimes thought of moving away, but as time went on it seemed more and more unlikely. It was convenient that the van made the weekly run into town, making it unnecessary for her to drive up to the city to fetch Rain for her visit.

"You wouldn't even *see* me if it weren't for the van," Rain would accuse Judith on Thursday afternoons as they walked back to the clinic, to catch the van back. "You just better keep voting for higher taxes so the county will keep the service running." She sounded delighted at the idea that her mother would have to pay more and more.

"Oh, honey," Judith would say, kissing her good-bye and brushing—even though she tried to refrain—her daughter's bangs away from her eyes. "Now call me when you get home, and you have a good week."

"Oh, Mummy." Rain would shake off Judith's hands and jerk away, springing into the van and sitting on the far side. The driver would slide the door closed behind her and wink at Judith, which always started Judith back on the path to cheering up. The van settled as he climbed in, and the engine started, and as the van started to pull away Rain would suddenly scramble into the back seat, her sullen, angry face crumpled into tears, and press her hands against the window in frantic good-bye waves to her mother. As the van carried her baby away, Judith would weep herself, waving her handkerchief, her heart growing lighter as the van grew smaller and smaller and finally turned the corner and was gone.

And besides the convenience of having her daughter delivered practically to her door once a week, she liked the town. She could walk anywhere, except to the mall, where she didn't want to go anyway. After coffee with Dickie she walked to work, crossing Washington Street and striding down Elm to College Place, where she turned and plunged under the maple canopy of the campus arboretum and slowed down to drift through fallen leaves, or bee-laden flowers, or squeaking snow, depending on the season, to her office.

There were only two problems with staying here. One was that her office was in a prize-winning newer building which had been cleverly designed by an architect who had never heard of either below-zero weather or sound-proofing. Half the year Judith was forced to keep her moonboots on and wear fingerless wool gloves, as if she'd just come in from ice-fishing. And the acoustics of the building were such that she knew most of the professional secrets, and many of the personal ones, of Professor Arvin, even though he was on the other side of the building and downstairs. They were attached by some convolution of heating vents. That Professor Arvin knew her secrets, too, she could tell by the way he either caught or avoided her eye during faculty meetings, when various topics came up.

The other problem was that after a nationwide search the college had turned its bleary eyes toward home, and Dreiser Smith, her former husband and Rain's father, had just been named president of the college. It was unlikely to be a major problem; Judith herself stayed out of campus politics as much as possible, and Dreiser would considerately pay as little attention to her as he found consistent with their respective positions.

That was how he put it when he called her, soon after the search committee had approached him with the offer. "I just wanted to let you know, Judith," he said. "I don't foresee that it will be uncomfortable in any way."

"No," she said, "I don't imagine you do."

"Jude," Dreiser whined then, "don't be that way."

"Congratulations, Dreiser," she said, relenting a little. "What an honor." To get a job no one else in the country would take, she didn't add.

"I'll have a chance to do some of the things we've always talked about," he said, sounding for a moment like the young instructor Judith had fallen in love with.

"Good luck," she said dryly. "I suppose Impy is quite proud."

Dreiser hesitated a moment, probably, she thought, trying to decide whether Judith was being sarcastic or not. In keeping with his new position he apparently decided to assume the best, and said, "Impy's pleased, of course; but she's so caught up in her own work that I'm afraid this will be quite an imposition on her time."

"I don't imagine she'll let it be, will she?" Judith said. "Her duty to God comes before her duties as first lady, doesn't it?"

"It's not as if she has a parish of her own yet," Dreiser said. "I would imagine she can make arrangements if she feels it's necessary."

"Well," Judith said, "I know Rain will be quite proud."

"Oh, yes," Dreiser said. "I'll have to let her know."

He was, really, as good a father to Rain as it was probably possible to be under the circumstances. As good a father as an administrator with no psychological insight, who thought that any person could *shape up* if he or she really wanted to, could ever possibly be. He spent an afternoon with Rain once a month, like clockwork; he paid his share of the bills that Medicaid didn't cover; and Judith suspected that because of Rain he had even declined to have a child with the young and fecund-looking Impy, thus causing her to turn to Christ for consolation. Judith did not *know* this last, but she thought it very likely, from the fierceness with which Impy sometimes shook her hand.

· · ·

"So," Dickie said, the Friday after Dreiser's appointment had been announced, "the big man's reached the pinnacle. Aren't you sorry you gave all that up?"

"If I was still married to him they never would have given him the job," Judith said.

"From what I hear, the priestly wife made them think twice," Dickie said, refilling his coffee.

"Nonsense," Judith said. "She's perfectly charming."

"My source says she's just a shade too earnest," Dickie said. "They think she'll try to convert all the alumni."

"Episcopalians don't convert people," Judith said. "Besides, it's her nature. It seems to me she was fairly earnest when she went about seducing my husband."

"Takes two to tango," Dickie said.

"You're right," Judith said. "I rather earnestly drove him into her arms." And she changed the subject.

Judith did not talk much about Dreiser or Impy to Dickie. All that was too long ago and had hurt her too deeply to discuss with anyone. Impy was just the proverbial blonde girl student, albeit one who was now turning into an Episcopal priest. Judith mentioned them sometimes in passing, but only lightly, or with a roll of her eyes, and Dickie responded just as lightly; and they went back to Judith's daughter, or to Dickie's mother, or sometimes to their imaginary futures, when they would be free.

Rain had her ups and downs. As long as she took her medication she was a joy to have around. She would go shopping with Judith, or to a chamber concert, and if they met any of Judith's colleagues she was as charming and forthright as any of the adult children that came back to town to visit their aging parents.

The problem was that Rain hated her medication. Judith could tell if Rain had gone off her meds as soon as she saw Rain's face through the window of the van on Thursday mornings, and her heart would drop like a stone into the bottom of her stomach.

"Don't you see, Mummy, that's not *me*," Rain would say,

when she was calm enough to discuss it. "I start to miss the voices."

"I don't understand that," Judith would say hopelessly. "How on earth can you miss them?"

"You're as bad as Daddy!" Rain would shout then. "You don't want to understand me! You don't even like the real me!"

But Judith thought she did understand what Rain meant; the bright, erratic, shimmering Rain was much more like Judith's old healthy child than the calm one that agreeably swallowed her pills every morning. But the drugs made it so much easier for Rain to function; no voices, no visions of hell, no people on the street conspiring against her and sticking out their demonic tongues. How could someone choose fear and—well, insanity, over the easy chemical path through life?

"She is an adult," Dickie would say. "She's not stupid."

And Dickie was right; he was repeating Judith's own words. Rain was twenty-six years old, and she was brilliant. Just because she couldn't stick to anything, or concentrate, didn't mean she was incapable of making her own choices.

"Okay," Judith said. *"Mea culpa.* It's just so much harder for me."

"Right," Dickie said, and he laughed. "Same with Mom. *She's* perfectly happy as long as they don't turn off her TV. Why should I worry?"

"Would your mother really know if you didn't come to see her?"

Dickie rolled his eyes. "That's the question I torment myself with at night. It would probably make not one iota of difference to her. My visits are like trees falling one by one in the forest. No one even knows they go."

"Except the trees themselves," Judith said. "And eventually so many trees fall that there's no forest left."

"There's something incredibly heavy in that," Dickie said, "but I think it may take me a lifetime to figure out what it is."

Judith had long ago relinquished the embarrassing secret hope that a man unlike Dreiser would show up on her doorstep, begging to take care of her and her mad daughter. But sometimes she still dreamed of an uncomplicated companionship with someone who, when Rain left on Thursday afternoons, would walk home with her through the lengthening shadows, swinging her hand, and, when they got inside the door of their own house, heave a deep sigh of relief, pin her to the wall by her shoulders, and say, "Let's go out for Thai, beautiful." Or pizza, or Greek. But such a man's turning up was about as likely as Dickie Partee's growing twelve inches overnight, or Rain's showing up on a Tuesday to announce, "Guess what, Mom! I'm cured!"

Judith was not a person who had friends. There was Dickie, and of course she went to lectures and concerts with colleagues, and attended her share of cocktail parties and retirement dinners; but she did not have any that she would call *close friends.*

"I blame myself," Dreiser had once sighed when Judith pointed this out to him in what she had thought was an objective fashion.

"Yourself?" Judith had said. "Of all the things to blame yourself for, why choose my personality?"

"Because I'm so socially adept," he had explained. "You neither feel the need nor have you developed the skill to make friends."

This had silenced her, as so much about Dreiser had silenced her: his self-centeredness, his attitude toward their daughter even before her illness struck, his very strange way of seeing the world, as if, if it had only consulted *him,* it would not be in such bad shape. It was not so much ego, Judith had finally decided, or even optimism, as it was a profound lack of understanding of what made people tick.

"Oh, come now," he had said to her when she ventured to tell him this, sometime toward the end of their marriage. "Your own field isn't exactly psychology."

"My field?" Judith said. "You think people's fields are all they understand?"

"You know what I mean, Judith," he had said.

"Anthropology is not entirely unrelated to human beings," Judith said.

"And where do you put God in all this?" he had said, looking at her over the reading glasses he had recently begun to wear.

"What on earth does God have to do with it?" she had said,

astonished; and it was at that moment that she began to suspect that something was going on with Dreiser that she had never dreamed of.

Sure enough, a few weeks later, there, casually dropped on Dreiser's bureau beside his keys and a well-used hankie, was the letter from Impy. The letter did not mention God, but Impy did write that she felt blessed to know Dreiser, and the way she capitalized "Know" seemed significant to Judith.

The rest of that year was as tawdry and painful as years like that usually are. But it was the year after, when Dreiser had married Impy and was on sabbatical with her in Italy, that 15-year-old Rain's illness washed over them all, upsetting—none of them dared to say *ruining*—what they had all started to plan for the rest of their lives.

Rain had been named Sarah, but when she got sick she told her mother that everything was now changed. "Sarah is dead," she had said, weeping, as she lay on the table in the emergency room where Judith had brought her. "I am clouds, I am storm, I am cold gray Rain." And Rain was all she would answer to.

"What?" Dreiser had shouted from the distant continent. "Rain? You're calling me about the weather?"

He had refused to come home after that first episode, because it was, after all, a professionally important semester for him as well as a honeymoon with the blonde Impy. "I can't rush back because Sarah's had a tantrum," he said. "She's jealous, *that* much I understand, Judith. She's a big girl now. She'll have to get used to the idea that Daddy's not always going to be available."

He had grown disgusted with Judith's calls, her descriptions of Rain's changed behavior. *"Make* her clean up her room," he'd said. "Tell her she's grounded until she straightens up. Don't let her go out on any dates."

"She doesn't have dates, Dreiser," Judith said. "She doesn't comb her hair and she doesn't bathe. Why would anyone ask her out?"

"Throw her in the shower, for God's sake," he said. "That's your department, not mine."

"Those years left me absolutely bruised," Judith told Dickie. "I thought I was crazy. Everyone dismissed what I said, as if I were a child or an imbecile."

"You know," Dickie said, "unless someone's lived with a crazy person, they just don't understand it."

"I'll tell you one thing, I know what Anita Hill went through," Judith said. "I would sit there describing Rain's behavior, and then some white-haired man would say, 'She'll snap out of it. Maybe we should talk about what's going on with Mother?' "

"Oh, my," Dickie said, burying his face in his little hands. "You poor thing." He looked at her through his fingers. "Speaking of Mother—" And they were off into his side of the story. She wouldn't eat, she demanded drink, she accused Dickie of stealing her money and keeping her a prisoner in the old folks' home. "Oh, God, Judith," Dickie said, "what would I do without you to talk to?"

"Talk to yourself," she said. It struck them both as hilarious, and they sat in the Village Inn shaking with laughter as their coffee grew cold and their waitress looked at her watch and stepped into the kitchen for a cigarette.

Well, they had all gotten used to it. Used, that is, to never knowing for sure where they stood, or what would happen tomorrow. And to the knowledge that they would never, any of them, be *quite* happy. Moments, maybe hours, maybe even days of happiness might occur, but in general they had to find their satisfaction in understanding that they were doing the very best they could, under the circumstances.

Human beings were so adaptable, Judith thought. The unthinkable so quickly became the accepted. The first few weeks in her new office, for example, she had been driven crazy listening to Professor Arvin's sneezes, and to his humming as he put his books on the new shelves and hung pictures on his walls. She had furiously called the Buildings and Grounds people, who referred her to the heating plant, who sent her to the chief of operations, who finally came up to her office and heard Professor Arvin's sneezes for himself, and said that perhaps the architect could redesign the air moving system. And a

week later Judith realized that not only didn't she mind anymore when Professor Arvin sneezed, she had begun to hum
along with him when she knew the tune.

And no doubt Rain was right—there was no way Judith
could really understand her life. Rain was the one who had the
voices and visions; she could never get away from them, never
go to a movie or on a honeymoon or spend a night at the office
in order to escape them, because they were always there. "The
drugs make me dopey," she told Judith, "but the voices are *in*
there. They're just dozing, waiting around. They know I'll give
in in the end and let them come back."

The same thing had happened with Impy. Judith had hated
the very thought of Impy for months. When Dreiser and Impy
came back from Italy she had felt like running off to Antarctica,
someplace where she would never have to see them. She had
dreaded the first faculty party, the first concerts and plays and
football games of the year, because she would have to see Dreiser and Impy together. But then she *did* see them, at an afternoon reception for a visiting historian. And although Impy
was quite pretty, she was so very *young!* Of course, by now she
wasn't young anymore; and over time Judith had come to
rather like her, in an odd and uncomfortable way. Impy was
part of her life, as much as Dreiser was.

That was the other thing—how easily people forget details.
Living with Dreiser had often been difficult, but now she was
hard-pressed to remember specifics, or, if she did remember
them, to bring back the desperate and helpless feeling she'd
had at the time. The Dreiser she knew now could have been an
entirely different person; the removal of intimacy between
them had changed not only the situation but the people in it.

Everything that fall seemed crystal clear, brighter and closer
than it had for some time. The brilliant red and yellow leaves
were untouched by crusty brown edges or spots; the children
Judith passed as she walked to campus were nicely dressed,
their hair combed, their clothes sturdy, and they smiled
politely at her and said, "Good morning;" the high school
band, marching past her house in the dark on the way to a
football game, played in tune and with a heavy pounding of

percussion that caught in Judith's chest and excited her, the way such things hadn't excited her for forty years. Perhaps, she thought, she was nearing menopause. But more likely it was the mild stress connected with the vague excitement on campus that made her feel more alert, a little on edge, a touch apprehensive.

The imminent anointment of the new president—even if it was just Dreiser—affected the whole college. Administrative assistants were busy planning a great, symbolic ceremony and accompanying gala events; the deans of things stood around in little knots in the halls, discussing the possibility of revamping lines of communication and authority; even individual faculty members, beneath the collective veil of academic cynicism, felt tiny surges of optimism at the thought that this or that long-hoped-for but long-despaired-of pet project—a new course in Hispanic Lesbian literature, an increase in the number of physics hours required for graduation, perhaps a dental plan— might at last be put into effect.

There was just a slight awkwardness in Judith's position, an inhibiting factor when it came to candid discussions of the new president's proclivities and failings. When she walked into the faculty lounge she felt just a touch *on display,* as if people had just been saying, "I wonder how Judith feels about all this," but nobody quite had the nerve to ask her.

"Daddy called," Rain said over the phone. "He asked me to come to his inauguration and then he had the nerve to say, 'If you think you can behave.' "

"Oh, dear," Judith said.

"Why can't he think of *me* for once?" Rain said. "Why can't he even imagine how I feel?"

"He's that way with everyone, honey," Judith said.

"Behave myself!" Rain said. "What does he think I'm going to do, stand up and start shouting? Rip off my clothes and dance around in the aisles?"

Judith laughed. "He means well, sweetie. It's just that it's a very important day for him. He's worried about everything."

"He thinks I'm insane," Rain said. "He said Impy's giving the invocation. Do you think she'll wear her priest outfit?"

"She's not ordained yet," Judith said. "But the faculty will be gowned, so I suppose she will too."

"I think I'll wear scarlet," Rain said. "Spangles and feathers. And dye my hair purple."

"If you want to, dear," Judith murmured. She had learned long ago that maternal protests sometimes made idle threats into stubborn promises.

And in fact when Rain arrived for the inaugural weekend, Judith was ashamed to realize how relieved she was that her daughter had brought a perfectly nice dress, red but unspangled, and that her hair was the familiar honey brown with golden highlights that she had gotten from Dreiser.

Saturday night Judith went to a dinner for Dreiser and Impy, and when she got home a little after ten every light was on and Rain was taking a shower in the upstairs bathroom. Judith sighed and wished again that Rain would now and then do the dishes or turn out a light when she left a room. She turned off the television and locked the doors, and thought about dinner. It had begun as a strained gathering of alumni and faculty on their best behavior, and Dreiser's rather stiff personality had dominated the room; but after Dreiser and Impy left, the party had livened up, and people had danced and drunk and conversation had been loud and loose, and Judith had found herself flirting with Professor Arvin.

As she stood in the dark living room and stared out the window a car pulled up in front of the house and Impy got out. "Good Lord," Judith said aloud, and she went to the front door and opened it.

"Judith!" Impy said, stopping on the top step. "I thought you might be asleep."

"Well, I'm not." Judith led her into the living room and turned on a light. "Impy, what's the matter?"

"I wrote it all down," Impy said. "Dreiser doesn't know I'm here. If you were asleep I was just going to leave it in your mailbox."

"Impy, what are you talking about?" Judith said.

Impy took a deep breath and sat down on the sofa. "Well," she said, "I'm about to be ordained a priest."

"Yes," Judith said, sitting down across from her. "Congratulations."

Impy shook her head. "My spiritual advisor—my confessor—and I believe that I should enter the priesthood with my soul as unburdened as possible. And with all the important things going on this weekend—well, I thought this was a good time." She looked damply at Judith. "I need your forgiveness, Judith."

"Good Lord," Judith said. "For what?"

Impy looked down at her hands. "I knew Dreiser was married when he first asked me out," she said. "And I went anyway."

"Oh, for heaven's sake," Judith said. "That was ten years ago."

"Time doesn't change it from being wrong to being right," Impy said. "I'm afraid you were terribly hurt because of me, and I want to apologize."

"Impy, I really don't want to discuss this," Judith said.

"We don't have to discuss it," Impy said, wiping her cheek. "I just need you to forgive me."

Judith had never felt farther from forgiveness than she did right now. She had never realized that Impy was such an incredible boob. "Oh, for God's sake," she snapped, and suddenly she thought that the shower had been running since she got home—she looked at her watch—over an hour ago. She stood up, said, "Excuse me a minute," and ran up the stairs.

She knocked on the bathroom door. "Rain?" There was no answer. She tried the knob, but the door was locked. "Rain? Honey?" She knocked louder, and a slice of fear tore through her heart. "Rain!" she screamed, and she shook the doorknob with both hands.

"What's the matter?" Impy said, running up the stairs.

"Rain," Judith cried, rattling the doorknob. "Help me open this."

"Oh, God," Impy said, and she threw herself clumsily against the door and bounced off. "Is there a window?"

"No," Judith sobbed. "Call someone. Hurry."

"Nine one one," Impy cried. "Where's the phone?" She rushed down the hall in the direction Judith pointed.

"Rain!" Judith called again through the door. If she could just get Rain's attention, she thought, she could keep her from slipping away. "Rain!"

"They're coming," Impy called, running back.

"Oh, God, let them hurry," Judith said, and she thought, I suppose Impy will think I'm praying. She pressed her ear to the door. It seemed to her that she could hear voices in the shower: conversation, and an occasional laugh.

Impy leaned against the door beside her, and together they pounded and called, "Rain? Rain?"

It was an eternity before they heard the siren, although it turned out later to have been no more than four minutes. Impy ran down to open the door, and Judith heard her saying, "Oh, hurry, hurry!"

Two policemen ran up the stairs. "Stand aside, ma'am," one said, and Judith jumped back as the men hurled themselves against the door. It broke with a crash, and sweet moist air burst into the hall as they ripped away the splintered plywood and plunged into the bathroom.

Rain, standing in the shower trying to cover herself with her arms, screamed.

One of the policemen, with what Judith later thought was remarkable presence of mind, took a towel off the rack and held it toward Rain, turning his head away.

The other one reached in and turned off the water. "Are you all right, miss?"

"Of course I'm all right," Rain shouted, clutching the towel.

"Why didn't you answer me?" Judith said angrily, wincing at the harsh sound of her own voice.

"I didn't *hear* you," Rain said, wrapping the towel around herself. Judith saw that she was covered with goosebumps, and her lips were blue. The hot water had run out long ago.

Two emergency medical technicians had run up the stairs and stood behind Judith, looking into the bathroom. The policemen stepped out through the broken door, both of them holding their hands up as if they were subduing a mob. "Just a misunderstanding," one of them said to the ambulance attendants, but Judith felt he was giving her a dirty look as he said it.

"You're kidding," one of them said.

"I'm sorry," Judith said. "I made a mistake." She stood looking at Rain as Impy went downstairs with the four men.

Rain had cut off most of her hair, and what was left stood

up in wet purple spikes. "What did you think I was doing, Mummy, slitting my wrists?" she said, stepping out of the shower and adjusting the towel.

Judith burst into tears. "You didn't answer," she said. "I called you and called you and you never answered. I never know what I'll find."

"Oh, Mother," Rain said irritably, and then she too began to cry. "Neither do I. I wish I were dead."

"No you don't," Judith said, putting her arms around her.

"Daddy will never forgive me."

"Of course he will," Impy said, appearing at the door.

"You don't understand," Rain cried angrily. "My father has never loved me."

A great wave of fatigue washed over Judith. "Rain," she said, "stop worrying about Daddy."

"But it's true," she said.

Judith looked at Impy over Rain's head. "It's not true," she said at last. "And if it were, purple hair isn't the way to win his heart."

Rain snickered in spite of herself. "Oh, Mother, what am I going to do?"

"You'll just have to let it grow."

"But I can't *go* tomorrow," Rain said, weeping again. "I can't let anyone see me this way."

"It won't wash out?" Impy said.

Rain shook her head. "I've been washing it for hours."

"You could wear a scarf," Judith said.

"Oh, right, Mom," Rain said, rolling her eyes. "Show up in a babushka. That wouldn't attract attention."

Judith looked at her watch. "Maybe I could call someone."

"Who?" Rain said.

"A hairdresser I know," she answered.

"It's an acceptable fashion in New York," Dickie said, walking around Rain and examining her head.

"I hate New York," Rain said.

"Do you think you can do anything?" Judith said from the doorway. "Make it less extreme or something?"

"Sure," Dickie said, "we can do something."

"Glue my hair back on," Rain said.

"Honey, Dickie can't work miracles," Judith said.

"He has to," Rain said, twisting around in her chair to look at him.

"You don't need a miracle," he said. "You just need a good haircut."

"And a dye job," Rain said. "I want my normal color back."

"That I can't promise," he said.

Rain turned around again and closed her eyes. "Don't touch my hair if you can't fix it."

"Rain," Judith said. "Dickie has come all the way over here in the middle of the night to help you. Do you have to be so rude?"

"Mother, this is my *life*," Rain said. "I feel so fragile right now, I'm just not responsible." She buried her face in her hands.

Judith shook her head at Dickie and beckoned him out into the hall. "I am so sorry," she said in a low voice. "I apologize for her rudeness."

Dickie shrugged. "I'm a hairdresser," he said. "I'm used to it."

"I just don't know where the line is," Judith said. "Is she really fragile, or is she just spoiled? Even after all these years I don't know what to do."

"You're talking about me!" Rain called. "Stop talking about me!"

Dickie patted Judith's arm. "Why don't you leave us now, Mother," he said, and he grinned. "Go have yourself a nice drink with your friend."

Judith went reluctantly downstairs. She couldn't imagine what Dickie could possibly do to salvage Rain's hair, and she was sorry she had called him. He would never forgive her for dragging him into this. And Rain would twist it all around so that Dickie's failure would be the root of all the trouble and it would be her, Judith's fault. Proving once again that she didn't really love Rain at all.

In the kitchen Impy was hanging up the phone. "I called Dreiser," she said. "I told him everything was under control."

"Why on earth did you call Dreiser?" Judith said.

Impy looked surprised. "It's nearly one in the morning."

"I hope you didn't tell him about Rain."

"Well," Impy said. "I had to give him some reason for being here."

Judith started to say something, but she thought better of it. She got a bottle of wine out of the refrigerator, and they sat drinking silently at the kitchen table until Rain called, "Here I come!" from the top of the stairs. With a look at each other, Judith and Impy went out into the hall.

Rain was marching down the stairs, her hair a mere dark shadow spreading over her skull. In spite of herself, Judith put her hand to her mouth. It was like seeing a vision of her daughter in death, the skin around her ears gleaming, her bones sharp under the thin white bathrobe.

Rain stopped halfway down. "Well?"

With her hair gone, there was nothing to distract from her marvelous green eyes. What a funny thing, Judith thought, to forget how beautiful your own child's eyes are. "Rain, darling, you look lovely," she said.

"She's got the cheekbones for it," Dickie said as he came down behind Rain.

"What do you think, Impy?" Rain said.

Without hesitating Impy said, "You look beautiful," and Judith forgave her everything.

Rain and Dickie came on down the stairs. "What are you doing here, anyway?" Rain said to Impy.

But before she could answer there was a knock at the front door and Dreiser walked in. "What's going on here?" he said, and then he saw Rain and said, "Good God."

"Hi, Daddy," Rain said. "It's the cancer ward look."

"Cancer?" he said, and Judith saw a look of terror cross his face.

She started toward him but Impy said, "Darling, it's a *fashion*," and moved over to kiss his cheek.

"It's all the rage in New York," Dickie said.

Dreiser looked down at Dickie, and Judith watched with awe and amusement as his social skills clicked into action. "I don't believe we've met," he said, extending his hand. "I'm Dreiser Smith."

"Dick Partee," Dickie said. "Congratulations on your big day tomorrow."

"Thank you," Dreiser said. "Are you an alumnus?"

"No," Dickie said, "I'm a hairdresser."

"I think I know your mother," Impy said.

"You do?" Dickie said, looking up at her in surprise.

"Mrs. Partee? Out at the Vercingetorix Nursing Home?" Impy said. "She always speaks very highly of you."

"She does?" Dickie said.

"Oh, yes," Impy said. "In her clearer spells she doesn't talk about anything else."

"Is that right," Dickie said, and a look that Judith had never seen came over his face. It was a slow smile that rose from his mouth into his cheeks, brightening his skin as it went, and it lit up his eyes and the tips of his ears, and even the scalp that showed between the dark strands of his thin hair, as if a floodlight inside him had been turned on.

Judith felt odd the next day. It may have been lack of sleep, but as she filed into the chapel and sat down in the front pews with the rest of the faculty, everyone seemed insubstantial and miles away. She might have been watching big-screen TV as Impy, her golden hair almost too bright to look at against the black of her gown, spoke a brief and, to Judith, incomprehensible prayer. Her eyelids drooped as trustees and alumni spoke, and then she perked up again as Dreiser was sworn into office, his hand resting on a Bible that Impy held. It seemed to Judith like Kabuki theater: a performance that had a great deal of meaning in some context, but not in hers.

She watched as Dreiser swept to the podium in his black gown and scarlet hood to begin his speech. He looked excited; he was probably very happy. Over in the choir alcove Impy sat in rapt attention, and beside her was Rain in her red dress, with the red velour belt from Judith's bathrobe tied around her head. She looked terrible. Probably everyone who saw her thought she *did* have cancer. Judith could imagine the comments—"All the trouble with that girl and now *this*." Maybe that's why people seemed so interested in Dreiser's speech— the bald daughter and the priestly wife made him a more sympathetic character.

She wondered if another hairdresser might have been able to do something less drastic with Rain's hair. Just bleach what was left of it blonde, perhaps. Maybe Dickie had been mad about being called out in the middle of the night, and had taken it out on Rain to get back at Judith. Dickie had probably thought it was just a bad haircut, not a matter of life and death at all.

When she ran up the stairs to her daughter last night, Judith had been convinced that the strange thing she'd felt all fall was a change in Rain, in her behavior or in her body chemistry; something that Rain herself was unaware of, a subtle clue that only Judith could detect, as mothers recognize the smell of their own babies as soon as they're born. But as she leaned on the door beside Impy, Judith had suddenly known that it was a change in *her*, herself. She was tired. And even if she could call Rain back this time, it might be the last time; she no longer had the strength to keep the world from collapsing.

And when the police broke open the bathroom door to expose Rain standing naked in the ice-cold shower, washing her hair, it was the happiest moment of Judith's entire life. It was the moment she would have chosen to live in forever: a flooding instant when everything she had ever wanted was granted, and she loved her daughter absolutely, just as she was—naked, screaming, and purple-haired.

Judith glanced around at the faculty. Everyone appeared to be absorbed in what Dreiser was droning on about. But perhaps they weren't listening to him any more than she was; they were lost in their own thoughts, planning lectures or vacations, or getting up the nerve to ask someone out, a blonde girl in one of their classes perhaps. As she looked around she saw that Professor Arvin was watching her from down the row. Before she could look away, he crossed his eyes at her.

She tried to stifle her laugh, and it came out as a horribly loud snort. Heads all around turned to look in her direction, and Dreiser faltered in his speech for a moment. She bowed her own head and fumbled in the sleeve of her gown, hoping she would find an old Kleenex from a long-past graduation; she didn't, but the new physics professor sitting next to her took a clean white handkerchief from her purse and handed it to her.

Judith held it over her face with both hands and sat hunched over as Dreiser droned on and on. She tried not to shake, or to make any noise. Maybe people would think she was overcome with emotion; maybe they couldn't tell if she was laughing or weeping. God knew, most of the time she couldn't tell herself.

Joyce Carol Oates

MARK OF SATAN

A woman had come to save his soul and he wasn't sure he was ready.

It isn't every afternoon in the dead heat of summer, cicadas screaming out of the trees like lunatics, the sun a soft, slow explosion in the sky, that a husky young woman comes on foot rapping shyly at the screen door of a house not even yours, a house in which you are a begrudged guest, to save your soul. And she'd brought an angel-child with her too.

Thelma McCord, or was it McCrae. And Magdalena who was a wisp of a child, perhaps four years old.

They were Church of the Holy Witness, headquarters Scranton, PA. They were God's own, and proud. Saved souls glowing like neon out of their identical eye sockets.

Thelma was an "ordained missionary" and this was her "first season of itinerary" and she apologized for disturbing his privacy but did he, would he, surrender but a few minutes of his time to the Teachings of the Holy Witness?

He'd been taken totally by surprise. He'd been dreaming a disagreeable churning-sinking dream and suddenly he'd been wakened, summoned, by a faint but persistent knocking at the front door. Tugging on wrinkled khaki shorts and yanking up the zipper in angry haste—he was already wearing a T-shirt frayed and tight in the shoulders—he'd padded barefoot to the screen door, blinking the way a mollusk might blink if it had eyes. In a house unfamiliar to you, it's like waking to somebody else's dream. And there on the front stoop out of a shimmering-hot August afternoon he'd wished to sleep through, this girlish-eager young female missionary. An angel of God sent special delivery to *him*.

Quickly, before he could change his mind, before *no! no!* intervened, he invited Thelma and little Magdalena inside. Out of the wicked hot sun—quick.

"Thank you," the young woman said, beaming with surprise and gratitude. "Isn't he a kind, thoughtful man, Magdalena!"

Mother and daughter were heat-dazed, clearly yearning for some measure of coolness and simple human hospitality. Thelma was carrying a bulky straw purse and a tote bag with a red plastic sheen that appeared to be heavy with books and pamphlets. The child's face was pinkened with sunburn, and her gaze was so downcast she stumbled on the threshold of the door and her mother murmured *Tsk!* and clutched her hand tighter, as if, already, before their visit had begun, Magdalena had brought them both embarrassment.

He led them inside and shut the door. The living room opened directly off the front door. The house was a small three-bedroom tract ranch with simulated redwood siding; it was sparsely furnished, the front room uncarpeted, with a butterscotch-vinyl sofa, twin butterfly chairs in fluorescent lime, and a coffee table that was a slab of weather-stained granite set atop cinder blocks. (The granite slab was in fact a grave marker, so old and worn by time that its name and dates were illegible. His sister Gracie, whose rented house this was, had been given the coffee table slab by a former boyfriend.) A stain the color of tea and the shape of an octopus disfigured a corner of the ceiling but the missionaries, seated with self-conscious murmurs of thanks on the sofa, would not see it.

He needed a name to offer to Thelma McCord, or McCrae, who had so freely offered her name to him. "Flash," he said, inspired, "my name is Flashman."

He was a man no longer young yet by no means old; nor

even, to the eye of a compassionate observer, middle-aged. His ravaged looks, his blood-veined eyes, appeared healable. He was a man given, however, to the habit of irony, distasteful to him in execution but virtually impossible to resist. (Like masturbation, to which habit he was, out of irony too, given as well.) When he spoke to Thelma he heard a quaver in his voice that was his quickened, erratic pulse but might sound to another's ear like civility.

He indicated they should take the sofa, and he lowered himself into the nearest butterfly chair on shaky legs. When the damned contraption nearly overturned, the angel-child Magdalena, fluffy pale-blonde hair and delicate features, jammed her thumb into her mouth to keep from giggling. But her eyes were narrowed, alarmed.

"Mr. Flashman, so pleased to make your acquaintance," Thelma said uncertainly. Smiling at him with worried eyes, possibly contemplating whether he was Jewish.

Contemplating the likelihood of a Jew, a descendant of God's chosen people, living in the scraggly foothills of southwestern Pennsylvania, in a derelict ranch house seven miles from Waynesburg with a front yard that looked as if motorcycles had torn it up. Would a Jew be three days unshaven, jaws like sandpaper, knobbily barefoot and hairy-limbed as a gorilla? Would a Jew so readily welcome a Holy Witness into his house?

Offer them drinks, lemonade, but no, he was thinking, *no.*

This, an opportunity for him to confront goodness, to look innocence direct in the eye, should not be violated.

Thelma promised that her visit would not take many minutes of Mr. Flashman's time. For time, she said, smiling breathlessly, is of the utmost. "That is one of the reasons I am here today."

Reaching deep into the tote bag to remove, he saw with a sinking heart, a hefty black Bible with gilt-edged pages and a stack of pamphlets printed on pulp paper—THE WITNESS. Then easing like a brisk mechanical doll into her recitation.

The man who called himself Flash was making every effort to listen. He knew this was important, there are no accidents. Hadn't he wakened in the night to a pounding heart and a taste of bile with the premonition that something, one of *his things*, was to happen soon? Whether of his volition and calculation, or seemingly by accident (but there are no accidents), he could not know. Leaning forward, gazing at the young woman with an elbow on his bare knee, the pose of Rodin's Thinker, listening hard. Except the woman was a dazzlement of sweaty-fragrant female flesh. Speaking passionately of the love of God and the passion of Jesus Christ and the Book of Revelation of St. John the Divine and the Testament of the Witness. Then eagerly opening her Bible on her knees and dipping her head toward it so that her sand-colored, limp-curly hair fell into her face and she had to brush it away repeatedly—he was fascinated by the contrapuntal gestures, the authority of the Bible and the meek dipping of the head and the way in which, with childlike unconscious persistence, she pushed her hair out of her face. Unconscious too of her grating singsong voice, an absurd voice in which no profound truth could ever reside, and of her heavy, young breasts straining against the filmy material of her lavender-print dress, her fattish-muscular calves and good, broad feet in what appeared to be white wicker ballerina slippers.

The grimy venetian blinds of the room were drawn against the glaring heat. It was above ninety degrees outside and there had been no soaking rains for weeks and in every visible tree hung ghostly bagworm nests. In his sister's bedroom a single-window-unit air conditioner vibrated noisily and it had been in this room, on top of, not in, the bed, that he'd been sleeping when the knocking came at the front door; the room that was his had no air conditioner. Hurrying out, he'd left the door to his sister's bedroom open and now a faint trail of cool-metallic air coiled out into the living room and so he fell to thinking that his visitors would notice the cool air and inquire about it and he would say, Yes, there *is* air conditioning in this house, in one of the bedrooms, shall we go into that room and be more comfortable?

Now the Bible verses were concluded. Thelma's fair, fine skin glowed with excitement. Like a girl who has shared her most intimate secret and expects you now to share yours, Thelma lifted her eyes to Flash's and asked, almost boldly, Was he aware of the fact that God loved him? He squirmed hearing such words. Momentarily unable to respond, he laughed, embarrassed, shook his head, ran his fingers over his sandpaper jaws, and mumbled, No, not really, he guessed that he was not aware of that fact, not really.

Thelma said that was why she was here, to bring the good news to him. That God loved him whether he knew of Him or acknowledged Him. And the Holy Witness was their mediator.

Flashman mumbled, Is that so. A genuine blush darkening his face.

Thelma insisted, Yes, it *is* so. A brimming in her close-set eyes, which were the bluest eyes Flash had ever glimpsed except in glamour photos of models, movie stars, naked centerfolds. He said apologetically that he wasn't one hundred percent sure how his credit stood with God these days. "God and me," he said, with a boyish, tucked-in smile, "have sort of lost contact over the years."

Which was *the* answer the young female missionary was primed to expect. Turning to the little girl, she whispered in her ear, "Tell Mr. Flashman the good, good news, Magdalena!" and like a wind-up doll, the blonde child began to recite in a breathy, high-pitched voice, "We can lose God but God never loses *us*. We can despair of God but God never despairs of *us*. The Holy Witness records, 'He that overcometh shall not be hurt by the second death.'" As abruptly as she'd begun, the child ceased, her mouth going slack on the word *death.*

It was an impressive performance. Yet there was something chilling about it. Flash grinned and winked at the child in his uneasiness and said, "Second death, eh? What about the first?" But Magdalena just gaped at him. Her left eye losing its focus as if coming unmoored.

The more practiced Thelma quickly intervened. She took up both her daughter's hands in hers and in a brisk patty-cake rhythm chanted, "As the Witness records, 'God shall wipe away all tears from their eyes; and there *will be* no more death.'"

Maybe it was so? So simple? *No more death.*

He was bemused by the simplicity of fate. In this house unknown to him as recently as last week, in this rural no-

man's-land where his older sister Gracie had wound up a
county social worker toiling long grueling hours five days a
week and forced to be grateful for the shitty job, he'd heard a
rapping like a summons to his secret blood padding barefoot
to the dream doorway that's shimmering with light and there
she *is*.

"Excuse me, Thelma—would you and Magdalena like some
lemonade?"

Thelma immediately demurred out of countrybred politeness as he'd expected, so he asked Magdalena, who appeared
to be parched with thirst, poor exploited child, but, annoy-
ingly, she was too shy to even nod her head yes, please. Flash,
stimulated by challenge, apologized for not having fresh-
squeezed lemonade—calculating that Thelma would have to
accept to prove she wasn't offended by his offer—adding that
he was about to get some lemonade for himself, icy-cold, and
would they please join him, so Thelma, lowering her eyes, said
yes. As if he'd reached out to touch her and she hadn't dared
draw back.

In the kitchen, out of sight, he moved swiftly—which was
why his name was Flash. For a man distracted, a giant, black-
feathered eagle tearing out his liver, he moved with surprising
alacrity. But that had always been his way.

Opening the fridge, nostrils pinching against the stale stink
inside, trying his best to ignore his sister Gracie's depressed
housekeeping, he took out the stained Tupperware pitcher of
Bird's-Eye lemonade—thank God, there was some. Tart chemical taste he'd have to mollify, in his own glass, with an ounce
or two of Gordon's gin. For his missionary visitors he ducked
into his bedroom and located his stash and returned to the
kitchen counter, crumbling swiftly between his palms several
chalky-white pills, six milligrams each of barbiturate, enough
to fell a healthy horse, reducing them to gritty powder to dissolve in the greenish lemonade he poured into two glasses: the
taller for Thelma, the smaller for Magdalena. He wondered
what the little girl weighed—forty pounds? Thirty? Fifty? He
had no idea, children were mysteries to him. His own childhood was a mystery to him. But he wouldn't want Magdalena's heart to stop beating.

He'd seen a full-sized man go glassy-eyed and clutch at his
heart and topple over stone-dead overdosing on—what? Heroin. It was a clean death, so far as deaths go, but it came out of
the corner of your eye, you couldn't prepare.

Carefully setting the three glasses of lemonade, two tall and
slim for the adults, the other roly-poly for sweet little Magdalena, on a laminated tray. Returning then, humming cheerfully
to the airless living room where his visitors were sitting primly
on the battered sofa as if, in his absence, they hadn't moved an
inch. Shyly yet with trembling hands, both reached for their
glasses. "Say 'thankyou, sir,'" Thelma whispered to Magdalena, who whispered, "Thankyou, sir," and lifted her glass to
her lips.

Thelma disappointed him by taking only a ladylike sip,
then dabbing at her lips with a tissue. "Delicious," she murmured. But setting the glass down as if it were a temptation.
Poor Magdalena was holding her glass in both hands taking
quick swallows, but at a sidelong glance from her mother, she
too set her glass down on the tray.

Flash said, as if hurt, "There's lots more sugar if it isn't
sweet enough."

But Thelma insisted, No, it was fine. Taking up, with the
look of a woman choosing among several rare gems, one of the
pulp-printed pamphlets. Now, Flash guessed, she'd be getting
down to business. Enlisting him to join the Church of the Holy
Ghost, or whatever it was—Holy Witness?

She named names and cited dates that flew past him—except for the date Easter Sunday, 1899, when, apparently,
there'd been a "shower from the heavens" north of Scranton,
PA—and he nodded to encourage her though she hardly
needed encouraging, taking deep, thirsty sips from his lemonade to encourage her too. Out of politeness Thelma did lift her
glass and take a chaste swallow but no more. Maybe there was
a cult prescription against frozen foods, chemical drinks? The
way the Christian Scientists, unless it was the Seventh Day
Adventists, forbade blood transfusions because such was "eating blood," which was outlawed by the Bible.

Minutes passed. The faint trickle of metallic-cool air
touched the side of his feverish face. He tried not to show his
impatience with Thelma, fixing instead on the amazing fact of

her: a woman not known to him an hour before, now sitting less than a yard away addressing him as if, out of all of the universe, *he mattered.* Loving how she sat wide-hipped and settled into the vinyl cushions like a partridge in a nest. Knees and ankles together, chunky farmgirl feet in the discount-mart wicker flats, half-moons of perspiration darkening the underarms of her floral-print dress. It was a Sunday school kind of dress, lavender rayon with a wide, white collar and an awkward flared skirt and cloth-covered buttons the size of half-dollars. Beneath it the woman would be wearing a full slip, no half-slip for her. Damp from her warm, pulsing body. No doubt a white brassiere—D cups—and white cotton panties, the waist and legs of which left red rings in her flesh. Undies damp, too. And the crotch of the panties, damp. Just possibly stained. She was bare-legged, no stockings, a concession to the heat: just raw, female leg, reddish-blond transparent hairs on the calves, for she was not a woman to shave her body hair. Nor did she wear makeup. No such vanity. Her cheeks were flushed as if rouged and her lips were naturally moist and rosy. Her skin would be hot to the touch. She was twenty-eight or -nine years old and probably Magdalena was not her first child, but her youngest. She had the sort of female body mature by early adolescence, beginning to go flaccid by thirty-five. That fair, thin skin that wears out from too much smiling and aiming to please. Suggestion of a double chin. Hips would be spongy and cellulite-puckered. Kneaded like white bread, squeezed, banged, and bruised. Moist heat of a big bush of curly pubic hair. Secret crevices of pearl drops of moisture he'd lick away with his tongue.

Another woman would have been aware of Flash's calculating eyes on her like ants swarming over sugar, but not this impassioned missionary for the Church of the Holy Witness. Had an adder risen quivering with desire before her, she would have taken no heed. She was reading from one of THE WITNESS pamphlets and her gaze was shining and inward as she evoked in a hushed, little-girl voice a vision of bearded prophets raving in the deserts of Smyrna and covenants made by Jesus Christ to generations of sinners up to this very hour. Jesus Christ was the most spectacular of the prophets, it seemed, for out of his mouth came a sharp, two-edged sword casting terror into all who beheld. Yet he was a poet, his words had undeniable power, for here was Flash the man squirming in his butterfly chair as Thelma recited tremulously, " 'And Jesus spake: I am he that liveth, and was dead; and, behold, I am alive for evermore; and have the keys of hell and death.' "

There was a pause. A short distance away a neighbor was running a chain saw, and out on the highway cars, trucks, thunderous diesel vehicles passed in an erratic whooshing stream, and on all sides beyond the house's walls the air buzzed, quivered, vibrated, rang with the insects of late summer but otherwise it was quiet, it was silent. Like a vacuum waiting to be filled.

The child Magdalena, unobserved by her mother, had drained her glass of lemonade and licked her lips with a flicking pink tongue and was beginning to be drowsy. She wore a pink rayon dress like a nightie with a machine-stamped lace collar, she had tiny feet in white socks and shiny white plastic shoes. Flash saw, yes, the child's left eye had a cast in it. The right eye perceived you head-on but the left drifted outward like a sly, wayward moon.

A defect in an eye of so beautiful a child would not dampen Flash's ardor. He was certain of that.

Ten minutes, fifteen. By now it was apparent that Thelma did not intend to drink her lemonade though Flash had drained his own glass and wiped his mouth with gusto. Did she suspect? Did she sense something wrong? But she'd taken no notice of Magdalena, who had drifted off into a light doze, her angelhead drooping and a thread of saliva shining on her chin. Surely a suspicious Christian mother would not have allowed her little girl to drink spiked lemonade handed her by a barefoot, bare-legged pervert, possibly a Jew, with eyes like the yanked-up roots of thistles—that was encouraging.

"Your lemonade, Thelma," Flash said, with a host's frown, "it will be getting warm if you don't—"

Thelma seemed not to hear. With a bright smile she was asking, "Have you been baptized, Mr. Flashman?"

For a moment he could not think who Mr. Flashman was.

The gin coursing through his veins, which ordinarily buoyed him up like debris riding the crest of a flood and provided him with an acute clarity of mind, had had a dulling, downward sort of effect. He was frightened of the possibility of one of *his things* veering out of his control, for in the past when this had happened the consequences were always very bad. For him as for others.

His face burned. "I'm afraid that's my private business, Thelma. I don't bare my heart to any stranger who walks in off the road."

Thelma blinked, startled. Yet was immediately repentant. "Oh, I know! I have overstepped myself, please forgive me, Mr. Flashman!"

Such passion quickened the air between them. Flash felt a stab of excitement. But ducking his head, boyish-repentant too, he murmured, "No, it's okay, I'm just embarrassed, I guess. I don't truly *know* if I was baptized. I was an orphan discarded at birth, set out with the trash. There's a multitude of us scorned by man and God. What happened to me before the age of twelve is lost to me. Just a whirlwind. A whirlpool of oblivion."

Should have left his sister's bedroom door shut, though. To keep the room cool. If he had to carry or drag this woman any distance—the child wouldn't be much trouble—he'd be miserable by the time he got to where he wanted to go.

Thelma all but exploded with solicitude, leaning forward as if about to gather him up in her arms.

"Oh, that's the saddest thing I have ever heard, Mr. Flashman! I wish one of our elders was here right now to counsel you as I cannot! 'Set out with the trash'—can it be? Can any human mother have been so cruel?"

"If it was a cruel mother, which I don't contest, it was a cruel God guiding her hand, Thelma—wasn't it?"

Thelma blinked rapidly. This was a proposition not entirely new to her, Flash surmised, but one which required a moment's careful and conscious reflection. She said, uncertainly at first and then with gathering momentum, "The wickedness of the world is Satan's hand, and the ways of Satan, as with the ways of God, are not to be comprehended by man."

"What's Satan got to do with this? I thought we were talking about the good guys."

"Our Savior Jesus Christ—"

"*Our* Savior? Who says? On my trash heap I looked up, and He looked down, and He said, 'Fuck you, kid. Life *is* unfair.' "

Thelma's expression was one of absolute astonishment. Like a cow, Flash thought ungallantly, in the instant the sledgehammer comes crashing down on her head.

Flash added, quick to make amends, "I thought this was about me, Thelma, about my soul. I thought the Holy Witness or whoever had something special to say to *me.*"

Thelma was sitting stiff, her hands clasping her knees. One of THE WITNESS pamphlets had fallen to the floor and the hefty Bible too would have slipped had she not caught it. Her eyes now were alert and wary and she knew herself to be in the presence of an enemy, yet did not know that more than theology was at stake. "The Holy Witness does have something special to say to you, Mr. Flashman. Which is why I am here. There is a growing pestilence in the land, flooding the Midwest with the waters of the wrathful Mississippi, last year razing the Sodom and Gomorrah of Florida. Everywhere there are droughts and famines and earthquakes and volcanic eruptions and plagues—all signs that the old world is nearing its end. As the Witness proclaimed in the Book of Revelation that is our sacred scripture, 'There will be a new heaven and a new earth, as the first heaven and the first earth pass away. And the Father on His throne declaring, Behold I make all things new—' "

Flash interrupted, "None of this *is* new! It's been around for how many millennia, Thelma, and what good's it done for anybody?"

"—'I am Alpha and Omega, the beginning and the end,' " Thelma continued, unheeding, rising from the sofa like a fleshy angel of wrath in her lavender dress that stuck to her belly and legs, fumbling to gather up her Bible, her pamphlets, her dazed child, " '—I will give unto him that is athirst of the fountain of life freely but the fearful, and unbelieving, and the abominable, and murderers, and all liars, shall sink into the lake which

burneth with fire and brimstone: which is the second death.' "
Her voice rose jubilantly on the word *death*.

Flash struggled to disentangle himself from the butterfly
chair. The gin had done something weird to his legs—they
were numb, and rubbery. Cursing, he fell to the floor, the rock-
hard carpetless floor, as Thelma roused Magdalena and lifted
her to her feet and half-carried her to the door. Flash tried to
raise himself by gripping the granite coffee table but this too
collapsed, the cinder blocks giving way and the heavy slab
crashing down on his right hand. Three fingers were broken at
once, but in the excitement he seemed not to notice. "Wait! You
can't leave me now! I need you!"

At the door Thelma called back, panting, "Help *is* needed
here. There is Satan in this house."

Flash stumbled to his feet and followed the woman to the
door, calling after her, "What do you mean, 'Satan in this
house'—there is no Satan, there is no Devil, it's all in the heads
of people like you. You're religious maniacs! You're mad!
Wait—"

He could not believe the woman was escaping so easily.
That *his thing* was no thing of *his* at all.

Hauling purse and bulky tote bag, her sleep-dazed daughter on her hip, Thelma was striding in her white wicker ballerina flats swiftly yet without apparent haste or panic out to the
gravel driveway. There was a terrible quivering of the sun-
struck air. Cicadas screamed like fire sirens. Flash tried to follow after, propelling himself on his rubbery legs which were
remote from his head which was too small for his body and at
the end of a swaying stalk. He was laughing, crying, "You're a
joke, people like you! You're tragic victims of ignorance and
superstition! You don't belong in the twentieth century with
the rest of us! You're the losers of the world! You can't cope!
You need salvation!"

He stared amazed at the rapidly departing young woman—
at the dignity in her body, the high-held head, and the very
arch of the backbone. Her indignation was not fear, an indignation possibly too primitive to concede to fear, like nothing in
his experience nor even in his imagination. If this was a movie,
he was thinking, panicked, the missionary would be *walking
out of the frame*, leaving him behind—just him.

"Help! Wait! Don't leave me here alone!"

He was screaming, terrified. He perceived that his life was of no more substance than a cicada's shriek. He'd stumbled as far as the driveway when a blinding light struck him like a sword piercing his eyes and brain.

He'd fallen to his knees then in the driveway, amid sharp gravel and broken glass, and he was bawling like a child beyond all pride, beyond all human shame. His head was bowed, sun beating down on the balding crown of his head. His very soul wept through his eyes for he knew he would die, and nothing would save him, not even irony. *Don't flatter yourself you matter enough even to be grieved! Asshole!*—no, not even his wickedness would save him. Yet seeing him stricken, the young Christian woman could not walk away. He cried, "Satan *is* here! In me! He speaks through me! It isn't me! Please help me, don't leave me to die!" His limbs shook as if palsied and his teeth chattered despite the heat. Where the young woman stood wavering there was a blurry, shimmering figure of light and he pleaded with it, tore open his chest, belly to expose the putrescent tumor of Satan choking his entrails, he begged for mercy, for help, for Christ's love, until at last the young woman cautiously approached him to a distance of about three feet, knelt too, though not in the gravel driveway but in the grass, and by degrees put aside her distrust. Seeing the sickness in this sinner howling to be saved, she bowed her head and clasped her hands to her breasts and began to pray loudly, triumphantly, "O Heavenly Father, help this tormented sinner to repent of his sins and to be saved by Your Only Begotten Son that he might stand by the throne of Your righteousness, help all sinners to be saved by the Testament of the Holy Witness—"

How many minutes the missionary prayed over the man who had in jest called himself Flashman he would not afterward know. For there seemed to be a fissure in time itself. The two were locked in ecstasy as in the most intimate of embraces in the fierce heat of the sun, and in the impulsive generosity of her spirit the young woman reached out to clasp his trembling hands in hers and to squeeze them tight. Admonishing him, "Pray! Pray to Jesus Christ! Every hour of every day pray to

Him in your heart!'' She was weeping too and her face was flushed and swollen and shining with tears. He pleaded with her not to leave him, for Satan was still with him, he feared Satan's grip on his soul, but there was a car at the end of the driveway toward which the child Magdalena had made her unsteady way and now a man's voice called, ''Thelma! Thelma!'' and at once the young woman rose to her full height, brushing her damp hair out of her face, and with a final admonition to him to love God and Christ and abhor Satan and all his ways, she was gone, vanished into the light out of which she had come.

Alone, he remained kneeling, too weak to stand. Rocking and swaying in the sun. His parched lips moved, uttering babble. In a frenzy of self-abnegation he ground his bare knees in the gravel and shattered glass, deep and deeper into the pain so that he might bleed more freely, bleeding all impurity from him or at least mutilating his flesh, so that in the arid stretch of years before him that would constitute the remainder of his life he would possess a living memory of this hour, scars he might touch, read like Braille.

When Gracie Shuttle returned home hours later, she found her brother Harvey in the bathroom dabbing at his wounded knees with a blood-soaked towel, picking bits of gravel and glass out of his flesh with a tweezers. And his hand—several fingers of his right hand were as swollen as sausages and grotesquely bruised. Gracie was a tall, lank, sardonic woman of forty-one with deep-socketed eyes that rarely acknowledged surprise; yet, seeing Harvey in this remarkable posture, sitting hunched on the toilet seat, a sink of blood-tinged water beside him, she let out a long, high whistle. ''What the hell happened to *you?*'' she asked.

Harvey raised his eyes to hers. He did not appear to be drunk or drugged; his eyes were terribly bloodshot, as if he'd had one of his crying jags, but his manner was unnervingly composed. His face was ravaged and sunburnt in uneven splotches as if it had been baked. He said, ''I've been on my knees to Gethsemane and back. It's too private to speak of.''

From years ago, when by an accident of birth they'd shared a household with two hapless adults who were their parents, Gracie knew that her younger brother in such a state was probably telling the truth, or a kind of truth; she knew also that he would never reveal it to her. She waved in his face a pulp religious pamphlet she'd found on the living room floor beside the collapsed granite marker. "And what the hell is *this?*" she demanded.

But again with that look of maddening calm, Harvey said, "It's my private business, Gracie. Please shut the door on your way out."

Gracie slammed the door in Harvey's face and charged through the house to the rear where wild, straggly bamboo was choking the yard. Since she'd moved in three years before, the damned bamboo had spread everywhere, marching from the marshy part of the property where the cesspool was located too close to the surface of the soil. Just her luck! And her with a master's degree in social work from the University of Pennsylvania! She'd hoped, she'd expected more from her education, as from life. She lit a cigarette and rapidly smoked it, exhaling luxuriant streams of smoke through her nostrils. "Well, fuck you," she said, laughing. She frequently laughed when she was angry, and she laughed a good deal these days.

It *was* funny. Whatever it was, it *was* funny—her parolee kid brother, once an honors student, now a balding, middle-aged man picking tenderly at his knees that looked as if somebody had slashed them with a razor. That blasted-sober look in the poor guy's eyes she hadn't seen in twelve years—since one of his junkie buddies in Philly had dropped over dead mainlining heroin.

Some of the bamboo stalks were brown and desiccated but most of the goddamned stuff was still greenly erect, seven feet tall and healthy. Gracie flicked her cigarette butt out into it. Waiting, bored, to see if it caught fire, if there'd be a little excitement out here on Route 71 tonight, the Waynesburg Volunteer Firemen exercising their shiny red equipment and every yokel for miles around hopping in his pickup to come gape— but it didn't, and there wasn't.

Daniel Menaker

INFLUENZA

I — Poison

It was a New York I'd never seen at close range before. I'd known it only through the squibs in the papers, which reproduced what I imagined attending society events must have been like: a background blur out of which emerged one rich or famous mug after another. The pictures that floated out of the inky blackness above these name blurts always made the people look abnormal—prognathous, narcoleptic, Tourretic, or as vacant as unlaid storm-drain pipes. This was strange, because when some of these same people drove in their limos or 190 SLs over to the West Side, to drop their sons off at the Coventry School, they were handsome and cheerful, the dads in slim business suits, the moms in pricey jeans and burgundy or wintergreen sweaters or sweatshirts. Every head of hair with a suave streak or swath of gray; good skin, with crinkles instead of wrinkles; amphitheatrically perfect white teeth. Maybe the combination of dusk and engraved invitations threw them into a gargoyle phase. I taught English in the Upper School at Coventry in the late sixties and seventies, and for the first three of those years, when I was in neurotic despair and was on the outs with the school's autocratic headmaster, W. C. H. Proctor—a socialite not only because of his capital-campaign obligations but out of native hobnobbery—the world of penthouses and summers at Niantic or Hyannis or Bar Harbor and of dressage and mixed doubles and poached salmon and charity bashes seemed as distant to me as a cloud to a clam.

In the early spring of my fourth year at Coventry, my gloom began to lighten. I'd tried to stop a fight in the locker room and got knifed, and Proctor saw it as some kind of courageous act. He began to call me "Jake" instead of "Singer" or "you." As time went on, he put me on this committee and that committee, and asked me to speak on behalf of the school to parents and prospective parents and groups of alumni. I found it uncomfortable under his wing, but I also began to feel more present in my life, at least my professional life, as if some psychic clutch had finally engaged and the neurasthenic idling—

Now, really, Mr. Singer—it is most embarrassing to listen to this narrative masturbation. I know that you had a good rhythm going as you flipped through the pages of your dictionary to find all your impressive words, and I'm so sorry to interrupt, but perhaps you could try a little harder to get to the point!

This would be the voice of Dr. Ernesto Morales, the psychoanalyst I saw three times a week for all but the first of my seven years as a teacher. I internalized his Spanish accent and speech patterns and the machete-like sarcasm that he wielded in the slash-and-burn process he tried to pass off as "interpretation," and I guess such internalization is part of the point of analysis. It's true that life improved for me as I went to him, but whether if I could do it all over again I would actually choose to have the homunculus of an insane, bodybuilding, black-bearded Cuban Catholic Freudian shouting at me from inside my own head I am not sure.

DR. M. (clearing his throat, his audible for boredom): *Please let me know when you* are *sure of something, Mr. Singer.*

ME: *Sorry.*

DR. M.: *I'm surprised that you didn't say that you* guessed *you were sorry.*

ME: *Sorry.*

DR. M.: (Silence).

ME: *What's wrong now, for Christ's sake? I said I was getting better—you should take it as a compliment.*

Dr. M.: *So you ask me to kiss your ass in gratitude as you waste my time with this interminable prehahmble? Even an analyst's patience has—*

Me: *Preamble.*

Dr. M.: *Pree-ahmble. Even an analyst's patience has some limit, Mr. Singer.*

Me: *O.K., O.K.*

So anyway, at school, things were going well. I gave these talks to groups of parents who were considering Coventry for their boys, and I seemed to be convincing a lot of them. Of course, I'd be so nervous I'd spend a half hour on the shitter beforehand, but—

Dr. M.: *Ah, honesty. It is always so refreshing, like a breeze through the palmettos in Havana. It is a pity we are still ninety miles off the shore of your subject.*

Anyway, there was a day in the middle of April when the air in New York was as cool and clear as—

Dr. M.: *And now we have the weather report! Isn't the news supposed to come first, Mr. Singer?*

As a day in October, while—

Dr. M.: *What about the rich and famous people?*

Me: *I'm getting there. I'm just setting this up, trying to give the whole picture.*

Dr. M.: *This giving of the entire picture, as you say, is your characteristic way of putting painful matters on the shelf for a while longer, preferably until they are stale and unappetizing. I would wager that you wish to speak of the problems that brought you to me in the first place—your rage at your mother for dying when you were six years old, the fact that months and months elapsèd when no woman even so much as glimpsèd your penis, the estrangement between you and your father, the compromises involved in your profession. Here they all are, still preying on your mind as if they were the eagle at the livers of Prometheus, no? This is what happens when a patient terminates the treatment before he should.*

Me: *But—*

Dr. M.: *But most of all you wish to avoid the recognition of the crucial role I played in your life. You cling still to the belief—no, the delusion—that one can be his own man, create himself, and as it were have no parent of any sort.*

Me: *But that's what this is about. If you'd just give me a chance to get started, you'd—*

DR. M.: Mr. Singer, you would put off the sunrise if you were not quite ready for breakfast.

ME: But—

DR. M.: But if we could not make progress in this area in our real work together, what chance is there, I ask you, of our getting anywhere in this absurd imaginary dialogue of yours? So proceed with your meteorology, if you feel that you must, but you must also forgive me if I catch forty huinks while you do.

There was a Sunday in the middle of April when the air in New York was as cool and clear as it is in late October. The trees in Central Park had gone blurry with buds, the Great Lawn had begun to lose the look of an old blanket thrown down to protect the earth, and the water in the Reservoir had a fine chop, like a miniature sea. A few people—the avant-garde of the jogging movement—beetled around the gravel path. It was all down there and I was up here, fifteen stories above Fifth Avenue, on the terrace of an apartment that occupied the top two floors of a magnificent Deco building between Eighty-third and Eighty-fourth Streets. To my left, in his usual blue blazer and gray slacks, stood Coventry's headmaster, nautical in appearance and demeanor.

"Ah, fresh air, Jake," Proctor said, putting his hand on my shoulder. Fresh air was his universal restorative. "There's nothing like it, even in New York City."

To my right stood Allegra Marshall, the hostess of this Coventry fund-raising lunch. Luncheon. My first point-blank encounter with the Manhattan of pure wealth and glamour. Five round tables of eight in a huge dining room with wainscoting and a "Close Encounters" chandelier. White maids in black uniforms and white, lace-edged aprons. Cutlery, linen, chased silver. Not a bell-bottom in sight, no ankhs, no zoris, no peasant blouses. It could have been the fifties. It could have been now.

Before I escaped to the terrace, one sleek fellow, the grandfather of a student of mine, asked me where I was going over spring break, and I said, "Nowhere," and he said, "Well, what a good idea!" He and I then discussed the Yankees' prospects for the coming season, and he pointed out a relative of Jacob Rupert's across the vast living room or parlor or whatever it was. "This is a man who won't touch a drop of anything," the sleek fellow said. "I've heard that he's ashamed of his fortune." My other conversation was with the mother of one of my advanced-placement seniors who simply could not get *over* how wonderfully *detailed* my comments were on her son's papers.

When Proctor and I arrived, Mrs. Marshall gave me an automatic smile but a firm handshake—the kind that a girl's rich, manly dad or independent-minded mom tries to install at an early age. She was wearing a short black dress and a black wristband. Her husband—Coventry '59—had died, of cancer, on New Year's Day, leaving her with a six-year-old son—in first grade at the school—an infant daughter, and his millions to add to hers. The apartment was beautiful and tasteful to the point of hilarity, and its mistress, with her tall, willowy stature, pale complexion, bright-blue eyes, and long, dark, ironed-looking hair, and her aristocratic imperfection of feature—a real nose with a real bump in it, one very white front tooth slightly overlapping the other—also seemed comically perfect for her role of young society personage gamely pressing on. Now, out on the terrace, in the presence of Proctor and his bromides, she seemed sad, and her perfection looked frayed at the edges, and after a fellow-blazer-and-gray-flannelsman hailed the headmaster back inside, I thought I saw her roll her eyes.

"Sometimes I think he'd make a better admiral than a headmaster," I said. "do you ever see any muggings down there?"

"You're Mr. Springer?" she asked.

"Singer. Jake Singer."

"You're the one who is going to do the sales pitch."

"Yes. I've done something like this three or four times now, but I keep getting stagefright. Especially here. I mean, I feel sort of out of place. And it's for money this time, not just to try to get people to send their kids."

"Proctor says you do it very well. When we set this thing up, he told me the applications pour in after you talk."

"You know, a year ago he was barely speaking to me."

"Why?"

"Oh, I was always arguing with him, always mouthing off. Nothing better to do, I guess."

"What do you mean?"

"You know, just trouble with authority."

"But he certainly likes you now."

"I just calmed down, I suppose."

"Just like that?"

"No, it probably has something to do with being in analysis, though I'm not supposed to talk about it and I don't like to give my lunatic analyst any credit."

"I'm in it, too, so you're safe."

"But you have a real reason, not just the vapors, like me. Anyway, one thing I am sure of is that it isn't Proctor who changed. He'd prescribe fresh air for you if your husband had died." Good work, Jake. "Oh, Mrs. Marshall, I'm so sorry. What an idiot I am."

"It's all right. I've discovered it's like having two heads. But when you collect yourself I hope you'll call me Allegra. And, by the way, these things make me as uncomfortable as they make you." She went back inside, leaving me alone with my clumsy self.

At lunch, Proctor and I sat on either side of our hostess, and I said how delicious the consommé was. "Actually, it's turtle soup," she said. It was difficult to eat the rest of the meal, with my foot so far in my mouth and the butterflies in my stomach. But I nodded and smiled and chewed as best I could, and I made what seemed to me an English teacher's joke—something feeble about cashing in Mr. Chips. Mrs. Marshall's frozen smile thawed into a real laugh—very musical—and I felt as if I'd done her a good turn. "Great chicken," I said when the veal chop was served, and she looked at me in proto-discomfiture until I shrugged, whereupon she got it and smiled a real smile again. Before dessert and after a trip to the bathroom, I made my speech: To afford the kind of diversity in our student body. All the way from catcher's mitts to calculators. Provide the brand of leadership that seems so sorely lacking in our nation. Instill the values, stem the rising tide of drugs. To defray cost of mandatory haircuts and install narrower and quieter ties. (*Polite laughter.*) To pay for the polish Proctor uses for his brass blazer buttons and his bald bean.

·   ·   ·

This last I said to Dr. Morales in his cold, cluttered office the next morning as I lay on the slab-flat couch with the cervically inimical jelly-roll headrest. It was a chilly, drizzly day, the bad side of spring. I had already told him about Allegra Marshall and my high anxiety and various faux pas. "You did not really say this about the polish, Mr. Singer," he said.

"No—it's a joke."

"I have asked you to tell me what you said in your speech and first you drone like an old priest and then you become saracastic—sarcastic and rude, if I may say, since I, too, am bald. Why do you suppose you cry in fear before the hand?"

"Beforehand. Who said anything about crying?"

"These attacks of cramps and diarrhea—you are weeping like a frightened child, but since you are a man you must do it through your asshole. And I shall ask the questions here. Why are you so frightened of something so boring and contempt-ible, Mr. Singer?"

"If I don't know the drill here by now, I really should be ashamed of myself. It's *not* boring and stupid. I act that way only because I care about it so much and want so badly to do well, to appease the spirit of my dead mother, whom I magi-cally think I must have killed when I was six, and to earn the respect of my father, who thinks I am a failure and wishes I had been a doctor like him, and to please you. Always to please you, of course."

"Again this same sequence—dull recitation with following it the scorn. Ho-hum and fuck you, is it not?"

"Well, I mean four years of—"

"No, it is thirty-two meenoose six years, Mr. Singer—twenty-six years of preventing yourself from genuine involve-ment in your feelings and your life. I swear to Christ that if Marilyn Monroe came to you with no clothes on and a wet pussy you would not know what to do with her. Now please listen to me. If you joke, I shall kill you and spare you the effort of this slow suicide. Is this school of yours a good school?"

"Yes. It could be—"

"*Is it a good school?*"

"Yes."

"Do your students respect you?"

"Yes." Satisfaction, as surprising as a twenty-dollar bill on the sidewalk, came to me with this answer.

"Tell me one important thing you have done for the school besides the teaching."

"Well—"

"It is dry, Mr. Singer."

"I'm helping to get scholarships for poor kids," I said, more proudly than I meant to.

"Good, there is feeling in your words at last. Anything else?"

"I'm convincing more people to apply, and now I'm helping to raise money. As of yesterday."

"Ah, your voice has fallen here. Why?"

"I don't know—the whole idea of raising money, being with rich people, glad-handing and putting on a show."

"*It is a good school!*" thundered Dr. Morales. "You are trying to make it better according to your convictions! Making a speech is not selling eslaves or torturing cute lambs! A President of the United Estates has attended this school, three or four *Nobelistas,* many professors and doctors, the director of the Peace Corps, I believe, the head of Sloan-Kettering, the man who designed—"

"How do you know all this?" I asked.

"I have looked it up. I should not have revealed this, perhaps—it is bad technique—but just maybe you will take a leaf from my tree, Mr. Singer. I am *interested* in my work. You are my work. I am *interested* in you. And one more thing—if there are rich people in the world, why should you not be among them? You yourself are hardly from the road of tobacco. If there is a rich young widow making goggle eyes at you, why should you not fuck her, I ask you. Why should you not marry her, when I come to think of it. Why didn't you mention how she looked when you were speaking of her?"

"Less Marilyn Monroe than Ali McGraw," I said. "But beautiful enough. Quite beautiful, in fact."

"In fact? I did not think it was in fiction. I do not know who is this Alice McGraw."

"She's the one in 'Love Story'—the girl who dies."

"Ah, yes. This is interesting. We must stop now, Mr. Singer, but have you by any chance happened to notice the corpses that have littered our conversation this morning like a battle-field, as if it were? Your mother, the husband of the hostess, the character of this movie."

"Marilyn Monroe."

"Very good, Mr. Singer. You are quite right, I have joined in this necrophilia. But it is *spring*, Mr. Singer. Time for the new beginnings, for the birds to tweeter and among the twigs to build their nests."

Dr. Morales's crude incitement concerning Allegra Marshall at the end of the session had not come out of nowhere. Near the beginning, when I mentioned her widowhood and the opulence of her apartment, I could feel him coming to attention like a setter behind me. I was surprised and annoyed to feel myself coming to attention the following week, when I was in the nurse's office at school, getting a Band-Aid for a wound inflicted by the staples that had interfered with my reading of "Hester Prynne: Hawthorn's Revolutionery Heroin." A little kid was lying on the cot looking green around the gills, and the nurse, a clinical type with a neurosurgeon's hauteur and the name Gladys Knight, of all things, was on the phone saying, "You and the babysitter probably have the same organism that George has, Mrs. Marshall, with the nausea and the vertigo. I'd bring him over for you myself, but George is the fourth incidence today, so I really should stay here."

I asked if it was Allegra Marshall she was talking to and she covered the phone and scowled at me. "This is important, Mr. Singer, if you don't mind," she said. "This child *and* his mother *and* the babysitter have all come down with gastroenteritis, and we're trying to figure out how to get him home."

"I met Mrs. Marshall last week. I'd be glad to take him home—I've got two free periods. Tell Mrs. Marshall it's me."

In another five minutes, George Marshall and I went out into the April sunshine and hailed a cab on West End Avenue, after a parting advisory from Miss Knight: "One of the other children had projectile vomiting." As we drove across the park, yellow with forsythia and daffodils, George sat still and regarded me. He was small for his age but built solidly, with blond hair and a turned-up nose with a few freckles sprinkled over it—he looked nothing like his mother. "My dad died," he said when we stopped for a red light at Ninety-sixth Street and Fifth Avenue. "I know," I said. "It's very sad for you and your family." "My sister doesn't realize it," he said. "She's too little. Are you a teacher in the upper school?" I told him I was. "I thought I saw you," he said.

The taxi started up again, and George faced forward, looking sick and unhappy. His feet didn't quite reach the floor. Even though I'd never met this boy before, I knew for a fact that he believed that he had done something to cause what had happened to his family, and I wanted to reach over with both hands and shake the innocent truth into him before the guilt worked itself too deep into his heart.

George said he could go up in the elevator by himself, but the doorman said that Mrs. Marshall had asked me to take him upstairs, if it wasn't too much trouble. So up in the elaborately scrolled and panelled elevator we went. When the door opened into the apartment's foyer, Mrs. Marshall was standing there looking very sick and forlorn herself, plain and ashen and lank-haired, so that the elegant dark-blue Chinesey house-coat she had on seemed as beside the point as the Aubusson on the floor and the modest Corot on the wall behind her. "I'm tired, Mom," George said, and he tottered away down the long hallway. "I'm going to lie down for a while."

"I'll be right there," Mrs. Marshall said.

"I hope your daughter's all right," I said. "The nurse told me your babysitter is sick, too."

"Emily is fine. And George's mother will be here in half an hour. She lives just over on Park. We'll be O.K."

"George's mother?"

"My husband's mother. My late husband's mother. Georgie is George Junior."

"Oh."

"It was nice of you to bring him home. Thank you."

"It was nothing. He's a sweet kid."

"Let me pay you for the taxi."

"Oh, no. that's all right." I looked over her shoulder at the living room, glowing with perfection in the morning light. "I know this is silly," I said, "but I wish there was something else I could do for you."

"Why is that silly?"

"I mean, I've only met you once, and—"

"Is it silly because I'm rich?"

"Yes."

"Ah—honesty. But it shows what you know." Tears were in her eyes now, and her nose looked more broken than distinguished, and she seemed skinny rather than slender and pathetic rather than tragic; and I felt ridiculous instead of gallant, and furious at Dr. Morales for his careless manipulations, and for regarding this woman so lubriciously and so lightly, like a personal ad, like a sitting duck. "I'm sorry if I've upset you," I said. "Don't worry about it," she said, pushing the elevator button.

"And I think you should be ashamed of yourself," I said to Dr. Morales the next morning, after telling him as calmly as I could what had happened with George Marshall and his mother the day before.

"I am," Dr. Morales replied. "I am truly ashamed." He rattled some papers around and cleared his throat a few times.

I sat up and put my feet on the floor and looked at him. He had a tax form over the yellow pad he used for taking what I assumed were scathing notes about me and his other victims.

"Filing late?" I said. "I hope you applied for the automatic two-month extension."

"This is against the rules, Mr. Singer."

"You mean the New York Psychoanalytic Society has an actual rule against doing your taxes during sessions with your patients? Why, that's positively draconian."

"I shall not explain myself to you, Mr. Singer. This is as forbidden to me as sitting up is to you. But God and Freud will pardon me, I feel certain, for occupying myself with other matters when a patient enters my office in an inappropriate rage, insults me further by thinking to disguise it, and then has the amazing condescension to tell me that I should be ashamed of myself, as if I were a four-year-old child who has deliberately belchèd during Communion."

"I would never have made such a fool of myself if you hadn't—"

"Had not what, Mr. Singer? Had not held a pistol at your

head to force you to volunteer to take the boy home? Had not squeezèd your heart in the taxi to make you recognize his psychological situation and sympathize with him? Had not transformed you into Sharlie McCarthy and then like Edgar Burgeon thrown my voice into you standing there in front of the mother and to diminish her humanity on account of her wealth? By the way, Mr. Singer, will you please lie down."

"You want it both ways," I said, continuing to face him. "You want me to behave the way you think I should, and then when I try and then fail you disavow any part in the matter. 'My advice is to jump, Mr. Singer, but if you break your neck, don't blame me.' "

"Had not, in general, as I was saying, miraculously reached into your soul and poured into it the poison that you are convinced is so powerful as to threaten also anyone whom you might love. Like your mother, your father, like a woman. Like me. You are not Siva, Mr. Singer, nor Attila nor Hitler, nor even Sharles Starkweather. You are not so lethal as you wish to believe. Now please lie down."

"No. I don't feel well. I'm going home."

"You know, I truly *am* ashamed that after four years of our work together you can still busy your mind with any amount of anger at yourself and at me to ignore what is really going on in your life—for example, the possibility that from the start this woman has taken some interest in you, and that this was why I tried gently and humorously to encourage your interest in her."

"*Gently?*"

"Why else would a person divulge within five minutes of meeting someone the highly intimate knowledge that she was in analysis, as you divulgèd it to her also—why else would she say this if she did not feel immediate trust and confidentiality? And why else would she have asked you to accompany her son in the elevator if not because she wished to see you again, and being in a very unattractive and weakened condition, what is more. Now please do lie down and try to address these matters."

"No, I really do feel ill," I said. "I'm leaving."

"So now the regression and withdrawal will be complete."

·   ·   ·

I called in sick and spent the rest of the day in or very near the bathroom in my apartment. From time to time I hazarded a walk into the living room to watch TV. I would doze on the couch, wake up to a soap opera or a game show, whose gaudiness the flu rendered almost hallucinatory, get up and turn it off. And before stumbling toiletward again, I once or twice looked around my place and took stock. In January, as my responsibilities grew at school, I had through an effort of will upgraded my domestic situation. I discarded the bricks and boards and sofa *trouvé* and card table, and the bottom half of a bunk bed sold to me by the building's gaunt Croatian super for thirty-five dollars, and the dieseling vintage refrigerator, which I called the Serf of Ice Cream—another English teacher's joke— and replaced them with Door Store merchandise and new appliances. A captain's bed, a blond wall unit or two, a big, round, tan hooked rug in the living room, an oak table with a chrome base, even a Zurbarán print and a Magritte poster— that kind of thing. All in all, it had become a decent bachelor's place on the eleventh floor of a nice building on West End Avenue—plenty of light and a nice breeze in the spring and summer—just around the corner from Coventry. Rent-controlled, which you could still get back then, especially on the fringe of a bad neighborhood. But so what? It was still a pocket of isolation—especially in illness, when you'd like to be able to call on someone—and I felt like a penny in the pocket. Whatever progress I'd made was in baby steps, or in a marionette's artificial, hinged gait, with Dr. Morales pulling the strings. I felt far less desperate than I had four years earlier, but the absence of desperation is not life.

The flu subsided. I took a longer, deeper nap, looked in listlessly as Thurman Munson and his teammates braved chilly April conditions at Yankee Stadium, ate a little chicken soup, drank a lot of water, stayed on my feet, barely, in the shower, and collapsed onto my bed into an even deeper sleep, which lasted the night.

I felt much better in the morning but couldn't face the red-letter discussion looming in my Advanced Placement class or the concluding negotiations over "A Separate Peace" in my regular junior courses, to say nothing of playing pepper with the baseball team in Riverside Park after school, so I called in sick again and read and dozed on the sofa. I was brought out of a semi-dream, in which Dr. Morales lobbied the halls of Congress on behalf of Cuban cigars, by the ringing of the doorbell. It hadn't rung in so long that I'd forgotten when the last time was. I opened it without using the little burglar scope or asking who was there. What can anyone do to me, after all, I said to myself in the self-pitying aftermath of my stock-taking and influenza.

It was Allegra Marshall, well beyond influenza and its aftermath—looking very beautiful once again, in fact, if nervous.

"I'm sorry, I should have called," she said. "I know you're sick, but you live so close to the school that I thought I would just stop by. And then the doorman said he didn't need to announce me or anything."

"It's the super," I said. "My friend the super."

"So here I am. I hope I'm not disturbing you."

"I'm much better," I said. "It's O.K. Is George all right?"

"I took him back to school yesterday, and I asked for you and they told me you were out sick. And when they told me you were out again today I felt even more guilty. You probably got this from George, or maybe even from me."

"Oh, it's going around."

"But that isn't why I was looking for you at school in the first place," she said. "I wanted to apologize for being so rude to you the other morning. Here you had done me this kindness."

"I was rude first—worse than rude," I said. "You caught me out. I asked for it."

"Well, I'm sorry anyway. Now I really should leave you alone."

She turned away and started back toward the elevator, and as she did I heard that insinuating voice, which had already installed itself in my mind, say, "Now, Mr. Singer, I ask you— what do you wish this woman to do, take out a full-page advertisement in the *New York Times?*" I drew a deep breath and said, just as she was about to push the "Down" button, "Wait, um, Allegra, as long as we're apologizing." She turned again, to face me. "I wasn't really doing you a kindness. I offered to take George home so I could see you. It was just an excuse. And my analyst sort of put me up to the whole thing anyway."

"You mean you *didn't* really want to see me?"

"No, I did, I probably did, or I would have, but this doctor of mine gets himself in the middle of everything, so it's hard to tell. He egged me on. He said *you* were interested in *me*."

"He was right."

"What?"

"He was right."

"He was right?"

"He was right."

I I — M o t h e r ' s   D a y

They wanted to have children right away, but she didn't get pregnant. The specialist she saw couldn't find anything wrong. Still, she and her husband had sex by the chart, she took hormones, they went on tense "relaxed" vacations. None of it worked. At length, her husband said maybe he was the one with the problem—she had to give him credit for that. The specialist he saw, who wore a bright-red toupee, said "Whee" when he looked through the microscope at the semen sample, and the subsequent, more scientific assay found nothing wrong. Now they had both no one and each other to blame. It was an open field. It's like a poison in a well that you're both drinking from, Allegra told me. They kept trying to conceive a child but meanwhile adopted a baby boy through Spence-Chapin. They gave up on biology, and on sex, a couple of years later, and a few years after that, in the midst of growing strain and louder silence between them, which they managed to hide from the Spence-Chapin social worker, they adopted another baby—a girl this time—in the hope that this would somehow solve their problems. Three months after that, her husband was diagnosed with pancreatic cancer, and three months after that he died. Their parents were friends. She had known him all her life, through Brearley for her and Coventry for him, Radcliffe for her and Yale and Wharton for him, summers at Sag Harbor,

winters skiing out West. They went out with other people from
time to time, but nothing came of that. They thought they were
comfortable with each other. They got married when she was
twenty-three and he was twenty-five. The comfort seemed to
evaporate overnight. Even without all the reproductive trouble, there would have been trouble, she was sure. She should
have learned something from the way the dark skinny boys
with the scraggly beards and the banjos and their protest songs
à la Phil Ochs attracted her in Cambridge. She should have
gone to graduate school in English at Berkeley and thrown
herself into the free-speech upheaval out there. She should
have done a lot of things. Until her husband died, she felt as
though her life had been written down before she was born, in
a novel so boring and predictable that even the writer realized
it and put the manuscript in some drawer and left it there.
Now she had despair to add to the tedium. No one would
come near her in her grief. Or maybe she pushed them away.
And she *was* grieving—you can miss someone you don't much
like, she had discovered. This was depressing all by itself. Men
stayed away out of propriety, and just as well, in most cases.
Her family and her husband's family seemed afraid of her. She
loved her son and daughter so much and so feared what
would happen to them if she couldn't give them what they
needed that she felt it almost guaranteed that she wouldn't be
able to. She sometimes had nightmares about having them
taken away. Her husband had been a good father—she had to
give him credit for that, too. As good as his long hours at
Thomson & McKinnon, Auchincloss permitted. He hadn't had
to work but he did, and that was really the only other thing she
would give him credit for. Though she realized it was not a
bad list and he was not a bad guy. Just the wrong guy. And she
had found herself wondering, out there on the terrace when
we first spoke, whether—dark and thin as I was and scraggly
as my beard might be if I grew one—I played the banjo.

"Now I should leave you alone," she had said in the doorway after confirming Dr. Morales's conjecture. "I wanted to get
another look at you—that's why I asked you to come up with
George when you took him home. I could have just written
you a note, after all."

"Well, would you like to come in?" I had said.

"Are you really feeling all right?"

"Yes."

"Then yes, I'll come in for a little while."

And that was when she sat down on my Door Store sofa and told me about herself. And then she asked me about myself. It got to be eleven-thirty, and I found I was hungry, for the first time in a couple of days, so I excused myself and went to the kitchen and wolfed down a bowl of cereal. When I went back, Allegra stood up and said, "I thought that talking to someone new or doing something different might help me out of this trap I feel I'm in."

"I'm flattered that you think of me as new and different. I feel more or less like the same old thing."

"I really should go now," she said, pulling at one of her cuticles.

"You don't have to."

"Then would you please kiss me?"

I went over to her and put my arms around her and kissed her. She tilted her head back a little and looked at me. She was so tall: eye to eye with me.

"Cheerios," she said. "Would you please really kiss me?"

I did my best.

"Good," she said. "Give me your hand." She took my hand and put it on her breast. She tilted her head back and looked me in the eye again, as if she were measuring something. "That feels very good," she said. "You don't know how long it has been."

"Yes, I do," I said. "But I think I can take it from here. I'm getting tired of people telling me what to do."

It turned out that she wasn't really directorial about sex but, as in that firm handshake when we met, just well mannered. "May I suck your cock?" she asked, with that unnerving look in the eye, and when I said "Sure" she said "Thank you." "Would you mind if we stopped for a second so that I can get on my hands and knees?" "Could you please hold my shoulders down?" "Would you put your finger in my ass." She sprinkled these courtesies among other, much more pre-verbal utterances, and the whole effect was wonderfully, almost over-whelmingly lewd. After a while, she didn't really have to ask but I let her every now and then anyway, for the pleasure of hearing her.

"Socialite widow Allegra Marshall, after copulating with prep-school pedagogue Jake Singer," I said, while we rested.

"What?"

"You know—those society-party pictures in the papers. I've probably seen you in them and had no idea who you were. And now here you are. And you turn out to be a regular human being. So regular that you probably came over to the West Side just to use me. But if you did, I must say that I can't understand why women are always objecting to being used."

"After we fuck a few more times and then I tell you I don't care about you, you'll find out," Allegra said.

"Is that likely to happen?"

"The fucking? Oh, yes, I hope so. Right now, in fact, if you can, please. But I'll have to be discreet. I am a widow, you know. As for the rest, I have no idea. Maybe your analyst does. He seems very smart. All mine says is 'Why is that, do you think?' and 'What does this bring to mind?' "

"That sounds pretty good to me. I don't know why you need analysis—you're so direct."

"The closer I am to people, the more distant I feel, it turns out. And don't you think it's just a little bit strange for some-one to tell all her secrets to someone she has had maybe fifteen minutes of conversation with before? And then beg for sex?"

"You didn't exactly beg," I said. "And anyway I don't think it's strange."

"Well, you should."

Three weeks later, after coaching third base in the varsity's last game, against Collegiate, I went down to Tiffany's and bought Allegra a silver-and-onyx bracelet for Mother's Day. She had discreetly come to my place again a week after the first time. And I discreetly had supper once at her apartment, late one night. She cooked some kind of chicken and I made some salad. Her kids were asleep. I dried the dishes afterward—I could hardly bear to use the dish towel, it was so exquisitely folded. I left just as the sun was hitting the tops of the buildings on Central Park West. Proctor told me I looked tired when he stopped by my classroom to ask if I would say a few words at graduation. He suggested I get some fresh air after school. Luckily, all I had to do that day was give final exams.

"Mother's Day is Sunday," I said to Dr. Morales when I lay down on the couch the morning after the trip to Tiffany's. "Too bad I don't have one."

"It is indeed too bad, Mr. Singer. It is not funny."

"Well, at least I don't have to buy a present or anything," I said. "So, do you think Nixon will be impeached or not?"

"For permitting you to employ him as a red herring, do you mean?"

"For abusing his power," I said, as pointedly as I could.

"I don't know, Mr. Singer. Can we return to Mother's Day? I know you were just being humorous, but here so sadly, as you know, there are no jokes."

"Why should we talk about it? What's the point? I remember making a card for my mother when I was in first grade in Bronxville, and she loved it. And then she died. Now I don't believe in it—it's just commercial. I think that's probably because my mother is dead. Just bitter, I suppose."

"Remove the 'probably' and 'suppose.' "

"Well, so there you are."

"What about your new lover? She has children."

"So? I'm not one of them."

"I shall tell you what, Mr. Singer. I shall make a bargain with you, not because I am feeling magnanimous toward you, the good Christ knows, but because my heart goes out to this woman, this poor woman who cannot have children naturally, this woman whose husband has died, this woman who is trying to fight her way out of depression and make changes in her life, this woman who would be cut to the quicks if she could hear you speak so coldly and callously about her, this woman who has what suddenly appears to be the further misfortune of taking you into her bed. The bargain is this, Mr. Singer: Take the fee for this session and get your narrow and self-absorbed ass off my couch and go to Tiffany's and with the money buy this woman something beautiful. And then give it to her. And do not come back here until you do."

"Free advice—a first for you," I said. "Well, even the analyst can have a breakthrough, I guess." I reached down to my briefcase, which was on the floor next to the backbuster, and took out the little blue box tied with a white ribbon and held it up over my head.

Dr. Morales was silent for a full minute. Then he said, "Why did you feel the need to tease me in this way, Mr. Singer? Could you not bear the idea that I have helped you to take such a step for once without having to get in the back of you and push?"

"I think you hit the nail on the head," I said. "When I went to buy this, I wouldn't have been surprised to find you driving the No. 4 bus down Fifth Avenue, and when I went into the store I could hear you whispering, 'Now, don't be a cheapskates, Mr. Singer,' and the only thing that almost kept me from going ahead was knowing how much satisfaction this whole thing would bring you." In the middle of this I had started crying, though my voice didn't break. Tears just ran out of my eyes as if from a spillway.

"Think instead of the person who will receive this gift and how pleased she will be."

"We even came up with the exact same store. You know, I could accept help from you a lot more easily if you were less constantly critical of me, less sarcastic about it all, and if I didn't suspect that you were getting some kind of perverted kick from disparaging me and trying to run my life."

"I think this is the *only* way you can accept help, Mr. Singer. I think I am doing what is right. I do have my own life, you may be certain of that. I am not living through you or my other patients, much as you wish to believe it so."

"Are you sure?" I said. "Was there an ounce too much protest in there somewhere?"

I walked back to the West Side through Central Park, trying to calm down. The morning was soft and warm; flowers were everywhere. I heard a padding behind me and the next thing I knew I was flat on my face and someone was running away with my briefcase. The next thing I knew, I was running after him and then catching up with him and knocking him flat on his face and taking my briefcase back. He got up and ran away.

"Of course you do," I said. "You have to take care of sick children even when you're sick yourself."

"That's love—it's different. Speaking of love—" she said.

"So this is love," I said when she was still again. To keep myself from coming I had been trying to think about how it would feel not to have to work. This beat my dusty old delaying tactic of mowing an imaginary lawn, even though in the middle of my reverie of wealth I felt Dr. Morales's influence seep into the room like swamp gas. *"Mr. Singer, I suspect and fear that you are about to open this gifted horse's mouth and inspect its teeth, is it not?"* I could hear him say. *"Can you not resist your impulse to piss on your good fortune?"*

"It might be," Allegra said. "I feel as though we would always get along well."

"But you don't know me at all," I was about to say, before Dr. Morales whinnied mockingly in my head to warn me away from honesty. "Would you mind if we turned the tables here again?" I said instead. "Because if it's all right with you I'd like to finish this off as if I were in control, pretty please."

Allegra laughed. "You're making fun of me," she said.

"Yes, but I really would like to do that."

"All right, turn me over now, and we can come at the same time. Let's watch each other, O.K.?"

"Sure," I said. "It would be a pleasure." And like an eight-year-old boy who has succumbed to wearing a tie for the first time, I silently added to the Dr. Morales inside my head, You win. I'll try to throw my lot in with this rich and interesting woman—who happens also to be a staggering piece of ass—and her wainscoted world. What would that world make of me, a neurotic school-teaching Jew without a Corot, Herreshoff, or nine iron to his name, I wondered—if it ever got to that point. Oh, well, I went on, I have nothing to lose. And I might have told myself that lie and forgotten about it and everything else for a little while if Allegra, holding me in her direct and at that point hectic gaze, hadn't said, "Jake, Jake, not yet, please" and I hadn't believed, for a split second, that she was begging me to cancel the calculating decision I'd just made. I did have something to lose, I realized then, as I tried to oblige Allegra— whether more for fun or strategy I was suddenly no longer sure. In fact, some part of myself had just gone out the window and was hurtling down to the sidewalk below, although I couldn't put a name to it. "Now, Jake," Allegra said, and, just before ardor obliterated all further thought, I heard my indwelling Dr. Morales say, *It is your innocence that you have lost, Mr. Singer, and for that it is a high time.*"

Lucy Honig

CITIZENS REVIEW

She was just one more mousy young woman in a town full of mousy young women. There was absolutely nothing to distinguish the town and nothing to distinguish her, and don't for heaven's sake confuse her with the mousy young woman who forged signatures on all those stolen welfare checks or the mousy young woman who let her three-month-old baby starve to death. It's true that in a town where nothing ever happens, a mousy young woman occasionally separates out, differentiates, and becomes, briefly, the front-page photo on the morning paper for a few days running. But this particular mousy young woman (her name is Eileen) did not make it to the front page.

She made it to the front porch of her rented first-floor apartment in one of the nondescript, gray-painted wood-frame houses that lined the block, all rented out and left to rot by landlords living somewhere else. On a summer evening like this one, everybody sat out on their porches, not because it was an exciting thing to do and certainly not because time had forged the warm bonds of community that we like to think draw folks together of an evening into an easygoing, down-home story-swapping banter that we also like to think occurs in other people's neighborhoods (the ones, that is, we wouldn't be caught dead in). No, it was just too hot inside and there was nothing else to do, not even a store in walking distance except for the Jamaican deli, not a movie theater downtown since everything had moved out to the malls—a phenomenon that seems as dated as oil lamps, say, or poll taxes, as if it had long ago stopped happening. Yet it does keep happening, this siphoning off of downtown economy and cultural lifeblood, leaving a desolation of no interest anymore to anyone except drug dealers in flight from Manhattan and a few sleazy entrepreneurs who've figured out how to cash in on HUD grants.

Eileen's apartment—but it was not really Eileen's, her husband Robert would be quick to point out, because he'd paid the rent even after he was laid off from the cleaning business and even now that his unemployment checks were done (and don't think a few souls on the block didn't wonder how he still managed, even if Eileen herself barely gave it a thought)— Eileen lived in an apartment on Jefferson Street, in the part of town where streets bore the names of presidents. The people here, of course, were no more ennobled by the names of their streets than the residents of streets named for trees (though often, if you've noticed, streets commemorating elms and oaks and maples and pines are in better shape, with fewer potholes, smoother sidewalks, tidier garbage pickup, and faster snow removal). The names of Adams and Washington and Lincoln, set against the desolate reality of their streets, lent an air of lapsed promise and poignant futility to the whole neighborhood. Even Eileen was aware of false hopes raised by names. She sometimes thought of her husband's mother putting so much store by calling him Robert as a young child, and never Bob or Bobby or Robby, so that by the sheer seriousness of his name he might transcend the destiny launched by his father being a hired farmhand, by the two-seated outhouse in back, by the whining, merciless teasing of his seven brothers and sisters: he'd been a thin, puny child of no redeeming sweetness or cunning and the older, bigger ones never came to his defense. His mother's hopes for the outcome of his naming, though, got nowhere. Robert, in fact, backfired on her; the skinny adolescent still called by that name lopped himself off

from the underpinnings of self-respect that had always sup-
ported and linked his parents, only to free fall into a random,
catch-as-catch-can, boundaryless life that a regular Bobby or
Bob or Robby might have sidestepped.

Now those other mousy young women—the check forger,
the baby-starver—had given the district attorney occasion for
splendid shows of outrage (as he quickly displaced them from
center stage in the local news)—outrage not only at the thousands of dollars stolen or the innocent life lost, but at their own
deplorable housekeeping habits, for if you saw him on TV, you
couldn't help wondering if it wasn't the squalid state of the
murderous mother's trailer that most offended him, and not
that she was really a child still herself, desperately poor, badly
abused, unequipped to think things out. But Eileen was not
made of felonious stuff. The apartment on Jefferson, though
hardly spotless, would not have made the DA bat an eyelash,
never mind gloat, since she dabbed around with a dustcloth
almost every day. The excess furniture she'd once laid in had
long ago been repossessed, and the remaining clutter was for-
givable, being mostly toys. In fact she now tripped over
Mickey's broken plastic tricycle thing as she came through the
doorway to the porch, can of beer and bag of cheese doodles in
hand, ready to plop down on the rusty old glider (which had
been abandoned by the previous tenant). She kicked the tricycle out of the way. In her circle of acquaintances on Jefferson
Street, no one was actually slovenly and some stood up, defi-
ant, to the inevitable shabbiness of their houses by being
downright clean. Eileen believed that the black women kept
their houses cleanest, but maybe this was just what Robert
called her habit of giving all the breaks to black people.

She didn't think she really did that. Did she? What breaks
did she have in her possession to give?

When she married him, and she thought he was good-looking then, his puniness having matured into a compact, sinewy
girth she found sexy, she didn't care that he made nasty comments about black people. It didn't occur to her that this habit
of his foreshadowed a capacity for meanness that might grow
in other directions, including hers—she figured that what she
saw was what she'd get, from now until doomsday. Change of

any sort had seemed unlikely to intrude in either of their futures. In fact, the future itself, as distinguished in any real way from the present, seemed hardly likely to make an appearance either.

What surprised her, when he threw the fit over the plaits in her hair, was not that he threw it but how much she hated it. Eileen had gone next door and walked into the kitchen—which sparkled, the crisp ammonia wafts of cleanser mixing with the earthy, fresh smell of greens heaped in the sink—just as Amander was finishing up Ayeisha's glorious head of cornrows. For fun, Amander wove five little plaits into Eileen's stringy, thin, mouse-brown hair, each with a strand of gold tinsel entwined, like plaiting a bit of life itself into dull, mousy Eileen. Eileen loved it. But when Robert saw those five little ropes of ornery fun radiating out from her forehead, he shouted louder than he'd ever shouted before, and she was sure that this time he was finally going to haul off and slam her one, like her father in that tone of voice would have long ago done to *her* mother. (He didn't, he still hadn't hit her, but she was still waiting.) And for all three days she kept in the glittering plaits, he refused to talk to her, and that's when she first realized, after being married more than two years, that she liked it, not having to listen to him, not being an iota lonelier when he didn't talk to her than when he did.

Theirs was a neighborhood of white folks and black folks living side by side in no particular pattern; the theme running through it was not race but income: low factory wages or low unemployment or low social security or low disability or low veterans' benefits or low welfare payments or low fast-food paychecks—no matter what it was, it was low. A lot of people in other parts of town thought of this one as the black neighborhood; they were wrong. Robert, on the other hand, also wrong, thought it was a white neighborhood with a lot of black intruders who had no business there.

"They should go back to where they came from," he said more than once.

"But Amander was born right on Washington Avenue," Eileen said.

"Keep away from that slut Amander," he retorted.

"Her cousin Tyrone was born in the same house he lives in now. Amander says his grandfather came up from the City and rented that house down on Lincoln, and then after he made some money he bought the house and built onto it, and then Tyrone's father got into trouble and lost the house, and when his father died his mother rented it again, and Tyrone—"

"Shut the fuck up about that Tyrone, that no-good drug-pushing bastard."

"Tyrone doesn't—"

"Shut the fuck up."

Amander's name had always been Amander—she had two great-aunts Amanda whose names got said Amander enough, long before she was born, that for her it finally got spelled that way, despite the irritation of her school teachers. Her own kids were named Tricia and Ayeisha and Keisha and, true to the family tradition of irritable teachers, Mrs. Cahill, who had both older girls in first grade, two years apart, called Ayeisha Tricia the whole year long, insisting it was the same exact name. Amander had a knack for things—for scraping together meals from crumbs, for getting people out of jail, for having babies only when she wanted them, for having gorgeous ones, for doing hair, for getting the Health Department to test for lead in houses up and down the block. She always knew the score, who was where and what was what. Eileen was happy (if Eileen could be said to be happy about anything) that Amander lived next door.

A police car with two pale, husky officers cruised down the block. Eileen picked at the frayed hem of her denim shorts, then absently traced a bluish vein in her thigh with her thumb, the red nail polish badly chipped. A squeal came from somewhere. Was Mickey crying? He had seemed fast asleep when she put him down. She leaned forward on the glider, held her breath, listened carefully in the direction of his room, heard nothing, leaned back, and took a large swallow of beer, which was already warm. The evening had become hotter and muggier; she was too listless even to push back and forth on the glider to stir up a little breeze. With her good thumbnail she bore down into the polish of her chipped nail until flecks of red crumbled off. A big old Buick went by, thumping loud with rap music. A few kids playing on the sidewalk shouted briefly, then quieted, hunkering down over dinosaur toys. From next door, Amander's scolding voice burst onto her front porch right behind Ayeisha, who flew out the screen door, let it snap shut with a bang, and ran to join the other kids. Three men were talking on a porch at the corner; occasionally their throaty, deep peals of laughter reached Eileen. A brand-new silver BMW slowly whispered down the block and stopped at that corner, obstructing her view of the three men. The car had dark-gray tinted windows; she could not see in. She took another swig of beer.

Amander stepped out onto her porch, rubbing a large orange plastic colander with a dish towel. She gazed at the parked BMW, then turned to Eileen. "Now what I tell you, Eileen," she called out, stretching and accentuating the *Ei* part. *"Do* I have a sixth sense about them dealers or *don't* I?" She shook her head. "Shit." Then she moved to the top of the porch steps. "Keisha, Ayeisha, get up here and outta that street!"

After one second, when they hadn't shown signs of responding, Amander bounded down the stairs, flinging the dish towel over her shoulder. She yanked Keisha up with her left hand, and when Ayeisha merely looked at her impassively, Amander exclaimed, "I gotta pull you up from the gutter too?" Then, to liberate her other hand, she set the colander on her head as if it had always been a bright orange plastic hat with handles and holes, and grabbed onto Ayeisha and dragged her to her feet and pulled the two girls up the stairs onto the porch.

"There!" Amander called out, releasing them. "You stay and play here. Your friends can come on up if they want, but don't you go out into the street again!" Her girls looked up at her orange helmet, their annoyance dissolving to giggles. Their playmates, clustered at the bottom of the steps, gawked at Amander, struck silent by the authority she still commanded even with (and maybe more so with) a colander on her head. "Whatsa matter, you guys?" said Amander, pretending to preen as soon as she caught sight of them. "Don't you like my new hat?"

Early on the fourth day of the plaits, Robert had finally spoken. "Get ridda them," he seethed, and then he hurled his coffee mug onto the floor, where it shattered into little pieces. Mickey had begun to scream in his highchair. Eileen felt the blood rising and pounding in her head, her temples throbbing from it, as she groped, unseeing, in the top drawer of the sink cabinet. She laid her hands on the scissors. Mickey was still screaming and Robert was still standing beside the table, doing nothing to comfort him. She didn't say a word, the blood was still pounding and her hands were shaking and her heart was beating hard and she felt for the plait that was closest to the front on the left side and she held it out and she rested her hand against her forehead and poised the scissor and made sure the plait was held firmly between the two blades and then she held the plait out taut and opened the blades and closed them fast and sharp and hard, making a thick, deep, loud scrunching sound alongside and inside her ear. She pulled with her left hand and the plait separated neatly from her head, not a hair resisting. She flung it at him. Then in exactly the same way she held out each of the other four plaits in turn and snipped them off, each one yielding the same scrunch of blades through hair as the cut was complete. One by one she hurled them at Robert.

"Jesus Christ," he said. "Look how you butchered yourself." He stomped out of the kitchen and out of the house as Mickey continued to scream himself into a purple frenzy.

She lifted Mickey from his chair, held him, ssshhed him, bounced him up and down, wiped the tears and snot from his cheeks, and rocked him in her arms until he quieted. She put him back in the highchair, gave him a piece of banana, washed her hands. Then she felt her head for the chopped-off stumps where the plaits had been. "Shit," she muttered. She checked herself in the bathroom mirror: five uneven mousy little paintbrushes stood up in a ragged crown from the top of her head. "Shit," she said again. Back in the kitchen, she picked up each plait from the floor, carefully flattened and straightened them, laid them on a piece of plastic wrap, rolled them up in it, and then slid the limp little package under the panties in her top dresser drawer.

Eileen swallowed the last mouthful of beer as a beat-up old mustardy colored Thunderbird drove past, much too fast, radio blaring. Alice Boatright and her two kids waddled down the block, slurping on melting popsicles. Alice waved to Eileen. Guffaws of laughter mixed with accusatory exclamations rolled down from the porch across the street where the little old white-haired guy (a fragile, shrunken gentleman, always bow-tied) played cards with two of his cronies. An electric company van whizzed by from the right at the same time a sleek red Honda Prelude came along from the opposite direction, very quiet, very slow. The Honda stopped right behind the BMW with the dark windows, still parked at the corner.

Eileen got up, went into the house, and checked on Mickey. Fast asleep, he breathed in noisy, congested little gasps, his face and neck mottled with heat rash. She straightened the flannel sheet that he'd mashed down to the foot of the crib and pulled it up over his shoulders. She plugged in the small plastic fan she'd found at a yard sale last week; groaning, its blades made a few slow, tortured turns, then stopped, emitting an ominous muffled buzz and burning smell. Eileen yanked out the plug. From the bedroom she padded into the kitchen for another beer, the last in the bleak tundra of her refrigerator. Just as she returned to the porch, Robert came racing up the steps. Inside, he said no hello, no nothing, but grabbed the can of beer from her hands, slurped it down fast, and threw himself on the glider, sprawling over the whole seat.

"That was mine," she said. He didn't answer. But in seconds he scrambled forward to sit on the edge of the glider, tapping his foot nervously and scanning the street with fast, jerky moves of his head.

"Shit!" he said, jumping to his feet. He pressed his face against the screen and stared at the corner for a few seconds. Then he darted back into the house.

Eileen reclaimed her place on the glider and fumed. She thought she heard him call to her: too bad, let him waste his breath. After a moment of quiet she heard him again and again she said nothing. But when he kept talking she realized he spoke in tones not meant for either her or Mickey, he must be on the phone and her smoldering silence was wasted. Angrily she thumped her foot against the side of the glider until her toes stung; when she stopped, all was quiet in the house.

Then Amander's cousin Tyrone came pedaling down the block on a too-small bicycle, his knobby knees pumping hard. "Cops on Lincoln!" he called out to no one in particular as he whirred past Eileen's porch. Slowing when he approached the corner where the fancy cars were parked, he repeated the warning, "Cops on Lincoln!" And then he pedaled round and round in the intersection, his big frame leaning at a precarious angle toward the center of the circle he made. "Buchanan and Lincoln, headed this way!" he shouted.

There was fast movement: car doors slammed, engines started. Tyrone pedaled out of his circle and stopped by the curb as the BMW and Honda Prelude sped away. He rested both feet on the ground as he caught his breath, wiped his forehead with the hem of his T-shirt, already splotchy with sweat, and then pedaled again, circling through the intersection, around and around. People stepped down from their porches and stoops and walked toward him.

"Whatcha doin', Tyrone?" asked the bent white-haired man who had teetered down without his cane from the porch across the street.

"Here they come!" Tyrone shouted. "Cops are comin'!"

"Mommy!" yelled Ayeisha, jumping up and down on Amander's porch. "Uncle Tyrone!"

Eileen rose from the glider and stepped toward the door. Robert burst onto the porch. "Watch that bastard fuck up everything!" he hissed.

Eileen scowled. "What's it to you, him out there?" She went out the screen door and stood on the stoop.

"A lot more'n to you!" shouted Robert.

Amander's door screeched open and snapped right back with a hard bang as she stepped out and took a quick look around. "Now what the hell is he doin'?"

Tyrone was still pedaling in circles and people were still coming to watch him when the cruiser pulled up from the south on Lincoln and squealed to a stop just inches from the bike.

"Shit!" said Amander, and she ran down the steps toward Tyrone.

"Stay here with Mickey," Eileen told Robert, and she rushed down her own stoop to follow Amander without even looking back, without even wondering how he'd look when *she* ordered *him* around for once.

The two cops got out of the cruiser, talking into their radio. They were both blond-haired and young, one stocky, one a beanpole type—good-looking guys, Eileen thought, but scary. They swaggered from the car toward the center of the intersection as other folks streamed slowly down the streets toward the same scene, Eileen one in a small crowd of thirty or so.

"Get outta our street!" Tyrone yelled at the cops. He gasped for air, still pumping hard on the bike in the same circle. "Whatcha always come botherin' *us* for?"

The two cops planted themselves in the weightiest of ways, legs apart, chins jutting, one bracing his fists on his hips, the other crossing his arms on his chest, the smirks that now spread along each of their smug boy faces silently staking a claim to the turf.

"Get the fuck out, we don't need no occupyin' army here!"

"You tell 'em, Tyrone!" shouted one young man in the crowd.

"Yeah! Get outta here!" yelled another.

The two officers approached Tyrone, but stopped in mid-swagger when he rose to a stand on the bike and pedaled faster, now circling the police car itself. Eileen didn't understand why Tyrone kept pedaling or why the cops gave a shit; it wasn't like there were cars jammed up waiting to get through, just Tyrone a little nuts on a bicycle, a hot, boring night, people milling around.

The cops turned to the crowd. "Everybody back!" commanded the tall one.

Amander's firm voice called out, "Tyrone, quit it and come in!"

"Why should he? He ain't doin' nothin' illegal!" said the old man, now standing next to her.

"That don't stop a man from getting into trouble with the law," replied Amander, more quietly.

"You all go back home now!" ordered the stockier cop. "I want these streets cleared, y'hear?" He tapped his billy club repeatedly into the palm of his hand, then made a brief, not-very-serious charging motion toward the crowd. "Get *back!*"

Still believing that when a cop said move, you moved, Eileen took a step back and stepped right on Alice Boatright's two big feet. "Whoa, girl!" said Alice, grabbing Eileen by the shoulders. Nobody else seemed to budge.

"Police state!" shouted one of the young men.

Emboldened, his buddy shouted louder. "Get the fuck off our street, pigs!"

A murmur of female disapproval hummed along one side of the gathering, cut off when Tyrone hollered, "We'll get Al Sharpton in here to straighten this out!"

The thin cop laughed derisively and muttered, "Crazy nigger."

Silence followed while a flinch of shock travelled through the crowd like a current. Then the old man took a shaky step toward the cop. "Whatidya say, fellow?"

"Back off, old man," yelled the other cop, holding the billy club out. The old man stayed precisely where he was, but Eileen—two or three rows back and nowhere near them—still ducked. Alice Boatright patted her on the shoulder from behind, laughing. "They never gonna hit no white girl, Eileen," she said softly.

"Did I hear someone say 'nigger'?" the old man rasped, turning to the neighbors just behind him.

"Lord help us!" called out an older woman from the back.

"You sure heard right!" said Amander.

The angry smile on Amander's face made Eileen scared and excited at the same time so that her spine tingled in a way she'd never felt before.

"Sharp-ton! Sharp-ton!" chanted several youngsters in the crowd. "Sharp-ton! Sharp-ton!" joined in a number of other voices.

Amander turned around to the folks behind her and hooted with laughter. "A lotta good Sharpton would do. As if he'd even bother with us up here!"

Nothing could have been more reassuring to Eileen than the sound of Amander's high-pitched laughter; Amander, the most real adult Eileen had ever known, would never let a bad thing happen here on her own street.

The crowd by now had grown to fifty or more, but you couldn't say it was a boisterous scene, hardly the mob the cops reported in the papers the next day. Now it's true, Eileen would probably not have known the difference between being in the middle of a mob and being in the middle of a crowd, so unaccustomed was she to being in the middle of anything at all. On the other hand, if it is in the nature of a mob to be threatening and hostile, it's likely that Eileen would have sensed the threat and felt the hostility and shrunk away from them in fear. But in fact as more people gathered near her, she grew even less scared, not more. Parents hoisted kids up on their shoulders so they could watch Tyrone, still circling. Young friends jostled and kidded each other. Teenage women in short shorts and skimpy halters clung together in a knot, unsure if their sexiness should be on display with so many of their elders all about. Boys teased and flirted more covertly too, sensing the gathering's moral edge. Heavyset grandmothers, oozing sweat, fanned themselves with wilted newspapers and talked about cousins down in the Carolinas. If theirs had been a neighborhood given to summer block parties (and it wasn't), the parties might have been like this—just add music and some covered dishes. So why were the cops so angry at them all? Eileen was confused. But confusion in the absence of fear and in the company of familiar people and softened by the heavy, muggy evening heat only seemed to make her more excited—excited, that is, in the subdued way Eileen got, with only a slightly faster thumping of her heartbeats and the strange tingliness at the back of her neck and an urge to keep rising to the tips of her toes.

When the ice-cream van came along, people cheered and Tyrone moved his circling away from the intersection and farther out a bit on Lincoln where the crowd was thinnest, letting the van cross over to do business. And then there was a noisy stirring of children and hands reaching for coins and passing of dollar bills along from adult to adult so that neighbors who'd run out of their houses with empty pockets could still take part.

"Whatcha doin' out here, Ayeisha?" Amander asked sternly as her daughter tugged at her hand. "You're supposed to be up at the house with the others."

Ayeisha grinned, guiltily stopped grinning, looked at her

feet for a few seconds, then looked back up resolutely, accepting of her mother's anger and the scolding it might bring forth. "We're hot. Can't I bring ice cream back?"

Amander sighed a long sigh while the stern reprimand etched on her face did visible battle with a crop of second thoughts and the sight of Ayeisha's forehead beading with sweat. At the end of the sigh, her expression softened, the conflict finished. "What can you do?" she said to Eileen as she fished money from her pocket. "Bring me a lemon ice first. You want one, Eileen?"

"Uh-uh, no thanks," said Eileen, not really meaning it, but embarrassed to accept.

Ayeisha ran back and forth to the van and, cradling an assortment of popsicles, rushed back to the house by the time the crowd—throats quenched, foreheads cooled with the bottoms of soda cans—collected its focus again as a second cruiser pulled up on the north side of Lincoln. A large, balding officer jumped out with a megaphone.

"This is an un-*law*-ful assembly!" he drawled gruffly. "Everybody disperse and go *home!*"

"What's unlawful about people standing around in front of their own houses talkin'?" asked one of the heavyset women.

A chorus of "Yeahs" followed. "What we doin' wrong?"

"Everyone disperse and go home!" bellowed the megaphone.

"Sharp-ton! Sharp-ton!" The chant started again. Even Eileen mumbled along this time. "Sharp-ton! Sharp-ton!"

The beanpole police officer from the first cruiser called out to Tyrone, "Get down from the bicycle immediately! Do you hear? Get off the bike at once! You are under arrest!"

"Ain't no crime to ride a bike," said the old man.

The arresting officer turned to him angrily. "Obstructing governmental administration, old man. That's a crime. You could be charged, too, if you don't keep that mouth shut."

A sudden hush descended briefly, then Amander spoke. "Officer, you should be ashamed of yourself, botherin' a helpless elderly gentleman." She took another breath. "When the drug dealers are here right under your nose and you never see 'em."

The stocky cop pointed at Tyrone. *"He* warned 'em off. You got yourselves to blame, lady."

"Pooh!" she retorted. "If you did your job, the dealers wouldn't be here in the first place, but no, you come here just to pester innocent folks."

"You said it, sister," said the old man.

"Tyrone's right," said Alice Boatright. "We need Sharpton."

The beanpole shouted, "Inciting a riot is unlawful!"

"If this be a riot," said a muscular young man in the back of the crowd, "then I must be Malcolm."

Lots of folks laughed, but the balding cop lowered the megaphone, pushed through the crowd and grabbed the muscular young man by the neck of his T-shirt. "Hey, boy, you better watch your mouth or we're gonna see *you* again behind bars."

"Ooooooh," sang a group of teenage women, mocking. Eileen was sure the cops would clobber everybody now. She knew she could get away if she wanted, but her spine tingled along its whole length and she was too excited and too curious and feeling too much for the first time in her life that she was *part* of something to leave it all now, so she braced herself, squeezed her eyes shut, and waited for blows to rain down on her. But nothing happened, except somebody's kid fell against her leg and left strawberry-flavored fingerprints on her knee. She opened her eyes and glanced around. Just in front of her, Amander chewed tensely on the paper from her lemon ice. The knot of young women was now standing taller and defiantly flesh-proud, the flirty young men had become a little louder, and the heavyset women had started again to fan themselves, moving their wrists in a brisk and deliberate unison that barely made a ripple in the thick night air.

And just then Jack Newton came jogging through the crowd in a small burst of power that *did* stir the air. She recognized him from the high-school track team years ago. He was a taut, wiry bullet of a man. People quickly opened up a path for him as he cut into the center of things, his bright fluorescent purple running suit stealing the focus of the scene so that even the cops backed off in order to watch. "That's my bike, dammit, Tyrone, gimme my bike!" he yelled. He ran right between two cops, right up to Tyrone, who kept pedaling, and he ran alongside the bike and reached out and grabbed it and forced the bike to stop and nearly forced Tyrone (though twice as big as Jack himself) to sail over the handlebars.

A lot of people booed at Jack Newton. "Leave 'im be, Jack!" someone cried out. But Tyrone made a pushing-back, calming-down gesture with both hands, and the crowd suddenly hushed. Tyrone sighed, then gave a sardonic laugh. "Shit!" he said, swinging his leg high as he dismounted.

"You took my bike, man!" hollered Jack.

Tyrone shook his head. "I just borrowed it, I was gonna give it back. Look, everybody know I got it. Everybody!" He laughed again, a sad winded hoarse laugh, and shot a quick glance around the crowd. The crowd, silent, stared back at him. And then he walked away. It was that simple: he walked fast through the throng along the path that had been cleared for Jack Newton and just kept going down Jefferson.

A third police car sped toward Tyrone from the other direction and stopped right in front of Eileen's house. Three more officers jumped out. The crowd began to move toward them, oozing like a hot, slow liquid from the intersection into the center of Jefferson.

"Everyone disperse and go home!" blared the megaphone.

Tyrone climbed up the stoop to Amander's porch and from this spot on higher ground turned to the folks and shouted, "You gonna let them *arrest* me? *Arrest* me for ridin' a bike and exercising my right to speak my mind?"

A loud, strong, and strangely happy "No!" rang out from the crowd.

"We're with you Tyrone!" the old man warbled, moving toward the house with what seemed like ease, despite pains of arthritis that must have been worsened by the humid, hot night; he advanced like a much younger man, buoyed up and carried along by this unexpected wave of solidarity.

And as intentional as the collective flow and movement now became, it was still so smooth and slow and easy that no one even feared for the small children who had managed to stay on and no threat of panic marred the mood as people arranged themselves by wordless instinct at the foot of the porch into one solid, spirited barricade between Tyrone and the police.

Holding up the megaphone, one cop spoke. "Let us through, this man is under arrest!" Five other officers prowled the fringes of the crowd, looking for breaks in Tyrone's shield.

"Forget it!" Tyrone called to the police.

"Tyrone's our man!" shouted a youngster.

"Get outta here, you motherfuckin' cops!" yelled another.

"Don't start that language!" warned a harsh female voice.

A moment of silence followed. Then one of the cops, mistaking the hush of caution for a dropping of guard, pushed and prodded between people with a billy stick. People shoved back—not with the outward force of arms and hands, but with the total weight of their resistance. Two more cops shoved more, but still could not break through. Eileen rose up on tippy-toes to catch a glimpse of them behind her, then settled back down on flat feet, her shoulders touching folks on either side. The crowd was close and hot and calm. A deeper hush fell. But then, over the crackly static of a radio, the voice of the beanpole officer calling for back-up became clear. A few seconds after he finished, Amander's loud, steady voice rose up from the middle somewhere. "Let me up there, that's my house," she said. "My babies are in there."

A low murmur eddied through the crowd as folks inhaled just enough and repositioned shoulders and elbows just enough to open not so much a path or space, but the most slender possibility for Amander to make it to the porch. Eileen watched Amander glide up the stairs, duck into the house, reemerge a minute later, then return to Tyrone's side. She talked to him softly, then laughed and tossed her head and stood tall and looked out into the crowd and looked out over the crowd and looked out beyond the crowd and straightened her broad shoulders and settled her gaze squarely yet calmly on the cops, like she was ready for anything. And Eileen (who was ready for nothing) felt something like a pang of envy all mixed up with fear and admiration and yearning—yearning for what, she would not have known. Nor could she have wondered very long, because the wailing sirens of three more cruisers now drowned out all talk and thought.

Cops jumped out, cops slammed doors, cops pushed, cops raised their clubs and jammed their way into the crowd, which, for a moment as one body, fell back and surged forward and fell back again. People hollered and some who could wriggle loose began to scatter and others tried hard to hold their ground. Eileen, paralyzed with confusion, looked to the porch: Amander stood exactly where she'd been before, watching out, seeing everything, somehow serene and somehow ferocious both at the same time. And as the crowd lost its bond and churned apart, Eileen let herself get bumped and shoved nearer and nearer to the steps and then pushed up the steps and up farther until she too was standing on the porch and saw out as the cops pushed in closer and closer and saw out as the fragile old white-haired man folded and recoiled from a blow and saw out as they got closer. And she heard right beside her Tyrone yelling and Amander cursing now and a shriek of cursing anger flew from her own throat and suddenly in what seemed like one fast rough movement she was yanked from the porch and handcuffed and dragged back through the crowd to a police car and shoved in.

Sitting side by side shackled to the bench at the police station, Amander and Eileen waited for a long time, silent. An old blotchy-faced officer sat at a desk looking away from them; he shuffled papers, spoke on the phone, occasionally buzzed another officer in or out, spoke more on the phone, and never once said a word to them.

"Jeez I'm hungry," Eileen mumbled, breaking the silence.

Amander stopped her right away. "Shush now, Eileen."

Eileen obeyed and shushed. They waited more. It was almost eleven o'clock and the room was eerily quiet. Eileen glanced at Amander, whose eyes were closed, her face smooth, cool, expressionless.

Then in a sudden burst of yelling and scuffling, three big officers entered the room with a cyclone in handcuffs: Tyrone. He shouted curses as they pulled and hoisted him across the room—passing close enough in front of Eileen and Amander so that even as he struggled the women saw the angry red bruises shining from his forehead and cheeks, the swollen, purple, cracked bulge of his lower lip, and the muddied, bloodied shreds of his T-shirt. And he was quickly dragged out of sight through another door.

For a moment Eileen stared, stunned, at that door, at that

space Tyrone had occupied so briefly and tumultuously, now a gaping emptiness. She let out a long, loud sigh. "They sure roughed him up, didn't they?" she murmured, and looked sideways into Amander's face. And there she saw an Amander she had never seen before. This Amander's face was a dark blue-brown, covered in droplets of sweat, and it quivered—quivered uncontrollably from the *not* saying, the not crying, and the not screaming. Her shoulders, too, began to tremble and quake from not lashing out to pound or hit. This Amander sat handcuffed and shackled and unable to do a single thing to stop what was being done.

Eileen drew in a quick gasp of air as her stomach tightened into a knot. She spun her head to the other side, away from Amander, and lowered her blurry stare to fix on a stain on the floor. Amander who could do anything couldn't do anything right now. And for the first time in her life Eileen felt the sudden welling up of tears of grief together with the nausea of deep shame.

A few minutes later the officer got off the phone, rose from his desk, stretched out his arms as he stifled a yawn, regained his posture, and sauntered over to the bench.

"You," he said. "You're outta here." He released Eileen from the cuffs and shackles.

Eileen stood beside Amander, waiting.

"C'mon, let's *go*," said the officer.

"What about her?" Eileen asked, letting her glance make a very brief stop on Amander's face, which was again transformed: immobile, eyes closed, impervious, giving away nothing. Eileen looked quickly back at the officer.

"She's not going anywhere," he said. Then he gave Eileen a little shove and guided her, alone, to another room. She caught sight of Robert and stopped in the doorway. It was as if she had not seen him in years and now suddenly he was inside the next room laughing with the desk sergeant. Or was he? Nothing was real, except the slice of pain in her stomach. The blotchy-faced officer pushed her not so very gently toward this man who was supposed to be her husband, and the door from the holding room clanged shut behind her before she could look back.

She looked back anyway, and saw the hard gray metal of

the door. A sour taste of failed regurgitation rose into her throat.

"You go home now," said the officer.

Robert turned slowly away from the desk sergeant. "Well, Charlie, I guess I'll see ya later." Facing Eileen, his features twisted with mock surprise. "Now jeez, look who's here." He looked her up and down coldly, as smugness darkened his eyes and curled his lip at one corner. "Now ain't this your lucky day, Eileen. You're free now. They made a mistake."

Eileen looked quickly around. The desk sergeant smirked. She glared back at Robert. "They didn't make no mistake," she said. "You know that."

"You better shut up about it," he said.

She rolled her eyes up to the ceiling. Then, even as an inkling of what he must have meant began to chew at the edges of her mind, she followed him out. For the time being, at least, she had no other way to get home and no place else to go.

Alice Adams

HIS WOMEN

"I think we should try it again. You move back in," says Meredith, in her lovely, low, dishonest Southern voice.

Carter asks, "But—Adam?"

"I'm not seeing him anymore." Her large face, not pretty but memorable, braves his look of disbelief. Her big, deep-brown eyes are set just too close, her shapely mouth is a little too full, and greedy. Big, tall, dark, sexy Meredith, who is still by law his wife. She adds, "I do see him around the campus, I mean, but we're just friends now."

That's what you said before, Carter does not say, but that unspoken sentence hangs there in the empty space between them. She knows it as well as he does.

They are sitting in the garden behind her house—their house, actually, joint ownership being one of their central problems, as Carter sees it. In any case, now in early summer, in Chapel Hill, the garden is lovely. The roses over which Carter has labored in seasons past—pruning, spraying, and carefully, scientifically feeding—are in fragrant, delicately full bloom: great bursts of red and flame, yellow and pink and white. The beds are untidy now, neglected. Adam, who never actually moved in (Carter thinks), is not a gardener, and Meredith has grown careless.

She says, with a pretty laugh, "We're not getting younger. Isn't it time we did something mature, like making our marriage work?"

"Since we can't afford a divorce." He, too, laughs, but since what he says is true, no joke, it falls flat.

And Meredith chooses to ignore it; they are not to talk about money, not this time. "You know I've always loved you," she says, her eyes larger and a warmer brown than ever.

Perhaps in a way she has, thinks Carter. Meredith loves everyone; it is a part of her charm. Why not him, too? Carter and Adam and all her many friends and students (Meredith teaches in the music department at the university), and most cats and dogs and birds.

She adds, almost whispering, sexily, "And I think you love me, too. We belong together."

"I'll have to think about it," Carter tells her, somewhat stiffly.

The brown eyes narrow, just a little. "How about Chase? You still see her?"

"Well, sort of." He does not say "as friends," since this is not true, though Carter has understood that the presence of Chase in his life has raised his stature—his value, so to speak—and he wishes he could say that they are still "close."

But four years of military school, at The Citadel, left Carter a stickler for the literal truth, along with giving him his ramrod posture and a few other unhelpful hangups—according to the shrink he drives over to Durham to see, twice a week. Dr. Chen, a diminutive Chinese of mandarin manners and a posture almost as stiff in its way as Carter's own. ("Oh, great" was Chase's comment on hearing this description. "You must think you're back in some Oriental Citadel.") In any case, he is unable to lie now to Meredith, who says, with a small and satisfied laugh, "So we're both free. It's fated, you see?"

A long time ago, before Meredith and long before Chase, Carter was married to Isabel, who was small and fair and thin and rich, truly beautiful and chronically unfaithful. In those days, Carter was a graduate student at the university, in business administration, which these days he teaches. They lived,

back then, he and Isabel, in a fairly modest rented house out on
Franklin Street, somewhat crowded with Isabel's valuable in-
herited antiques; the effect was grander than that of any other
graduate students', or even young professors', homes. As Isabel was grander, more elegant than other wives, in her big hats
and long skirts and very high heels, with her fancy hors
d'oeuvres and her collection of forties big-band tapes, to which
she loved to dance. After dinner, at parties at their house, as
others cleared off the table, Isabel would turn up the music and
lower the lights in the living room. "Come *on*," she would say.
"Let's all *dance*."

Sometimes there were arguments later:

"I feel rather foolish saying this, but I don't exactly like the
way you dance with Walter."

"Whatever do you mean? Walter's a marvellous dancer."
But she laughed unpleasantly, her wide, thin, dark-red mouth
showing small, perfect teeth; she knew exactly what he meant.

What do you do if your wife persists in dancing *like that* in
your presence? And if she even tells you, on a Sunday, that she
thinks she will drive to the beach with Sam, since you have so
many papers to grade?

She promises they won't be late, and kisses Carter goodbye
very tenderly. But they are late, very late. Lovely Isabel, who
comes into the house by herself and is not only late but a little
drunk, as Carter himself is by then, having had considerable
bourbon for dinner, with some peanuts for nourishment.

Nothing that he learned at The Citadel had prepared Carter
for any of this.

Standing in the doorway, Isabel thrust her body into a
dancer's pose, one thin hip pushed forward and her chin, too,
stuck out—a sort of mime of defiance. She said, "Well, what
can I say? I know I'm late, and we drank too much."

"Obviously."

"But so have you, from the look of things."

"I guess."

"Well, let's have another drink together. What the hell. We
always have fun drinking, don't we, darling Carter?"

"I guess."

It was true. Often, drinking, they had hours of long, wonderful, excited conversations, impossible to recall the following day. As was the case this time, the night of Isabel's Sunday at the beach with Sam.

Drinking was what they did best together; making love was not. This was something that they never discussed, although back then, in the early seventies, people did talk about it quite a lot, and many people seemed to do it all the time. But part of their problem, sexually, had to do with drink itself, not surprisingly. A few belts of bourbon or a couple of Sunday-lunch Martinis made Isabel aggressively amorous, full of tricks and wiles and somewhat startling perverse persuasions. But Carter, although his mind was aroused and his imagination inflamed, often found himself incapacitated. Out of it, turned off. This did not always happen, but it happened far too often.

Sometimes, though, there were long, luxurious Sunday couplings, perhaps with some breakfast champagne or some dope; Isabel was extremely fond of an early-morning joint. Then it could be as great as any of Carter's boyhood imaginings of sex.

But much more often, as Isabel made all the passionate gestures in her considerable repertoire, Carter would have to murmur, "Sorry, dear," to her ear. Nuzzling, kissing her neck. "Sorry I'm such a poop."

And so it went the night she came home from Sam, from the beach. They had some drinks, and they talked. "Sam's actually kind of a jerk," said Isabel. "And you know, we didn't actually do anything. So let's go to bed. Come, kiss me and say I'm forgiven, show me I'm forgiven." But he couldn't show her, and at last it was she who had to forgive.

Another, somewhat lesser problem was that Isabel really did not like it in Chapel Hill. "It's awfully pretty," she admitted, "and we do get an occasional good concert, or even an art show. But, otherwise, what a terrifically overrated town! And the faculty wives, now really. I miss my friends."

Therefore Carter was pleased, he was very pleased, when Isabel began to speak with some warmth of this new friend, Meredith. "She's big and fat, in fact she's built like a cow, and she's very Southern, but she has a pretty voice and she works in the music department, she teaches there, and she seems to have a sense of humor. You won't mind if I ask her over?"

Meeting Meredith, and gradually spending some time with her, Carter at first thought she was a good scout, like someone's sister. Like many big women (Isabel's description had been unkind), she had a pleasant disposition and lovely skin. Nice long brown hair, and her eyes, if just too closely placed, were the clear, warm brown of Southern brooks. With Carter, her new friend's husband, she was flirty, in a friendly, pleasant way—the way of Southern women, a way he was used to. She was like his mother's friends, and his cousins, and the nice girls from Ashley Hall whom he used to take to dances at The Citadel.

Meredith became the family friend. She was often invited to dinner parties, or sometimes just for supper by herself. She and Isabel always seemed to have a lot to talk about. Concerts in New York, composers and musicians, not to mention a lot of local gossip.

When they were alone, Carter gathered, they talked about Meredith's boyfriends, of which she seemed to have a large and steady supply. "She's this certain type of Southern belle" was Isabel's opinion. "Not threateningly attractive, but sexy and basically comfy. She makes men feel good, with those big, adoring cow eyes."

Did Isabel confide in Meredith? Carter suspected that she did, and later he found out for certain, from Meredith, that she had. About her own affairs. Her boyfriends.

Although he had every reason to know that she was unhappy, Carter was devastated by Isabel's departure. Against all reason, miserably, he felt that his life was demolished. Irrationally, instead of remembering a bitter, complaining Isabel ("I can't stand this tacky town a minute longer") or an Isabel with whom things did not work out well in bed ("Well, Jesus Christ, is that what you learned at The Citadel?"), he recalled only her beauty. Her clothes, and her scents. Her long blond hair.

He was quite surprised, at first, when Meredith began to call a lot with messages of sympathy, when she seemed to take his side. "You poor guy, you certainly didn't deserve this" was one of the things that she said at the time. Told that he was finding it hard to eat—"I don't know, everything I try tastes awful"—she began to arrive every day or so, at mealtimes, with delicately flavored chicken, and oven-fresh Sally Lunn, tomatoes from her garden, and cookies, lots and lots of home-made cookies. Then she took to inviting him to her house for dinner—often.

As he left her house, at night, Carter would always kiss Meredith, in a friendly way, but somehow, imperceptibly, the kisses and their accompanying embraces became more pro-longed. Also, Carter found that this good-night moment was something he looked forward to. Until the night when Mere-dith whispered to him, "You really don't have to go home, you know. You could stay with me." More kissing, and then, "Please stay. I want you, my darling Carter."

Sex with Meredith was sweet and pleasant and friendly, and if it lacked the wild rush that he had sometimes felt with Isabel, at least when he failed her she was nice about it. Sweet and comforting. Unlike angry Isabel.

They married as soon as his divorce was final, and together they bought the bargain house, on a hill outside town, and they set about remodelling: shingling, making a garden, mak-ing a kitchen and a bedroom with wonderful views. Carter, like everyone else in the high-flying eighties, had made some money on the market, and he put all this into the house. The house became very beautiful; they loved it, and in that house Carter and Meredith thrived. Or so he thought.

He thought so until the day she came to him in anguished tears and told him, "This terrible thing. I've fallen in love with Adam." Adam, a lean young musician, a cellist, who had been to the house for dinner a couple of times. Unprepossessing, Carter would have said of him.

Carter felt, at first, a virile rage. Bloodily murderous fanta-sies obsessed his waking hours; at night he could barely sleep. He was almost unrecognizable to himself, this furiously, righ-teously impassioned man. With Meredith he was icily, en-ragedly cold. And then, one day, Meredith came to him and with more tears she told him, "It's over, I'll never see him again. Or if I do we'll just be friends."

After that followed a brief and intense and, to Carter, slightly unreal period of, well, fucking: the fury with which

they went at each other could not be called "making love."
Meredith was the first to taper off; she responded less and less
actively, although as always she was pleasant, nice. But Carter
finally asked her what was wrong, and she admitted, through
more tears, "It's Adam. I'm seeing him again. I mean, we're in
love again."

This time, Carter reacted not with rage but with a sort of
defeated grief. He felt terribly old and battered. *Cuckold.* The
ugly, old-fashioned word resounded, echoing through his
brain. He thought, I am the sort of man to whom women are
unfaithful.

When he moved out, away from Meredith and into an
apartment, and Chase Landau fell in love with him (quite rapidly, it seemed), Carter assumed that she must be crazy. It even
seemed a little nuts for her to ask him for dinner soon after
they met, introducing themselves in the elevator. Chase lived
in his building, but her apartment, which contained her studio,
was about twice the size of Carter's and much nicer, with balconies and views. "I liked your face," she later explained. "I
always go for those narrow, cold, mean eyes." Laughing, making it a joke.

Chase was a tall, thin, red-haired woman, not Southern but
from New York, and somewhat abrasive in manner. A painter
of considerable talent and reputation (no wonder Meredith
was impressed). Carter himself was impressed at finding
inquiries from *Who's Who* lying around, especially because she
never mentioned it. In his field, only the really major players
made it.

Her paintings were huge, dark, and violent abstractions, incomprehensible. Discomforting. How could anyone buy these
things and live with them? As they sat having drinks that first
night, working at light conversation, Carter felt the paintings
as enormous, hostile presences.

Chase was almost as tall as Carter was, close to six feet, and
thin, but heavy-breasted, which may have accounted for her
bad posture; she tended to slouch, and later she admitted,
"When I was very young I didn't like my body at all. So con-
spicuous." Carter liked her body, very much. Her eyes were
intense and serious, always.

As they were finishing dinner she said to him, "Your shoulders are wonderful. I mean the angle of them. This," and she reached with strong hands to show him.

He found himself aroused by that touch, wanting to turn and grasp her. To kiss. But not doing so. Later on, he did kiss her good night, but very chastely.

Used to living with women, with Isabel, and then with Meredith, Carter began to wonder what to do by himself at night. He had never been much of a reader, and most television bored him. In the small town that Chapel Hill still was in many ways, you would think (Carter thought) that people knowing of the separation would call and ask him over, but so far no one had. He wished he had more friends; he should have been warmer, kinder. Closer to people. He felt very old, and alone. (He wondered, *Are* my eyes mean? Am *I* mean?)

He called Chase and asked her out to dinner. "I know it's terribly short notice, but are you busy tonight?"

"No, in fact I'd love to go out tonight. I'm glad you called."

His heart leaped up at those mild words.

During that dinner, Chase talked quite a lot about the art world: her New York gallery, the one in L.A., the local art department. He listened, grateful for the entertainment she provided, but he really wasn't paying much attention. He was thinking of later on: Would she, possibly, so soon—

She would not. At the door, she bid him a clear good night, after a rather perfunctory social kiss. She thanked him for the dinner. She had talked too much, she feared; she tended to do that with new people, she told him, with a small, not quite apologetic, laugh.

From a friend in the law school, Carter got the name of a lawyer, a woman, with whom he spent an uncomfortable, discouraging, and expensive half hour. What it came to was that, in order to recover his share in the house, Carter would have to force Meredith to sell it, unless she could buy him out. None of this was final, of course; it was just the lawyer's temporary take on things. Still, it was deeply depressing to Carter.

Coming home, in the downstairs lobby of his building he ran into Chase, who was carrying a sack of groceries, which of course he offered to take.

"Only if you'll come and have supper with me." She

flashed him a challenging smile. "I must have been thinking of you. I know I bought too much."

That night it was he who talked a lot. She only interrupted from time to time with small but sharp-edged questions. "If you didn't want to go to The Citadel, why didn't you speak up?" And "Do you think you trusted Meredith at first because she's not as good-looking as Isabel?" The sort of questions that he usually hated—that he hated from Dr. Chen—but not so with Chase; her dark, intelligent eyes were kind and alert. He felt safe with her, and appreciated. He almost forgot his wish to make love to her.

But then he remembered, and all that desire returned. He told her, "It's all I can do not to touch you. You're most terrifically attractive to me."

By way of answer, she smiled and leaned to meet him in a kiss. For a long time, then, like adolescents, they sat there kissing on her sofa, until she whispered, "Come on, let's go to bed. This is silly."

Carter had not expected their progress to be quite so rapid. He hardly knew her, did he really want this? But not long after that, they were indeed in bed, both naked. He caressed her soft, heavy breasts.

Pausing, sitting up to reach somewhere, Chase said, "You'll have to wear this. I'm sorry."

"Oh, Lord, I haven't done that since I was twenty. And look, I'm safe. I never played around."

"I know, but Meredith did. A lot."

"I don't think I can—"

"Here, I'll help you."

"Damn, I'm losing it, I knew I would."

Strictly speaking, technically, that night was not a great success. Still, literally they had gone to bed together, and Carter's feeling was that this was not a woman who fell into bed very easily (unlike—he had to think this—either Isabel or Meredith).

The next day he had another appointment with the lawyer, who had talked with Meredith's lawyer, who had said that things looked worse.

"I don't know why I'm so drawn to you," Chase told him,

"but I really am." She laughed. "That's probably not a good sign. For you, I mean. The men I've really liked best were close to certifiable. But you're not crazy, are you?"

"Not so far as I know."

Chase did not seem crazy to him. She was hardworking, very intelligent. Her two sons, with whom she got along well, were off in school, and she was surrounded by warm and admiring friends; her phone rang all the time with invitations, friendly voices. But, as Carter put it to himself, she did sometimes seem a little much. A little more than he had bargained for. Or more than he was up to right now.

Their sexual life, despite her continued insistence on—hated phrase—"safe sex," was sometimes great, then not. Chase complained, though nicely, only that out of bed he was not affectionate. "I could use more plain, unsexy touching," she said, and he tried to comply, though demonstrativeness was not at all in his nature.

Carter's broker called with bad news, quite a lot of bad news. Carter, like most people in the market, had taken a beating.

Even Chase would admit that her work habits were a little strange. She liked to get up late and to spend a couple of hours drinking coffee, phoning, maybe writing a letter or two. She would then go into her studio (a room to which Carter was never admitted). At times she would emerge to eat a piece of fruit, heat some soup, or, less frequently, go out for a short walk along the gravelled paths of old Chapel Hill. Back in her studio, immersed in her work, quite often she would forget about dinner until ten at night, or eleven; she did not forget dinner dates but she sometimes phoned to break or to postpone them.

Carter argued. "But if you started earlier in the morning you could finish—"

"I know. I know it's impractical, but it's the way I seem to have to work. I'm sorry. It's not something I can change."

Along with feeling some annoyance, Carter was moved and a little alarmed by her intensity, her high purpose.

Sometimes, in bed, Chase cried out quick, impassioned words of love to him—which Carter did not answer in kind, nor did he take what she said at those moments too seriously. In fact, as he was later forced to recognize, he gave rather little thought to Chase's deeper feelings. "You didn't want to deal with what I felt," she accused him, and he had to admit that that was entirely correct.

"Adam and I aren't getting along at all," said Meredith to Carter, over the phone. "I don't know—he's a lot more neurotic than I thought he was."

"Oh, that's too bad" was Carter's response. Not saying, *Now* you find this out, after wrecking our marriage and costing God knows what in lawyers' bills.

"He's very dependent," Meredith said. "I don't really like that. I guess I was spoiled by you."

"I don't know why she's telling me this stuff," Carter said to Chase when she called; the old instinct of compulsive honesty had forced him to repeat the conversation with Meredith.

"I think she wants you back," Chase told him. "You wait and see."

"You think so? Really?"

"Jesus, Carter, you sound sort of pleased. If she did, would you even consider it?"

"Well, I don't know." As always, the literal truth: he did not know.

"God, Carter, she slept with everyone. Everyone in town knows that. Why do you think I insisted on safe sex?"

She was furiously excited, almost hysterical, Carter thought. She was out of control. A little frightening—but he only said, "Oh, come on, now."

"How tacky can you get!" Chase cried out. And then she said, "Look, don't call me, I'll call you, O.K.?" And hung up.

True to her word, she did call him—once, very late at night. "I've had some wine," she said. "I shouldn't be calling, I mean, otherwise I wouldn't. But I just wanted you to know a couple of things. One, I was really in love with you. God, if I needed further proof that I'm seriously deranged. I always fall in love with the most unavailable man anywhere around. Emotionally. Mean eyes, good shoulders. *Shit*, why did I call? Good night!" And she hung up, loud and clear. A ridiculous and quite unnecessary conversation, in Carter's view.

.   .   .

Now, in the afternoon sunshine, Carter looks about at all the roses, and the scented white wisteria—at their lovely house and at unlovely, untrustworthy, but deeply familiar Meredith. He finds that, despite himself, he is thinking of Chase. Of her passion (those cries of love) and her scornful rage and of her final avowals (but she was drunk). Is it now too late? Suppose he went to her and said that he was through with Meredith, would she take him back? Would she ask him to come and live with her? (So far, she has never suggested such a thing.) Could they marry?

No is the answer that Carter gives to all these questions. No, Chase would probably not take him back, and no, there is no way he could afford to marry her. Even if he were sure that he wanted to. Chase is crazy—she must be crazy. Look at those paintings. There in the warm sunlight he suddenly shivers, as though haunted.

"Yes," he says to Meredith, although she hasn't spoken for a while. "Yes, O.K. All right."

Ellen Douglas

GRANT

This is a story that may have been waiting for me until I was
old enough to tell it. Not that I had forgotten. How could I
forget what had happened in my house, under my nose, to me?
I even thought from time to time about telling one of the stories that lay next to it, so to speak. There were the bees the
night he died. There was Rosalie, who sat by him every day
when he was dying, beautiful Rosalie, who had five children
and sometimes came to work with a cut lip, a battered nose, a
bruised temple. There were the day walks, the night walks. But
I didn't want to tell those stories. Nothing came of thinking
about them.

My husband's uncle came to live with us during the last
year of his life. He was eighty-two. His wife had died several
years earlier and he had no children. He had cancer.

He could have gone to a veterans hospital—he was an An-
napolis graduate, a retired naval officer. And there were other
possibilities. Once he was too feeble to look after himself, he
could have hired live-in help or gone into a nursing home. But
we invited, insisted, and he came.

I knew Grant as one knows uncles-in-law who live in the
same town—as a genial enough fellow who brought his fiddle
to family Thanksgiving gatherings and played badly to my

husband's piano accompaniment. I can see him now on those occasions, fiddle tucked under his chin, standing over the piano, stooping to read the music, an expression of deep but clearly ironic concentration on his face, his head bent, light bouncing off the balding scalp. They'd play easy pieces from a collection of violin and piano duets: "None but the Lonely Heart," "Humoresque," a Schubert serenade. After they finished a piece he'd sit down, lay the violin across his lap, and smile. "I always have trouble with the triplets in that one," he might say. And his mother, nearly ninety then and nodding in her wheelchair: "Grant plays so well. It's a pity his violin squeaks."

That was a family joke.

So . . . Why did we invite him in? Well, again, family—he was family. One couldn't send him off to a veterans hospital or put him in a home, could one? But I'm misstating the case. No one could send him anywhere. He was perfectly capable of sending himself anywhere he wished, or of staying where he was, in the house his wife had left to her own niece and nephew.

Now there's another story. His wife Kathleen, who was fifteen years younger than he was, had died suddenly of a stroke. She'd doubtless always believed he would die first (he'd been retired early from the navy after a coronary) and had consequently left him nothing. The house and what other modest property they had was in her name. His name was not even mentioned in her will.

Grant could have contested it, of course: In our state you can't leave all your property away from a spouse. But he would never have done such a dishonorable thing. In her will she had said what she wanted. It would be done.

In their dealings with him, the niece and nephew were correct, but they were a cold pair to my way of thinking. Or maybe it's just that they were like me, had other things to think about besides aged uncles-in-law. They gave him permission to live in the house for the rest of his life. So that there could be no confusion about the title, they paid the taxes and he reimbursed them. They didn't charge him any rent. He paid repairs and upkeep.

Now I ask you, no matter how much younger you were than your husband, no matter if he'd had a coronary, would you leave everything away from him? Wouldn't you think he might by chance survive you? You might get run over by a truck or stung to death by hornets or drown or get trapped in a burning house, or God knows what. Surely you would mention in your will the name of your husband of forty years.

The only light he shed on this story came when he moved in with us and was clearing out of her house the things that belonged to him. He brought with him his clothes, a couple of canvas-covered wicker trunks from his tour in the Philippines before the First World War, a beautiful Japanese tea set, some brass trays from India, a huge piece of tapa cloth, his easy chair. Everything else: the furniture, his wedding silver, china, linens, even the lovely carved cherry bed he'd had made for them by a local cabinetmaker, "All that stuff," he said, "I got it for her. It was hers. She left everything to them. So . . ."

He brought his navy dress uniform and his cocked hat, circa 1911. They're still in a closet somewhere in our house, the uniform in a moth-proof bag, the hat stored in its leather case.

His sword he had given some years earlier to one of our sons. His violin he gave to my husband.

I think of one ray of light his wife shed on their marriage, although, I don't know, it may be misleading.

She was one of those large, soft-looking women, fair-haired and blue-eyed, who, statistical studies indicate, are most vulnerable in middle age to gallbladder attacks and diverticulitis. And indeed she did have the latter, although not for long, since she died when she was sixty.

In any case, what she said surprised me. She'd always seemed an easy-going, lively lady, ready for a good time, and I would have thought her tolerant of other people's foibles and failures and moral lapses. Not so, or not everybody's. We were talking of a man in the county who had left his wife for a woman who was widely known to have had in the course of her life a number of open love affairs—not so common among the small-town gentry of a couple of generations ago. I mean, people had *clandestine* affairs, of course, but not open ones. "She's filth," Grant's wife said to me when I commented once on this lady's charm and wit. "Filth. That's what they both are." She shivered and looked straight at me. (This was when I was quite a young woman, still focused almost to the exclusion of everything else on those lovely nights in bed.) "Men," she said. "There's only one thing men want and she gives it to them."

So, as you see, there's the story of their marriage, if one could dredge it up. And then . . . There's Rosalie.

But I think, instead, of the day Grant gave his sword to our second son. This was after his wife's death, but long before he came to live with us. As I've said, he had no sons of his own and my husband was the only child of his brother. There were no children of his blood except ours. He came walking slowly up the driveway the afternoon of our son's tenth birthday, bearing the sword in its leather scabbard with the gold tassel attached at the hilt. He didn't have a particularly soldierly bearing, looked more like a slightly seedy, gentle-mannered farmer than a potential admiral. Ross, our son, and three or four of his friends were sitting around a trestle table eating ice cream. Ross had been alerted ahead of time that his great-uncle intended to give him his sword and we had explained that this was a significant gift and he should feel honored. He stood up very straight and looked solemn and said, "Thank you," but it was clear to me he was unimpressed—didn't quite know what use this sword, almost as tall as he was, would be to him. He and his friends were organizing a war with another neighborhood gang for the next day. Mudballs and BB guns would be their weapons of choice. We invited Grant in and he sat and had a drink with us. He was always convivial, happy to join you in a drink, never at a loss for words, often the butt of his own jokes.

So he came to live with us the last year of his life. He had refused treatment for the cancer. "I'm too old to let somebody cut on me," he'd said. "It's out of the question." He knew that he probably had less than a year to live.

The first few months he used to take a long walk every morning through the humming, buzzing, late-spring world, bees swarming around the honeysuckle vines on the back fence, towhees calling, flickers drilling for bugs in the bark of the pecan tree, squirrels chasing each other up and down the trunk. He'd walk slowly, head a little forward, determined to go as far as he could; and then he'd return even more slowly, going to his room by the side door into the wing. He'd stop there sometimes and watch the squirrels. One day he pointed out to me that a wren had built her nest in the potted fern by the side door.

I never joined him on these walks. I didn't have time.

In the afternoon one of his friends or his brother might come to sit with him for a while; at night he and our youngest son sometimes played bridge with my husband and me. Grant was a good bridge player—indifferent, though, whether he won or lost. Or, some nights, he'd go back to his room and watch TV.

Later, as he grew weaker, he walked up and down our front sidewalk every day, too feeble to risk getting far from the house. Then he began to walk at night, up and down the long hall that led from the main part of our house past the two bedrooms where our sons were asleep, to his room and bath at the very back of the wing.

I still slept lightly, a habit most women keep after the years when the least sound from a child's room will wake you, and of course I heard Grant tramping up and down the hall. The first time, I got up and went back to see what was the matter. He was in his bathrobe, his sparse gray hair disheveled, his face drawn. For the first time I noticed how thin he'd gotten.

"What's the matter, Grant?" I asked.

"I'm getting a little exercise," he said. He gave me the same look of ironic concentration I'd seen on his face when he was playing the violin, as if to say: I don't expect you to think I'm good, but I'll give it a try. This time it was: I don't expect you to believe me, but act as if you do.

Or was that what his look said? Might there have been a question in his eyes? An invitation to join him? Or was it deep knowledge of my fears, my self-absorption?

I knew he was in pain. He wasn't walking up and down the hall for exercise. I said to myself that I didn't want to invade his privacy and went back to bed. Next day I called the doctor and told him Grant needed something stronger, morphine or

Dilaudid; and he called in a new prescription. For some weeks Grant continued to walk every night. I would hear him and put my pillow over my head.

It was during this period or a few weeks later that Grant hired Rosalie. She had worked for him and his wife a couple of days a week for several years, and then, after his wife died, had cooked for him. She was a splendid cook and the kind of woman who could take charge of a household—intelligent and aggressive. She could have been an office manager or a clothes buyer in a department store (had a flair for style) or perhaps a lawyer (she knew how to get what she wanted from almost anyone). Unfortunately none of these careers had been open to her. She was an illiterate black woman and the year was 1964.

When Grant had moved in with us, he'd given Rosalie a month's severance and a bonus and recommended her to several friends. She'd had no trouble getting another job. Then, when he began to weaken, could no longer trust himself alone in the bathroom, needed help with dressing, he arranged with the family for whom she worked to share her time. She came every morning for a couple of hours, helped him with his bath, made his bed, and, if he wished, fixed a cold supper and left it for him in the refrigerator.

Sometimes she would stay for a while after he was bathed and dressed and comfortable. She was a talker, loved to visit—and so did he. He may already have been talking to her about dying. Or maybe she began it. She was a devout Christian, offered up a marvelous strong soprano voice to God every week at church, and was president of the choir.

In any case during those morning visits he began to teach her to read, using the Bible as his text. Oh, how deeply Rosalie wanted to learn to read the Bible—more, I think, than wanting the changes that reading might make in her life. It was reading the Bible, I'm sure of it, that she was focused on. She needed it, needed the support of religion, I mean. She was trapped in her life, not just because she couldn't read, but because she had five children and an abusive husband who she couldn't leave as long as he paid the rent and made a contribution to the household expenses.

And Grant was bored, of course.

So he occupied himself teaching her. Some days I'd go back and find them sitting side by side, him in his easy chair, Rosalie with a straight-backed desk chair drawn close to his. Together they leaned over his battered King James Bible, turned the onionskin pages. It must have been easier for her to begin to pick out words because she knew so much of it by heart. He'd move his finger along a line: " 'I sink in deep mire where there is no standing I-am-come-into-deep-waters-where-the floods-overflow-me.' " Or: " 'Bless the Lord, oh my soul; and all that is within me, bless his holy name.' " She could read that easily or pretend to, moving her finger from word to word once he started her with "Bless." "Look at every word," he'd say, and they'd do it again. " 'B-b-bless—Bless the Lord-oh-my-soul.' "

One day, putting away clothes in my son's room I heard him laughing and then Rosalie, raising her voice, "Now you know that ain't it, Mr. Grant." I stopped to listen.

"But there it is," he said, "and you ought to like it. 'I am black but comely, O ye daughters of Jerusalem,' and 'I am the rose of Sharon, the lily of the valleys.' And how about this: 'Stay me with flagons. Comfort me with apples: For I am sick of love.' That's the bride talking."

"Oh, Mr. Grant," she said, "that's talking about Jesus and the church. The church is the bride of Jesus. That's not about what you're talking about."

He laughed again. "Anyhow," he said. "It's poetry. It's beautiful poetry."

"It's the Word of God," Rosalie said.

I tiptoed away.

I don't want to wander here. I want to stick with the long, agonizing last months of Grant's illness. Still, I have to tell you before I go on how beautiful Rosalie was. It would be commonplace to compare her profile to Nefertiti's and, remembering her—the full lips, the heavy-lidded eyes, and slightly flattened nose—I think she's more like those elegant attendant ladies on the wall of one of the Rameses' tombs. But there was nothing stiff or narrow or Egyptian about her body. You admired her face when she walked in, and then, when she swung a strong, round hip against the kitchen door to bump it shut, you'd begin to wish your waist was as supple, your legs as shapely, your breasts as softly ample as hers. What a pleasure to have such a person to look at every day.

But one day she would come to work sullen, turning her face away, an eyelid darkened, not with kohl but with the greenish purple stain of a bruise, her sensuous lips cut where her husband's fist had crushed them against her teeth. She'd threaten to leave him or to swear out a restraining order against him and for a while everything would be quiet.

As the weeks passed, it became more and more difficult for me to walk down the long back hall in our house, to raise my hand and knock on Grant's door, to hear his breathy voice saying, "Come in," to listen to his labored breathing, look into his gaunt face.

There he was, a huge presence in our house, and he was family; but I didn't want to see him or to think about him. Every day, morning and afternoon, I forced myself to go back to his room and stay for at least ten minutes. I felt the weight of my watch on my wrist and willed myself not to look at it, but I knew to the minute when I could leave.

During this period several of his friends abandoned him. At first their visits would be less frequent—once a week, once every two weeks. Then they stopped coming altogether. If I saw one of them in the grocery store or in the post office picking up mail, he'd inquire for Grant and say, "I've been out of town." Or, "He's so weak, I don't want to disturb him. But give him our love."

"Yes," I'd say. "All right. I will."

His brother, my father-in-law, still, and to the end, came every day.

There can be only one reason why I hated so deeply the ordeal of going back to visit with this lovely old man. He was dying. His dying was a terrible disgrace, an embarrassment not to be endured. That's the story I could not tell. I abandoned him too.

In the middle of it, I didn't know I was abandoning him, did I? I was busy. I had three children. I had my own work to do, my obligations. And I needed to go fishing, to see my parents, to go out with my friends, to lie beside my husband in our warm bed.

The town where we lived was on a cutoff bend of the Mississippi River, a man-made lake, long and still on windless summer days between its confining levees, fringed with willows and cypress and cottonwood trees, jumping with bream and bass and crappie and catfish. When they were younger, the children and I had picnicked and fished and skied and swum its waters. Now that the eldest was in college and the two younger in high school, they were not interested in picnics with Mama, but I still needed, as I always had, to be out on the water, to hear waves lapping the green sides of my fishing boat, to lie on the sandbar with my friends and watch the sun go down behind the cottonwood trees. I was busy, caught up in my life.

It sometimes seemed to me in those days, as I told a friend when we were out on the lake together, as if our house were panting, the walls swelling and shrinking—as if it were breathing sex. I'd hear the boys come in on weekend nights, would pretend not to hear the soft voices of the girls they sometimes brought with them. In the kitchen, in the morning, I would hear Rosalie teasing them about their girlfriends, asking about this one or that one. And at night, when they came in from a party, from skinny-dipping off the sandbar, from lying on the levee with the radio on . . . What can I say to tell you how alive that household was?

One night, Ross came in at two or three in the morning, disheveled and half-buttoned, lipstick smeared across his cheek, and found Grant sitting on the floor in the hall, conscious, but unable to get up. Half-asleep, I heard them talking to each other and tiptoed out to see what was the matter. Ross was buttoning his shirt. "Well . . . ," he was saying.

And Grant was laughing. "I was waiting for you," he said. "I knew you'd get here eventually. But look at you!" And then, "Don't try to pick me up. Don't pull on me. I might come apart."

I stood appalled. Ross should not have to face this.

But he stooped without a word—strong as a stevedore he was in those days—and slipped one arm under Grant's shoulders, the other under his knees, lifted him, as it appeared, without effort, and carried him back to his room. I heard them laughing together, waited a minute, then pretended I had just gotten up, walked back to Grant's room, stuck my head in, and asked if I could help.

"No, no," Grant said. "We're okay."

It was shortly after this that he said he needed someone with him at night and from then on he had round-the-clock sitters, Rosalie in the morning and two other women who came in from three until eleven and eleven until seven.

One morning during those last weeks, not so long before he lapsed into a coma, just as I raised my hand to knock at his door, I heard him say to Rosalie in a measured, thoughtful way, "Yes. Yes." A pause, and then, "I do. I do. I don't try to know what it'll be like, but I know I'll see Kathleen."

Rosalie said, "Amen."

"But what will *see* mean?" he said. "I don't know. Somehow she and I will be . . ." Again a thoughtful pause. ". . . She will be there with me."

"Yes, Lord," Rosalie said. "Amen, Mr. Grant."

He did not speak of those things with me.

There is one more thing about Rosalie and Grant. I had thought I could leave it out, but I find that I can't. It happened after he was entirely bedridden, after everything had to be done for him.

I realize now it's usually the case that one hires men to take care of male patients, but curiously enough I didn't think about that at the time and apparently neither did Grant. We'd started with Rosalie and it seemed natural to keep on with her, and then to find two other women, one a cousin of hers who came with a string of recommendations, the other a trained LPN.

In any case, I came into the kitchen one morning from the car, bringing bags of groceries and found Rosalie standing, her back to me, at the sink.

"Morning, Rosalie," I said and turned to go out for another load.

"I got to leave," she said. "I can't nurse him anymore."

"What?" I stood in the doorway staring at her. "What's the matter?"

"He wants me to touch him," she said.

"Rosalie!"

"He wants me to touch him."

Grant was already at the stage where he spent much of the day dozing, drifting in and out of sleep. Last time the doctor had come to see him, I'd gone back to his room and stood by to make sure we were doing everything we should. The doctor had touched his arm, raised it and lowered it, helped him sit up, pressed the soles of his feet, tapped his knees. Afterwards, as we walked to the car, he'd said, "It's in his brain now. I don't think it will be long. I'm increasing the morphine. We don't want him to suffer."

"He wants me to touch him," Rosalie said. "I can't see after him anymore."

"Oh, Rosalie, Rosalie."

She was weeping. I put my arms around her, patted her shoulder distractedly. "It's in his brain," I said. "The cancer. And the pain medicine. He doesn't know what he's saying."

"I'm scared of him," she said. "I don't want no part of that."

"Rosalie, he's so weak, he couldn't possibly hurt you," I said.

"He says, 'Come on, help me. Let's see if I can get it up.' And then he laughed. I got to go," she said.

But of course she didn't. She stayed to the end.

And I was going to leave out the bees too. The bees seemed, to begin with, no more than a bizarre detail of what happened the night Grant died.

It was towards four o'clock in the morning when the night nurse came to our bedroom door and roused my husband and me. "Mr. Grant has passed," she said.

We got up, put on bathrobes, tiptoed, so as not to wake the boys, down the long hall to his room. He had been unconscious for many days. His body, under the sheet and light blanket, was barely an outline, thin to emaciation, his cheeks sunken. But he seemed now no less alive than when I'd looked in on him the day before. He was still himself, the lines that his life had made vivid in his flesh, his dignity untouched. I even seemed to see that ironic half-smile on his face: *Well, I'll give it a try then.*

I laid my hand on his chest, feeling for a heartbeat, thinking the sitter must be mistaken, put my fingers on his lips to catch a breath. But Grant was dead—as she knew quite well. She had already cleaned him up after the sphincter relaxed; had changed his pajamas before she called us; had opened the curtains and the windows to air out the room and turned on all the lights in the hall. She had even opened the outside door to the mild spring night. She knew her job.

Now she said that she had done all she needed to do and, if we were agreeable, she would go on home.

"All right," my husband said. "Certainly." And he walked with her to the door, thanking her, saying he'd call her in the morning, put her check in the mail, let her know about funeral arrangements. She'd told us that she was a nurse who always attended her patients' funerals. "I show respect," she'd said.

It was at the door, when she couldn't go out, that we saw the bees.

The bees, part of the colony that lived in a high hollow of the pecan tree in the side yard, were swarming. How could such a thing be? Swarming in the middle of the night? But there they were, a heaving mass of them clustered on the screen door, sheets of them clinging to the window screens in the long hall. My husband saw the nurse out through the front door and came back. What should we do?

"If we turn off the lights," he said, "maybe they'll decide to move. They can't start a new hive on a screen door."

So we turned them off, groped our way to our bedroom, sat down, stared at each other. What do you do at four o'clock in the morning with your dead uncle cooling toward rigor in his bed and a swarm of bees on the door?

After a while my husband said, "I should call Daddy."

"It's too early," I said. "Let's wait until six o'clock. He's usually up by six."

"The doctor," he said. "The death certificate. We forgot. And maybe we should call the funeral home to come and get him. I mean, before the boys wake up."

"Yes," I said. "I think we should."

"But what about the bees? How will they get him out the door?"

We went back to check. The bees were still there.

And then we found ourselves outside with burning spills of

newspaper flaring in the darkness. We would smoke them into docility and then brush them away so the undertaker could come in with his gurney. But the bees clung and buzzed and crawled over each other and stayed.

We called the doctor and then the funeral home. Of course they managed well enough, rolling the gurney out the long way, down the hall, across the living room, negotiating the sharp turn into the entrance hall, and out the front door.

He was gone.

By then it was almost six and we called my husband's father. The sun was up. The wren was calling from the fern by Grant's door where she'd made her nest. While we were in the kitchen making coffee, talking about arrangements, about who we needed to call, who would be pallbearers, the bees must have decided to leave. They were gone when we went back to the wing to wake the boys.

It was Rosalie who told us why they'd swarmed.

"That fool should've known," she said, talking about the night nurse. "Any fool ought to know. You got to tell the bees immediately when somebody dies." But then she thought better of what she'd said. "Maybe she didn't know there were bees up in that tree," she said. "I saw them, but there wasn't any reason for her to have noticed. She don't come on 'til eleven. How she's going to see bees going in and out in the middle of the night?"

"But what do you mean, Rosalie?" I said. "Why do you have to tell the bees when somebody dies?"

"I forget y'all are not from the country," she said. "In the country they say you got to tell the bees or they'll swarm, they'll leave the hive. I don't s'pose it makes no difference whether it's a hive or a tree. You got to go out right away and say, 'The master is dead,' and then, maybe, something like, 'I'm the new master,' so they'll know somebody is in charge or . . . I don't know."

I sat down at the kitchen table and put my head in my hands and she sat down across from me. We looked at each other and wept.

About Rosalie. Soon after Grant's death she began to go to night school, leaving her fifteen-year-old to look after the younger kids. She got her high school equivalency diploma; and then she got a much better job and she left her wicked husband for a while, although I've heard that every now and then she went back to him. At least she was freer, able to leave him if she liked.

And, as it turns out, the will, Rosalie, the bees, all those tales, are a part of the story I didn't tell when Grant died. Now, twenty-odd years later, I can tell that story. Death has become, so to speak, family.

Sometimes, in the morning, when the bees are just beginning to stir (I wake early these days, as old people so often do), I fill my coffee cup and stand listening in the kitchen. The boys are long gone now on their separate ways; the house is still, no longer breathing and swelling with their energy. I take my cup then and go out into the yard and listen to the raucous cries of the jays, the flicker's jackhammer drill, the *tchk tchk* of the squirrels chasing each other through the high branches of the pecan tree. The wind lifts the leaves and there at a fork I see the dark hole where years ago a limb was torn away in a storm and where now the bees still make their home. They've filled the hole with comb, and comb hangs down against the tree trunk. Singly, the bees drift out, circle, drop downward, and begin to draw nectar from the daffodils, to pollinate the clover on the ditchbank, to tumble like drunken bawds in the deep, intoxicating magnolia cups. I lay my hand against the bark and tell the bees that I, too, will die. I admonish them not to swarm, not to leave us, but to stay in their hollow in the pecan tree, to keep making for us all their golden, fragrant, dark, sweet honey.

David Wiegand

BUFFALO SAFETY

A man walks into the gallery on a sunny afternoon carrying a fistful of golf clubs. I'm aware that there's been some kind of traffic thing going on outside for the last few minutes, but I haven't gone to the window to check it out—happens all the time around here. The softening silence of the gallery is protective that way, I guess. Anyway, the guy walks in with these golf clubs, maybe four of them, looking like some kind of whacked-out classical god with thunderbolts when he steps out of the elevator.

It's around four-thirty or so, maybe later—you lose a sense of time keeping watch over an art gallery; Keats notwithstanding, this stuff isn't eternally on the move. Anyway, I'm paying only scant attention because in this part of town, we get all kinds. Some you keep an eye on, to be sure, but the guy seems harmless enough, and I've seen him around the streets.

The gallery is located in downtown San Francisco, the last resort of the rich and the homeless alike, the edge of all kinds of worlds. No, that's too poetic. It's just San Francisco. I suppose a lot of people have this sort of other-world, romantic idea of San Francisco, but after you live here for a while, you realize it's just another city. Maybe we do have more than our share of crazies, people who haven't come down from that last great acid trip of '68, or drifters figuring it's warmer here and you don't have to spend half your life looking for a heating grate. I don't know. There was a time I probably ascribed more meaning to the place than there is, but that was a long time ago. Maybe the only thing left to say about San Francisco is that it's a good place to get used to most things. Some say it's tolerance. I think it's probably closer to indifference. Or maybe that's the same thing but not worth thinking further about.

The place I work is called the Gallery of Western Realism. Yes, we get our fair share of tourists wandering in looking for Remington statues, but that's not what we mean by western. It's contemporary realism that celebrates the culture of the western U.S., but we stop short of bronzed horseback riders. Over the years, I've made a habit of tracing trends from one group show to the next, and I've found that disaster seems to play a leading role. Lots of paintings of the Golden Gate snapped in the middle or a high-arched bridge on U.S. 1 ending in midair, freeways coiled like DNA and men kissing against a backdrop of crashing trains. A sense of anticipated, if not invited, disaster. I don't know many people who sit around out here worrying about the Big One, but that's the general impression, I guess. Mostly, we sell stuff to people from the East, and I figure it's because it probably makes them feel comfortable thinking they live in a safer place.

So, anyway, I'm behind the desk, lost in mindless thought trying not to think about Nick and, of course, thinking about nothing else, and the elevator door opens, and this guy walks into the room with the golf clubs in one hand, and he's got a shoulder bag on the other side, sort of a Navajo tapestry thing with ratty fringe, overflowing with papers and leaflets and God knows what. The only reason I recognize him as one of the regulars among the army of homeless who work this part of the city is that his thing when you pass by is to ask for "home for the changeless." The first time I heard that, I actually dug down and handed him a buck.

I'd say he's around thirty or thirty-five, maybe younger, kind of wild, sticky-looking hair, wire-rims on the point of his nose, but they're pretty bent up, so they slice across his face on an angle. He's wearing the same thing he always wears: baggy red-plaid pants and an aquamarine bowling shirt with the name "Sal" stitched in white over the pocket.

The elevator door closes behind him, and he stands there a minute and then launches himself into the gallery, marches right past the desk without even looking at me, and keeps on going until he reaches the other end of the room. He stands there a second or two, then pivots like he's on guard duty or whatever, and strides back to the elevator.

I'm watching closely now and for once really not thinking about Nick, because even though this banana seems harmless enough, he's got those golf clubs and might all of a sudden start slashing away at the paintings with his four-iron, or whatever. But he just pushes the down button and stands there waiting, and all the time I'm watching but trying to be a little careful about it, too—subtle, I mean—because you never know what's going to set them off. I hear the elevator make its usual slow, groaning ascent, and then, just as the door slides open, Changeless Sal picks up one of our brochures from the Lucite holder on the wall, looks at it a minute, and then turns to me and says, without even a trace of a smile, "So, I guess realism is the theme of the day. Right?"

At first, I want to chuckle, like it's a joke or something some rich airhead might say at an opening to be clever, but then I figure we're not chatting up Robert Hughes here, you know? So I just smile and say, very politely, "That's right. Realism is the theme of the day."

And he nods, real serious, like he just learned something important, something momentous, and scrunches up his face like he's thinking very carefully about what I've said. And he gets into the elevator, and the door closes, and that's it.

I sit there for a minute or two, wanting to laugh at first, but I don't because I almost expect the doors to open again and Changeless Sal to reappear for an update on realism. But he doesn't come back, and after a while it's almost like he was never there, like the whole scene was just something I imagined or dreamed.

As usual on a slow afternoon, the gallery seems more empty now than before. You get used to the solitude, then people come in and you have to interact, smile, answer questions, try not to look as though you're listening to their whispered comments—and it's a blip on the screen. So when they go, you feel the emptiness more acutely for a minute or two until you readjust to the silence.

I can still hear the traffic on the street, horns honking more frequently because rush hour is starting. But the sounds are soft, muffled, like they're coming from far away. I look around at the triangles of light descending from the ceiling over the paintings, forming a row of almost-touching semicircles on the floor along each wall. Now I'm thinking of Nick again, and it's all mixed up with Changeless Sal and the golf clubs, and for a second or two, nothing makes any sense. It's as if the order of things, the stuff you take for granted, has just gone haywire. I wish there were other people here right now, or that at least the phone would ring. I glance toward the elevator door, as if I can make it open just by looking at it. I almost expect the figures in the paintings to start whispering the way they would in some old *Twilight Zone* episode, telling me everything's going to be okay again, that things will all float back down to where they belong.

I am thirty-one and have worked at the gallery for two years. Before that, I lived in Seattle and then in Portland. Sometimes I figure I'm working my way down the coast, but until recently, I've felt more settled in San Francisco than anywhere else. Now, I don't know. Nothing feels settled at all.

I am attractive enough, I guess—dark-haired, black-eyed by virtue of my father's Armenian-born grandparents, and I work out regularly at a gym in Hayes Gulch, which is on my way home. My life is very patterned, but I like order to things. I broke up with a boyfriend I'd been living with for three months in Portland because he never bothered to close the doors to the kitchen cabinets. No joke. Well, it did start out as a joke between us, and he'd sometimes leave them open on purpose, just to get to me, and it did. Of course, there was a lot more to why things didn't work out, but the open cabinet doors became a symbol of everything else that was wrong. On the day he moved out, I came home to find every cabinet door in the kitchen wide open. I remember thinking there was something obscene-looking about all those gaping cabinets.

Now, I admit if you're looking for order to your life, San Francisco wouldn't be the first place to come to mind. This is a city that thrives on chaos; because people have come here to get away from so many things, there's this kind of universal empowerment against getting locked into anything again. But what can I say? I moved here with Nick, and now he's not here, but I am, and I do the best I can to keep things together. We met in Portland, after the kitchen-cabinet boy moved out, and I needed a roommate, put an ad in the local gay paper, and he answered it. Simple. To the point. We were roommates—I almost said "only" roommates, but of course there was always more to the story.

Maybe I was always in love with Nick because being in love with Nick meant I didn't have to be in love with anyone else. I never told him, but came close enough that he probably knew. If he did, he was at least kind enough not to acknowledge it, I guess. I don't know.

Anyway, Nick was the kind of guy everybody falls in love with. Yes, part of that had to do with his looks. Greek on his father's side, Czech on his mother's, he had dark blond hair that seemed somehow black and gold at the same time, olive skin, and pale green eyes. Everything made him smile, it seemed, and whenever he smiled, you did, too. He wasn't tall, but he was one of those guys who seem taller than they are, who seem to occupy more space. A presence, I guess you'd say. I remember every feature of his face, of course, but mostly the strange delicacy of his hands, delicacy that somehow always surprised you. More than once, I watched someone talking to him, and they'd be held for a minute or two by the smile, but then, invariably, they'd see the hands. Perfect hands, like hands Rodin once carved and somehow made more alive in marble than they ever could have been in life.

Okay. More now. I'm afraid to get involved with other men unless I really know them for a while. No, that isn't true, although it's what I've told myself from time to time as an excuse. It would be easy enough to say that in recent years I have learned to be very cautious about dating, and I'm sure that would make perfect sense, given what's going on out there, what we all know—our common Fear of the Great Known in the nineties. But still, it would be misleading if I said that: It wouldn't be the whole truth or even a very significant part of it. Death isn't what I'm afraid of. It's something else, something I always thought I was searching for, but I'm not sure that's true anymore.

I have said and thought and almost convinced myself in the past that the goal here is to surrender the heart, because love is all that counts and all that really lasts. How many times did I say that to Nick, aching for him to agree but secretly relieved, I suppose, when he changed the subject? I thought I never wanted to be one of his flings, one of his one-night stands, and the fact is that I never was.

I've made love, yes, and surrendered myself to another person, and of course everyone practices safe sex, but lately, I can't help wondering if there's another kind of safety going on, a kind that isn't safety at all but something that keeps us too safe. If so, Nick didn't believe in it. Nick took square aim at life without the slightest hesitation or doubt, and if he fucked up, certainly there were never apologies or regrets. I don't mean to imply that he was a callous person, just that he didn't believe the point of it all was to think too much about anything in advance or pick over what had already moved into the past tense, wondering if he did the right thing or if he could have made another choice. Of course, he practiced safe sex, too, but that's not what I'm talking about: What I'm saying is that it never occurred to him to play it safe with life. If you didn't really know him, you might say that Nick was reckless, or that he used sex as an excuse for not falling in love and somehow missed out on something, but I don't think I could agree with that. I think he was always in love. You can fill in the object of that sentence yourself.

I would ask, "Are you dating anyone special these days?" And he'd laugh and invariably answer, "Baby, I'm always dating, and they're always special."

We'd say that all the time to each other, like a private knock-knock joke. And I'd laugh, of course, but there was often enough truth in Nick's answer to cause a secret pain to snake through my stomach. He'd have relationships of a sort that would last several weeks or even a couple of months, and he'd be gone from the apartment a lot more then. After a while, I stopped feeling like I'd been kicked in the gut, praying that they would end soon and not turn into something permanent that might crowd me out of Nick's life. Maybe if there had been more time, that would have happened eventually. Hard to say.

Anyway, in between, the briefer flings came and went, and I didn't mind them as much, believe it or not, because I never figured those men had much interest in the part of Nick I wanted, the part I was always sure would one day be mine, if I could just get through, if I could just wait it out until Nick finally understood that temporary intimacy with visiting strangers was nothing compared to the kind that came with trust and abiding loyalty. I really believed that then.

Sometimes we'd be out on the street when he'd catch sight of a former trick walking toward him, and it would make me feel oddly secure, somehow, almost smug, the way they'd look at each other at a distance, maybe trying to place the face atop a clothed body. And then they'd get close enough to greet each other, maybe still not sure of the "where" or "when" but willing enough to concede the "what." They'd talk a minute or two about nothing at all, and I'd be introduced but then left to stand there to study the other guy. And I'd be thinking the two of them sounded like a couple of salesmen who met casually at a business convention in another city. Nick always called these encounters "the street dance of the one-night stands."

But of course I would be the one walking away with Nick. The other might even take me as Nick's lover. They'd be wrong, of course, but it didn't matter, because I'd tell myself I had something none of them ever could have, something that would last beyond the next morning.

I don't mean to imply that I didn't have flings of my own, but sometimes I have to admit I'd get interested in someone else only as a defense against waiting for Nick, or maybe to gauge his reaction when I told him about the really hot guy I'd met at Badlands the night before. I would have given anything then to have seen even the slightest flicker of jealousy or regret in his face, but he'd just laugh and clap me on the back, thrust his fist into the air, and shout, "He scores!" like a hockey announcer.

Even before I or anyone else knew about Nick, I would read the paper every day and get choked up over death notices of total strangers. Yes, I would see that some had achieved certain things in their abbreviated lives, others showed promise of one kind or another, and it would hit me particularly hard if they were young. I should be ashamed to admit that, because death is sad at any age, but it's human nature, I guess, to feel it's particularly cruel when it comes too early. Well, we should be used to that by now, especially in this city, but I always figured it kept me human, so I'd put myself through the daily exercise.

I would study the bare facts in the obits and try to use them to flesh out a real life, kind of like those paint-by-numbers kits you'd get as a kid. I'd try to imagine that certain awkwardness growing up, the feeling of not fitting in somehow, then the emergence and realization, followed by a kind of explosive defiance and energy. If the obit listed a lover among the survivors, I'd think kindly about the dead man's family for accepting their son or brother, at least in part, for who he was. It doesn't always happen that way. I've heard so many stories of surviving lovers who've been cut off and kept away from the grieving process, as if it was all their fault somehow.

Now I could tell you that I went through this daily ritual in order to grieve for the injustice of it all, for life cut off at the stem, but that would only be part of it. Sure, I'd feel sad about the obvious irony of love being the eventual cause of death, but then in my mind, I would see them couple, open to each other, these lives I had created out of the agate type on newsprint. All shame and doubt would be cast aside, all hesitation, and there was no time then, no past or future, just the bellowing, split-second now of it, and of two bodies and lives, slamming into another, leaping dancers crossing in midair, forming a connecting arc that could never be duplicated in just the same way and therefore could never be broken again, either.

Imagining those moments of crossing, it wasn't the possibility or even the certainty of death that broke my heart, but the understanding that even though at least one of them was dead now, they had been more alive than I had ever been or maybe ever could be. I envied the dead for having lived, but my safe heart slept on while I kept telling myself I was waiting for Nick.

Nick told me he was sick on a September afternoon in Golden Gate Park while we stood by a wire fence, watching sleepy-eyed buffaloes munching grass and lifting their tails to piss from time to time. I don't know why he picked that time or place. Knowing Nick, he probably didn't give it much thought.

Maybe I shouldn't have been surprised at the news, but of course you always are. I felt my body give way and my forehead press into the fence, my eyes pinch shut against the damned unretractable fact of it. I almost wished the fence wire would cut into the skin of my forehead, as if real physical pain could somehow block out the silent scream I felt in my chest.

I turned to hold him, but I could feel his body tense up, so I stepped back. And I remember taking a very deep breath and then trying to say some hopeful things, but they all sounded lame. I was trying hard to be what I thought Nick wanted me to be, but then I lost it, and it was Nick's turn to hold me and tell me it was okay, that it was just the luck of the draw or some such. I suppose, for him, it was okay, in a way, because he'd never been afraid of living, so why should he be unduly afraid of dying?

We sat down on the bench facing the buffalo pen and talked or didn't. In time, we even found a few funny, macabre things to say. And then there were these long silences with words swirling in my mind, but they wouldn't settle down into sentences the way I wanted them to. At some point, I guess I must have assured him I'd stick by him, because I remember him saying, "I know." Finally, it was getting dark and too cold to stay there anymore, so we got up and started back to the car.

I remember how Nick laughed a little as we set out and said something about how he always used to think as a kid that all the buffaloes had been killed off. It was something he believed growing up in the East, that they were almost extinct except for a very few that he'd seen once in the zoo in Buffalo, New York. Of course, he'd learned otherwise somewhere down the line, but still he said he'd been surprised when he first moved to San Francisco to find a small herd of them calmly grazing and pissing in Golden Gate Park.

"Reports of their demise were greatly exaggerated," I remember him saying in a phony Mark Twain Southern accent. I think he was trying to break the tension—Nick was good at that. I probably laughed out of habit, but I don't remember.

Nick died last month. You wouldn't say it was a peaceful or noble death if you had been there and didn't know him. And yet, because of the way he lived his life, I guess it was both of those things for those of us who loved him. No, he did not go gently, even when there was so little of him left to keep fighting. Pictures of every hour and minute are burned into my memory, and I don't think they'll ever fade. I thought I would be haunted by them above all, but if you've ever lost someone from your life, you know that something much worse takes over, a hole in the middle of you deeper and darker than anything you could have imagined. There are even times when you'd give anything just to relive that last second together, no matter how awful it was, because even the worst moment is better than knowing there will never be any others.

I spent as much time with him as I could, and finally near the end, they just gave me a leave from the gallery because I wasn't doing much good there anyway. I'd take care of the medical stuff, attach the new IV bags when it was time, make sure the refrigerator was well stocked with syringes, change the bedding several times a day. It helped to have visitors, if only because there'd be someone else to share waiting for him to wake up for a while. And Nick knew everybody in town, so thank God there were a lot of visitors. At last, I wasn't jealous of sharing my time with him.

If I had to be out of the apartment for any period of time, Nick would write notes for me and leave them scattered among the pill bottles next to the bed—sometimes just reminders of things that needed doing, people who had to be contacted, silly things he'd seen on a talk show that afternoon. Other times, he'd just write down things he was thinking, so when I came home later, and he'd be asleep, it was almost like we were having a conversation.

The other thing he had, on the table next to the bed, was this stupid poetry box someone had given him a long time ago. It's a long wooden box with eight cubes in it and a separate word in different typefaces on each side of the cube, so you can make up sentences depending on how you arrange the cubes. Sometimes, Nick would leave me a message, usually suggestive, before he went to sleep at night, so I'd find it when I came in later to check on him. At other times, visitors would play with it while they sat there waiting for Nick to wake up.

I didn't pay attention to it over the final weeks, but then, when it was over, and we were cleaning things up, I noticed it: "GOD—*%#,?—*please*—do—ev erything—to—TRUST—*love.*" Like I said, other people used to play with the poetry box when they came to visit, so I don't even know for sure that it was Nick's arrangement, but obviously I like to think it was.

I wish I could say now that I learned what Nick tried to teach me by the example of his life. I wish I could say I so envied him for having truly lived that I have finally broken free of this half-life safety, that I have finally stopped waiting, or that I think I can at least try to break free as time goes on.

Mostly, since Nick died, I've tried to get through from one day to the next. I don't read the paper every morning anymore and cry over strangers, so maybe that's a good thing. I have a real loss to try to make sense of, I guess. I go to the gallery, I work out, I see people, but I'm still waiting—at least for the time when I'm not always thinking about Nick.

Sometimes I do think about moving, to another apartment at least, another job, another city, but it's too soon to make those kinds of decisions. I guess I'd think about the job thing first, because the real problem with the one I have now is that I have too much time to think about things. It's not as though I spend all day smothering in a cloud of grief. Actually, I sometimes feel very pissed off at Nick, because wishing he'd never come into my life in the first place is easier than wishing he'd never left it.

Is that bad? Maybe, but it's how I feel.

Anyway, at the end of the day, I do the close-up routine at the gallery—answering machine set, security system activated, lights dimmed on my way out.

I did go back to the park a couple of weeks ago, just that one time, maybe in an attempt to focus or something. I stood for a few minutes and watched the buffaloes, still there. Maybe I thought I'd find some comfort in knowing they aren't extinct after all, that life goes on, or that I would look at the high fence that keeps the buffaloes safe and remember Nick and the feel of the wire pressing into my forehead that day. I sat for a while on the bench where we'd sat, wondering things like how long a fingerprint lasts on painted wood, but I didn't focus anything or feel anything I haven't felt every minute since Nick died. And the fact is that right now, at least, I don't give a shit that life goes on and the buffaloes are still safe in their pen.

There's still a trace of daylight when I leave the gallery and start walking toward the subway. I know I should go to the gym, but there's time for that later. There are so many people on the sidewalks, it's hard to move, but I'm in no hurry. I remember one other time, leaving the gallery with Nick at the end of the day, not too long after we'd moved here, how he'd laughed and said, "Imagine if all these people were insects with silk threads coming out of their butts. How long do you think it would take to sew up the whole city like a cocoon?" It was just some silly, throwaway thing he said, but I often seem to remember it when I leave the gallery at night and the side-walks are crowded. When you lose someone from your life, you want to remember some big important thing they said, but sometimes all you come up with are throwaway lines.

What I am also thinking about now, walking along, is the banana with the golf clubs, wondering if I'll run into him at his usual spot on the corner. Good old Changeless Sal. I look, but he isn't there, and I find myself wondering where he's gone, how he lives when he's not asking for "home for the change-less." And the more I think about him and how he looked when I assured him that realism was the theme of the day, I can't help feeling a little envious. It's not like how I used to feel about Nick's life or even the lives I used to make up to go along with the obit data in the morning paper. But still, there's this odd connection in my head somehow. Maybe it's hard to see the point, but at this moment, at least, I think about the crazy guy and how his head is all mixed up, how he lives on some separate plane from the rest of us where nothing we probably think of as "normal" ever registers or is acknowl-edged. And one day he comes into an art gallery with his golf clubs, asks a simple question, gets an answer, and leaves.

Bingo. His day is made. And when he's outside again, the world might still seem pretty mixed up to him, but maybe not entirely. It may make no sense to anyone else, but at least that poor son of a bitch has been given one small answer, one tiny truth, and no matter how crazy it gets for him later on, maybe he can hold on to that just for a while.

I'd give anything for that.

Becky Hagenston

TIL DEATH US DO PART

1

When Joyce was seven, the Reverend Sewickley performed the second of her mother's four wedding ceremonies, to the first of three stepfathers. Joyce was disappointed to realize that her mother's new husband would be Fat Henry; she'd thought that the Reverend would marry her mother, that he would live with them in their apartment in Baltimore and take her to the zoo. "He's already married, dummy," said Kathy, who was ten and didn't want a stepfather. "Besides, he's about fifty years old." Joyce didn't care. If the Reverend married their mother, he would let her ring the church bell every Sunday.

Their mother made her own dress from a Butterick pattern, and miniature versions for Joyce and Kathy. The fabric was called seashell pink, and with the leftover scraps their mother made herself a wide pink headband. Joyce and Kathy got bows for their ponytails. While Aunt Gretchen played guitar and sang a song she'd written herself, Joyce walked down the aisle, feeling like a princess even though her shoes pinched her. She fluttered pink petals from her basket and waved at her Sunday School teacher, Mrs. Cook.

Joyce thought that getting married was a fine thing to do, as long as you could hold still. She was under strictest instructions not to scratch herself or yawn. It wasn't easy. The Reverend looked over at her once and smiled, and she could almost hear his voice in her head, saying her name in his gentle drawl: "Joy-ous," he called her, and she was.

The reception was in the Ebenezer Church hall, where last month they'd had the big Oyster Fry, like they did every March. White, foldout paper bells were thumbtacked to the ceiling, and pink streamers wound their way around the bookshelves and paintings of Jesus. Doris Sewickley had made cream cheese and olive sandwiches on pink bread, cut into little triangles. The silver punchbowl was filled with Hawaiian Punch.

After the cake, Joyce and Kathy went outside and hunted for toads in the mulchy ditches by the basement windows, which is what they did every Sunday after church while their mother was talking with the Reverend and Doris. They each caught one, and Kathy's left a damp brown smudge in the palm of her white glove when she let it go. Joyce deposited hers in her pocketbook. Later, she would give it cake.

They walked up the weedy hill and through the iron gate to the cemetery. Joyce stomped over to a gray marble gravestone three rows down, bunched up her skirt and threw herself down on her knees in the prickly grass. "Hello, Agnes," she shouted to the ground. Even though Joyce and Kathy didn't know who she was, they felt sorry for Agnes, for having to go through an entire life with that name.

Mrs. Cook said that when you died you went to heaven, where flowers bloomed all the time. Joyce preferred to think of it as a zoo. In her heaven, camels stepped carefully among the roses and pandas nibbled the daffodils. She wasn't clear if they were under the ground or in the clouds, but she liked to believe that heaven was beneath her feet, so that if she stomped hard enough, all the dead people would pause on their elephants and wonder what it was. Her father—who was farther north, under dirt much colder and harder than this—would call out her name, and sad Agnes would start to laugh.

Kathy was sitting on her knees in a way their mother said destroyed ligaments. "I won't call Fat Henry Dad, no matter what," she said. "And I won't move to that stupid house in the middle of nowhere."

Joyce had her ear to the ground. "Shh," she said. "I'm trying to hear the dead people."

2

Joyce and Kathy's mother married George on a Saturday in November. They had moved back to the city, out of Henry's house in the middle of nowhere. Joyce was back at her old school, and they didn't have to drive an hour to get to church anymore. Not that they'd been going much—Christmas and Easter, mainly. Fat Henry said religion was boring.

"I don't go for the religion," said Joyce's mother. "I go for the rest of it." She'd made George promise to go, too. George had a little boy named Andrew, who was just big enough to toddle up the aisle with the ring.

"I bet he swallows it," Kathy said. Joyce giggled. "And they have to get it out of his poop." Kathy frowned. Kathy was fourteen, and suddenly things offended her. Joyce had to be careful now, especially where boys were concerned. The mention of certain boys would send Kathy flying to her room, an unrecognizable whirl of hair and shrieking. Then she would lock the door and get on the phone until their mother threatened to call the fire station to break the door down. Joyce didn't know what to make of it.

In the vestibule before the ceremony, the Reverend Sewickley called Joyce a lovely young lady, and Joyce blushed because she knew it was true. Her mother had splurged on turquoise taffeta gowns and pearl chokers. The dress—scoop-necked—looked better on Kathy, who was beginning to poke out in front, but Joyce felt radiant. Her hair was swept up on her head, and little ringlets bounced beside her pearl earrings.

She was the only flower girl this time. Kathy was a bridesmaid, positioned between Aunt Gretchen and George's sister. George's brother was the best man, and the ushers were Uncle Ted and Cousin Charlie. As she walked down the aisle, behind little Andrew, she imagined that the entire wedding party was giving off a pale light that the people in the congregation could see. The Reverend's smooth head gleamed like something holy. Joyce thought she might die from happiness.

George was a bank teller, and he had already taken them to Ocean City and King's Dominion. And Joyce had always wanted a brother; admittedly, not one like Andrew, who cried when you looked at him, but he would grow up eventually, and perhaps they would be friends.

As she was thinking this, tossing out her white and turquoise flowers, little Andrew stopped short, as if realizing that he should have been afraid a long time ago. Joyce collided with his tiny tuxedoed back.

"Keep moving," she hissed, and gave him a push. Andrew swung around, opened his mouth, and bleated. His lips were shiny with drool.

The ring box fell off its velvet pillow and landed at the puffy feet of Mrs. Cook, who picked it up and tried to push it back into Andrew's fist.

"No!" he screamed, batting her hands away. He plopped down in the aisle, legs straight out in front of him, and howled. George rushed over and swept the boy up by his armpits.

"He's wet himself," he announced, and Andrew screamed louder. Joyce's mother ran from her place at the end of the procession and hefted Andrew into her arms, heedless of his damp bottom.

"I told you he was too young," said Kathy loudly. Their mother swung around and mouthed, "Shut up." The Reverend Sewickley stood with his hands on his thick hips, shaking with laughter. Joyce glared. He was in charge here; he was supposed to settle things down, put everything back in order. He could ask Mrs. Cook to cart Andrew off to the nursery, where he could cry all he wanted. But Andrew stayed. George joggled him in his arms while they said their vows. When they kissed, squishing Andrew between them, the congregation murmured "Awww" and clapped. Joyce squeezed the handle of her empty basket and stared at her shoes. As far as she was concerned, the wedding was ruined.

Kathy was no longer interested in looking for toads or visiting Agnes. She was preoccupied with applying lipgloss and flirting with Robbie Russell, whom she had known since she was six and had, until recently, only addressed as Turd Face. Joyce found it sickening. She went outside and peered in the ditches by the basement windows. It was cold, and she couldn't squat comfortably without ruining her dress. "Here, toad," she said half-heartedly, but no toad came.

The clouds were thick like milk behind the steeple, and the weathervane—a brass rooster—twisted creakily this way, then that, as if it didn't really care if the wind blew or not. There was the faraway smell of burning leaves. A jack-o-lantern, damp and rotten, grinned a mush-toothed grin on the porch steps of the house across the street. Joyce wondered why anyone would want to get married in dreary November—or, for that matter, at all.

3

"This is it, I swear," said the girls' mother. It was the night after Christmas, and the church glowed with white candles and smelled of pine air freshener and wax. The day before, the Sunday School had had a pageant, and there was still hay on the floor by the altar. The girls' mother was standing in the vestibule, under the rope that led to the bell tower. She was wearing a white suit and a white velvet hat, which Joyce was bobby-pinning to her hair. The short veil reached just past her chin.

"Ow, you jabbed me," said her mother, turning around. She pulled the veil back from her face. She and Joyce were almost the same height. "Anyway," she continued, "if this doesn't work out, I'll just stay single. Not that I think it won't work out," she added hurriedly. "I'm sure it will." She cast her eyes down at Reverend Sewickley, who was picking tinsel off the carpet. "You must think I'm pathetic."

"Not at all," said the Reverend. He stood up, looked about vainly for a trashcan, and put the tinsel in the pocket of his robe. "I think your persistence is admirable. You're grasping happiness when you find it." He clutched at the air. "And if we don't go after happiness, what're we here for?"

"Is that what I'm doing?" said the girls' mother. "I should hope so," said the Reverend. "There, you're done," said Joyce, sliding in one last bobby pin. She took a step back.

"You look beautiful."

Joyce was sixteen. She was, to her complete shame, in love with her cousin Charlie, seventeen. She hoped to dance with him at the reception—which was going to be at the Holiday Inn—but not if she had to do the asking.

Her mother touched her veil. "Well, I am happy, some of the time," she said. "I just know that I deserve better than a husband who ignores me or yells at me."

Life with George and Andrew had proven more trying than life with Henry. While Henry would lapse into trances over Cheerios, staring dumbly at a Popular Mechanics flopped under his bowl like a placemat and not speaking for hours at a time, at least he was docile. George had a temper that Little Andrew—as he would forever be called—was fast beginning to inherit. Sometimes they would both throw figurines.

George got a job in Nevada and wanted the girls' mother to go with him. But in the end, he and Andrew went alone, and the girls' mother moved her daughters to an apartment in the suburbs. She met Jerry at a yard sale, pricing end tables.

Joyce's mother had erased all traces of George and Andrew, the same way she had disposed of any paraphernalia that might evoke memories of Fat Henry. She didn't even buy Cheerios anymore. "A person needs to start fresh," she'd said grimly, tossing her wedding album into the trash. Then she bought other people's discarded objects to fill the spaces left by her own.

Moving around so much had made it difficult for Joyce and Kathy to keep friends—particularly boyfriends—and Kathy had once accused their mother of deliberately destroying their own chances for love, out of petty bitterness. "It isn't fair," she said. "Just because you're a failure at relationships, why do you have to make us suffer?"

"Because I can," said their mother. Joyce had stayed out of her mother and Kathy's battles. She preferred to shut herself away in her room with her unique tragedy, which no one could possibly understand or appreciate, and which Joyce herself could not even define. She sat on her bed and smoked, blowing clouds out her open window and watching them vanish into the maple tree above the roof. While Kathy and her mother screamed in the kitchen, Joyce lay on her floor and wished her real father was still alive so that she could go live with him. She used to believe that, had her father lived, he and her mother would still be married. She was no longer so sure.

Her father had died when Joyce was one and Kathy was four. Kathy said she could remember him, or parts of him—a gold watch, brown leather shoes, his voice floating down the hallway, singing "I Feel Pretty." Joyce's mother hadn't thrown away all remnants of her father; there simply weren't any. Except the wedding picture, which showed a tall, geeky boy with snaggle teeth grinning beside a poofy-haired girl in a dress that looked like it was made of icing. Sometimes Joyce doubted that these were actually her parents. She wondered if her mother had found the picture at one of her yard sales.

Now that Kathy was away at college, Joyce and her mother had reached a kind of understanding: Joyce would not smoke in her room and her mother would not make her change high schools for her senior year. She and Jerry were going to get a larger apartment in the same complex, and in a year and a half Joyce would go away to college, to live the kind of life she was meant to be living. To meet some boy besides her cousin she could fall in love with.

When the service was over, the lights came on, and smoke from the white candles hung in the air like a low fog. "I don't suppose anybody has a fan?" the photographer wanted to know. Nobody did. The photographer was a friend of Jerry's. He dabbed his eyes with his hanky. "I'm not crying," he said to Joyce. "Although it was a gorgeous ceremony, and I did feel a little weepy partway through. Did you?"

"Kind of," said Joyce. "But it's not like it's the first time I've seen my mother get married. Are you all right?"

"It's my contact lenses, I'll be fine when the smoke clears. Would you mind pointing me in the general direction of the tree?"

Joyce took the photographer by his bony elbow and escorted him to the tall artificial mountain pine, from which dangled the handiwork of Mrs. Cook's Sunday School class: clothespin shepherds, pipecleaner wise men, popsicle-stick mangers. This was the first year the Reverend had invested in an artificial tree—to the outrage of several elderly members of the congregation, who declared it a "sacrilege." Old Mrs. Ely called it "spitting in the eye of God," but somebody pointed out that she'd said the same thing about television and now she had three. Still, the Reverend was sensitive about it.

"It really looks just as nice as a real one, if not nicer," he was saying now to Cousin Charlie, who was admiring a tinfoil star. "And there's no pine needles to pick up."

"It's less of a fire hazard," Joyce added, depositing the photographer at a nearby pew so he could squeeze out his hanky and change his film. At home, her mother and Jerry had put up a horrifying aluminum tree that Jerry's family had used in the fifties. It had its own spotlight, which rolled rainbow colors across the silver branches. It made Joyce think of something from a cruise ship disco.

"OK, I think I've got everything under control," the photographer announced. "If you all don't mind, I'd like to get a couple shots in front of the tree. You two." He pointed at Joyce and Charlie. "Why don't you just stay right where you are, and if we could only find the bride and groom—"

"Here they are!" cried the Reverend, herding them over. Joyce's mother and Jerry allowed themselves to be arranged in front of the tree, between Joyce and Charlie. The photographer pulled out a piece of mistletoe from his pocket and handed it to Jerry. "Now, Jerry, what I'd like you to do is hold this over your lovely bride's head and steal a kiss. And these two are going to lean in—that's right—lean in and make kissy faces toward the bride and groom!"

"You're kidding," said Charlie. "How hokey," said Joyce. She felt suddenly sick. "Oh, come on," said the photographer. The flash went off, freezing Joyce, Charlie, her mother and Jerry in a photograph that would make Joyce wince every time she saw it, for the rest of her life.

"That was really stupid," Joyce said to Charlie, but he had already wandered off to talk to Kathy's boyfriend, Philip, whom she'd brought home for Christmas break. Philip was tall and gaunt in a way that made Joyce think of Abraham Lincoln. She wasn't envious of Philip himself, but of the way he looked at her sister, and the way when they were watching TV in the den he would rub her knees distractedly, as if he couldn't help it.

Joyce pushed her way past the people milling in the aisles and went outside. There was a limousine parked by the curb. The driver was reading a magazine. Pieces of slate rolled off the church's roof and landed with soft thuds in the old snow. People began pouring out of the church, hugging Joyce, their voices launching puffs of steam into the darkness. Jerry and her mother emerged, laughing and waving, then scrambled into the limousine and were whisked away. Joyce crunched across the church parking lot with her sister and Philip, under the frosty stars.

4

You're the same age I was when I had you," Joyce's mother said to Kathy after her bridal shower. They were cleaning up the wrapping paper in Kathy's living room. Joyce had started off folding it neatly like her mother insisted, but finally gave up and stuffed it all in a Hefty bag.

"I know. You've said that before." "I'm just glad you didn't run off without finishing college, like I did." "You've said that before, too." Joyce had been noticing a certain irritating sentimentality about their mother lately. It was as if, by pointing out the way her daughters' lives differed from her own, she was holding up her failures for their inspection and forgiveness. Assuring herself that she had been a good mother, successfully steering her girls clear of the minefield of her own mistakes.

"I hope you like the book. Joyce, you might want to read it, too." Joyce nodded and carried a tray of empty cups into the kitchen. Her mother had given Kathy a book called *Making Love Last*. Now that she was happily married, she had become preoccupied with searching out the root of her previous unhappiness and bad luck. She read self-help books and went to retreats where everyone cried, hugged, pounded pillows and ate candy for four days. Joyce couldn't talk to her at all anymore; every complaint had some corresponding chapter in a book about people just like herself.

When she came out of the kitchen, her mother was moving aside a Victoria's Secret box so she could sit on the sofa. "You know," she said, sinking into a pile of tissue paper, "it's not so much marrying the right person as being the right person."

"Oh, for Christ's sake!" said Kathy. "No offense, but I'm sick of all this really helpful advice. I know what I'm doing."

"I think you should have married Philip," said Joyce. "You've only known Brian six months."

After two and a half years of Philip, Kathy had accused him of being predictable and average. "If Philip were a color," Kathy had said, "he would be beige. You can only live with beige for so long."

"There are worse things," was all Joyce could think to say. "If you like Philip so much, you marry him," said Kathy now. "I'm crazy, wacko in love. Isn't anybody happy for me?" She stood swaying in the middle of the living room floor, under the hanging light. It occurred to Joyce that there were certain words that could knock her sister over, and she wanted to use them. She wanted to hurt her mother, too, sitting amongst the tissue paper like some ceramic figure held together by glue. She felt the words rising like a tornado from her stomach: You're turning out just like her, casting people off like clothes that are suddenly the wrong color.

Knowing she possessed this power to wound her mother and sister made her feel dizzy, and she was opening her mouth to see what might come out of it when her mother spoke up loudly.

"Of course," she said, rustling on the sofa. "We couldn't be happier."

Jerry gave Kathy away when she married Brian. They got married in a small Methodist church in Pennsylvania, in a town between the Amish farms and Hersheypark. It was May, and the air smelled of pasture when the wind blew from one direction, chocolate when it blew from another. "A land of con-

trasts," the Reverend had sighed appreciatively. "Glorious."
The Reverend was not going to perform the ceremony, but he
and his wife Doris sat holding hands in the third pew, beside
Aunt Gretchen and Uncle Ted. The Reverend had retired, and
he and his wife had moved to the country. The Reverend had
told Joyce and Kathy to call him Dan.

As a child, Joyce hadn't considered this other life of the
Reverend, the life that existed apart from Sundays and her
mother's weddings. And she had always viewed Doris Sewickley with undisguised animosity—she was, after all, the woman
who kept the Reverend from falling in love with and marrying
her mother. "Say hello to Mrs. Sewickley," Joyce's mother
would say. Then, helplessly: "She's shy," as Joyce untwisted
herself from her mother's arm and ran off.

"It's all right," Doris would tell her mother. "I was shy,
too." Joyce had tried to make amends, without ever mention-
ing the reason for her hostility.

Doris had been in and out of the hospital for chemotherapy,
and Joyce made it a point to bring her magazines and catch her
up on the kind of things the Reverend wouldn't think to tell
her—like how old Mrs. Ely had boycotted the new red
hymnals because red was the color of the devil, and how one
of the men fixing the roof had fallen in love with Ellen Wilcox,
the organist, when he'd heard her practicing one Saturday afternoon. She did this partly out of guilt, partly out of genuine
affection. Doris accepted Joyce's sudden kindnesses with the
same calm smile she'd withstood her rude stares.

Two rows in front of Doris and the Reverend—she could
never bring herself to think of him as Dan—Joyce's mother sat
proudly, her gloved hands reminding Joyce of a day long ago,
when she and Kathy had hunted for toads in the mulch.

Kathy's reception was held in an old barn that had been converted into a restaurant.

Waiters and waitresses dressed in black and white drifted
between the tables, refilling champagne glasses and baskets of
warm bread. The deejay, a friend of Brian's, was telling everyone to get up and dance. Joyce's mother kicked off her shoes
and hauled Jerry to the floor, where they twisted until she got
a splinter and they had to sit down.

Joyce was sitting between Brian and Charlie, for whom she still harbored a mild, residual crush. She had never danced with him at the Holiday Inn and so, having revealed nothing, could now chat easily about classes and her plans for the summer. She'd won a scholarship to the University of Connecticut, where she was studying English literature. She had no real plans for the summer, but she told Charlie that she was thinking about going to Spain, to see the running of the bulls. Joyce lied when she drank. She took another gulp of champagne.

"Not that I would run with them, of course," she told him. "I'm not an idiot." "That's so cool, though," said Charlie. "I'd love to do that." "You know," Joyce confided to Charlie's ear. "Kathy says that if Brian was a color, he'd be magenta. That's why she married him!" It had never seemed so ridiculous before. "Personally, I think it's lust," she added, and felt her face flush. She had never said the word "lust" to a young man before.

"Looks like your sister's getting sloshed," Charlie said. Kathy was laughing too loud. "I got rice all over my sleeve!" she shrieked. She held up her arm for Brian to inspect the damage.

"Don't worry," he said. "Who's worried?" Kathy said. "Next time, I'm wearing blue." "Next time?" said Brian. Charlie was leaning in close to Joyce, watching. "Blue." Kathy nodded and took another swig of champagne. She held up her glass. "Yoo-hoo, Mr. Waiter Person!"

Kathy's mother came over and stooped down beside her daughter. "Honey, why don't we cut the cake now? You don't need any more champagne."

"Let them eat cake," Kathy agreed. Her mother helped her to her feet, and Brian strode ahead of them to the cake table.

The deejay cut off the music and tapped his microphone. "Hey, everybody! It's cake time!"

"What's she doing?" Charlie asked. Kathy, instead of following Brian to the cake table, had run laughing past the stunned deejay, out the front doors and into the cornfield behind the restaurant. The guests rose to their feet and shuffled as a mass to the window. Joyce stood next to the Reverend, who was shaking his head in bewilderment. She could see her mother's face, blank and pale as an egg. Jerry was behind her,

holding both of her shoulders as if she might split in half if he
let go. Joyce wondered if there was some bulleted list in one of
her mother's books with instructions on what to do when your
oldest daughter runs away from her wedding. What to do
when—as Joyce watched with a strange thrill—your oldest
daughter trips through a cornfield in the late afternoon sun,
leaving her shoes and veil in the stalks.

Brian sagged against his father's shoulder. The best man ran
outside and, as everyone watched, Kathy threw her arms
around his neck and kissed him on the mouth, hard.

All those tuxes look the same, she said later. How was she
to tell?

5

Joyce watched Adam and his father playing horseshoes with
Jerry and the Reverend, under the gold-washed trees. Adam's
parents had insisted on having the rehearsal dinner at their
house, and there were cubed cheeses, baby quiches, and
shrimp cocktail laid out on picnic tables on their wooden
patio.

Adam hadn't swept Joyce off her feet or made her forget
herself. She would not describe herself as "crazy, wacko in
love." She loved him—not madly, not crazily, but sanely and
contentedly. It didn't matter that certain young men made her
feel woozy, like Cousin Charlie had, or that she sometimes fell
in love in elevators. That, she decided, was a sickness similar to
the flu. It passed soon enough, and then you recovered and
went on with things. It was what got people like Kathy and her
mother into trouble.

Joyce's mother was pleased because Adam came from a
"healthy family environment." His parents had been married
for 34 years, and he'd grown up in this farmhouse on a country
road that was still unpaved, five miles from Nathan Hale's
house. Joyce couldn't remember what Nathan Hale had done,
but she liked that his house was still there, after so many years.
There was something reassuring and permanent about it.

Adam had grown up climbing these same trees, playing

with the horseshoes that were now thudding and clanging across the lawn. In this place, Joyce had the same feeling she sometimes got when she went back to Ebenezer Church—that it could be ten years ago, or sixty, or a hundred. That every moment was present and intact, swirling seamlessly into right now.

Sometimes it seemed to her that she had left pieces of herself under furniture that had never belonged to her, and in schoolyards with children who had never learned her name. It made her sad, as if there were small ghosts that looked like her, wandering lost in places they didn't recognize. She had tried to explain this to Adam once, when he was showing her the remains of a rocket he and his brothers had built in the barn when he was nine.

"I don't have any relics of my childhood to show you," she'd said. "I couldn't take you to any tree houses or point out any tire swings I used to play on. It was like, with every new father, everything just began again. My mother would give a lot of stuff away, so she wouldn't be reminded of whoever it was she had just divorced. And she threw away a lot of photo albums, so I'm not even sure what certain people looked like anymore."

"Well, you've turned out great," Adam had told her. "And maybe if your life hadn't gone that way, you wouldn't be the person you are now."

"Maybe," said Joyce, doubtfully. "Besides, we've got about sixty years ahead of us to collect relics." Joyce was always relieved when he said things like that, even if she herself was not entirely convinced. Now, pulling a cube of cheddar cheese from its red-frilled toothpick, she squinted toward the lawn and imagined her sons and daughters playing on this same grass. It was much easier to picture these people who didn't exist than to imagine the older version of herself who would be right here, watching them.

Joyce could see the absence of Doris in the Reverend's face, in his sudden jowliness and pale cheeks. His smooth head still reflected the stained glass greens and blues of saints and saviors, but his eyes sagged at the corners. It had been easy to

convince the Reverend to come to New London for the wedding. He and Doris had lived just across Long Island Sound in
Providence, he told her, fifty-two years ago. The service was
held in a 19th-century church with dark beams and windows
that flared in the August afternoon light. Adam's uncle was
performing the ceremony, but the Reverend was giving what
he called a Marriage Meditation, between the scripture reading
and the exchange of vows.

"We are here," said the Reverend, "not only to celebrate the
marriage of Joyce and Adam, but also to celebrate our own
vows, our own commitments." His voice caught. He cleared
his throat. "To ourselves, to each other, and to God."

Joyce thought of Kathy in the cornfield. She thought of
Henry, of George and Little Andrew, and of all the vows made
and broken in the search for happiness. She knew that if she
turned around, she would see her mother and Jerry holding
hands in the first pew. If she turned to her left, she would see
Kathy, tall and lovely in lavender. Kathy had decided that—at
least for now—her particular brand of happiness did not include a husband. Next week, she was going to England to
study business at the University of London. Joyce and Adam
would spend two weeks at Cape Cod and then fly out to visit
her.

She thought of the Reverend, on his knees in front of Doris'
grave in the Ebenezer churchyard, four rows away from sorry
Agnes.

And there was a moment, as Joyce waited for the preacher
to say "Do you, Joyce, take Adam," when she believed herself
entirely capable of saying no, she didn't; no, she wouldn't, and
running down the aisle and out the wooden doors, into that
less predictable life. She thought of the pastor's three vixen
daughters, blonde and sulky in the third pew, turning around
to watch her go. And their mother, a beat behind, rising to her
feet; her own mother clapping a hand to her mouth; Adam's
parents rattling their pew with astonishment; the ushers tripping over each other and the bridesmaids dropping their white
and lavender bouquets. Adam wilting in his white tuxedo. By
the time she'd finished rolling out this scenario in her head, the
time had come to say the expected things, and she said them.

Adam pulled back her veil and kissed her, and she knew she had never really had a choice at all.

After the reception, Joyce and Adam put on shorts and sweaters and made their way down to the beach, where the other members of the wedding party were drinking beer and throwing themselves into the Sound. The best man, Adam's brother Todd, was running down the sand toward Kathy, who stood knee-high in the surf, giggling in her underwear. She shrieked as Todd lunged at her. They fell into the water and Joyce could see, flashing between the gray foam, a heel, Todd's denim rear end, and a white knee. Then two dark heads rose out of the water, attached to two sets of shoulders. Kathy and Todd started paddling toward the floating dock, where three of the ushers and two more bridesmaids were huddled together, half-naked, whooping and shivering.

"Come on." Adam tugged at Joyce's sweater. "Let's jump in." "It looks kind of cold," said Joyce. The Reverend was toddling down to the beach in his pale blue swim trunks, black shoes and black socks. "You two should be out there," he said. He had a yellow towel draped over his shoulder; it swooped out across his white belly like a kiddie slide.

"That's what I've been telling her," Adam said, squeezing Joyce's hand. The Reverend shook his head. "You don't know what you're missing." He shuffled on down the sand. Moving faster, he kicked off his shoes, threw down his towel and, gaining momentum, flicked off his socks in a few quick hops. He threw himself face-first into the water and splashed out to the dock, where the young people were now jumping up and down and clapping. Todd caught hold of the Reverend's wrist and hauled him aboard.

"Amazing," said Adam. "He's seventy-three," said Joyce proudly, feeling almost as if she had created these happy human beings gamboling in the waves, the way she'd made herself see her future children on the lawn. The way, years ago, she'd populated her zoo heaven with daffodils and elephants. There was something mirage-like about the scene. If she tried to step into it, it might shatter like glass, or melt. Or perhaps the people would be not quite as happy as they seemed from here; perhaps Kathy and Todd were really arguing on the dock and the Reverend was horrified at all these young people galli-vanting half-naked.

"You're worrying," said Adam. "Your forehead's doing that twitchy thing. We just got married! What could you possibly be worrying about?"

"Nothing!" Joyce laughed. "Maybe my forehead just does that on its own now." She took a breath and tried not to think anything. When she'd asked her mother what she'd thought on each of her wedding days, she'd said she'd been too happy to think. But then, look what had happened to her. Wasn't it bet-ter to be rational, and clearheaded, and recognize the risks involved? Wasn't that better than plunging blindly into for-ever, only to have forever last three years? Or, in her sister's case, six months?

The sky was turning the blue-gray of dusk, and the light-house cast a rippling light over the water and across the curve of beach. The wind blew cold and damp, and Joyce sneezed. She and Adam were huddled at the picnic table, under a blan-ket Todd had left behind. The members of the wedding party began to make their way back to the shore. They pulled on their clothes and scurried back to the inn at the top of the hill.

"He's still out there," said Adam softly. The Reverend was a pale shape, fading to gray. Big Band music floated down the hill from the inn and out across the water—or at least Joyce imagined that it did, that it reached the Reverend and re-minded him, as he stood facing Rhode Island, of a night like this fifty-two years ago.

The Reverend raised his arms in the air and twirled in a half-circle, then back again. "Is he dancing or praying?" Adam asked, and Joyce shook her head. From here, it was impossible to tell.

Julie Schumacher

DUMMIES

The second time my mother started dying, my brother and sister and I were sent to live with a woman on the edge of town. Mrs. Edna McLeod was a widow who often misapplied her makeup: the dark-red lipstick and dots of rouge were slightly out of place, as if she had looked in the mirror, gotten a fix on her features, and then jiggled her head to the left, placing the colors where her lips and cheeks had recently been.

Dan was fifteen, Bea was twelve, and I was nine.

Our parents had wanted to send Dan back to Maywood—an institution—but Bea had fought hard against it, saying that if Dan had to go, she would leave everyone behind and ride to Cleveland on her bike and stay in a homeless shelter there. She said we were supposed to stick together.

My father pointed out that Dan actually didn't mind Maywood; he had lived there off and on for seven years.

"That isn't the damn point," Bea said. She was just old enough to swear. Rudeness was a brand-new coat she was trying on.

I understood how she felt. With our mother sick again, all of us seemed to be in danger. We were flying apart, crumbling, with no one to protect us but ourselves.

"When is Mom coming back?" I asked.

"Soon." My father looked tired. He would have to go with her, but told us the week before that he was sure she would be all right. But our mother was always dying. The process took years; for half our childhood she was rehearsing. Then she was gone.

On a map of northern Ohio you see Toledo to the west, a small ring of roads around it, and the vast blot of Cleveland toward the east, a tangle of interstates and suburbs all around. In between those two cities, below the southern bulge of Lake Erie, you see a grid of smaller roads, the land cut into perfect midwestern squares by the cars going north-south and east-west in orderly progression. The terrain is as flat as a tabletop. If you could zero in even closer, you'd see that each of the small towns, marked by a tiny dot, is built the same: cut in squares and then bisected into smaller blocks, so that any street with a bend in it is called something like Mount Curve or Winding Trail. From where we sat, we thought that getting anywhere should be easy: hang a left to the redwood forest, hang a right to Plymouth Rock.

Edna McLeod lived on the outer edge of Kenford, about a hundred yards from the sign that said POPULATION 9,600. Other than the graveyard and the car wash, her house was the last piece of Kenford you drove by on the way out of town.

When my father left us there, forgetting to kiss anyone good-bye, Dan stood next to his duffel bag on the pock-marked driveway and pulled his lip. It was one of those things that he needed to do over and over, as if he thought that doing it long enough would make whatever was bothering him pass on by. We had explained the situation to him more than once, but usually Dan didn't understand what he didn't want to hear. He was sensible that way, Bea said; she said that most people who were smart were really stupid, and that IQ didn't matter next to common sense.

Mrs. McLeod, her fingers bent at an odd angle where they joined her hands, waved at the dust already settling down the road and said that she hoped we'd get along. She shook hands with Bea. (Bea was easy to remember: thin and pointed, like her name, with freckles and nervous hollows beneath her eyes. Most people didn't remember me, on the other hand: I was large and soft, with a regular face—brown hair and no deformities, that's about all.) Then she patted my shoulder and nodded quickly at Dan. People who weren't used to the way he looked seemed to think that meeting his eyes would be impolite. But Dan was very friendly when you knew him. His teeth were pretty messed up and his gums were bad, but he was more normal than people liked to make him out.

"Do you all bathe yourselves?" Edna McLeod's voice was reedy and thin.

I had a sudden vision of this crooked woman taking off my clothes and lifting me into a round steel tub of boiling water. I stepped back into the shade of a walnut tree. I craved my mother's soft smell, the cool palm of her hand like a magic cup.

"I'll take care of everything," Bea said. Dan was rocking back and forth beside her in the sun. She kept trying to take his hand, but he shook her off, looking down Route 20 for my father's car.

I figured things would probably get even more depressing pretty fast, but then we started toward the house. It was a light-brown clapboard, and didn't give a clue from the outside as to what we'd find within.

"Jesus," Bea whispered, when the door was opened and we stood on the threshold with the polished light of September streaming in. On every wall and surface were shelves and cases spilling out plastic flowers, old shoes, ladies' gloves, quilts, pictures, broken kitchen tools, eyeglasses, telephones, crumbling books, ancient underwear, and what must have been the largest collection of Bell jars and thimbles in the world.

Mrs. McLeod closed the door, and I felt encapsulated, cut off from my life as if I'd entered a late-night movie on TV. She nudged a rolling step-stool out of the way and handed me a card from the nearest shelf: "E. McLeod, Antiques and Collectibles." Next to her phone number was a drawing of a jack-in-the-box resting on a stack of books. "I don't sell retail from the house," she said. "I don't want to be bothered. Several times a year I have the dealers come to me."

"Who would want this stuff?" Bea asked, forgetting to whisper.

Mrs. McLeod showed us down a hallway toward our

rooms. "The junk of the world recycles itself," she said. "I'm part of the process. You two will sleep in here, and your brother can have the room across the hall." She rubbed her lips together. They were bright red and made her face look as white and pale as a turnip.

Dan was holding a vase he'd found out in the hall.

"Don't worry," Mrs. McLeod said. "There's nothing very expensive here that can break."

"He wouldn't break anything," Bea said, just as the vase thunked hard on the wooden floor. Dan picked it up again.

I gripped the hem of my yellow shorts so that I'd know where my fingers were. Then Mrs. McLeod put a beautiful pink beaded pocketbook in my hands.

"It's so pretty," I said, touching the shining surface. That was probably why Bea didn't trust me. That was probably one of the reasons, later on, I felt her affection for me vanish into thin air.

People used to ask me what having Dan in the family was like. It was fine. A lot of the time he was away, but when he was home, he was always cheerful, and he liked to play almost any kind of game. Sometimes, when Bea and I played marbles or even dolls, he'd come up behind us and pretty soon he'd be hogging the shooter or bending the dolls' skinny legs to conform to chairs, or tucking them into the beds we made of tissue boxes and washcloths. He liked to play with the neighbors' cats, and he raked leaves and shoveled walks for almost everyone we knew. When he turned eighteen, he was going to move to a different school, to a place where he could learn to have a job.

Even though we liked having Dan home, I'm not sure we knew our brother well. In his own way he was private, and what he liked best was to lie on the couch and have my mother comb his hair. Bea liked to pretend that she and Dan were very close, but I don't think they were. He had gone away from home when she was five. She said she remembered playing with Dan when they were kids, before I was born, and that they grew up together. But I don't think Dan remembered that. Bea and I were close instead. Only when Dan came home again, two months before our mother went away, did my sister suddenly seem to love him best.

On our first full day at Mrs. McLeod's, Bea made a point of explaining Dan's routine. While he was brushing his teeth (noisily) in the bathroom, Bea explained that during the time she and I were in school, Dan would probably like to stay outside if it was sunny; that he liked peanut butter for lunch; and that he would walk to the old bus stop near our house to meet us, because he was used to it and it was something he liked to do. She had warned me the night before that we would not get off the bus near Mrs. McLeod's, because Dan would get confused.

"I think I should keep him here." Mrs. McLeod had set out a breakfast of mandarin oranges, hard-boiled eggs, toast, and black sugared coffee, which would make Bea shake until afternoon.

"What do you mean, 'keep him'?" Bea asked. "He's fifteen."

"He may not know the route from here. It's quite a bit farther."

"It *is* pretty far," I said, because my legs got tired after school.

Bea acted as if I hadn't spoken. She looked toward the open cupboards and kitchen shelves, which contained the largest collection of unmatched dishes I had ever seen. "The way is straight. All you have to do is point him in the right direction."

Dan came in to show us his teeth, most of which overlapped one another and were hard to clean. Usually he stuck the end of the toothbrush in his mouth and stretched his lips away from his gums, but today he was shy, or maybe nervous, so he made a kind of grin instead. The belt on his pants was wrong side out.

"Good job," Bea said, repeating what our mother and father said at home. She seemed to have aged ten years in just a day. She had smoothed her hair with water and fastened it into a red barrette. To Mrs. McLeod she said, "I'll take the responsibility."

"You don't have the responsibility." Mrs. McLeod spoke

softly. "Your parents have given that to me." She looked at my watch. "That's an old-fashioned piece. It's almost time for you to go."

"Dan will meet us whether you want him to or not," Bea said.

Mrs. McLeod looked at my sister. Bea was pinched, narrow, as if someone had been squeezing her all her life. "I'm sorry this is hard for you," she said.

I helped Dan spread butter on his toast. His fingernails were a mess; no one had clipped them.

"It's not hard for me," Bea said. "I'm used to it now."

Mrs. McLeod sipped her coffee. I wondered whether she had ever been pretty: she had watery blue eyes and a square forehead, and a lacy pattern of veins on either side of a delicate nose.

We picked up our books and said good-bye to Dan, who was looking down at his toast so intently that he didn't even seem to hear. On the way to the bus stop I was relieved to be alone with Bea. I realized I had been waiting for a chance to cry ever since we had said good-bye to our mother on the porch and I had put my face against her dress and tried to memorize her smell. I had lost it already. I thought I could keep her alive by remembering her smell. Bea looked at my wrinkled dress and my ugly brown shoes and said that if I wanted to cry, I could walk alone, that she had had enough crying to last for the rest of her life. That afternoon Dan was waiting for us as usual, happy to carry our books and walk us home.

At dinner that night we sat down at the table, reached for our napkins, and found on our plates an elaborate meal: brown rice cooked in gravy; carrots glazed with honey and wild herbs; and four miniature birds, one for each of us, nestled in the center of our plates. Bea and I stared at the birds in astonishment. It was like having a three-inch cow appear on your plate, or sitting down to a pig small enough to fit inside a drinking glass.

Mrs. McLeod had clearly dressed for the occasion, with a clean white apron and a cameo on a chain around her throat. Her white hair was curled like a private garden; orange lipstick overflowed the small perimeter of her mouth. It occurred to me that usually she was lonely.

"Excuse me," Bea said. "Could you please tell me what these are?" She touched a bird with the back of her spoon.

"Cornish hens." Mrs. McLeod severed a two-inch leg from the tiny creature on her plate. She wielded her knife with a butcher's skill.

Bea looked at Dan, who was staring down at his plate with enormous eyes. He'd had a pet parakeet once.

I felt a cool and steady nausea creep from my stomach to my chin.

"I don't want to offend you," Bea said, "but I really doubt we're going to eat these."

"Are they tough?"

At home we usually ate fish sticks, hamburgers, casseroles, spaghetti, and other things whose origins didn't so clearly show.

"We just can't eat them, that's all."

Dan pushed the bird off his plate and made a tent for it with his napkin. He ate his rice and carrots with a serving spoon. When he was done, he scraped back his chair and went to the den to watch TV. He seemed to scowl at Mrs. McLeod. Bea had asked him to say "Thank you," but he probably forgot.

We had a hard time thinking of anything to talk about. The three of us in the cluttered kitchen were a small Bermuda Triangle: anything dropped in the midst of us would be lost, would disappear. Bea shoveled her bird aside with a tarnished fork.

"Tell me," Mrs. McLeod said, "what do you two want to be when you grow up?"

I said "A dog trainer" right away, because I loved dogs and because I was not allowed to have one. Bea shook her head. She hated to be asked that question by adults.

"Bea wants to live in a city," I said. At home, when Bea and I talked in our room at night, she used to whisper her plans to me. She hated Kenford and hated Ohio, where there was never anything new; she was going to move to New York when she was eighteen. She would live in an apartment and wear her hair long, and when she walked down the street, people would think she was someone famous. But she would be a veterinarian and a stewardess—all our parents' friends would be amazed. I would visit her from Ohio, and the two of us would eat in restaurants every night.

"Alice doesn't have the slightest idea what I'm going to be," my sister said. She drank her milk and asked for more. She had told Mrs. McLeod that we had to have milk with at least one meal.

I looked at my plate, which had pictures of little Dutch people in hats holding hands around the rim.

"I might run a group home for retarded adults," Bea said. "Maybe in town." She ate a tiny mouthful of rice and a miniature carrot. "You know, if things don't work out here, we could probably stay with my friend Carla's family. The Strommens."

Mrs. McLeod nodded. "I know Bill Strommen well. He's an alcoholic. I suspect he abuses his wife." She wiped her mouth and pointed out that three extra children to feed was a lot. "And then there's your brother." She looked up, her eyes filmy and light, searching for Bea's.

"My brother's fine," Bea said.

Mrs. McLeod looked down the hall to the den where Dan was watching TV. "He didn't touch what I made him for lunch. I think he imagines it's my fault your parents are gone."

"I think he probably wasn't hungry," Bea said. "He's really fine."

Mrs. McLeod leaned over her food to be closer to Bea. "Whether your brother is fine or not, you aren't to blame. Blame is only destructive. Why don't you try the Cornish hen?"

Bea opened her mouth and closed it. Then she picked up the bird on her plate in a paper napkin and slammed through the door. My stomach was rumbling, but I didn't move.

Mrs. McLeod had her back to the picture window by the sink and couldn't see Bea head toward the compost heap in the back. But I watched my sister take her dinner spoon from her pocket and begin to dig with it, the small bird next to her on the ground.

"Explain to me what she's doing." Mrs. McLeod reached for the gravy.

"Digging," I said, feeling the tears inexplicably start in my eyes.

"Oh." Mrs. McLeod poured some gravy over her bird and then over mine. She sliced the meat from the carcass on my plate and cut it all into little pieces, putting the skeleton on the counter at her side. The food looked good. "Your sister's a very bright girl, Alice."

"I guess so," I said. I tried the meat; it was tangy and chewy. I wondered if Mrs. McLeod was a kind of good witch, who could cure you with her magic cooking powers. "My mother says she needs to apply herself."

"That's true. It isn't right to spurn a gift. I don't like to see people sacrifice themselves. Does she have very many friends?" Mrs. McLeod put the largest of a basket of muffins on my plate. Bea was skinny and I was round, but I always thought of our shapes as givens—our job was to maintain them, good or ill. I added butter.

Bea was still crouching in the yard; digging with a spoon must have been hard work.

"No, not many. Not anymore."

Outside, it was getting dark.

"Sickness like your mother's is a challenge." Mrs. McLeod leaned over and put her cool, dry, powdered cheek on mine. I thought she would whisper to me some secret, some way of getting through the weeks to come. But she said, "Your sister is struggling; you can help her," and pulled away again.

When she excused herself from the table and left the room, I stood by the window eating leftovers from the pots—the sticky rice with too much pepper, and the buttered carrots with flecks of basil clinging to their sides—waiting for my sister to come in out of the dusk and tell me the ways in which I could help her, and when, and how I could lift the burden she'd taken on.

When our parents called that night, we were already in bed, so Mrs. McLeod answered the telephone in the hall. Bea and I lay in the four-poster double bed in the guest room, looking up at the ceiling and hearing a report about our day. Mrs. McLeod even told them about the hens. She didn't say anything incriminating about Dan.

Bea lay as still as a rock.

"Shouldn't we get up and talk to them?" I asked. I was half asleep, but I could imagine the feel of my mother's hand in the dark, her long nails parting the hair at the nape of my neck. She owed it to me to stay alive, and I'm ashamed to admit that I used to bargain with God about how long I would need her: until the end of elementary school, or until I turned fifteen, or until I married, or until I had a daughter of my own.

Bea said I could make my own decision about whether I wanted to talk to them. She sounded choked, as if she were smothering.

I looked at the collection of things on the wall: colored glass bottles, boxes marked "gloves" and "antimacassars," and books with the bindings gone. Then, just as Mrs. McLeod knocked softly on the bedroom door, I saw the small white statue: two girls holding hands, swinging and pulling each other in a circle, their white porcelain skirts flared out, their heads tilted toward the sky. It had been our grandmother's once. She kept it on her dining-room table until she died. I almost pointed it out to Bea, but she had probably already seen it. Why would our parents have given it away?

"If you don't talk to them, I won't either," I said. "I think we should go together."

Bea turned over. "It's not like that anymore. You have to decide things on your own."

Slowly I put my feet on the cold wood floor. Mrs. McLeod hung up the telephone in the hall.

On Saturday morning Mrs. McLeod said she needed our help on an errand in Bastion, ten miles away.

"I'll stay here." Bea was working on a puzzle she had brought from home.

"No, I need you all to come." Mrs. McLeod was rubbing lotion on her hands, over and around the swollen knuckles. "Is your brother still in bed?"

Bea looked at me quickly. We had gone into Dan's room before breakfast and found the sheets and blankets off the mattress, the mattress off the bed, and his clothes on the floor. We'd picked them up while he stared at himself in the mirror.

Bea said she wasn't going to leave him anymore to go to school.

She unbuttoned Dan's pajamas and helped him get dressed. I didn't like to see him even partly naked, with his underwear loose around his thighs. Bea put his legs into jeans and said, "Stand up and zip, Dan," and he did.

I said that Mrs. McLeod wouldn't let anyone skip school.

"I might just be sick," Bea said. She pulled a shirt over Dan's head and he said "Bitch." I had never heard him swear.

Bea turned on me before I could say a thing, her narrow face like a needle. "Mind your own business, Alice. Come on, Danny, stand up." She used our mother's voice to talk to him, and someone else's voice to talk to me.

Now, finally, Dan walked into the kitchen, his hair standing straight up on his head. He was pulling his lip again.

"Daniel." Mrs. McLeod spoke slowly and distinctly. "We're going to drive to Bastion on an errand."

"He isn't deaf," Bea said.

When I asked what we were going to buy, Mrs. McLeod said she'd rather we be surprised.

By ten o'clock we were riding in the back of a pickup truck toward town. Mrs. McLeod sat alone inside the cab, her head barely clearing the steering wheel, and Bea and Dan and I rode in back, our legs straight out in front of us like two-by-fours.

It was cool in the back of the truck, and we bounced along on the metal bed over the potholes, which hadn't been repaired for years. Riding backward we saw the things you usually see on small Ohio roads: animals flattened into disks, mobile homes, the blue sky like a lid about to open up above. The pavement rolled beneath us, uncurling under the wheels as we jounced along. Dan seemed better now that Bea and I were with him. We closed our eyes when the sun turned a corner and suddenly faced us; Bea kept hers shut even when we got to town.

The three of us stayed in the back of the truck while Mrs. McLeod walked in the service entrance of Eugene's, the only department store in Bastion. Dan smiled as soon as she left, looking happy, his old self. He stood up and jumped out of the truck. He could be unexpectedly graceful. "I can lift it," he said, too loud. In the past six months his voice had gotten low; because he didn't talk very much, his voice was always surprising when it came out.

"Maybe you can," Bea said.

"Watch, Bea." He yelled, "Alice!"

We watched. He hunkered down by the tailgate, red in the face, the cords in his neck stretching out to make him look webbed.

Bea turned to face me. "It could be she's mean to him," she said.

"Mean to who?"

"To Dan. That could be the reason he's upset. How do we know what she says to him when we're at school?"

"She wouldn't be mean to him," I said.

Bea chewed her nail. Her hair was as straight and stiff as straw. "We don't know that. He doesn't like her, anyway."

I stood up and checked on Dan, who was head-down in effort, the sweat making a path down the back of his neck. I touched him. "It's too heavy," I said. "That was good."

He spat on the ground.

"We didn't ask you to lift it," Bea said. "Don't spit."

He held up his open palms. At the best moments, outdoors, when there was happiness in his face, I could picture him as a handsome grown man. His hands were dented where he'd hooked them beneath the truck.

I looked back at Bea, crouching behind her knees and elbows. It occurred to me that maybe she was afraid of growing up. Maybe she didn't have enough faith in Dan and me.

"I think everything's going to work out," I said, hopefulness coming over me like a breeze.

Mrs. McLeod was waving to us from the entrance of Eugene's.

"I don't see why you suck up to her," Bea said.

I waited, even though Mrs. McLeod was calling. I wanted Bea to know that I would stick by her; I would be like one of those birds that mates for life. "She's taking care of us," I said.

"She's being paid."

Dan had run up to Mrs. McLeod and run on back, feet

clomping in his heavy shoes. He climbed up the tailgate and grabbed my wrist, bringing his face too close to mine—Bea and I had given up trying to teach him how far away you were supposed to stay from someone else. "Dummies!" he yelled. At first I thought he was yelling at me, or insulting Mrs. McLeod and Mr. Buehl, the Saturday manager, who was now wheeling a large cloth bin through the parking lot. "Dummy" was a word my mother didn't allow at home. But Dan was pointing at the bin. *Mannequins.* Soon Dan and Mr. Buehl were tossing nearly a dozen life-size dummies into the truck with us, some of them whole, some of them missing heads or limbs, and all of them singed or charred and smelling of the fire that had nearly destroyed Eugene's six months earlier. Most were naked and lay obscenely spread around us in the truck, impassive faces hard against the metal floor.

Bea curled up against the cab. When the truck started, she pulled her sweater up to her eyes as though anyone on the street would notice one pale girl, hunkered down, amid the stack of naked figures and the crooked-toothed boy, standing, laughing, and waving at the passersby.

At first we played with the dummies out of boredom, and because Dan was always with them when Bea and I got out of school. (Dan had still been asleep when it was time to leave on Monday, so Bea lost her nerve and walked to the bus with me.) We'd drop our books and head for the garage, separate from the house and out of hearing of Mrs. McLeod. The dummies were always waiting, sitting patiently on the cold cement floor in a careful row. They seemed to need us, and each of us had our favorite. Bea adopted a frail bald girl with a wire waist, and with breasts that pointed upward toward the sky. She was blackened on the arms and legs, but she was intact. She looked off to the side, so no matter which way you turned her, she refused to meet your eyes.

I chose a woman who was more in need: she was missing an arm below the elbow and one of her legs was twisted, so she couldn't stand up straight—she leaned forward, as if stumbling, or as if trying to catch up to someone in front of her to hear what they said. I liked her better for the game leg and the missing arm; I imagined her coming to life, needing me to help her through crosswalks, leaning on my shoulder with the stump of her arm. I named her Louise. Dan singled out the smallest of the dummies, a four-foot sexless child with a missing chin. He clearly loved it, and I let him dress it in my clothes as long as he gave back whatever I wanted to wear.

Dan worked hard cleaning the dummies. He washed each mannequin scalp to toe, methodically wiping off the grime with a washcloth dipped in water and lemon soap. He was serious: he washed the eyes and stiffened lashes as though expecting the rigid dolls to come to life, to wrap their arms around his neck and call him Prince Charming, Rescuer Divine. He didn't talk to us anymore. After inserting arms into sleeves and legs into pants he took a comb from the pocket of his shirt and smoothed the sticky, matted hair. Bea and I watched him arrange the hairstyles with his hands, sometimes licking the tips of his fingers to pat a wayward section into place. The dummies seemed to be getting ready for something. The ones he'd worked on looked like conservative farmers, neatly groomed.

One day, when Mrs. McLeod moved his favorite dummy so that she could get a shovel for the garden, Dan stood up and hit her in the eye. Bea and I went to check on her in the kitchen and found her sipping a glass of wine.

"Let's be honest," she said, holding an ice cube to her temple. A red half-moon was rising beside her eye, which was clearly on its way to swelling shut. "I haven't given your parents any real news about Daniel, which in most people's minds would constitute an enormous mistake. Partly I don't want to worry them. They don't need it. But I'm not sure that's the right strategy anymore."

"He didn't mean to hurt you," Bea said. "I'm going to make him apologize." She was pale from not sleeping well, and I knew that she'd gotten in trouble with her teachers at school.

Mrs. McLeod pushed her wineglass out of the way—I wondered which Kenford family had gotten rid of it—and dabbed her injured eye with a paper towel. "I don't care about this," she said. "And I'm not concerned about his etiquette; he doesn't need to apologize."

"He will, though," Bea said.

Mrs. McLeod leaned across the table. "Your brother's a miracle, I know, a beautiful boy."

I had imagined, before this, that once my mother came home, we would visit Mrs. McLeod every now and then and look at the things she had to sell; I would show my mother where I'd slept for three long weeks and we'd buy a beaded purse and look for the small albino squirrel out in back. But possibilities, it seemed, were disappearing. Or maybe they were getting smaller.

"They'll be home in six days," my sister said.

Through the screen door we could see the yellow light of the garage. Dan was sitting there, alone.

"He needs to eat," Mrs. McLeod said.

"I'll get him to eat," Bea said. I'd already watched her, after lunch, tear a sandwich into pieces and put the pieces into Dan, holding his jaw and begging him to chew.

I said I would help. When Bea stood up, I stood up with her. But I wanted to throw myself into Mrs. McLeod's broad lap and wait for the world to come undone.

Bea had told Mrs. McLeod that school was closed for the rest of the week for teachers' conferences. I don't think Mrs. McLeod believed her, but she didn't try to make us go to school. We spent our time in the garage with Dan and the dummies. Sometimes he still combed their hair, but at other times he sat with them doing nothing, just touching them now and then: their chipped hands, their starchy hair, the places where they had been injured or damaged or burned.

Mrs. McLeod had a junk dealer in the house—a middleman, she said—and Bea was afraid she would sell the dummies.

"Ask her not to," I said, looking at Dan. "Tell her not to sell them until we're back home."

Bea rolled a penny on her tongue. Ever since I could remember, she liked to hold things in her mouth: coins, bobby pins, bits of stone. "She makes her money on this stuff. I don't want her doing me any favors."

"I could ask her," I said. "I don't mind."

Bea looked fierce. "No, we'll buy one. We'll ask her how

much she can get and then we'll buy one. How much money do you have?"

I wanted to buy a new set of markers and a Frisbee. "Not very much."

"How much?" Bea grabbed my arm.

Dan was sitting on the floor. He was a good brother but he hardly seemed to notice us. He stirred his fingers in the oil on the ground. I could feel Bea's fingers leaving their imprints on my skin. "Two dollars," I said. But I had ten.

At lunch we ate on trays in the garage, because Mrs. McLeod was still busy with the buyer. Bea forced a piece of tuna salad into Dan's mouth and when he spit it out, she slapped him. She and I ate his lunch—she told me I had to finish half his sandwich as well as mine—and then she gave me the empty plates and eleven dollars, telling me to say that Dan had eaten everything.

When I went inside with the dishes and the money to buy the smallest dummy for Dan, Mrs. McLeod was counting a stack of twenties. The buyer was gone. I saw bare spots on the shelves along the wall. I had dirt and food on my hands and oil in my hair.

"You miss her, Alice, don't you?" she asked, putting her money loose on the counter. I didn't know if she was talking about my mother or about Bea, but I suddenly thought, What if I am the one to move away and Bea stays here? Will she visit me the way I would have her? I put the dishes in the sink and thought of my sister caring for Dan the rest of her life while I lived alone, and I remembered what Mrs. McLeod had said about helping Bea. I started to cry.

When Mrs. McLeod dialed the telephone in the hall, I didn't object. I watched her crooked finger find the long-distance number and I held out my hand when she pulled the heavy black receiver into the kitchen, over to me.

I talked. I had never, I thought, talked so long.

Mrs. McLeod stood behind me, quiet as dust. When I hung up, she rested her old woman's head on top of mine. "Come and wash up in the bathroom," she said.

I thought of the circle of artificial men and women in the yellow light of the garage, cripples and victims every one. I wished they'd all been sacrificed in the fire.

She ran hot water in the tub and helped me take off my clothes. She handed me a washcloth. I handed her my money.

In only four more days my father would bring my mother home.

In the middle of the night I woke up to find Bea putting on her raincoat and her boots, and tucking all of our money—about twenty-two dollars; she had found my ten—into the pocket of her jeans. I got up and dressed as she dressed; we didn't talk. Earlier I had offered to let her hit me, but she wouldn't even answer. Now I was a shadow she didn't try to leave behind. The two of us, in the dark, left our room and walked down the hall toward the front door.

Mrs. McLeod sat in an armchair blocking the way. "I don't think anyone will ask me to babysit again," she said. "I assume you have food, and your raincoats, and some money?"

I nodded, forgetting we were nearly invisible in the dark.

"Good. At least you feel prepared. That's important. It's an illusion, but it can help you through the day."

Bea was staring at the place in the flowered chair where Mrs. McLeod's face was bound to be.

"You girls tried your best. That's what counts if anyone wants to judge you. You were heroes." Mrs. McLeod sounded worn out. The outline of her hair was in disarray. "I'm sure you know enough not to accept a ride with anyone outside of Kenford. You'll find two sandwiches in the refrigerator on the shelf."

Bea stepped around the chair and opened the door.

"It was the right thing to do," Mrs. McLeod said.

We stumbled out.

The air was cool and wet with mist. We got our bikes from the side of the house; I kept an eye on Bea the entire time. I would watch over my sister now.

We rode without looking back. I could hear Bea's breath beside me and the whirr of her gears as they clicked along. Soon the muscles in my legs were aching and my hands were cold in the morning air. I tried to imagine a day when Bea and I would remember our time at Mrs. McLeod's with a sense of fun. Dan would be gone and we would miss him, but Bea and I would be close, the way I had always hoped we'd be. But I couldn't picture it very well. Generally I have found that the future is useless. It doesn't help; at times it may as well not exist. I was stuck on the seat of my bicycle, hearing Bea begin to cry and slow down behind me. I kept pedaling away from her; I didn't stop. Some moments you can't escape from. With the shallow taste of freedom in my mouth, I am still whispering Dan's name on that black receiver in the hall; I am still riding; I can still feel my sister's hatred spurring me on.

Tom Paine

WILL YOU SAY SOMETHING, MONSIEUR ELIOT?

After the eye passed over, the shivering Concordia Yawl Bliss was picked up and tossed sideways down into a trough. For a moment in the dark that had been a brilliant noon two hours earlier Eliot saw a light on the horizon and knew it was the light at the top of his own mast. The light flickered and went black, and there was nothing but the white noise of the storm. The wooden yawl shuddered deep in her timbers, and Eliot was catapulted from the cockpit and landed chin first on the deck and heard his molars shatter. Weightless for a moment as Bliss dropped, Eliot again cracked down against the deck like a fish. The bow rose up the face of a mountain of water, and Eliot fell head first toward the wheel. His heavy arms locked in the spokes, and his Adam's apple crunched on mahogany, and he was upside-down, bare feet to the sky. Bliss paused at the crest before her bow came down hard, hurtling Eliot backward through the companionway and down onto the teak floor below, where he rolled in a soup of seawater and motor oil and caulking.

The creaking of the hull planks rose to a moan and subsided and rose again. The garboard plank was wrenching away from the keel, and the sea overwhelming the pumps. Eliot caught

his breath and lifted his head. The storm paused. In the pause
Eliot heard a distant *plink*, the single sharp piano *plink* of the
lower shroud snapping, and then the crack of the main mast as
it folded at its midsection into the sea. Bliss rose and twisted
against the storm. The seaborne mast was buffeted, still wired
to the hull. Eliot was braced against the sink in the galley
reaching for the bolt cutters when the mast rammed through
the after-hull. He crawled behind the companionway toward
the hole with a red flotation cushion for a potential patch and a
broken paddle for a wedge. The sea poured in against his
knees. The mast broke through again, and Eliot was driven
backward on a river, into the cabin. He crawled to his feet and
slid an orange life jacket over his head, and Bliss was thrown
from the sea into the air and turned turtle and the sea rushed
into the cabin and she righted again. Climbing up the companionway, Eliot saw in the west the vaporous glow of the end of
the storm working toward him. He thrust his arms through the
wheel and watched the light grow, and a rogue wave dropped
from the heavens and drove Bliss down into the sea.

Eliot's shoulders and head bobbed in the sea like a red bottle.
He was shirtless and stripped of his life jacket, and his face was
bloated from twenty-four hours of exposure and oozing from
cuts and abrasions. His eyes were swollen half shut. The sharp
nubs of his broken teeth lanced at his tongue, and Eliot
counted six—three to starboard and three to port. Once a dolphin flew out of the sea not far from Eliot, but it didn't come
again, and the sea was mute. Eliot's lips fissured and the fis-
sures spread red and raw. At night he watched the sky for a
shooting star but he didn't ask to be saved when he saw the
first one, and there were dozens, as if every star in the sky were
thrown down. He floated on his back all night and missed Bliss
more than anyone because Bliss was perfection. Eliot exhaled
and sank under, down to his blistered lips and nose, and when
he filled his lungs the white island of his belly emerged, breaking the black surface, and he let the breath go in a gasp and
sank down again and then pulled the night again into his
lungs. It went on and on, this rising and falling. Morning
pinched the stars from the sky one at a time, and Eliot watched

them go, and slowly the gray turned to yellow and then gold, and the sun burned at the edge of the Atlantic Sea.

On the second day, Eliot saw something long and shiny in the sun, and he paddled to it. It was the boom of Bliss, yellow varnished Sitka spruce rolling in the sea. Eliot removed his belt from the tight loops of his bunched shorts. He tied the belt around the boom and looped his arm through the sling and fell back with a groan and hung in the water. He slid his burning face under the sea and looked up through its lens at a cloud quivering like mercury and blew silver bubbles to the surface. His face turned down toward the depths, and his puffy hand drifted before his face, and his Princeton ring sparkled gold in the airy blue. Eliot pointed downward and cried out with the last air in his lungs, and the cry warbled in the water, and his breath bubbled up his forehead. He broke the surface gasping and flopped up across the boom with his face in the sea. Eliot looked down into the water ten metres, where there was nothing, just liquid blue fading into black. He turned his head and sucked in a loud breath and searched the deserted sea. Skin shrivelled off his shoulders and drifted down and away as Eliot held his breath and watched the sails of skin battered in the invisible eddies.

On the day before leaving for this single-handed sail—out of the Bahamas and bound for St. Barts—Eliot had stood over his secretary's desk with his bag over his shoulder and written a check for fifty thousand dollars. Eliot told her to send it to David Mercer at Fleet, with best regards. Eliot's tenth Princeton reunion was in June, and he had been taunting David— threatening not to give any money this year—and one night was watching David squirm in his chair at the Princeton Club when David said out of the blue, What if something happened?

What if something happened when?
On your trip, David said. Your sailing trip.
Like what? Eliot said.
Like something could happen.
Like *what* could happen?

David raised his mineral water to his lips. Eliot, don't you see something could go wrong?

I've single-handed Bliss dozens of times.

So you're not afraid.

Not really.

You think it's impossible?

What?

You know.

I never think about that.

Never?

I think about dropping twenty pounds. Wasn't this dinner about money?

Eliot, do you mind my making a personal comment?

No more than usual.

That's kind of fucked.

Yes? You think so?

Yes. I do.

Let me tell you something, David.

I'm listening.

You won't understand this at all.

Say it, Eliot.

I don't really understand it myself.

Understand what?

The world loves me.

David stared at Eliot, and the waiter arrived and stood over their table, looking from one man to the other.

Ready to order, sirs?

David shook his head and rubbed at the creases in his brow. He looked at Eliot, who hadn't aged since Princeton.

Eliot finished his drink and looked up at the waiter and ordered another. The waiter nodded and turned to David, who looked at Eliot and repeated, *The world loves you?*

The waiter's gaze swivelled back to Eliot. Eliot laughed and shook his beautiful strawberry head. The laughter rolled up out of him as if he were a child being tickled.

What, David said. What's so funny?

The third day the sea was glass, and then the wind whispered at noon and feathered the glass in running swaths. For hours,

Eliot watched the swaths dapple in the sun, and once a dolphin rose against the horizon. Eliot hooked the belt around his head, using it as a sling under his chin, and slept lightly for a few hours with his head against the boom. When he awoke, his throat was on fire, and he wanted to drink from the sea and he swallowed, and the salt burned like acid down his throat. Soon the sun was slipping away and the breeze blew cool on the burned skin of his face and shoulders. The sun dropped out of sight, and Eliot saw the green flash, and the green flash was a sure sign to him. When he closed his eyes he saw the solar phenomenon lingering like green lightning on the glowing red interior of his swollen eyelids.

Tomorrow, Eliot said, nodding to the universe with closed eyes.

At dawn, Eliot took the metal edge at the end of the belt and carved a line next to the other three scratches. He tried to think of something dramatic to scratch in the mast for posterity and could only think of adding his name, Eliot Swan. He closed his eyes and saw the boom over the fieldstone fireplace in the pastel living room of his house in Locust Valley and saw himself standing under it telling the story of his shipwreck. There were many people in the room listening, but they were all strangers. Eliot tried to picture the face of his former wife, Claudia, or his former partner, Clive, or one of his former mistresses, Ilena or Mandy, or his doubles partner, Henry, or his broker, Dutch, but Eliot could not recall a single face. For a moment Eliot thought he saw the face of the green-eyed Florentine waitress he was screwing when the sink broke and Claudia came in screaming and he went on pumping and laughing on the floor of the *gabinetto,* tossing Claudia all the lire in his pocket—but it wasn't the waitress, and Eliot gave up and opened his eyes.

The wind started up after sunrise and whipped a spray off the tops of the waves. Eliot's boom bobbled against his bruised ribs, and he looked up at the clouds filling the sky. He cinched his belt tighter against the mast so there was no gap, and rode the slap and bounce of the agitated sea. The clouds darkened during the day and soon a low front appeared and sheeted across under the cumulus in long raked strips of black. A drizzle fell, and Eliot opened his mouth and drank as the drizzle became a downpour and then a wooden pounding of raindrops, filling his mouth as fast as he could swallow. Then the rain stopped as if a conductor had sliced his baton through the air and with his white-gloved hand swept away the clouds and calmed the sea.

Eliot felt the life from the rain pass into his wilting body, down his arms to his hands, and he ran his fingers through his hair. The strawberry hair came off in clumps and spread on the water. It floated with him and clung to his chest when he rose from the sea. Eliot loosened a canine tooth for hours with his tongue, and it fell out when he was face down in the water. It waggled through the chalky blue, sparkling in the shafts of underwater light until it winked and was swallowed by the dark below. Eliot ran his tongue over the bloody, wet crater until the taste of blood was gone and his mouth was dry and he smelled bile in his throat.

Eliot raised his chin to the setting sun. Tomorrow then, he said.

Eliot heard voices—not the voices in the wind, but voices from a radio far away that faded and then crackled again. He heard a splashing sound and the creaking of timber and was sure it was a boat. He cried out, but there was nothing, not even the sound of the waves slapping against his boom. Eliot pulled on the boom and twisted his head slowly like a radar receiver. It was morning. He lowered his head and shielded his eyes with his forearm.

Eliot heard muffled foreign voices, and wood splashing in the water. He tried to call out, but his voice snapped and there was only a croaking. The boat's waves splashed toward him, and Eliot heard a jumble of voices overhead. The shadow of the bow fell over him, and his boom was banging against the boat.

Eliot felt feet on his shoulders and toes searching under his armpits. He reached upward slowly. His hands touched thin ankles but slid down and fell back into the water. The voices were loud now. Eliot clung to the boom. A rope fell on his head. Eliot raised his arms and understood and pulled the rough rope over his burned shoulders. He was dragged up the side of the boat, wood against his belly. A woman yelled, and Eliot felt something sharp on the side of the boat catching his foot. The sharpness pulled deeply in the skin of his instep as he was yanked upward and Eliot scraped over the gunwale and flopped like a large dead fish onto the deck.

The sun burned through his blind eyes. There were yellow spots on the backs of his eyelids. The yellow broke up and scattered into a thousand small suns, and Eliot saw ideas whipping around his head as if in a hurricane, taunting him and then fading. A woman's voice was in his ear. There was a cloth and warm water, and she was wiping his eyes tenderly. The woman was singing a lullaby. The others were quiet while she sang in his ear and wiped his eyes. Her breath steamed on his ear. The boat creaked, but there was no motion on the deck.

Eliot tried to get up on his elbows. There was a clamor of voices, and he lay down again. Water was poured into his mouth and it curled warm down within him. Eliot felt a thumb on his eyelid, pushing upward. His eyelid opened, and Eliot saw a yellow eye.

Monsieur, parlez-vous français?

The thumb held his eye open, and Eliot saw a black face with cracked red lips and broken teeth. Eliot moved his head to the side, releasing the thumb, and blinked. He rubbed his eyes with his aching hands and he could see dozens of black faces crowded over him, waiting silently. A man in a torn light-blue dress shirt with dirty white ruffles said, *Parlez-vous français?*

Eliot opened his lips and said, I am American.

The faces turned to the short man with the ruffles and he waved his hand like an impresario and pointed at Eliot and said triumphantly, U.S.A.!

The faces, open-mouthed, looked down at Eliot, and the man in the ruffles nodded like a king and pointed at him and repeated, U.S.A.!

Their faces floated down to him and bobbed in the air, and Eliot felt dozens of dry hot hands patting his belly. The old woman who had sung the lullaby to him cried, her hands over her face, and ran her wet palms lightly over his forehead. Eliot saw many in the crowd make the sign of the cross and raise

their eyes to the heavens, and the man in the ruffled shirt cut
through the crowd and his face drifted down. He took Eliot's
hand and said, I am Alphonse.

Eliot.

Monsieur Eliot, said Alphonse. We are happy to see you
now.

Where are you from?

We are left from Haiti.

How long at sea?

We are at sea twenty days.

Does this boat sail?

There is a storm, Monsieur Eliot. We have no good sails.

Shit.

We are very happy to see you now.

Eliot looked up at a mast and saw it was a telephone pole
and the boom was a series of boards lashed together with black
rope. A patchwork sail hung limp against the mast, and broken
ropes hung loose like vines. The rough wood on the side of the
boat was covered with the cryptic destinations of old shipping
crates. Eliot could see the sea, flat and silent through the
cracks. A small boy with a large head pushed through the
crowd and looked at Eliot and poured a bucket of dirty seawater over the side of the boat.

Alphonse looked down at Eliot and smiled.

Now we are saved, said Alphonse.

Eliot looked up at the empty blue sky, and for the first time
it seemed foreign and unknown to him. He looked at it and
closed his eyes and retreated into the shell of his body.

Because you are American, we are saved.

Alphonse took Eliot's hand in his own and pressed it to his
heart. You have a big boat? said Alphonse.

She sank.

You are very rich?

Eliot said nothing, but his throat burned.

Alphonse spread his hands wide and his face snapped into
a fiery grin. He turned and spoke rapidly in Creole to the other
faces. All the Haitians spoke at once, and some of the old
women raised their hands to the sky, and a few of the men
cried.

Alphonse raised Eliot's hand and kissed his Princeton ring. What did you tell them?

I tell them you are a rich American and very big in America and now the President of the United States will make them look for you and we are saved. They are very happy to hear this good news.

The Haitians hugged one another and scanned the horizon and beamed at Alphonse. Eliot looked up at the sky and closed his eyes.

The sea was light-blue ice. The sun was insolent and bitter. The Haitians were silent, sprawled on the burning wood of the deck as if struck down. They had placed Eliot on a platform in the center of the boat, and Alphonse had used his pale-blue shirt to rig an awning over Eliot's head. An old man grunted from the front of the boat, and other voices were praying with a sound like cicadas. A woman stood in the bow, fishing with a string. When Eliot moved his head he saw faces twitch and look up at him from the deck with expectation. The sail quivered occasionally as if possessed.

Eliot's right foot throbbed for the first two days. A nail sticking out of the planks on the side of the boat had gashed jagged and deep. A faded little girl came to look at Eliot and ran her soft fingers down the length of his body until she came to his foot, where she stopped and lowered her face and sniffed. She went back to Eliot's head and knocked on his skull lightly with her hand balled into a fist. Then she pointed to his toe and pinched her nose. The girl looked at Eliot and Eliot looked at the girl. Eliot turned his head, and Alphonse, who was always watching from nearby, where he squatted inside a cardboard box, stood slowly and hobbled over. Alphonse took Eliot's hand and pressed it to his chest and squinted at the horizon with his yellow eyes.

Alphonse, said Eliot.

Oui, Monsieur Eliot?

My foot is infected.

Alphonse looked at Eliot's foot and held it between his fingers and twisted it from side to side.

Monsieur Eliot, said Alphonse. It is not bad.

It *is* bad, said Eliot. It is infected.

Alphonse looked out across the sea, still holding Eliot's toe.

You are a big man in America, said Alphonse. They will come for you.

Alphonse let go of Eliot's foot and returned to his box. A wrinkled woman shuffled over and poured a few drops of water into Eliot's mouth from the good edge of a broken glass. A few minutes later a young girl carefully poured a few drops into his mouth from a rusty can. Alphonse watched them and nodded from his box. Eliot kept his mouth open, and one by one Haitians came to him and offered a few drops of their supply.

In the evening, the woman who had sung the lullaby in his ear hummed a song and laid her cool hand on Eliot's hot forehead, and Eliot closed his eyes and nodded. She stopped and pulled back her hand and looked down at him and her hand in surprise. In the melody or the touch Eliot had remembered something, something as rare in his life as the green flash at sunset. Others came during the evening and spoke in Creole and touched his body, and sometimes they cried and wiped their tears on his chest. Alphonse came and took down the awning when it was dark and gave Eliot a few gulps of water. Then he went back to his box and watched Eliot look up at the stars.

On the fifth day no one brought him water, and he knew there was no water, and on the sixth day he heard the Haitians lying near him scuttle away. He knew it was the smell of his rotting foot. Alphonse stood over his foot and with his thumb traced the blue lines of poison up Eliot's calf to his knee. Eliot saw only a shimmering black form moving like liquid in the glare, but Eliot smelled the rot from his toe and had seen the blue lines of the poison creeping along his veins toward his heart.

Monsieur? said Alphonse.

Cut it off.

Monsieur, you know the Americans will come. He pointed out to sea.

Cut it off, said Eliot. Above the knee.

Non, non, Monsieur Eliot. We wait for tomorrow.

Do it today. You have a machete?

No, Monsieur, not today.

Alphonse?

Monsieur Eliot?

Take my ring.

Alphonse shook his head sharply and hobbled back to his box. The sun was egg-shell blue through the shirt-awning above Eliot's head. The boat whispered with the sounds of scorched lungs, and Eliot wanted to say he was a skeleton bleaching in the sun. Eliot did not understand. With his eyes closed, he saw the skeleton lying on the deck, bleached and white. He tried to open his eyes and hold them open, staring at the strange sky; he tried to count to a hundred, but when his eyes fell closed he saw the skeleton. At dusk Eliot turned his head to the side in time to see a dolphin leap and the sea flat again.

The first Haitian died on the night of the sixth day. Eliot heard grunting and a splash and turned his head to see Alphonse and another man leaning over the side of the boat. In the morning when the sky was still pink Eliot heard another splash, but before this splash there was a sharp shout and another shout from Alphonse in the box. Alphonse hobbled to his side and said, It is the husband of the woman from the night.

Alphonse took Eliot's hand, and Alphonse's head and face were red and on fire.

I love America, he said. I teach myself to speak English. I listen to English on the radio for many years. We make this boat. We go to America. My daughter with me. You will see, Monsieur Eliot.

Take off the leg, said Eliot.

Tomorrow, said Alphonse.

Alphonse, said Eliot. Take off the leg or I'll die.

If you die, Monsieur Eliot, many will die.

Alphonse.

They see you, Monsieur Eliot. You are here. *C'est un miracle.* The sea is big, and you are here from America. *Un miracle.* You see?

I'm going to die.

You will not die, Monsieur Eliot. Many pray for you. Do you pray, Monsieur?

Shit.

Alphonse stayed with Eliot and held his hand through the day. The sun hammered, and there was no air. The smell of his foot was strong and the two of them wheezed through their mouths. Alphonse held Eliot's hand and sat exposed to the sun on the edge of the platform. In the afternoon Alphonse wet a rag on a string over the side of the boat and wiped Eliot's forehead. Alphonse emptied water from below over the side of the boat and hobbled around the boat every hour and whispered to the Haitians the word "America" and pointed at Eliot. At dusk, Alphonse brought a little girl no more than five to his side, holding her up from behind as if teaching her to walk, and she watched Eliot. Her ribs showed through her torn shirt. She looked up at Alphonse, who smiled, and the girl smiled, and Alphonse walked her away.

On the night of the seventh day, Eliot heard more bodies going over the side. Those that went with a splash and grunts Eliot knew were already dead, but many more went with a sucking sound and Eliot knew those had jumped, and some cried out and there was no question. Alphonse sat with Eliot all day on the eighth day and even found a few drops of water for his lips. On that night the bodies again jumped or were dropped over the side, and Alphonse came to him at dawn and held Eliot's foot gently in his hands.

How many on the boat? said Eliot.

I do not know. We are many.

How many? A hundred?

We are many. I know everyone. We are many, and many are family.

How many are gone?

They are gone, Monsieur. The others are alive.

How many?

Alphonse shrugged. It is too late for them. I pray for those who live.

The woman who had sung the lullaby to Eliot died at noon and was carried by three men to the side of the boat. Her body was rested on the railing and rolled slowly over the side, and her splash cut through the heat. The splash echoed in Eliot's skull and he closed his eyes and a green flash turned to black.

Alphonse went to the railing and looked down at the sea and made the sign of the cross. A young woman with a scar on her nose stood on shaking legs in the center of the boat and sang in slow Creole. She swayed and sang with eyes closed, and other voices from the floor of the boat rose up in the sun. The woman collapsed after hanging like a puppet with a look of surprise. Alphonse hobbled to her and he carried her in his arms and dropped her over the side of the boat. On the way back to his box he stopped and looked at his feet and said, My daughter.

Eliot closed his eyes.

Monsieur Eliot, my daughter.

Eliot turned his head away.

Alphonse sat with Eliot and cried with no tears and asked him to say something please about the President of the United States and how the boats would come to take them all to America.

Tell them, Monsieur Eliot. They believe you.

At night the Haitians flew over the side like black ghosts and Eliot heard their footsteps as they passed his platform and heard them go into the sea. Eliot heard the feet pass him and then the hands on the edge of the boat and only once a shout and a loud splash, and in the morning watched a body floating near the boat. A foot stuck up stiff in the air. Alphonse was sitting in his box with his face in his hands, and Eliot thought Alphonse was dead.

Eliot heard a fly. He tried to see the fly but he could not turn his head, and the sound of the fly grew louder. Eliot looked up, and the sound of the fly became the sound of an engine, and he heard the helicopter coming and the helicopter was right over his head, whooshing over the boat. The helicopter swung around again and blocked the sun. Eliot saw the American flag on the side. Two seamen in white helmets looked down from the wide door, and one waved. The men swung a net down to the boat with dozens of plastic jugs, and Eliot could feel feet moving on the boat toward the supplies. Eliot felt the cool wash from the blades. An aluminum gurney rocked down from the helicopter. Hands slipped him into the gurney, and it rose swinging in the air.

Eliot was pulled into the empty cave of the helicopter. The

pilot turned his blue eyes to Eliot and raised his thumb as he spoke rapidly into a small rectangular microphone over his lips. A seaman hanging from a strap leaned forward and yelled into the pilot's face, motioning with a jerk of his head toward the boat below. The pilot shook his head and with two flicks of his forefinger pointed to Eliot and the horizon. The helicopter suddenly swung around, banking hard, and Eliot's head rolled to the side and he was looking down at the deck. He saw them waving up to him, five Haitians standing and supporting each other, passing a jug of water. Many others were crawling toward the water jugs, and even some of those on their backs were waving and smiling. The helicopter circled around again and slipped down, and Eliot saw Alphonse emerge from his box. Alphonse stood stiffly, face raised, and turned slowly on his bare feet, watching the helicopter circle. The helicopter circled again, and Alphonse swivelled on the deck, never taking his eyes off the helicopter, his arms limp at his sides, and when the helicopter circled a final time Alphonse slowly raised his arms. Eliot blinked and Alphonse collapsed on the deck and Eliot looked down at the crumpled form until his face was pulled around gently by the chin. A smiling medic looked down at Eliot. The medic stuck an I.V. into Eliot's arm and wet his face and dribbled cold water into his mouth from an eyedropper. Eliot closed his eyes and closed his stiff lips around the long plastic nipple. The helicopter levelled and shot low across the turquoise sea.

Jane Smiley

THE LIFE OF THE BODY

I had been going to call my sister Rhonda when the phone rang, and even then, when I heard her voice, I thought that I could just open my mouth and tell her, but when she heaved a blue, premenstrual sigh and said, "So what are you going to do today," I just said what I always say, oh nothing. I thought, another day. Just another day. Then the time will be more right, somehow.

The fact is that I am in about the worst trouble I have ever heard of anyone being in. After Rhonda hung up, the phone rang four separate times. There is no one I dare to hear from, and so I let it ring. If I had picked it up, I would have said to anyone on the other end that I am pregnant, that Jonathan Ricklefs is the father, not Jake, my husband, and that everything inside me is about to be revealed, layer by layer, to Jake, to Jonathan, to Rhonda and our parents, to my son Ezra and my daughter Nancy, to people who care about me and to people who barely know me. What is it that will shame me most when it is revealed? Maybe it is the crazy force of my desire for Jonathan, the full extent of which I have kept from him and which makes me squirm with discomfort even as a secret. But maybe it is something else, something that has not even been revealed to me yet.

I used to have three children. The third was Dory. Five months ago, when she was almost three, she fell head over heels down the stairs. She went over three times, we think. She broke her neck at the bottom and died that afternoon. Various children around the country have her liver, her kidneys, her corneas. There was no one to receive her heart at that moment. A heart is something that can't be saved for very long. She had a little book in her hand when Jake found her at the bottom. It was a habit we couldn't break her of, "reading" on the stairs. Really, she didn't know how to read yet, but she loved to look at the pictures.

I was getting dressed in our bedroom, Jake was ironing his shirt, Nancy and Ezra were eating breakfast. We all heard the long cry of surprise and fear, the thump of limbs toppling and hitting, the utter silence of the house around those noises. All struck dumb, all thinking, *What's that?* all listening. The rustle of buttonholes, stopped, the swish of the iron, stopped, the interior crunch of cereal and toast, stopped.

I can't say what I would have given to have been standing at the bottom of the stairs, holding out my arms to catch Dory. My inner life isn't very mysterious or symbolic. I often dream that I am there, that she is saved. Some part of me, in the dream, always asserts that even if the last time was a dream, this time it is true. It isn't.

Jake wouldn't let me speak at the funeral. He was afraid I would say something outrageous. I might have. I might have said, What right do I have to grieve, having lost only one? Isn't the society of mothers who have lost some many times bigger than the society of mothers who have kept all theirs? I would have said a lot of contradictory things, since I was very confused. Instead, we thanked God who took her away for giving her to us in the first place. That was Jake's idea. He is a religious person, more so now.

Jonathan is a fatalist rather than a providentialist. Things come and go. Forces arrange themselves so that he will, for example, eat granola instead of a peach. When I think of the way he sees himself, I imagine a kind of pinpoint at the vortex of a whirlpool. Blakean swirls above his head. Streaks of light moving through darkness. He is not a very hopeful person. I used to tease him about it. When I tell him I am pregnant, he will nod slowly, his expectations of the worst confirmed.

Maybe that is what I hate most about this, all the suspicions confirmed, especially the suspicions about me that everyone seems to harbor—that Dory's death has made me crazy, that Jake and I have never gotten along, that I would do anything to tie Jonathan to me, that I wanted to replace Dory at any cost, that women are by nature evil, irresponsible, and deceptive. What does it say in the Bible? *And I find more bitter than death the woman, whose heart is snares and nets, and her hands as bands: whoso pleaseth God shall escape from her; but the sinner shall be taken by her.* All that stuff. Once on the *Today* show, I saw a man who had written a book about the Dionne quintuplets. When they were born, their mother was ashamed. She said, "People will think that we are pigs." So much intercourse revealed to the world. Well, I was never proud of my pregnancies. Just by looking at you, people knew what you were thinking about.

I could have told Jake last night. I could have told Jonathan last night, too, when he brought over some lettuce from his garden. It doesn't make it any easier that this will be the first news Jake has had of my affair with Jonathan. Jonathan talks well to Jake. Not many people do—Jake is antisocial and impatient, and his idea of a serviceable conversational gambit is "What do you want?" Someone else who talks well to Jake is Rhonda. I am tempted to tell her, and let her tell them all. She is a great moaner. "Ooooh, Sarah. Ooh, Sarah." That is how she listens to confidences, moaning those wordless cries that you would like to be moaning yourself. "Ooh, Sarah. Ooooh, Sarah." I try it out, out loud, but it isn't the same. I know I should be finishing the sentence, "Oooh, Sarah, you shithead," which is something Rhonda would never even think of doing.

There is the crunch of wheels in the driveway, Jake returning from work, as he often does. He will find me standing over the sink, as he often does. I get up and position myself there. He comes in and runs up the stairs. There is the slamming of closet doors upstairs, the thump of his heavy feet. He really has forgotten something, he always really has, but he never did before Dory died. The manifestation of his grief is more than forgetfulness, it is perennial searching. Though he gave up smoking years ago, his hands wander his pockets in search of cigarettes. He is always making sure he has his keys, his wallet, his checkbook. I find him in closets looking for sweaters and pairs of slippers and magazine articles we threw out years ago. He turns over the cushions, puts his hands in the cracks, comes up with pennies that he gives to Nancy. He calls his mother and asks if his old yearbooks are at her house, his swimming trunks from high school, his old Bo Diddley records. We are patient with this searching, his mother and I. Even Jake knows what he is searching for, but he can't stop just because he won't find her.

He appears in the kitchen doorway. I have my hands in the water, as if I were doing something, and it might be that, not looking at him, looking out the back window at the peonies blooming in the yard, I will say, "I'm pregnant." I know the words, I've said it before. But of everyone in the whole world, Jake is the only other person who knows that we haven't slept together since the week before Dory died. It is also possible that I will tell no one, just wait for them to notice, and ask. It may be that social nicety will prevent most people from asking. It may be that fear will prevent Jake from asking, and even greater fear will prevent Jonathan from asking, and a year from now I will say, in a cocky voice, "Ever wonder where I got this baby?"

Jake says, "I forgot the reports. I can't believe I actually forgot the reports."

"It's okay."

"Of course it's okay. That isn't what I'm talking about. I just can't believe it. I'm just remarking on that, is all."

"I know."

"What are you going to do today?" He asks suspiciously, because he thinks that my grief is to loiter around the house for hours, then hurry and clean up just before Ezra and Nancy get home. It was. Lately my grief has been to go to bed with Jonathan Ricklefs as much as possible, on every flat surface in his apartment. I say, "I'm going to go to Rhonda's dance class with her again, then I'm going to order meat at the locker, then bake cookies with Nancy for the day camp birthday party. How about cooking out for dinner? It's already getting hot enough."

"Will you make potato salad?" He glides up next to me, kisses me on the neck, as if bribing me. I turn and put my hands on his shoulders. I smile, as if being bribed. "I'll boil the potatoes as soon as you leave."

"The day camp counselor thinks Nancy seems fine. She's playing with everyone, and the shyness has worn off completely. She's making a belt in the crafts class."

"Good."

"Ezra is being more reserved."

"Ezra *is* more reserved."

"How much more?"

"Sweetie, I wish I knew. He likes the horses. Yesterday he told me about the horses for about twenty-five minutes. His favorite is named Herb. He got to go into the stable and give Herb his oats." We smile at Herb. Jake smiles at me. He thinks we are coming out of things when in fact we are just getting started. Another day. I will let him go another day. He pecks me on the cheek and leaves with a number of slams: the kitchen door, the garage door, the car door. He is a noisy man.

Rhonda dances every day. Lately I have been going with her. This is not aerobics, it is serious modern dance. The other students are mostly in their teens and early twenties. The teacher is a black man who dances in a local company. I don't know why he lets me come, except that he is a friend of Rhonda's, and she is my sister. Rhonda, although she is thirty-two and has two children, turns out to have considerable talent for the dance. The first day I came, she warmed up, without shame, by stretching and then doing three slow cartwheels and a couple of handstands. I was amazed. I keep up well with the slower third of the twenty-year-olds, and mostly Henry doesn't pay any attention to us. We pay attention to him, though. Pas de cheval: Henry says, "You know how a puppy licks your arm? So that every pore and hair gets wet? Well, make the sole of your foot lick the floor." Deep second position: "You are in water! Your head is floating upward! Your knees are floating outward! Lift! Lift!" He tells us not to mimic him, but to feel ourselves, our muscles and tendons sliding and rolling, our balls and sockets rotating.

Today we have hamstrings and adductors for half an hour,

then chaîné turns for half an hour. My days here, as every-where, are numbered, and so when we lie on our backs and rotate our hips outward and find the place on each side where the tendons split, I am careful to note what it feels like. When we then curl up to standing, I think only of my spine, catlike, and my long, furry tail anchoring me to the floor. When we step and pivot across the floor, I push my toes through the wet mud Henry evokes, and leave long swathes filling with water behind me. After four times across the floor, we lie down and slither through that same mud, chests first, trying not to get our chins wet.

The first to go are Nancy and Ezra, who are active and well taken care of. Then I stop thinking about Rhonda, even though she is just ahead of me in line. Jake vanishes next, with his expectations that are soon to be betrayed. Now Dory, who never knew me as a dancer, who has no associations with this room or these people (they know my first name only, if that). After that, I forget I am pregnant, and at last, sometime in the triple prances ("Sli-i-ide snap! snap!" says Henry), even Jona-than lets go. Henry becomes Henry the dancer rather than Henry the man. We are panting. Henry tells the accompanist to speed up the tempo, and we are running. Henry goes first, down-up-up, arms and chin swooping then lifting. Someone in red and black does it after him, a flute passage on the heels of a bassoon passage, and then it is me, and the only thing I feel is the slick floor under my feet and the rush of my fingers through the air, up-up!

The one in red and black, of course, is Rhonda, who is damp with sweat from ponytail to heel, and when class is over, she says, "God, let's shower and eat at my place. I've got spaghetti left over from last night."

It is words that bring them all back with a suffocating rush. "God." "My place." "Last night." We are fixed in place and time after all. Henry passes us on the way out. "Lovely," he says. He is a big man, happy, Rhonda says, because he gets a lot of oxygen to the brain.

I should tell her in the locker room, naked in the shower, but I make excuses. Now that she is right here, it seems like Jonathan should be the first to know, then Jake, then her. Then our parents, then the children. That's the obvious order, just as Rhonda-Jake-Jonathan was last night, when Jake and Jonathan were standing with their hands in their pockets under the hackberry tree, considering ways to save it from whatever is infesting it.

There is this space, of course, this carefully made space in the day when I will see Jonathan. After the meatlocker, after lunch, before Nancy and Ezra get home from day camp. I enter the downstairs door quickly, and run up. The door opens at the first brush of my first knock. Jonathan is grinning. "Hi," he says, "Hi, hi, hi." He locks the door behind me. He looks me up and down. I catch sight of a pot of tea steaming behind him on the coffee table and I burst into tears. It isn't the first time, nor does it come from the press of present circumstances. All of this sadness has been there from the beginning. I think, in fact, that this affair was begun as a tribute to sadness, gathered force through sadness, and will result in more sadness for everyone than we can possibly stand.

I feel utterly comfortable weeping here.

Perhaps more important, Jonathan feels utterly comfortable with my weeping. I sit on the couch and he pours the tea and then he sits beside me and folds me into his chest, and soon I am weeping and kissing him, and he is wiping my face with a paper napkin and kissing me, and that is how it has gone for months, salty kisses, passion, and grief. I am, as they say, shameless. Often we don't make love, but today we do. Today when he kisses me with his lips, I give him my tongue, only my tongue, and then I feel his, meeting mine, and instantly my nipples, tender with pregnancy, stand up, burning. As much as they hurt, I long to have him lick and suck them, and when I think of that, they tingle suddenly, as if milk were about to come down. They haven't done that since Dory was nursing, and it is the most intense feeling of physical longing, the longing to give suck. I almost tell the news, but I don't.

Jonathan kisses my neck and shoulders, and his erection presses against my leg, presses into my imagination, the thick, smooth shape, the reddish color—I am as familiar with it as I am with my own hand, more familiar, since I have looked at it, tasted it, touched and held it, smelled it. A weighty, living object. Sometimes at night, after Jake goes to sleep and I am lying awake in fear and guilt, I just open my mouth and put my tongue out, wishing, thinking how I would lick the little crease and then run my tongue under the cap, marveling always at the warm shape of it. He sucks my breasts and I push both hands into his pants, unsnapping them, forcing the zipper down. He hops a little on the couch, then pulls my T-shirt up. It tangles in my arms and hair. I am still weeping. I am happy to be trapped inside this shirt with my nipples burning, my cunt throbbing. I open my mouth and put my tongue out.

"Sarah!" he moans. "Oh, Sarah oh oh." And then he strips off my shorts and shoes and sucks my toes and after that he licks my cunt, and licks and licks, parting the lips and putting his fingers in, licking, finding, at last, the spot that burns so that I push him away, his head, his shoulders. He pushes back, licking, his tongue fastened to that spot. My legs turn to water, and my back arches, and for a moment he is gone, and then he eases into me, slow and slick, and his tongue is in my open mouth and his fingers are in my ears and his chest, smooth and firm, in its way, as a penis, is sliding along my chest, and then he does something I always like, which is to lift my legs to my shoulders so that he can get in and in, and he gets in, so far that he relaxes a little, and closes his eyes. I push him off, out. He is shocked, his flesh is shocked at the suddenness of it, but before he realizes, I have it, his penis in my mouth, as I have wanted, and I am licking and stroking. I like to feel this, that he cannot stop himself. He does not. I swallow. He falls back on the couch, pulling me with him, holding me tight, panting. This is the way it has gone for months. I cling to him in desperate fear, but I am no longer weeping.

Sometimes I dream that I am just a torso, and blind, born that way, skin, a mouth, breasts, a cunt more open than any cunt ever, and Jonathan is engulfing me as well as penetrating every orifice. I dream that all I can do in life is fuck and suck and kiss and be embraced, and that I orgasm over and over and never get enough. Sometimes I daydream it.

The tension flows back into his flesh. I feel it along my chest, in his shoulder where my ear and cheek rest. His arm tightens over my back, and his other arm moves. When I lift my head to look at him, I see that he has covered his eyes with his elbow. I lower my head gently and wait, as still as possible. His heart has not relaxed, and is pounding steadily faster. As I open my mouth to speak, he says, "Sarah, talk to me."

I lift my head. "You want me to open the conversation."

"It's hopeless."

"What is hopeless." I can't make it a question, must make it a denial.

"Sarah—"

"Don't say anything, just don't say anything. Do you love me?"

He answers without hesitation but not without pain, "I tell you I do over and over. I do."

"Then don't say anything."

"Do you love me?"

"I think of you without ceasing, day and night."

"Do you love me?"

"You possess me."

"Sarah, do you love me?"

After minutes go by and I don't answer, he sits up and puts me away from him and pours the tea. I reach for my T-shirt and pull it on, but I don't stop shivering. I watch him drink his tea, catching tea leaves on the tip of his tongue and picking them off with his finger. He knows I am looking at him and from time to time turns his gaze to mine. This is another thing that we feel comfortable with, staring and being stared at. He is a big man, broad and muscular, utterly defeated, *as an ox goeth to the slaughter*. When we met, I was attracted to his self-reliance, his detached outlook. Both of those are gone now. I wonder how much he wants them back. He says, "I am terrified."

"Are you terrified that it will go on or are you terrified that it will stop?"

"Both."

"Are you frightened of me or for me?"

"Both."

"Will love find a way? If we stick together, can we make it?"

"Sometimes I think so. Weaker moments. Oh, Sarah." He

covers his eyes again. A moment later I see tears on his cheeks. I look away. He goes on. "It's too painful. Sometimes I feel like our clothes are lined with nails and the tighter we embrace, the more blood we draw from each other."

I say, "It was fun at the beginning. That's important. A book I read says that you draw on the strengths of the relationship when you remember the beginning. I used to be known for my sense of humor, actually. Jonathan, suspend choice, all right? No action, no decision, just endurance." But he is slippery. As soon as he admitted fear, I felt it myself, telegraphed from him to me. I felt the size of the betrayal that would be possible just to escape that fear. Which arm, which leg, which sense would I have given just to escape that fear the moment I saw my daughter at the bottom of the stairs?

"A day," I say. "Only another day. Don't make up your mind or even think anything for another day. Go canoeing. Go to the movies. Eat something soothing, with lots of B vitamins. If I leave now, I might beat Nancy home by a minute." I run out the door, down the steps, out the lower door. I know he is watching me from the window. He fell in love with me when Dory died. That is why my chest closes up when I try to say that I love him. I don't want to be loved for my belongings, even if that belonging is only an enlargement that springs from tragedy.

I make a lot of mistakes. This time it is the potato salad, which I forgot, though Jake asked for it specifically. I forgot about it all the way until he looked in the refrigerator and said, "Didn't you make the potato salad?" and so there was no evasive action possible. I say, "I'll do that thing."

"What thing?"

"That thing where I go to the deli and get some of theirs, then redress it. You like that."

"You were going to put the potatoes on as soon as I left."

"I forgot."

"How could you forget? You were standing right here in the kitchen. All you had to do was turn around and take the potatoes out of the cupboard."

"I forgot."

"I'm not mad. I just don't understand you."

"You forgot your reports."

"I was working on them last night. I put them aside."

"I don't want to argue about fine points."

"It means something," he says. "The way people act means something. You know that."

"I forgot."

He shakes his head and goes outside to start the fire. Before he addressed me on the topic of potato salad, I was standing over the dishwater, as always, washing up the cookie things and pondering the recollection of Jonathan sucking my breasts, thinking that I would like him to kiss all of my skin at the same time. Jonathan knows in his heart that what I crave from him are impossibilities. That is why he is afraid of me.

Out the kitchen window, Jake comes into view, carrying the charcoal and the lighter fluid. Most people, including Jonathan, feel lots of sympathy for him. Soon they'll feel more. They think he must grieve a great deal for Dory. I don't know. I wish I had seen the first look on his face when he got to her, but I started from back in the closet in our bedroom upstairs, and by the time I reached them at the bottom of the stairs, he was already practical, had already covered her with the afghan and was calling the ambulance, wouldn't let her be moved. He has never cried in my presence. Nor have I cried in his presence. But we do not pretend that everything is normal. We strive with all our might to make a routine, a little thread that will guide Ezra and Nancy, and maybe ourselves, out of the labyrinth.

That our sex life ended did not surprise me. Jake does not seek comfort in the flesh of others. He has to feel good to reach out. When he does not feel good, he avoids people. All of his brothers are the same way. When their father died three years ago, they gathered in Tallahassee for four days, five men. They built a bathroom out of the downstairs porch of their mother's house, taking maybe four hours out for the funeral and the burial. I asked Jake if they talked about their father in there, while they were grouting and caulking. He said, "Ralph did, a little." He didn't touch me for four months. I didn't mind. I think about Jonathan putting his face between my thighs and licking, sticking his tongue in; Jake comes up behind me and says, "Are you going to get the potato salad now or not?" and I start violently. He turns me around, his hands on my shoulders, and looks into my eyes. His face is very close to mine, and he is serious. He says, "Sarah, can't you pay attention? That's not an accusation. I want to know. Is that the problem, that you can't pay attention?"

"I'm trying. Don't watch me."

"I wish I could help myself."

I pull away. "I'll get the potato salad now, okay? Nancy is over at Allison's house, and Ezra is watching television."

"Don't get distracted. Half an hour, okay? Be back in half an hour."

"I will."

"I mean it."

"I *will*." It is for my own good, so I won't wander, so I'll keep my mind on the business at hand.

That is the beginning. The second incident takes place when I am coming out of Nancy's room after putting her to bed. Jake is in the hallway, looking at the bookshelves. I turn to say one last thing to Nancy, and Jake's arm goes around my waist. Distracted, I stiffen. Then I relax, but the stiffening doesn't go unnoticed. His arm drops. We stand there for an awkward second, then he chooses a book, and I turn and go down the stairs.

In the end, we argue about religion rather than sex. It is dark when I come into our bedroom, and I think Jake is asleep, but he speaks in a firm, clear voice, surprising in the dark. "Can I tell you something?" I push the top drawer of the dresser in, and he takes this for assent. I stand quietly, looking at the parallelogram of moonlight on the top of the dresser. "There was this time, when my mother's younger sister died of complications of childbirth. I guess I was about fourteen. Anyway, we had just moved to that house in Tallahassee, and I came in from doing something outside. Maybe we were helping Dad move that shed. That was one of the first things we had to do. It was almost dark, and Mom was sitting in the dark, snapping beans for dinner, and everyone else was outside, and when I went to turn on the light, she said, 'Jake, leave it dark,' so I left it dark, and she said, 'The Lord helps a man be good, Jake. If you let Him come inside you, He is a tide that carries you to goodness. But you've got to open the door yourself.' That was all she said, and then Richie came in and turned on the light and pretty soon we had dinner. Sarah, I know it's hard to find the door. It took me ten years to find the door, but I found it.''

''It's not a door I want to find, Jake. Your mother was a religious woman, and she raised you, and so she was preaching to the converted. Before we got married, she said you'd come back to it, and you did. Big surprise.''

''I tried the other way.''

''You always thought of it as the other way. I don't believe, Jake. It's not in me. My brain doesn't have that bump. It's not in my horoscope. I went to Sunday school and read the Bible and it didn't take. If you didn't bring it up, I wouldn't think about it.''

''But maybe me bringing it up is the Lord's way of trying to get your attention. I can't stop doing it. *I am moved* to do it. Don't you understand what that means?''

By now I have gotten, without realizing it, into the dark corner between the dresser and the wall. I open my mouth, but I know perfectly well how Jake's life looks to him: in retrospect, a series of perfectly timed nudges toward the right path that his mother would have, and often had, called miracles—a moment of despair, and then she looks up to see the minister on the porch, about to ring the bell. That happened more than once. I didn't necessarily discount her interpretation. It does seem to me that the world and the inner life mesh in mysterious ways more often than not.

I run my finger around the edge of the moonlight. More than anything, I want him to stop badgering me. I say, ''I understand that you are driving me nuts with this God shit. I got some tracts in the mail again yesterday. Did you send them?''

He is out of bed in an instant, moved to rage by everything unbearable that we have to bear. I find that I am in a tight spot, between the wall and the dresser, and as I am trying to get out, he takes me by the shoulders and bumps my head on the wall. I press against him. His grip tightens, and I can feel the panic roll up from my toes all at once. I know he won't hurt me, but I feel that he will kill me. The walls behind me and to my left are unyielding, cold, terrifying. I bend down. His hands press harder on my shoulders, weights that I cannot evade. I do the only thing that I can possibly do, which is to push hard against the wall with my hip, and hard against the dresser with my hands. It falls over with a crash, and the stained glass box Jake keeps pennies in flies toward the window. I see this out of the corner of my eye. Jake does it again, bumps my head against the wall, this time hard, and simultaneously with the sound of breaking glass. Then I get out from under him, clamber over the dresser, and flee the room. For the rest of the night, which I spend on the sofa, every time I fall into a doze, I seem to feel my head being slammed into glass, and I wake up expecting to reach up and find blood pouring down my face.

When I loved Jake, when our relationship wasn't too complicated to have a label like that, it was this absolute quality that I loved, this straightness, this desire for goodness, and mostly the struggle he put up with himself, the manly difficulty of that. I didn't know anyone like him. I don't know that this appreciation is reciprocated—when he talks about me to his pastor and other men he likes who are religious, they will have a long tradition of misogyny to consult. He will not be guided to see things from my point of view. Well, deep in the night, curled up on the couch with the pillow over my head, somewhere in the realm of sleep, I do feel what he felt and see what he saw and hear what he heard: the flippant and dismissive tone of my voice, the indifference of my face in the half light, the inviting and unusual way I was wedged into that space, easy prey, and deserving of punishment too. I feel again the corner enclosing my flesh, the panic surging out of me in a flood, and I wake up with a start. Containing both points of view at once makes me short of breath. I sit up and gaze around the living room. For the first time in weeks, I don't want Jonathan. I try to make myself think of him, but my mind won't fix.

Jonathan used to run a millworks, producing hardwood moldings for lumberyards. He made some money and sold the business, and now he goes to school in horticulture and landscape architecture. He taught an extension course in tree fruits, which is where I met him, and which is why he has his days free and why he can talk to Jake, whose only ambition in life is to run a market garden with his brother Richie. Richie would grow only corn, Jake would do the other vegetables and press cider in the fall. I would do fresh-cut flowers in season and apples in the fall. Right now Jake and Richie have other jobs: Richie manages a big A & P in the next town and Jake works for the county government as an accountant. Jake and Richie and I own 57 acres, free and clear. Next summer, the five brothers are going to begin building a house on the land. Every weekend, all spring, Jake and Richie have gone out to the property and walked its every inch, looking for the best site for the house and the garden and the garden buildings. That gave Jonathan and me four or five extra hours every week that we wouldn't have had, and it was on one of those weekends, when I forgot my diaphragm, that I got pregnant. In the ten years of marriage, I have forgotten it off and on, without consequences, and each of the other pregnancies took a number of months, and so I was careless. Careless and lazy: I realized I had forgotten it before I was to the end of our street, but I couldn't bear to turn back and thought I would trust to luck, as I had in the past. Careless and lazy and possessed. There have been times in the last seven months when putting off seeing Jonathan for even ten minutes was the cruelest torture.

We bought the property two years ago, with savings and with Jake's and Richie's portions of their father's estate. I like Richie. All that summer he would come over about dinnertime and sit on the porch swing, talking to Jake about what sort of house they would build and watching Dory. Dory was sixteen months when we bought the land. When Richie was here, we would prop open all the doors and she would charge through all the rooms and in and out of the house. He would help her down the front steps, and she would tear around the yard, which was fenced. She was utterly safe and utterly free, and maybe for that reason, much happier than Nancy and Ezra were at that age. Rhonda and Walker came over a lot too. We have all known each other for a long time. Lots of times, Rhonda would go into the kitchen and open the cabinets and start making dinner, and though I had disagreements with

Jake that everyone knew about, there was a largeness and comfort to family life that soothed me. It spread in every direction,
over the landscape, from the past into the future. It was
enough to buy land and plan, to care for the children, to dig
and plant. Richie and Walker distracted Jake, engaged him in
conversation, made him feel at ease. Whatever was missing
between us got to seem like just a certain coloring, a certain
way the landscape might be lit but wasn't, nothing particular,
considering everything else that was there. Richie, after all,
wasn't even married, had never, as far as we knew, had a
steady girlfriend.

Usually, these days, it seems like nothing, what we had at
all those dinnertimes, but just now, when I am cold and tired
and frightened of sleep, it seems like a thing of substance and
weight, safe as a vault, with the child rolling through it like a
golden ball.

I don't know anyone who has had an abortion, but it can be
done. Rhonda would know all about it. And if this were the
moment when it was to be done, I would do it, because no one
else is here, not Jonathan or Nancy or Ezra or Jake or Richie or
Rhonda or my mother. Only I am here, and for the moment
Jake has pounded sentiment out of me. Nothing in this room,
which we bought and filled with our purchases, means a thing
to me, not even the pictures. Nothing I have ever felt or
thought or given voice to remotely interests me just now, no
principle or affection or intention. I sit against the arm of the
couch, waiting to make up my mind to have an abortion.

Instead it must be that I fall asleep, because Ezra wakes me,
and it is daylight, though just barely. Ezra always comes down
early and expects to have the house to himself for an hour. He
says, "Mommy, can I turn on the TV?" and the day is begun. I
look at him for a long moment, until he smiles in self-defense,
and then I say, "Do you have riding again today?" and he
grins. He says, "Alan, you know, the head of riding, he said I
could ride Herbie every time, if I asked." He goes and turns on
the TV, then glances back at me. "He's a real good horse, Mom.
And he's a horse, not a pony."

"Hmm."

"Do you know the difference?"

"I do, actually."

"Well, he's a horse."

"Good, sweetie." I pull myself up the stairs and into the bathroom.

At breakfast I act as if nothing has happened, and Jake can think he is getting away with something if he wants. I put his eggs in front of him and meet his gaze, and I am nearly as tender with him as I am with the children, brushing their shoulders or hair with my hand. And then they are gone, and I pick up the phone and I call Jonathan and make a date with him for lunch. His voice is distant, distracted. After that I make sure that Rhonda is going to her dance class and that I can come along. Then I do the dishes and sweep the kitchen. In fact, I get down on my hands and knees with the butler's brush and sweep like I've never swept before, getting the dust and sand of seven years out of the corners, off the top edge of the moldings, out from under the stove and refrigerator. When I am finished, I am dusty and sweaty. I go around and open the windows, catching what breeze there is. After that I take another shower.

The fact is that this is the last hour of the old life. Things that are soft are about to harden and take the simple shapes that may last them the rest of my life. For example, I don't hate Jake and I don't love Jonathan. Whatever I feel for each of them is like one of those dye baths that you dip the endpapers of books in—a riot of colors swirled together, compounded of everything each has confided in me and everything I have confided in each of them. At this moment, I have the feeling that each time I have looked at each one of them is distinct and significant, that I know some discrete grain of truth about each of them as a result of every glance. The large thing that I know about them is that they are not each other, but that large thing is compounded of the numberless small ways in which they are not each other. I don't blame them for not being each other, but as soon as I speak, they will move into position. Jake, betrayed, will become my enemy. Jonathan, responsible, will become my partner. I would be deluding myself if I didn't know that he will consider my pregnancy a moral outrage in addition to an injury to himself. If he doesn't tell his brothers, and probably my children, that I am a whore, then he won't be the Jake I have known for ten years. And so the children will move into position too: confused at first, judgmental later, damaged forever. And Jonathan. Well, Jonathan. Just because I know that he will do the right thing, does that mean I planned for him to? At lunch I'll tell him I'm pregnant before he tells me we have to end our affair, and for a lot of reasons, he will swallow his doubts, and I will swallow mine, and sometime soon I will tell him that I love him, because I will love him. I will move into position too. Maybe.

A week after the funeral, when the children were back in school, I walked to the library and then to Jonathan's house. It was the day before Valentine's Day, warm and sunny, with snow melt trickling down every gutter. I had thrown away the valentine I intended to give him—it was one of those cynical and sexy ones, and when I found it in my purse the day after the funeral, it seemed to be cursed, so I tore it up, tore it up again, took it down the street, and threw it into some dry cleaner's Dumpster. I was chastened. Everything having to do with Jonathan Ricklefs frightened me. We hadn't slept together very often—our friendship was more teasing and drinking tea than anything else. He seemed invulnerable, possibly dating someone else, though I wasn't sure. Jake was at work, my mother had left, the children were back in school, and I was walking down the street, glad to be put back together a little bit, glad that the previous night was over and the night to come wasn't yet upon me. I climbed the step and rang the bell, and I remember turning and looking down the street, idly, thinking of nothing for a moment. And then the door opened, and Jonathan was there, and his hand closed around my elbow, and he pulled me into the hallway where he hugged me and looked at me and put his hand on my face and then hugged me again, and just at that moment when he looked at me, I knew two things at once, that Dory was dead and that Jonathan loved me as he had not loved me ten days before. I don't know that any relationship can survive that sort of birth for long. Or maybe the root is this, that when I was standing in the closet that morning, buttoning my shirt, it was Jonathan I was thinking of, Jonathan who had delayed me in the closet, taking off one shirt and putting on another. I was thinking about him sucking my breasts; I could feel my nipples rise against the cotton of the shirt as I thought, *What's that noise?*

In the first hour of the new life, I will speak and act and justify and choose. I will summarize and simplify, in order to make the new life. I will start forgetting what I know in the last hour of the old life. I don't think this is the least of the things that will be destroyed.

I am pulling up my tights in the locker room when Rhonda comes in. She is lovely, my sister. She has two dimples, still, one just under her left eye, the other just to the right of her smile. In the humidity, her hair springs out of her bun with curly abandon. "Sary!" she roars. Her voice is always gravelly and ironic, because in spite of everything she still smokes cigarettes. "Am I late? I had to buy these new tights! Look at this! Is that shine? Don't you love it?" She goes over and stubs out her cigarette in the sink, then wets the end and throws it in the trashcan. "Shit. We've got to hurry. Henry always notices if you're late. Last week he wouldn't let one of them dance, that one who always wears the silver leotard."

I run after her. She snaps the front of her leotard as we trot down the hall. At the door, I put my hand on hers, holding it closed. She looks at me. I say, "Rhonda. Wait a minute." And I tell her. Then I open the door and walk in. Henry has started pliés. I take my place in line. Two minutes later, I feel Rhonda behind me, everything about her, her sadness and her fear as well as her presence. She gives out a little moan. Henry casts her a glance.

He says, "There is a thread attached to that spot on the back of your head where the hair swirls around. You know that spot? Just a thread. If you let your spine stretch upward as your buttocks drop down, you won't break that thread." My chin drops, the vertebrae seem to release one another and float. This is it, isn't it, what Jake calls God and Jonathan calls passion. I lift my arms and drop and spread my shoulders, then turn. Rhonda is there, and her face is white and her expression dismayed. She would like a cigarette. This is it, isn't it, this movement, movement, only movement, only the feeling of life running through the tissues. After all, it makes me smile. A second later, my sister smiles back.

Walter Mosley

THE THIEF

Iula's grill sat on aluminum stilts above an open-air, fenced-in auto garage on Slauson. Socrates liked to go to the diner at least once a month on a Tuesday because they served meat loaf and mustard greens on Tuesdays at Iula's. The garage was run by Tony LaPort, who had rented the diner out to Iula since before their marriage; it was a good arrangement for Tony so he still leased to her eight years after their divorce.

Tony had constructed the restaurant when he was in love and so it was well built. The diner was made from two large yellow school buses that Tony had welded together—side by side. The front bus held the counter where the customers sat, while the back bus held the kitchen and storage areas. The banistered stairway that led up to the door was aluminum also. When Iula closed for the night she used a motor-driven hoist to lift the staircase far up off the street. Then she'd go through the trapdoor down to Tony's work space, let herself out through the wire gate, and set the heavy padlocks that Tony used to keep thieves out.

If the locks failed to deter an enterprising crook there was still Tina to contend with. Tina was a hundred-pound mastiff who hated everybody in the world except Iula and Tony. Tina sat right by the gate all night long, paws crossed in a holy prayer that some fool might want to test her teeth.

She was waiting that afternoon as Socrates approached the aluminum stairs. She growled in a low tone and Socrates found himself wondering if he would have a chance to crush the big dog's windpipe before she could tear out his throat. It was an idle thought; the kind of question that men discussed when they were in prison. In prison studying for survival was the only real pastime.

How many ways were there to kill a man? What was more dangerous in a close fight—a gun or a knife? How long could you hold your breath underwater if there were policemen looking for you on the shore? Will God really forgive any sin?

Thinking about killing that dog was just habit for Socrates. The habit of twenty-nine out of fifty-seven years behind bars.

As he climbed the aluminum staircase he thought again about how well built it was. He liked the solid feeling that the light metal gave. He was happy because he could smell the mustard greens.

He could almost taste that meat loaf.

"Shet that do'!" Iula shouted, her back turned to Socrates. "Damn flies like t'eat me up in here."

"Shouldn't cook so damn good you don't want no notice, I." Socrates slammed shut the makeshift screen door and walked up the step well into the bus.

The diner was still empty at 4:30. Socrates came early because he liked eating alone. He went to the stool nearest Iula and sat down. The musical jangle of coins rose from the pockets of his army jacket.

"You been collectin' cans again?" Iula had turned around to admire her customer. Her face was a deep amber color splattered with dark freckles, especially around her nose. She was wide-hipped and large-breasted. Three gold teeth decorated her smile. And she was smiling at Socrates. She put a fist on one hip and pushed her apron out, making an arc that brushed her side of the counter.

Socrates was looking at those breasts. Tony had once told him that the first time he saw those titties they were standing straight up, nipples pointing left and right.

"Yeah, I," he said, in answer to her question. "I got me a

route now. Got three barmen keep the bottles an' cans on the side for me. All I gotta do is clean up outside for them twice a week. I made seventeen dollars just today."

"Ain't none these young boys out here try an' take them bottles from you, Mr. Fortlow?"

"Naw. Gangbanger be ashamed t'take bottles in a sto'. An' you know as long as I got my black jeans and army green I don't got no color t'get them young bulls mad. If you know how t'handle them they leave you alone."

"I'ont care what you say," Iula said. "Them boys make me sick wit' all that rap shit they playin' an' them guns an' drugs."

"I seen worse," Socrates said. "You know these three men live in a alley offa Crenshaw jump me today right after I got my can money."

"They did?"

"Uh-huh. Fools thought they could take me." Socrates held out his big black hand. The thick fingers were the size of large cigars. When he made a fist the knuckles rode high like four deadly fins.

Iula was impressed.

"They hurt you?" she asked.

Socrates looked down at his left forearm. There, near the wrist, was a sewn-up tear and a dark stain.

"What's that?" Iula cried.

"One fool had a bottle edge. Huh! He won't try an' cut me soon again."

"Did he break the skin?"

"Not too much."

"You been to a doctor, Mr. Fortlow?"

"Naw. I went home an' cleaned it out. Then I sewed up my damn coat. I cracked that boy's arm 'cause he done ripped my damn coat."

"You better get down to the emergency room," Iula said. "That could get infected."

"I cleaned it good."

"But you could get lockjaw."

"Not me. In the penitentiary they gave you a tetanus booster every year. You might get a broke jaw in jail but you ain't never gonna get no lockjaw."

Socrates laughed and set his elbows on the counter. He cleared his throat and looked at Iula watching him. Behind her was the kitchen and a long frying grill. There were big pots of beef-and-tomato soup, mashed potatoes, braised short ribs, stewed chicken, and steaming mustard greens simmering on the stove. The meat loaves, Socrates knew from experience, were in bread pans in the heating pantry above the ovens.

It was hot in Iula's diner.

Hotter under her stare.

She put her hand on Socrates's arm.

"You shouldn't be out there hustlin' bottles, Mr. Fortlow," she said. Her voice was like the rustling of coarse blankets.

"I got t'eat. An' you know jobs don't grow on trees, I. Anyway, I got a bad temper. I might turn around one day an' break a boss's nose."

Iula laid her finger across his knuckles.

"You could work here," she said. "There's room enough for two behind this here counter."

Iula turned her head to indicate what she meant. In doing so she revealed her amber throat, it was a lighter shade than her face.

He remembered another woman, just a girl really, and her delicate neck. That woman died by the same hand Iula stroked. She died and hadn't done a thing to deserve even a bruise. He had killed her and was a little sorrier every day; every day for thirty-six years. He got sadder but she was still dead. She was dead, and he was still asking himself why.

"I don't know," he said.

"What?"

"I don't know what to say, I."

"What is there to say?" she demanded. "All you could say is yeah. You ain't got hardly a dime. You need a job. And the Lord knows I could use you, too."

"I got to think about it," he said.

"Think about it?" Just that fast Iula was enraged. "Think about it? Here I am offerin' you a way outta that hole you in. Here I am offerin' you a life. An' you got to think about it? Look out here in the streets around you, Mr. Fortlow. Ain't no choice out there. Ain't nuthin' t'think about out there."

Socrates didn't have to look around to see the boarded-up businesses and stores; the poor black faces and brown faces of the men and women who didn't have a thing. Iula's diner and Tony's garage were the only working businesses on the block.

And he hated bringing bottles and cans to the Ralph's supermarket on Crenshaw. To get there he had to walk for miles pulling three grocery carts linked by twisted wire coat hangers. And when he got there, they always made him wait; made him stand outside while they told jokes and had coffee breaks. And then they checked every can. They didn't have to do that. He knew what they took and what they didn't. He came in twice a week with his cans and bottles and nobody ever found one Kessler's Root Beer or Bubble-Up in the lot. But they checked every one just the same. And they never bothered to learn his name. They called him Pop or Old Man. They made him wait and checked after him like he was some kind of stupid animal.

But he took it. He took it because of that young girl's neck; because of her boyfriend's dead eyes. Those young people in Ralph's were stupid and arrogant and mean—but he was evil. That's what Socrates thought.

That's what he believed.

"Well?" Iula asked.

"I'd . . . I'd like some meat loaf, Iula. Some meat loaf with mashed potatoes and greens."

From the back of her throat Iula hissed, "Damn you!"

Socrates was heavyhearted over the thoughts he had. He was sad, even depressed, over the guilt he could not escape.

But that didn't affect his appetite. He'd learned when he was a boy that the next meal was never a promise and that only a fool didn't eat when he could.

He laced his mashed potatoes and meat loaf with pepper sauce and downed the mustard greens in big noisy mouthfuls. When he was finished he looked behind the counter hoping to catch Iula's eye. Because usually Iula would give Socrates seconds while smiling and complimenting him on the good appetite he had.

"You eat good but you don't let it turn to fat," she'd say, admiring his big muscles.

But now she was mad at him for insulting her offer. Why should she feed the kitty when there wasn't a chance to win the game?

"I," Socrates said.

"What you want?" It was more a dare than a question.

"Just some coffee, babe," he said.

Iula slammed the mug down and flung the Pyrex coffeepot so recklessly that she spilled half of what she poured. But Socrates didn't mind. He was still hungry and so he finished filling the mug with milk from two small serving pitchers on the counter.

He had eleven quarters in his right-hand jacket pocket. Two dollars and fifty cents for the dinner and twenty-five cents more for Iula's tip. That was a lot of money when all you had to your name was seventy-two quarters, four dimes, three nickels, and eight pennies. It was a lot of money but Socrates was still hungry—and that meat loaf smelled better than ever.

Iula used sage in her meat loaf. He couldn't make it at home because all he had at home was a hot plate and you can't make meat loaf on a hot plate.

"Iula!"

Socrates turned to see the slim young man come up into the bus. He was wearing an electric-blue exercise suit, zipped up to the neck, and a bright-yellow headband.

"Wilfred," Iula said in greeting. There were still no seconds in her voice.

"How things goin'?" the young man asked.

"Pretty good if you don't count for half of it."

"Uh-huh," he answered, not having heard. "An' where's Tony today?"

"It's Tuesday, ain't it?"

"Yeah."

"Then Tony's down at Christ Congregational settin' up for bingo."

Wilfred sat himself at the end of the counter, five stools away from Socrates. He caught the older man's eye and nodded—as black men do.

Then he said, "I done built me up a powerful hunger today, Iula. I got two hollow legs to fill."

"What you want?" she asked, not at all interested in the story he was obviously wanting to tell.

"You got a steak back there in the box?"

"Shit." She would have spit on the floor if she wasn't in her own restaurant.

"Okay. Okay. I tell you what. I want some stewed chicken, some braised ribs, an' two thick slabs'a meat loaf on one big plate."

"That ain't on the menu."

"Charge me a dinner for each one then."

Iula's angry look changed to wonder. "You only get one slice of meat loaf with a dinner."

"Then ring it up twice, honey. I got mad money for this here meal."

Iula stared until Wilfred pulled out a fan of twenty-dollar bills from his pocket. He waved the fan at her and said, "Don't put no vegetables on that shit. You know I'm a workin' man—I needs my strength. I need meat."

Iula moved back into the kitchen to fill Wilfred's order.

Socrates sipped his coffee.

"Hey, brother," Wilfred said.

Socrates looked up at him.

"How you doin'?" the young man offered.

"Okay, I guess."

"You guess?"

"It depends."

"Depends on what?"

"On what comes next."

When Wilfred smiled Socrates could see that he was missing one of his front teeth.

"You jus' livin' minute t'minute, huh?" the young man said.

"That's about it."

"I used to be like that. Used to be. That is till I fount me a good job." Wilfred sat back as well as he could on the stool and stared at Socrates as if expecting to be asked a question.

Socrates took another sip of coffee. He was thinking about another helping of meat loaf and his quarters and Iula's nipples—and that long-ago-dead girl. He didn't have any room for what was on the young man's mind.

Iula came out then with a platter loaded down with meats. It was a steaming plate looking like something out of the dreams Socrates had when he was deep inside of his jail sentence.

"Put it over there, Iula." Wilfred was pointing to the place next to Socrates. He got up from his stool and went to sit behind the platter.

He was a tall man, in his twenties. He'd shaved that morning and had razor bumps along his jaw and throat. His clothes were bulky and Socrates wondered why. He was thin and well built. Obviously from *the 'hood*—Socrates could tell that from the hunger he brought to his meal.

"What's your name, man?" Wilfred asked.

"Socrates."

"That's somebody famous right?"

"Long time ago."

"In Europe right?"

"I guess."

"You see?" Wilfred said, full of pride. "I ain't no fool. I know shit. I got it up here. My name is Wilfred."

Socrates breathed in deeply the smells from Wilfred's plate. He was still hungry—having walked a mile for every dollar he'd made that day.

His stomach growled like an angry dog.

"What you eatin', Socco?" Wilfred asked. Before giving him a chance to answer he called out to Iula, "What's my brother eatin', Iula? Bring whatever it is out to 'im. I pay for that, too."

While Iula put together Socrates's second plate, Wilfred picked up a rib and sucked the meat from the bone.

He grinned and said, "Only a black woman could cook like this."

Socrates didn't know about that, but he was happy to see the plate Iula put before him.

Socrates didn't pick up his fork right away. Instead he regarded his young benefactor and said, "Thank you."

"That's okay, brother. Eat up."

Halfway through his second meal Socrates's hunger eased a

bit. Wilfred was almost through with his four dinners. He pushed the plate back.

"You got some yams back there?" he called out to Iula.

"Yeah," she answered. She had gone to a chair in her kitchen to rest and smoke a cigarette before more customers came.

"Bring out a big plate for me an' my friend here."

Iula brought out the food without saying a word to Socrates. But he wasn't worried about her silence.

He came around on Tuesdays, when Tony was gone, because he wanted Iula for something; a girlfriend, a few nights in bed, maybe more, maybe. He hadn't been with a woman since before prison when, in a blind rage, he'd slaughtered a man, raped that man's girlfriend, and then broke her neck for whining about it.

When the judge asked him for an explanation he couldn't give it. What was there to say? That he'd been mad as hell every day of his life and then that one day it all fell into place?

He had the right amount of Jim Beam and reefer, he was in the man's house, and the man's girlfriend was giving him the eye. When Socrates looked back at her the boyfriend wanted to fight.

Fight him! When it was his woman smiling and flirting like some whore.

It just all fell into place like a royal flush, like a perfect left hook.

And when it was over he didn't even know what he had done. He woke up the next morning with barely a notion of the crime. He'd hit the man pretty hard. He choked the girl till she stopped that crying.

But it wasn't till the prosecutor showed the police photographs in court that he knew for sure what he'd done.

He wanted to tell the judge that he didn't mean it, that he was sorry, but the words didn't come. They didn't come for a long time. When they finally came out, he'd been in prison for a dozen years.

And when they'd let him out of jail, because it was his birthday and because he hadn't killed anybody white, he was afraid; afraid of his hands on a woman. Afraid of the photograph of that girl.

Iula was petulant, but she didn't understand how scared he was even to want her.

But he did want her; partly because she wanted him. She wanted a man up there on stilts with her to lift tubs of shortening that she couldn't budge. She wanted a man to sit down next to her in the heat that those stoves threw off.

If he came up there he'd probably get fat.

"What you thinkin' about, brother?" Wilfred asked.

"That they ain't nuthin' for free."

"Well . . . maybe sometime they is."

"Maybe," Socrates said, "but I don't think so."

Wilfred grinned.

Socrates asked, "What kinda work you do, Wilfred?"

"I'm self-employed. I'm a businessman."

"Oh yeah? What kinda business?"

Wilfred smiled and tried to look coy. "What you think?"

"I'd say a thief," Socrates answered. He speared a hot yam and pushed it in his mouth.

Wilfred's smile widened but his eyes went cold.

"You got sumpin' against a man makin' a livin'?" he asked.

"Depends."

" 'Pends on what?"

"On if it's wrong or not."

"Stealin's stealin', man. It's all the same thing. You got it—I take it."

"If you say so."

"That's what I do say," Wilfred said. "Stealin's right for the man takin' an' wrong fo' the man bein' took. That's all they is to it."

Socrates decided that he didn't like Wilfred. But his stomach was full and he'd become playful. "But if a man take some bread an' he's hungry, starvin'," he said, "that's not wrong to nobody. That's good sense."

"Yeah. You right," Wilfred conceded. "But s'pose you hungry for a good life. For a nice house with a bathtub an' not just some shower. S'pose you want some nice shoes an' socks don't bust out through the toe the first time you wear 'em?"

"That depends, too."

" 'Pends on what? What I want don't depend on a damn thing." Wilfred's smile was gone now.

"Maybe not. I mean maybe the wantin' don't depend on nuthin' but how you get it does, though."

"Like what you mean?"

"Well, let's say that there's a store sellin' this good life you so hungry for. They got it in a box somewhere. Now you go an' steal it. Well, I guess that's okay. That means the man got the good life give it up to you. That's cool."

"Shit," Wilfred said. "If they had a good life in a box you know I steal me hunnert'a them things. I be right down here on Adams sellin' 'em for half price."

"Uh-huh. But they don't have it in a box now do they?"

"What you tryin' t'say, man?" Wilfred was losing patience. He was, Socrates thought, a kind benefactor as long as he didn't have to see a man eye to eye.

"I'm sayin' that this good life you talkin' 'bout stealin' comes outta your own brother's mouth. Either you gonna steal from a man like me or you gonna steal from a shop where I do my business. An' ev'ry time I go in there I be payin' for security cameras an' security guards an' up-to-the-roof insurance that they got t'pay off what people been stealin'."

Socrates thought that Wilfred might get mad. He half expected the youth to pull out a gun. But Socrates wasn't worried about a gun in those quarters. He had a knife handy and, as he had learned in prison, a knife can beat a gun up close.

But Wilfred wasn't mad. He laughed happily. He patted Socrates on the shoulder, feeling his hard muscle, and said, "You got a good tongue there, brother. You good as a preacher, or a cop, when it comes to talkin' that talk."

Wilfred stood up and Socrates swiveled around on his seat, ready for the fight.

Iula sensed the tension and came out with a cigarette dangling from her lips.

Wilfred stripped off his exercise jacket and stepped out of the gaudy nylon pants. Underneath he was wearing a two-piece tweed suit with a suede brown vest. His silk tie showed golden and green clouds with little flecks of red floating here and there. His shirt was white as Sunday's clothesline.

"What you think?" Wilfred asked his audience.

Iula grunted and turned back to her kitchen. He was too skinny for her no matter what he had on.

"Come here," Wilfred said to Socrates. "Look out here in the street."

Socrates went to the bus window and crouched down to look outside. There was a new tan car, a foreign job, parked out there. Socrates didn't know the model, but it looked like a nice little car.

"That's my ride," Wilfred said.

"Where it take you?" Socrates asked, but he already suspected the answer.

"Wherever I wanna go," Wilfred answered. "But mostly I hit the big malls an' shoppin' centers up in West Hollywood, Beverly Hills, Santa Monica, and what have you. I get one'a my girlfriends to rent me a car. Then I get all dressed up like this an' put a runnin' suit, or maybe some funky clothes like you got on, over that. An' I always got me a hat or a headband or somethin'. You know they could hardly ever pick you out of a lineup if you had sumpin' on yo' head."

Socrates had learned that in jail, too.

"I grab 'em in the parkin' lot." Wilfred sneered with violent pleasure. "I put my knife up hard against they necks an' tell 'em they dead. You know I don't care if I cut 'em up a li'l bit. Shit. I had one young Jap girl peed on herself."

Wilfred waited for a laugh or something. When it didn't come the jaunty young man went back to his seat.

"You don't like it," Wilfred said, "too bad."

"I don't give a damn what you do, boy," Socrates answered. He sat back down and ate the last piece of meat loaf from his plate. "I cain't keep a fool from messin' up."

"I ain't no fool, old man. I don't mess up, neither. I get they money an' cut 'em up some so they call a doctor fo' they call the cops. Then I run an' th'ow off my niggah clothes. When the cops come I'm in my suit, in my car comin' home. An' if they stop me I look up all innocent an' lie an' tell 'em that I work for A&M Records. I tell 'em that I'm a manager in the mail room over there. No sir, I don't fuck up at all."

"Uh-huh," Socrates said. He put a yam in his mouth after dipping it in the honey-butter sauce at the bottom of the dish; it was just about the best thing he had ever tasted.

"Motherfuckah, you gonna sit there an' diss me with yo' mouth fulla the food I'm buyin'?" Wilfred was amazed.

"You asked me an' I told ya," Socrates said. "I don't care what you do, boy. But that don't mean I got to call it right."

"What you talkin' 'bout, man? I ain't stealin' from no brother. I ain't stealin' where no po' brother live. I'm takin' the good life from people who got it—just like you said."

"You call my clothes funky din't ya, boy?"

"Hey, man. I din't mean nuthin'."

"Yes you did," Socrates said. "You think I'm funky an' smelly an' I ain't got no feelin's. That's what you think. You don't see that I keep my socks darned an' my clothes clean. You don't see that you walkin' all over me like I was some piece dog shit. An' you don't care. You just put on a monkey suit an' steal a few pennies from some po' woman's purse. You come down here slummin', flashin' some dollar bills, talkin' all big. But when you all through people gonna look at me like I'm shit. They scared'a me 'cause you out there pretendin' that you're me robbin' them."

Wilfred held up his hands in a false gesture of surrender and laughed. "You too deep for me, brother," he said. He was smiling but alert to the violence in the older man's words. "Way too deep."

"You the one shovelin' it, man. You the one out there stealin' from the white man an' blamin' me. You the one wanna be like them in their clothes. You hatin' them an' dressed like the ones you hate. You don't even know who the hell you is!"

Socrates had to stop himself from striking Wilfred. He was shaking, scared of his own hands.

"I know who I am all right, brother," Wilfred said. "And I'm a damn sight better'n you."

"No you not," Socrates said. A sense of calm came over him. "No you not. You just dressin' good, eatin' like a pig. But when the bill come due I'm the one got t'pay it. Me an' all the rest out here."

"All right, fine!" Wilfred shouted. "But the only one right now payin' fo' somethin' is me. I'm the one got you that food you been eatin'. But if you don't like it then pay for it yourself."

Iula came out again. Socrates noted the pot of steaming water she carried.

"I do you better than that, boy," Socrates said. "I'll pay for yo' four dinners, too."

"What?" Wilfred and Iula both said.

"All of it," Socrates said. "I'll pay for it all."

"You a new fool, man," Wilfred said.

Socrates stood up and then bent down to pick up Wilfred's stickup clothes from the floor.

"You always got to pay, Wilfred. But I'll take this bill. I'll leave the one out there for you."

Wilfred faked a laugh and took the clothes from Socrates.

"Get outta here, man," Socrates said.

For a long moment, death hung between the two men. Wilfred full of violence and pride and Socrates sick of violent and prideful men.

"I don't want no trouble in here, now!" Iula shouted when she couldn't take the tension anymore.

Wilfred smiled again and nodded. "You win, old man," he said. "But you crazy, though."

"Just get outta here," Socrates said. "Go."

Wilfred considered for the final time doing something. He was probably faster than the older man. But it was a small space and strength canceled out speed in close quarters.

Socrates read all of that in Wilfred's eyes. Another young fool, he knew, who thought freedom was out the back door and in the dark.

Wilfred turned away slowly, went down the stairwell, then down the aluminum staircase to the street.

Socrates watched the tan car drive off.

"You're insane, Socrates Fortlow, you know that?" Iula said. She was standing on her side of the counter in front of eighteen stacks of four quarters each.

"You got to pay for your dinner, I."

"But why you got to pay for him? He had money."

"That was just a loan, I. But the interest was too much for me."

"You ain't responsible fo' him."

"You wrong there, baby. I'm payin' for niggahs like that ev'ry day. Just like his daddy paid for me."

"You are a fool."

"But I'm my own fool, I."

"I don't get it," she said. "If you so upstandin' an' hardworkin' an' honest—then why don't you wanna come here an' work fo' me? Is it 'cause I'm a woman? 'Cause you don't wanna work fo' no woman?"

Socrates was feeling good. The food in his stomach had killed the hunger. The muscles in his arms relaxed now that he didn't have to fight. There was an ache in his forearm where he'd been cut but, as the prison doctor used to say, pain was just a symptom of life.

Socrates laughed.

"You're a woman, all right, I. I know you had that boilin' water out there t'save me from Wilfred. You a woman all right and I'm gonna be comin' back here every Tuesday from now on. I'm gonna come see you and we gonna talk too, momma. Yeah. You gonna be seein' much more'a me."

He got up and kissed her on the cheek before leaving. When his lips touched her skin a sound came from the back of her throat. The sound of satisfaction that takes a lifetime to understand.

Socrates only had four dimes, three nickels, and eight pennies left to his name. If he took a bus he'd be broke, but he was just as happy to walk. On the way home he thought about finding a job somewhere. He thought about making a living from the strength of his hands.

Elizabeth Graver

BETWEEN

For Juda

It is hard to tell among so many bodies—and some of them in skirts—but I think I am the only woman in the bar. Dancing there, close up to the go-go boys on their boxes, the men gleaming like seals, eyes only for each other. It used to be I was a stiff, small dancer, one leg forward, one leg back—jerk, jerk, a tight nod of the head, a bird bobbing for seed. How do I know? I could see my limbs lit red with awkwardness. Now I do not see myself, too small among the bodies, and mine the wrong kind.

I dance myself outside myself. No one looks.

Why does Paolo bring me to the bar? I'm not sure. Sometimes I think it is because he loves me. Other times I think it is because I am a fashion accessory, like the dachshunds or Chihuahuas the other men parade down Commercial Street. I do, in some ways, fit the part, small and lean, almost like a boy, now that we have cut my hair. "Time for a new you," said Paolo this morning on the beach, snip snip on each long strand, and then the ceremonial flinging of my locks into the sea. Sheared I was, cropped close. Paolo held my tiny, light skull between his hands and told me where my hair would go: wrapped around the *Titanic*, swallowed by sharks, part of the great blue.

"I'm ugly now," I said, though I could not see myself on the beach. "No one will ever want me."

"You're adorable, you could be the cutest little dyke."

I shook my weightless head.

"OK, then, just enough boy in you to excite the boys."

"You think?"

He snipped at stray hairs on my neck. "Of course. I could almost have a conversion experience over you."

"Right."

"No, I mean it, with angels and the works. A hundred naked cherubs."

I tried not to smile. "By the time you get through with them, I'll be past menopause."

Paolo brushed off my neck with his towel, backed up and surveyed his work. "Exquisite," he said, turning me around. "I get dinner for this. Let's go home."

When we got back, I saw in the mirror how smooth I had become, my neck longer, my eyes somehow darker than before. And in the shower I was a boy, almost, my hands smoothing away the lines of breast, the hip curves. In the soap dish was a nub of lemon soap, a present Tim had given me before he left. What would he think now, I wondered. Would he want me more, like this, or less?

Paolo and I are in many ways the perfect couple. In the winter, when the town is almost empty, we play at being married, at "Honey, you forgot the coupons," or "No more heavy cream, you need to watch your cholesterol." The locals love us, for we are gentle and playful with each other and look a pair, both of us dark and smallish. "A deal for you," they'll say at a garage sale, "since you're just starting out." It has been five years now since we met through a roommate ad in the paper, and still we cook and clean together, to Bonnie Raitt played loud. At eleven-thirty on nights when both of us are home, we watch "Love Connection" and lament the cruelty of dating, and over the long, bitter winters, we read aloud to each other, mostly from children's books. This winter Tim took turns reading too, from *Alice in Wonderland*. One night tucked between them on the couch, the three of us wrapped in a quilt, I realized that for the first time since I was a tiny child, I knew what the term "well-being" meant.

Sometimes I think Paolo brings me dancing for protection; it has been over a year since he has had a lover, though he is pretty as can be, and even at thirty-eight he is taken for a boy. We have our signals all worked out—the head scratch, the biting of the lip, the yawn. And then, on the way home, his regrets—how this one was all over him, how that one asked him for a walk on the beach. "Why not?" I coax. He has a thousand answers: too old, too young, too queeny, not smart enough, too trendy, never leaving, leaving the next day. All around us men are dying. "It's OK," I tell him, "if you're careful." But under my words I am afraid for him, and even further down, someplace fierce and selfish in my gut, I want him just for me.

We live two lives here. Summers we dance till late at night, then stop at Spiritus for an ice-cream shake. The nursery school where I teach closes for two months, and I spend my days sleeping, reading or making jam. Summer is Paolo's time, men everywhere, and I cook dinner for his friends, lie with them on the jetty, take boat rides with them when Paolo waits tables. They are fond of me; "fond" is the right word, not like Paolo, who loves me. These are men from the city—doctors, lawyers, and models who come down for the weekend. When I sun on the end of their sailboats, they spray water on me and heap careless compliments on my breasts.

Winter is my time. There are fewer men around, but they *see* me as I walk down the street, and I live the life of a fishing village girl, a date here, a date there, and then, when something goes a little bit right, a nice tousled, salty man in my bed, and then—careful, careful, each step could be the last—maybe another night and maybe I find out what he likes to read and who he voted for, and Paolo says, "This one sounds good" or "A man who hates his mother is bad news."

Tim he approved of from the start. "Notice his chest," said Paolo, "when he comes out of the shower and the hair curls in those little blond tendrils. Plus he's totally in love with you; he picked up your fingernail clippings and *played* with them. He probably saved them to light a candle to."

And Tim, like me, a teacher, tall and bulky and a man, but

playful when he rolled down hills with his second graders and did the floppy scarecrow dance in their production of *The Wizard of Oz.*

In the beginning it was fine between the three of us—almost, for a while, perfect. Sometimes I would go to Tim's, a few streets away, and eat dinner with him and his two roommates. More often he came to our place, and somehow the three of us fit into the narrow galley kitchen, where we cooked fish stews and chowders, apple and cheese omelettes. When I told my friend Emily how we were together, she said it sounded great, the best way not to scare Tim off.

"Break him in gradually," she said, and I pictured Tim tossing his hair like a mane, stomping his hoof. "You'll be moving in together before he realizes what's happened."

But the thing was, three was a number that pleased me. I loved being in the middle, the frosting inside the cookie, the door hinge, the go-between. I loved feeling *surrounded*, like a kid between her parents: one, two, and—swing—aloft over the curb. I loved the safety of our threesome, but also the shiver: between Tim and Paolo, maybe even between Paolo and me—nothing strong enough to act upon, but enough to put a gentle buzz of static in the air. With each of my two men I discussed the other, late at night in bed with Tim—"He thinks you're beautiful"—or at dinner alone with Paolo—"The longest time he's been with anyone is a year." And for a time, they liked it too, Paolo happy to have a man dripping in his shower, Tim pleased, I think, to be admired by the both of us, titillated, almost, to be safely with me and yet tousle Paolo's hair goodnight before we went to bed.

And in bed—this perhaps the strangest part—the way we played was not a play of two, but three, although Paolo never came inside the room. It began one night when I made my voice gravelly low and told Tim I liked his chest hair. I was joking, but he kept coming back to it: "My long-haired hippie boy," he called me. "My little sailor." Maybe, I told him, you want to sleep with men, with Paolo, but he said no, he was only fooling around, it was me he wanted. Yet I, too, could feel Paolo's presence through the wall, lying there sad, stiff, and alone, trying not to hear our sounds. And if it hadn't been a move into the outrageous (for Paolo and I were, in our way, the most domestic, conventional of people, with our canisters which said Sugar, Flour, Tea, correctly filled), I would have opened the door and asked him in, if he would come. Then Tim could be in the middle, the boy we both desired. It was too terrible, a house buzzing with sex and loneliness at the same time.

It was my mother who began to worry first.

"You'll never get really involved in a romantic relationship," she said, "as long as you live with Paolo."

"What are you talking about?" I said. "I have a boyfriend. Paolo doesn't keep me on a leash."

"I know you have a boyfriend—this boyfriend, that boyfriend. What about marriage? Children? You're already thirty and if I've understood you right, you want children and a full life."

What she meant was, you must work hard to guarantee yourself a better life than your mother's. Already she was unhappy about the fact that I had done so well in college and was now working for low wages in a nursery school. "It's just for now," I had told her—and myself—at first, but the truth was I loved reading aloud to a ring of sleepy four-year-olds, watching them plunge their fists into tubs of finger paint, seeing how they came into my classroom as stunned toddlers and left as resolute children. Whole families had passed through my classroom in the seven years I had been there.

A good job was one way to a better life in my mother's eyes; the other was a man. First, she thought, I had to transform my boyfriend into a husband. Then (this the trickier part), I had to make sure he did not die on me the way her husband, the way my father did—leaving her alone with me, a girl of six who got too many nosebleeds and would not be good company for many years.

I know, I know, I wanted to say to her. Like you, I feel the world as a fragile, teetering place, your fears all tangled through my veins. But don't you think there are other ways around this? My mother raised orchids, coaxed miracles from plants which have no roots and live in pots filled with stones. Last year she drove from Utica, New York, to Oxford, Mississippi, with her friends Miriam and Charlotte and slept under the open sky. What, I wanted to ask her, is a full life?

"I've got plenty of time," I told her instead. I did not tell her how, when I pictured my children, they sometimes had black hair and brown eyes, slender ankles, Paolo's clever hands. Paolo and I had discussed it, even, but always as an if—if I wasn't with someone when I reached the eleventh hour on my ticking clock.

Then it was Tim who began to worry.

"Listen," he said after we had been together for eight months and both had a spring vacation coming up. "What do you think about spending a week away somewhere, just us?"

"Sure," I said, "I'd like that." But when we began to plan a trip to northern Vermont, I couldn't bear the thought of Paolo home by himself.

"He'll be fine," said Tim. "He's a grown man. He lived for years without you."

No, I thought, no, you don't know him, how fragile he is under all his joking. But as we drove to a cabin in the mountains, I began to wonder who, really, I was protecting. How would we cook, just the two of us? How would we sit at dinner, across from each other or side by side? And when we went to bed, what would we do without that feeling of closing the door away from someone else, of being alone but not?

In fact I did sleep, did cook and eat and make love and feel my life begin to take a slightly new shape, like a bubble blown from a child's wand that gets caught by a sideways wind. From the cabin you could see a birch grove on one side, a brook out in front, not another house in sight.

"Someday," said Tim one morning as we walked through the woods, "I'm going to build a place like this, out here somewhere. All by hand—you can help if you want."

It was a voice he used to talk about things he planned to do, which usually involved either wandering the earth or building things. Soon after we'd met, he had pulled out a wooden crate filled with brochures and articles on World Teach, mountain gardens, homesteading, and trekking. At the time I had been half-charmed by his enthusiasm and half-worried by the fact that the one constant theme in the box seemed to be *not here*, *not you.* Lately he had begun to include me a little more, but his plans still made me nervous for their far-flungness. I pictured the two of us in a country where we were the only ones to speak each other's language, or perched on a mountaintop where the only light for miles was our own.

"It can't be too much fun out here in winter," I said.

He shrugged. "You just stock up on wood and get a car with four-wheel drive. It'd be great."

"You wouldn't miss the sea?"

"The Cape is becoming a zoo," he said. "Look at all these mountains. It's like no one even knows they're here."

"I'd go crazy."

"How do you know?"

How did I know? Maybe it would be peaceful; perhaps I would learn to live more comfortably under the vast arch of sky. But I doubted it. "I just know."

Each night I called Paolo. Each night he told me he missed me and filled me in on pieces of our life: the dryer had broken, a mouse had gotten into the pantry, my mother had called and sounded thrilled to learn I was away with Tim. The first few times I dialed the phone, I don't think I even noticed that Tim left the room, or sat humming tunelessly, picking at the lint on his sweater. On the third day when I hung up, though, he let out a sigh so loud I could not miss it.

"What?" I asked from the couch.

"How's your husband?" Tim was crouched by the fireplace peeling the bark off a log.

"What?"

"Your husband. Is he managing all alone in that great big house? Has he found out about us?"

"Come here," I said, but he only hunched closer to the log. I went over to him, leaned up against him, and kissed the back of his neck.

"Cut it out," he said, shaking me off. "I'm trying to talk to you."

"Jesus." I went back to the couch. "Look, I don't know what you're reacting to so strongly. I never thought you seemed jealous and anyway there's no need to be—"

"I'm not jealous," Tim said.

"Then what?"

"I'm not jealous, I just—you don't worry about me being lonely, you don't call me up to talk about the dryer—"

"We don't share a dryer, do you want to share a dryer?"

"Don't be an idiot."

"I'm sorry," I said. "If I don't worry about you being lonely it's because you have me."

But in my stomach I could feel fear beginning to stretch and unravel. He would leave me, said a voice in there; I had known it all along, from the day I saw his box of travel plans. And then another voice: But who can blame him, he's right, he should be jealous. You don't want to move to a far-off place where nobody breathes on the other side of the wall and the only way to Paolo is through a stretch of telephone wire.

"You do know," said Tim, "that he'd ditch you in a second if he found the right person."

In his voice I heard a hardness I had never heard before.

"You don't even know him," I said.

"Almost a year and I don't even know him? I've done everything but fuck the guy."

"In your dreams."

In my own voice I heard that same hardness. This, I wanted to say, this is what I'm afraid of—how easily, with these men I made love with, I came to be a snarling animal, claws flexed, baring all my teeth. This was nothing, compared to where we might end up. I had been there before—had made the long, cruel lists detailing another person's faults; kept secret count of gifts received, money spent; smashed pottery like a character in a TV movie.

With Paolo, too, I fought sometimes, but it wasn't like this, maybe because we couldn't *break up* (in my mind I saw a stick being cracked in two). I didn't know the smell of Paolo's hair, the feel of his spine, the slippery smooth wall of the inside of his mouth. With Tim—with every man I had ever slept with—I came so close to letting myself be turned inside out. Now I could feel an emptiness in my sternum, my pelvis, everywhere bones came together and formed a space.

"Come here, please?" I said again, and this time he did, though he sat turned away from me, and I wrapped myself around his back and spoke close to his ear.

"It's partly," I tried to explain, "it's maybe really screwed up, but it's partly because I *want* us to work out that I need to have Paolo. Otherwise I get too scared, like I'm putting too much weight on a bearing wall or something—"

Tim squirmed. "I'm glad you have such faith in us."

"It's not us, it's the whole thing, expecting that much of one person, it doesn't work, it shouldn't have to work. I mean, look around. But also—" I pictured Paolo stirring soup, tying the tomato plants to stakes with strips of his old shirts, curled before the TV. "Also I do love him, not like I love you, but he's my best friend. I thought you really liked him too."

"Of course I like him. Do I want to marry him? I'm not sure."

I pushed the words out of my mouth. "And me?"

He turned around and looked at me. "I'm not sure. Really I have no idea, but it seems pretty hard to figure out anything the way things are. I want—" He trailed off.

"What?"

"I want to travel again, I told you that before, and maybe end up someplace like this, or someplace else, where there's room to think. The Cape is hardly the most amazing place on earth, you know."

"I like to travel," I said, but my words came out weak. The truth was I loved to sit at home and watch how the dunes shifted, the shoreline changed shape, the summer people came and went and still I stayed.

"Maybe the real problem is you want to marry your roommate," said Tim.

"Stop."

"I don't think you'd leave him."

"It's not him, I'm settled, I have a whole life there."

"What if I decide to go to India?"

"I don't know." I pictured him with a walking stick, trekking somewhere. A place where there's room to think, he had said, as if thinking couldn't happen in a room. "Would you invite me?"

"Maybe. But not Paolo."

"Paolo hates to travel. He always gets sick." I turned away from Tim; outside the birches were shining in the dark. "Do you think we'll be OK?"

"I guess we should just go slowly," he said, "and wait and see."

I nodded, but as we lay in bed that night I could feel how guarded we had both become. It always happened after eight or nine months, the same time it took to make a baby. Suddenly it was almost a year you'd been together; everything tightened, crystallized. Before I started living with Paolo, I was the one who kept dragging my reluctant boyfriends to look at apartments. My mother, who now told me to want more, used to caution me: "Push too hard, Annie, and they'll run away."

I remembered the Pushmi-Pullyu beast from the Dr. Dolittle story Paolo and I had read aloud two winters before. If I was the one pushing, probably Tim would pull away. And if neither of us pushed or pulled? I wanted to see something lovely, cantering across the sand, but instead I saw a waterlogged, dead beast sinking down into the waves.

What happened instead was the world crashed in, Tim's father in Denver diagnosed with liver cancer. Tim got a month's leave from work and I drove him to the airport and gave him a long, tight hug good-bye.

"I don't know how to handle this," he said just before he got onto the plane. "I honestly have no idea."

"I know. But you will, you'll be OK, I know you will. Call me when you get there, do you promise?"

He nodded. "Listen—"

"What?"

"I don't know. If, I mean if I really flip out or something, do you think you might come out there, I'd help you pay for it—"

My mother crouched in the garden sobbing at night because she thought I could not hear her from my bedroom, but I could hear her, could see her bent shape as I knelt on my bed and bit into the chalky paint of the windowsill. The day of the funeral, she told me later, I brought out crackers into the living room where the aunts, the uncles, my mother sat; I passed around oyster crackers and patted backs, said don't worry, it'll be OK.

"Of course, just let me know," I said to Tim, but I was not thinking the right things. At least you'll know who he was, I was thinking. At least you'll have someone to remember.

After he got to Denver we talked on the phone every few days. "I miss you," I told him, and I did miss him, but I told him so extra, as if the word itself could save a space for us on his return. He did not ask me to come out there, and I did not offer. Sometimes when we were finished, he asked to speak to Paolo. Once, hearing in my silence some kind of hesitation, he said, "What? He's my friend, I can't talk to my friend?"

"Of course," I said and tried not to listen in or ask Paolo for a report after he hung up.

When I got the letter from Tim it was already July, and I thought, seeing my name on the envelope in his tiny, neat print, that it would tell me his father had died. The letter was short: "Annie, I've realized you're not someone I feel like I can depend on in times like this and so I think we should call things off. I'm too wiped out to explain any better. I'm sorry. Love, Tim."

"What does he mean?" I said to Paolo. "Did he want me to come out there? I said I would—he didn't bring it up again. I should have just gone. He's right, he can't depend on me."

I started crying, the slack sobs of a child.

"He's just going through a hellish time," said Paolo. "He'll be back, he just needs time to figure out his own stuff. Shhh— Stop." He sat me down on the porch steps, rubbed my back. "Don't cry, goose, it's OK. Come inside, we'll cook. Don't cry. The neighbors will think we're getting a divorce."

That night I called Tim. His voice sounded far away and blurry, the voice of my mother when I was six and she came back from the hospital at night, paid the baby-sitter, looked down at me from a great distance, and said, "Hi, Annie, how was school?"

"Hey," said Tim. "How's everything going out there?"

"All right. I mean, not so great, really. I got your letter."

"Yeah—"

"I said I'd come out," I blurted. "I want you to be able to depend on me."

"In the airport, you mean, before I left."

"Yes."

There was a long silence.

"Please talk to me," I said.

"You might have offered again, you could—"

"I will come out. I am offering. I'm sorry, I was waiting for you to ask. I'll come there as soon as you want."

"Look," he said. "It's not just this. I think it would have ended sooner or later anyway, I've thought that for a while."

"Since when?"

"I don't know. Our trip, maybe. Before that, even. I should have talked to you more about it, I just—it just seemed like it had to end."

"Why?"

"I don't know," he said. "A lot of things. I'm not even sure when I'll be back there, or for how long. Look, the hospital might call, I can't tie up the phone. Someday we'll talk about this, I just can't right now. I've really got to go."

"I'm sorry," I said. "You have enough to deal with. Will you call me, if you need someone to talk to?"

"OK," said Tim. But we both knew he would not.

August came. Each morning I woke thinking Alone. Thinking it, but not the way I would have before I met Paolo. The thought felt more like a habit now, a reflex I didn't quite believe. I missed Tim, his hands on my back, his voice in my ear, but I did not feel like a stick snapped in two. Maybe my mother was right. Maybe I was cushioning myself too much; perhaps I needed to live on the thin, sharp edge of desperation in order to find and keep a man. I wrote letters to Tim trying to mend things, read them to Paolo, tore them up. I could not write about lovers' spats to a man whose father was dying.

This morning Paolo said it was time to cut my hair.

"Shorter," I told him when the first clump fell. "Keep going, still shorter."

Paolo snipped and looked and snipped. After dinner he came into my room and pulled out a purple silk shirt from my closet.

"This," he said and grabbed some earrings from my dresser. "And these. And your black jeans."

"No." I burrowed down in my bed.

"Get up," he said. "Get dressed."

Now they make a circle around me, the only woman in the

place; they form a ring and clap and have me dance there in the middle. They are not watching so much as protecting me— I can feel it—the way the male whales form a ring around the nursing mothers and circle while they feed their calves. I do not know how they can tell I need that just now. These are men who have been forced to grow good at sensing rawness, at dancing around loss, or maybe Paolo told them about Tim. I know I must look beautiful, that I have found some sort of grace, and for a moment I pretend that with my short hair I am a boy, and they all want me, each and every one of them. But when I start to feel desire in that crowd, my limbs grow stiff and unfriendly, and a few seconds later the circle breaks apart.

When I look for Paolo to go home, I cannot find him.

"Have you seen Paolo?" I ask first this one, then that one, leaning up to their ears, close to their sweat. Finally I start home alone, make my way through the crowds on Commercial Street and then turn down our side street where everything, all at once, is from a different world: the rose hips, shingles, crushed shells, the rusty bikes and creaking gates, not even an echo of music, just the sound of sea and wind.

"Paolo, Paolo?" I sing inside my head, trying to pronounce it the way his mother, born in Italy, does, his mother who wants him to marry so badly that she brought a ring for me when she visited last fall.

"No, no," I tried to explain one morning when I got up early and found her sitting on the porch. "It's not like that. We're just good friends."

"He's a good boy," she said. "I don't care what anyone says."

I gave her back the ring and she tried to slip it onto her own finger, above her wedding ring, but it would not fit.

"Just take it," she said. "Maybe he'll change his mind."

I told her I couldn't, I had a boyfriend already.

"But you live with Paolo. Will you marry this other one? Has he given you a ring?"

I shook my head.

"Just take it," she said, "I have no use for it," and out of awkwardness or maybe something worse, I did take it, and never told Paolo. It is a pretty ring, a tiny diamond chip on a band of braided gold, and though I do not wear it and rarely look at it, it lies in a box inside my drawer.

In the morning when I wake up he is still not there, and by the time he comes home in the evening I have rehearsed what I will say so many times that I am not surprised when it comes out right.

"You met someone," I say. "That's great! That's so great, let me guess, the guy in the yellow shirt, the gorgeous one with the beard, I could see him checking you out all night, and then you disappeared. Tell me everything—"

He throws himself down on the sofa. "What am I doing, Annie? I'm too old for this, what am I doing?" He stretches out his legs, looks down at himself fondly, like someone who has just been tumbling in love. "He's just a kid, he's in his early twenties."

"What happened?"

"He—you know, we just kind of hit it off. I don't even know what happened, you know how petrified I am of all this stuff, we just started talking, it took forever for something to happen, I'm like a goddamn virgin starting all over again—"

"And?"

I know he will not tell me, can feel how a space is opening between us. *I told you everything*, I want to say, but I know it is not quite true, remember how when Tim and I used to close the door at night, Paolo was shut outside of a liquid, salty dark that could not fit inside words.

"He's sweet," Paolo says. "He *is* pretty gorgeous, isn't he? He has a terrible name, Harry, I've got to come up with something else to call him. He's even local, he works in Hyannis, and I guess—I think he likes me, the poor man doesn't know what he's getting into. God, I'm beat." He looks up at me. "Are you OK? Your hair looks great."

I nod. He sits up and glances at his watch. "I'm meeting him at ten at the bar. I've got to go rest for a couple minutes and then jump in the shower. You want to lie down?"

We do this sometimes, lie down together in his room with its gauzy white curtains, white sheets, blue speckled floor. It started when we only had one fan, but it was nice to nap together, to hear another person breathing, watch the curtains billow out, and even when we got another fan, we kept doing it. I tried to explain it once to Emily—how it wasn't sexual, how I didn't want to have sex with him but just liked to lie there. How safe it felt. But she kept saying how cute Paolo was, how could I keep my hands off him? He's not into women, I said, and anyhow, once we did it, it wouldn't feel safe anymore.

"That's OK," I tell him now.

Instead I go down into the basement to do my laundry. It is damp there, the place lit by one dim bulb, but after I put in the load, I drag over an old chair and sit beside the machine for a while with my hand on its belly, feeling its pulse. In my laundry are two shirts that used to be Tim's, one that was Paolo's, a camisole my mother gave me when it shrank. I try to picture which clothes have been mine from the beginning, the ones I bought and have been the only one to wear. The underwear, certainly, but I cannot remember what else is in there, now that it is all sloshing together in the tub.

I am startled by Paolo's voice calling, "Annie? Annie?"

I stand and lean up the stairs. "Down here. I'm doing laundry."

"I'm going to the bar," he calls down. "Do you want to come?"

"Do you want me to?"

"Of course. If you want."

"I might, but not right now. Maybe I'll show up later."

"All right, I'll see you."

I run up the stairs. "Paolo?"

He turns, bright and scrubbed in a turquoise shirt, on his way out the door.

"Huh?"

"Have fun. I hope it works out. He sounds nice." I must look dazed, blinking in the light.

"Yeah," he says. "It'll probably fall apart, he's probably fucked up, I'm probably fucked up." He puts out his hands, palms up. "I'm not any good at this."

"Sure you are," I say. "You'll be great."

And I do want him to be great, do want him to have someone to soothe the places I'll never be able to reach, at the same time that I can already imagine how sweetly he will include me for a while, how we will all three do things together until Harry gets too frustrated, how nicely Paolo will ask me to move out. Or maybe Harry will last two days, or two months; it almost doesn't matter, because eventually someone will come along, if not for Paolo, then for me.

I want to sit him down, then, before he leaves for the bar, and ask him if he thinks three is impossible, if it always comes down to two, or one. I want to ask him if he will marry me in a certain way, or just never stop cooking dinners with me or lying down for naps before the fan.

But this is not the sort of question you ask your friends, not the sort of promise you exact without a contract and a ring. I think of my mother, alone at my age with a skinny little girl who was me, of Paolo's mother, whose husband drank himself to death. I think of Tim's father who is dying like my father has died and all fathers will, and of Tim who is across the country and cannot depend on me.

And then I go down to put my laundry in the dryer. As I sat by the washing machine, I sit now by the dryer and feel my clothes tumble, arms tangling with legs, all of it pressed close around the circle of the sides. Later I will go dancing at the bar. First I will wait for my clothes to come out, and they will be warm and clean, and I will fold them, piece by piece, one by one.

Leonard Kriegel

PLAYERS

Lecture over, he begs off from the reception, the prospect of bouncing like a ping-pong ball between faculty and graduate students a shadow-dead alley in his mind. He has given the two lectures—obligation honored, money in the bank, reputation on the table. He will scarcely be missed. Besides, he hasn't seen San Francisco since his return from Korea almost thirty-six years ago.

He sighs. Invoking Molly's soliloquy to audiences intent on his every note, he feels himself choking on a surfeit of words. Alone at night in the desert stretches of Moabite Kingdom University, Bay Ridge gnaws like a termite at his dissatisfaction. Imagination dancing to secret rhythms—unknown languages, wild gyrations, furtive mustached scholars with faces as stiff as the turn-of-the-century boxers he remembers from worn copies of the *Police Gazette* he would thumb through as a child in the barbershop. Words exploding against the past. *If I forget thee, O Dublin, let my right hand forget its cunning.*

Maneuvering the rented Cutlass onto the freeway, he ignores the Berkeley hills slipping behind him. Fifty-six. One of the more eminent Joyceans in the country. "And what good?" he says aloud in the Cutlass. "Where does my life split off from the old man's?"

For months now, an elegiac crabbiness ballooning through him. Haunted by that time he chose the future that now chains him. Twenty years old and just back from Korea's dun-colored mountains. His prospects—to work the docks with his older brother or put time in with the city, as the dead father had done. Only the choices already turning on themselves in 1954. Brooklyn's docks dying. The city promising a death as meaningless as his father's.

In 1954, Margaret Rose Killian's black patent-leather shoes burn in his mind like onyx. Not so long a road back to eighth-grade dreams. Torturing himself at night, the killing times of love. Alone in the Ft. Hamilton library—Shakespeare, Joyce, secret gardens in his mind. Words let him breathe. Words and basketball. In both playground and library, ancestral voices claim him. Bay Ridge streets evaporate into Dublin nightmares.

At fourteen, words are snapshots framed in memory. At fifty-six, memory is beyond words. "Let me see if I can understand," Phil says in the office they share on Kissena Boulevard. "You're fourteen, you memorize the Clongowes Woods sermon, and that frees you? Charlie, you were just frightened. At fourteen, everybody's frightened."

But it wasn't fear. He would never again be afraid. Not of the church, not of the timid mother nor the dead father locked in tin piety. Not of the bitter brother. Nor memories of Margaret Rose's black patent-leather shoes.

How explain to Phil that Joyce had brought him home to Bay Ridge? The prospect of life on the docks or in the bowels of the subway holding neither terror nor promise. Brother and mother blown away like dried-out reeds. The gandy-dancer father just another Irishman who put his time in with the city until his heart exploded. The smell of death—like chewing gum or stale overheated air—clinging to the subway. *Carry me home, taddy, like you done at the toy fair.* Dead ends. Redemption's demands. "God made you the smart one in the family, Charlie. You owe God," his mother cries out. His mother wants a priest in the family.

Patches of sun and fog. He had come west wanting a break from the past. He would not find it among Mormons or in guest lectures at Berkeley. The last gandy dancer in New York a meaningless anachronism in Utah. Reputation appraised, compared. Fungible currencies. "After Richard Ellmann," a reviewer writes in *Twentieth-Century Realism*, "Mr. Dolan is the most distinguished Joycean of our time."

A far distance from late autumn in Leif Erickson Park. Racing into space, whispering into the wind and trees and the pallbearer-shrouded sky, "Charlie Dolan is my name, Margaret Rose Killian is my game." Kneeing grass, mind-humping his dream of pleasure, not yet the scholar focused on the main chance.

Had he been wrong to leave New York? Nothing left for him there. Diving for cover in a foxhole marriage. He had wanted out—of marriage, of a city so intent on feeding aspiration it expected him to feel failure with each new success. Moving west the solution, even when he couldn't find Moabite Kingdom University on a map.

"Utah," he murmurs to Phil, fingering the letter, "Utah." With each repetition, the prospect less incredible. Twenty-eight years with Eileen reduced to nightly encounters in which they tear at each other's weakness like belly-butting sumo wrestlers. All three sons, strangers allowed to go their way at birth, siding with Eileen. Arguments, recrimination. In marriage, he is judged and found guilty.

Eileen demands a divorce, the boys drift out of sight, almost out of memory. The war wearing down to an exhausted truce. And then the voice on the telephone. "You can help us, Professor Dolan. We Westerners can be a bit provincial, you know." Negotiations about money, housing, how many dissertations he will supervise. Whistling at the six-digit salary, the spin still up for the son of the subway system's last gandy dancer. Americans move west. He moves.

Earlier, he had turned down Harvard. "I'm not a damn curio," he tells Phil. "Can you see me at the Widener?"

"A desert, Charlie. Filled with revelation-seekers."

"They'll love me in Moabite Kingdom, Phil."

"In Moabite Kingdom, they're going to love Bay Ridge? And in Cambridge, they won't? Think, *boychik*, think."

"In Cambridge, Bay Ridge doesn't matter. That's the problem."

Eight months in rugged canyons raked over by god's own fingers and still searching for streets to give memory shape. He frowns. The move west isn't working. After this weekend, he will finish the semester at Moabite Kingdom and resign as Remsen Meredith Professor of Humane Letters.

He parks in the hotel garage, deposits his overnight bag when he registers, then wanders off through crooked streets his tourist eye searches for imperfections. Soothed by the streets, he does not stop walking until his eyes catch the marquee. 8:00—VANCOUVER VS. GOLDEN STATE. He sniffs at the brisk evening air. He hasn't seen Terry since high school. But he follows his career: St. Bonnie, ten years of coming off the bench in the pros, then a coach. Two years ago, named head coach by the expansion team in Vancouver. He meant to write, to congratulate Terry. He hadn't written.

They had played against each other in high school and in the CYO. He learned early on to watch Terry's shoulder. All through high school, right shoulder dipping just before Terry drove the basket. He could fold Terry in his pocket then. High school, CYO, half-court games on the rutted summer asphalt court behind the Swede cemetery—the two of them going one-on-one against each other.

Terry was the player. But no one could face him down the way Charlie could. When they graduated—Terry from St. Michael's, Charlie from the school for scholarship boys the Jesuits ran in Manhattan—Terry had offers from Siena, De Paul, Niagara, and St. Bonnie. His choice was between induction in the army or the subway to Brooklyn College. Talent not enough to command a scholarship. A schoolyard player, defined by what he could keep others from doing.

On impulse, he slips into the cluster of adolescent boys and middle-aged men and bored women in front of the Cow Palace box office. Inside, a sparse crowd, even for an end-of-season game between teams not in the playoffs. Less than a quarter of the seats occupied a half hour before game time. He buys a hot dog and beer from the bored man behind a counter punctuated with banners and balloons. He leans against the concession stand, surveys the arena.

Grown extraordinarily fat, Terry stands at courtside, green linen jacket draping his thick oversized frame like a tent. Huge, maybe a size sixty. He himself only ten pounds heavier than the hundred and fifty-five he weighed in high school. He never tried to out-muscle Terry. Wait for his shoulder to dip, and trust your hands. He had quick hands. Terry angry and flustered, moving against the one player in the neighborhood who can take him.

A player in love with the curve of liquid flesh springing from Margaret Rose's shoes. Love's rolling fantasies, secret promises guiding fingers that strip the ball from Terry. He took Terry, lusted after Margaret Rose, the world fading off into a sweetness so thick it cloys.

In Korea, still a player. Firing barrage after barrage of 105s into the dun-colored mountains and then going off with three or four others to drive against patchwork baskets mounted to spent shell casings. Thirteen months of firing howitzers, reading Joyce, driving against baskets mounted to shell casings. The world intruding only with his mother's neat careful handwriting telling him how she prays daily for his safety and healthy return. On his cot, he searched the sports pages of the *News* she encloses for names he once played against. He feels no envy, his talent limited.

Gray Korean sky flattening into the white of his mind. No longer mourning the dead gandy-dancer father or hungering for a pussy peek up Margaret Rose's dress or shooting baskets in late November with the chill wind slapping his face. A section of life ended. Beginnings await him.

Sipping beer at the concession stand, he watches Vancouver warm up. Give-and-go working rhythmic joining of arms, legs, backs, thighs. Indians circling a wagon train. Terry's massive bulk jiggles against the controlled temperature in the Cow Palace. Joy bubbles his body as Terry claps his hands together, shouting to his players. Circling the basket faster, players drive right and left and down the key, unleashing a storm of basketballs that rain against the net and threaten to explode into each other.

Happy not to be making small talk with faculty wives and

eager graduate students, Charlie Dolan jogs in place, beer in hand, at the concession stand. Charlie Dolan of Bay Ridge, now in the Cow Palace in San Francisco, away from the lamentations of his living mother and the ghostly demands of his dead father. Leaping every crack in the sidewalk of his mind, the blind messiah points the way to the world.

Terry a courtside Buddha, folds of neck fat following each other in sybaritic progression. Impulsively, he places his beer on the concession stand and runs down the stairs leading to courtside. He takes the stairs two at a time, jockeying in his refurbished imagination the way he used to charge down stairs to the gym, the nuns in their black-and-white habits screeching like maniacal penguins.

Enormous rolls of fat. A man of fifty-six, like him. A player. Only now so thick his flesh seems sculpted to the court. He envisions players coming to Terry to be judged. Ponderous and god-like, Terry guides them. He hears Terry's barking voice, deeper now than he remembers from Bay Ridge days. "Move it, Eddie. Move! Move! Move! Keep the flow, Reggie! Keep the flow!"

"You probably don't remember me . . . ," he begins to the huge back enfolded in the green jacket.

Terry spins around, quicker than Charlie imagines so fat a man can move. "I saw you in the stands, you bastard! Charlie Dolan from Bay Ridge. Who would steal the hair from my balls." Terry's huge embrace pulls him back in time. "I hear you're some kind of professor now."

"Can't find another way to make my dollar," he says.

Terry points to the players circling the basket. "I ever tell them how clean you picked me, Charlie, they laugh me out of a job." Fat hands shaping the round of a basketball, palms sweat-brushed, Terry gestures obscenely toward his scrotum. "Whatever you couldn't do, Charlie, you could have made a living playing against me."

"There was only one you, Terry," he says.

"That was then," Terry laughs, throwing open his jacket to display his massive girth. "Take a look now."

"You've put on a few."

"A few!" Terry howls. He opens his arms as wide as possible, as if praying to the enclosed God of the Cow Palace. "Christ, Charlie, I dipped my soul in butter."

Terry insists he watch the game from a seat directly behind the bench. Two mediocre teams playing out the season—and he is surprised at the pain he feels. Fifty-six years old, the most prominent Joycean after Ellmann, and he feels cheated because he will never again play a boy's game. He remembers Mickey's return ten years ago to the small frame house on 74th Street after a drying-out session in the upstate sanitarium the longshoremen ran, when Charlie and his mother and Eileen and their sons and Mickey's wife Katy and their three daughters gathered to welcome him. "Never again," his brother laughs. "Until the next time. So help me, never again." Dismissing their protests, "I'm no victim. But I can't get out of the way of the train."

Vancouver plays with discipline and surprising enthusiasm—limited talents who understand they are better as a team than as individuals. Charlie focuses on a small forward—one of two whites on the team—while Terry pleads, cajoles, exhorting refs not even trying to hide how bored they are by the game's lack of consequence. He likes the way the small forward passes, finds himself on his feet, cheering, as the forward cuts to the basket, hangs in mid-air as if he were about to shoot, then slaps the ball between the legs of the man guarding him to the center under the basket who stuffs it home.

Terry turns, winks. "You should have seen him before he blew his knee. Instinct. He's still good. But when he came up, he figured to be as good as anyone. Now the really fast boys go past him like I should go past a banquet. He's like you, Charlie. A reader. A goddamn philosopher."

"I'm no philosopher," he protests. "I teach English."

"And he's a one-knee jock who does it from instinct. Spinoza, Charlie. Imagine, a player who reads Spinoza."

Terry's massive body jiggles, like ice melting. The face of a fat man dying. Born within a month of each other in 1934 and Terry now fat, gross, led by the hand by a boy's game. As he is led by Joyce and a river of memory that threatens to drown him. Eyes closed, he blots out the court, trying to envision the face of Margaret Rose. Himself in his passion, before he made the choices he made.

Vancouver loses by four points. Terry and he shake hands as he leaves. "You could take me, Charlie."

Holding Terry's enormous hand in his own, he fights the urge to hug this man he knows will soon be dead. "I could, couldn't I? Maybe that was the problem, Terry."

Wilson Emmett frowns. Charlie Dolan has just resigned as Remsen Meredith Professor of Humane Letters. A year ago, Wilson had convinced fifteen Mormon elders to make the offer and put Moabite Kingdom's English Department on the map.

Wilson Emmett's thin blue eyes frame Charlie's angular face. "Is there something wanting, Charlie? Is it us?"

"You don't play one-on-one, Wilson," Charlie suggests.

"One-on-one," Wilson Emmett repeats, puzzled.

"I'm a New York Irishman, Wilson," Charlie sighs. "A half-court player. I just don't fit in here."

Wilson wipes his brow. He wishes Charlie would blame the heat. An Easterner who couldn't take the heat would evoke sympathy. "Any possibility you'll change your mind?"

Charlie stares at the desert outside the window. He had loved it when he first came west. As if he could reach out and tear a piece off. Now he rarely thinks about desert or heat or jagged rocks or scooped-out canyons. There are many things he rarely thinks about now. The divorced wife, the three sons he never hears from, the great-uncle in Asbury Park his mother would take them to visit every day-after-Christmas, parading them before a tiny man who looked like a regal Barry Fitzgerald sitting in an oversized wooden rocker. He no longer remembers his great-uncle's name. He is no longer certain of why he must leave Moabite Kingdom. But leave he must. "I miss New York," he says lamely.

Wilson Emmett frowns. "I'll take care of the paperwork. I want you to know I understand, Charlie."

But he doesn't understand. Not on that hot late-April morning in 1991 and not a year later when he opens his day-old air-mailed *New York Times*—Wilson Emmett makes it a point to subscribe to the New York edition—and reads

Few Happy Hour customers at Ireland's Anguish in Brooklyn's Bay Ridge know their bartender as the famous Joyce scholar, Charles A. Dolan. Author of *Joyce's Lost Dublin* and *Molly in Her Chambers: Sense and No-Sense in Joyce,* Mr. Dolan resigned a year ago as Remsen Meredith Professor of Humane Letters at Utah's Moabite Kingdom University. When asked why he had given up an endowed university chair to tend bar in Brooklyn, Mr. Dolan said, "I've gone from teaching the reality to living it."

Wilson Emmett shakes his head, puts the paper down. He wipes his glasses once again. He will never understand New Yorkers. He likes them well enough—the Irish, the Jews, the Italians who flock like wintering geese to the Medieval Studies sessions at the annual MLA convention. *Lasciate ogni speranza, voi ch'entrate.* But the city is beyond him, beyond the nation. A man as distinguished as Charlie Dolan serving drinks. Wittgenstein as a hospital orderly—*that* he can understand. But a bartender. He sighs, wipes his glasses again. He feels betrayed. Too much imagination running loose in the world. Rage clouds his eyes as Wilson Emmett angrily dismisses Charlie Dolan from his thoughts.

The mass scheduled for 9:30. He hails a taxi. To see the city shape itself as it prepares for the burial of the dead. He leans back in the cab, eyes on graffiti-scarred droppings that crust brick and concrete, roads and streets and roofs of Queens. Where he tends bar in Bay Ridge, the streets are also breaking beneath the onslaught of jagged reds, purples, yellows, blacks, paint slapped on every surface. The sky a brilliant blue, sun about to break the chill of morning.

Terry had died at courtside. A year after he saw him, Terry molded a team that made the playoffs. Exhorting his team in a playoff game, only to keel over as if struck by an invisible hand. "Dead before his head hit the floor."

"We're here, mister," the Pakistani cabbie says. The red-brick facade looms in front of him. He pays, checks his watch: 8:36. Too early to go inside. He walks down the unknown street bordering the park until he comes to a diner. At the counter, a waitress with too much lipstick and stringy blonde hair holds out a menu. He waves it away and says, "Coffee and." He likes to say "coffee and," and he grunts with irritation when she asks, "And what?"

"A doughnut," he snaps.

He tries to remember Terry moving toward the basket in the broken court behind the Swede cemetery. Only it is not the high school player that comes to mind but Terry as he last saw him, a mountain of flesh planted in the Cow Palace. "He smoked, he drank, he fucked all night!" Chanting at a passing funeral cortege from behind the Swede cemetery, daring death in their adolescent imaginations.

Small knots of mourners. A television crew pulls lights and cables from a van. The mourners are curious. Death rules in whispers. A sense of ending for the six o'clock news. Faces lament time's passing in a gathering of homeboys. Like in the bar, morose pallbearers to dead ambition. "If only I laid off the damn booze. I fought in the Gloves. A right that could kick a bull's ass."

A handsome woman walks up the four stone steps of the church. Turning to face him, she smiles. A year one side or the other of fifty, she still commands admiration. He wants the woman to be his lost love. Only Margaret Rose was tall. This woman is neither tall nor short but prim and solid in a well-tailored navy blue suit, light yellow scarf breaking the line of mourning. She waves. He crosses the street. She extends a white-gloved hand. "I'm Loretta Foster. Terry's cousin. I used to watch you two play."

"I remember," he says. A girl with bright red hair behind the cyclone fence. "I didn't know you were cousins."

"It's as if we were all related back then," she smiles.

Inside St. Benedict's, he guides her to a corner pew, past a bearded man holding a salt-and-pepper tweed topcoat. He is surprised at the interest he feels. The grad students and junior faculty at Moabite Kingdom University had left him indifferent. Like making love to textual analysis.

You're some kind of professor now. An archaeologist digging for artifacts, an ichthyologist classifying the sea's fullness, an astronomer mapping heavens freed from binding ties, the earth itself just another round ball.

Loretta weeps. "There should be more," she says.

A player, a dipping shoulder. Not the reason for friendship but friendship itself. "Maybe there should be," he says, pulling Loretta to him. "But there isn't."

And what more could there be? he wonders, massaging stains of beer into the gleaming oak bar. Dreams and ambition fathered by games. A child's game transformed into a game for adults. A lifetime deciphering Joyce as if he were trying to crack the Japanese code. How explain that to the *Times?* "You lose count of bodies in Beirut and Belfast, but the games remain." Attention for a dipping shoulder.

The bar awaiting patrons in the soft light of twin brass sconces. Comforted by the gleam of polished oak, the owner's thirty-year-old son, fearful of those he serves, ties his apron and sighs. "A rush soon," he says.

"It pays our keep, Brendan."

"I suppose," the son grunts. "But there are times money be damned. A quiet evening in front of the tube. Which one of the girls tonight?"

"Ellen." Ellen is one of the two Belfast illegals who work the tables with Brendan. A parade of aliens in Bay Ridge now. At the far end of the bar, Miller Time is 3:53. Terry in the Cow Palace, timer in his head. Myths encrusted, body dripping fat. Like his gandy-dancer father, the heart blown apart. He examines the glasses racked overhead. No longer a player, no longer the most distinguished Joycean after Ellmann. Just a bartender preparing for Happy Hour.

A rush of happiness. Since the funeral, he has been thinking about Loretta. Even the memory of Terry does not make him somber. Neither player nor professor now. Endings liberating body and soul. *Old father, old artificer, stand me now and ever* . . . He giggles. He is to meet her tomorrow at the Central Park Zoo. At fifty-seven, love's apprentice.

Later, he remembers noise and smoke and gossip, drunken laments, laughter reminding him he no longer needs to hump the park grass. Flesh is not grass. It is simply flesh. But for tonight, he feels he could tell Joyce himself about exile and coming home. To have once been, now enough. At fifty-seven, he pours shots and stands ready to dispel fervor and longing. He himself, Charlie Dolan. Not the dead writer. Not the dead father. Not the saints haunting his old mother. Not the dead player. But himself alone.

He is not surprised at his brother's sudden appearance. In the center of his white hair, Mickey's bald spot crowns his head like a monk's tonsure. At sixty-five, Mickey Dolan still demands filial obeisance from the living.

"What will it be for you, Mickey?" he asks.

"Double Jameson." Mickey draws himself up to his full five-foot-five. "So this is where you work. A real goddamnit in his own time. My brother, keeper of the keys."

He pours the double and stands it in front of Mickey. "God, Charlie," Mickey sighs, "the money them Mormons paid you. You could've bought this place. Ireland's anguish, my ass. The anguish is yours, not Ireland's. A professor, no less." Furious, he drains the double in one long gulp.

Charlie Dolan smiles and reaches across the bar. Hand on Mickey's shoulder, he says, "I'm just making my nut."

"You made us proud, Charlie," Mickey whispers, pushing Charlie's hand from his shoulder. Eyes fill with tears as he presses against an indifferent world pressing against him. "You were our pride."

"You were never a player, Mickey," he says. "And I was." And as if that were explanation enough, he leans across the bar and kisses his surprised brother on the bald spot in the middle of his head, a rush of grief and splendor wafting him clear of all players, all professors, exile no longer.

Frederick G. Dillen

ALICE

Alice propped herself, and balanced her box of stationery against her knees. She opened her pen, held sheets of stationery against the top of the box with her thumb, and wrote:

Dear Sam,
    Your first letter at college from your old mother. I expect by now you are pleasantly ensconced in your dormitory and have a few classes under your belt. I am ensconced in my suite here at the hospital. Not quite a suite, but a private room, which is elegant for me. Doctor Meyers insisted, and so I thought I would go ahead and be grand this time around.
    The day after you left, I packed my cooking whiskey under my robe and slippers, and moved in, but they'd no sooner gotten my clothes off me than I realized I had half a pack of Winstons in my handbag to last me God knows how long. Well, I've been in and out of hospitals enough to know better than to ask the nurses, so I asked one of the nurse's aids if she wouldn't get me a carton, and I would give her a dollar for her trouble. She was looking reluctant, hoping for another dollar no doubt, and you know I was feeling a little devil-may-care, so I

just offered her a drink of whiskey, and that made her stand right up.

She's a great big black woman, and she said, "Do you have whiskey in here? Oh my. Where you hiding it?" And she rooted up in the closet until she found it (behind the wig and its little stand). I told her it wasn't expensive whiskey, but she said, "Whiskey's whiskey and good enough for me. Unless you're drinking it all the time." I told her I just had my one good jolt every evening, and she said, "Well then, I'll join you. Yes, I will. I like a little something before I go off. Sounds very nice to me, thank you."

In the evening, she brought the Winstons and wouldn't hear of taking my extra dollar. She poured a glass right up to the top and took a gulp and sat down on the bed and passed the glass and there we were. Now she comes every day. Flora. She's as nice as can be, and she does the bartending so she can be sure there's enough to go around. Well, you can see that I've arranged myself to my best advantage. I only worry that we may run out of whiskey, since Doctor Meyers won't tell me how long I'm in for this time. But I'm sure if an emergency arises, Flora will do another bit of smuggling. She doesn't seem worried about getting in trouble, and we're very peaceable. Fortunately she didn't carry out her threat to bring in a couple of men on her day off.

And aside from Flora's welcome attentions, the doctors come on and off all day, armies of them, to pinch and poke me, and of course tell me nothing. Maybe it's just Henry Meyers showing off how important he's gotten, but even so I feel exotic when I don't feel like a laboratory frog.

Also, the girls from the shop have come, my nice Martha several times. She says the boss is having all sorts of trouble finding someone to fill in properly until I get back. I don't know how the world got on without me all those years I didn't work. Your Aunt Susan called up from Washington and said she might be up to see me, which I thought was odd until she told me she was trying to stay away from some Major or other. She's

always good company. Simon McGruder came
yesterday. You remember meeting him again this
summer. He even manages to make me feel a little sexy,
heaven forbid. I haven't a clue about how he knew I
was in the hospital or where he'd come from, but I
didn't ask. At my stage of the game, you take your
beaux where you find them.

Finally, you'll be pleased to hear that your gang all
came in to see me yesterday when Mr. McGruder was
on his way out. Terry and Peter and a friend of Terry's
whom I don't remember. And Terry brought his girl,
Patty, which I thought wasn't in the best of taste since
you liked her first, but I forgave him because he is so
nice to me, and besides Patty looks a little fat in the
fanny these days. They're all starting their schools some
time this week. I think they were looking for a little
sympathy from me so I gave them that. I even would
have offered a little cooking whiskey to soothe over the
end of the summer, but I thought they might have been
embarrassed, and preferred beer. I told them I expected
them all to raise hell and enjoy themselves without
wrecking the cars or getting thrown out. That seemed to
cheer them up a little bit, and they told tales on you to
get you in trouble and I pretended to be horrified. When
the nurse chased them out at the end of visiting hours,
Terry said that they'd come and see me again over their
Thanksgiving vacation. I certainly hope it isn't here that
they'll have to come see me.

That's my news for the time being. I realize letter
writing is frowned on in college, as it was in boarding
school, but if you ever are overtaken by the lunatic urge,
indulge me. By the way, Flora tells me she has a lovely
niece who would be just right for you. I don't
discourage her, but I have my doubts.

Love,
Mother

Alice folded the letter and put it in an envelope and addressed it. She closed her eyes to her discomfort, screwed on
the top of the pen, and slid the Crane's box and the letter away

from her on the bed, then let her knees down and lay back and was still.

Alice was used to hurting. That was one of the things she was good at. She sat with it until it was too much, then she buzzed the nurse.

"Here I am, Mrs. Armstrong."

She couldn't speak.

Henry Meyers had gotten her onto a good floor. They kept an eye out for her. She was lucky to have Henry Meyers. The nurse swabbed her arm, and Alice felt the coolness, and then the quick needle.

"A couple of the girls brought in some more mysteries for you, Mrs. Armstrong. We've got them down at the station."

And when the nurse came back with the books, Alice was better. She could push herself up and brighten. She had probably read all the books, but she would read them again. This was an attractive young nurse. She was sweet and Alice was fond of her. Alice smiled at the thoughtfulness of the books. She would have liked to squeeze the nurse's hand. It didn't seem such an odd impulse. She wasn't embarrassed of her silence in the pain. You lose embarrassment after a point. Now she was better.

"Flora left this one for you. She asked me to bring it in especially."

"Oh my goodness. Did I miss Flora? I didn't realize I had slept so long. Isn't that silly."

"No, it's still too early for Flora to be off. She left the mystery for you this morning. I'll stack them all for you on the table. Would you like one now?"

"Let's see what treasure Flora brought for me. *Nightgown for Murder.* Marvelous. Just what the doctor ordered. You go ahead now. I'm fine. And thank all the girls on the station for me."

The book was the usual off the rack. The cover showed a redhead sprawled on a rumpled bed, boobies about to pour out of a black nightgown, a dagger through the hem of the nightgown.

Alice used to have a good bosom. For years after she and

Vic were married, Vic wouldn't let her wear a thing to bed. Three years ago she'd had the right one taken off, but by then of course she and Vic were apart, and didn't do anything anymore anyway.

When she was little, Alice wore flannel nighties in winter, cotton in summer.

And slippers with pompoms, year around.

Her father was a doctor, and if he came home late from the hospital, she liked to wait up for him in her nightie and slippers. If she had to go to bed, she put her slippers beside the bed and stayed awake to hear him, and if he was not too late he came up to give her a kiss good night and a hug. If he was very late, then her mother would tell him not to go up because Alice needed the sleep.

On the nights when he did come up to kiss her, Alice pretended to be asleep as soon as the footsteps of his big shoes opened the door. She was very still as he tiptoed across the room and leaned over to kiss her. She loved his smell, part from the hospital and part from him. Then as soon as he kissed her, she put her arms around his neck and hugged him. On nights when it was too late, she listened to the peepers and worried that summer would be over soon.

Once when it was so late she must have woken from sleep, Alice heard his car outside, and then her mother's heels on the floor in the hall. And Alice wanted her father to come up no matter how late it was. It was too late, but Alice listened, and thought about him coming upstairs. He said, "I suppose Alice has been down for some time," and her mother said it was much too late, and Alice thought about him coming up, and didn't think about them turning and going into the living room, which they always did, and her father said, "Well, I'm just going to peek in." His steps came up the stairs, and Alice heard her mother whisper something from below, but her father said, "Shh," and came to the door.

Alice whispered, "I'm awake," but she didn't dare say it loud enough for him to hear outside the door. As he opened the door, she whispered it again, "I'm awake," and he came in and came over to the bed quietly and she held out her arms to hug him before he even got down to kiss her. When she had her face against his neck she started crying, and she tried to whisper that she wasn't crying because anything was wrong, but she couldn't say it. She didn't want her father to think she wasn't glad he came in.

Of course Sam would not need to be kissed as Alice had had to be. That would have been too easy for a mother. She went up every night just the same, to hear his prayers and tuck him in, and to kiss him whether he needed it or not. And she managed usually to look in on him later, hoping that he might call out to her, but not really expecting it. He was not a boy who called out for love. Boys would be different, and she told herself that. If she asked him for a hug, he always gave it to her, as long as she remembered not to ask for it in front of other boys or anything as foolish as that. But he never did come first with a hug, and those are the things a mother lives with. Maybe he already understood about Vic, that long before Alice understood.

It didn't seem long at all before someone else looked in the door. Alice thought it would be Flora, and smiled and tried to put her hand on Flora's book. But it was the same pleasant nurse.

To say that Susan was here.

"That's fine, Nurse. I'm awake."

And when Susan came in, Alice felt as she always did. Susan was getting older and fatter, but she had it, and she would have it until the day she died, and the men knew it instantly. Alice had never had it like that. Not at all now. Now she was too tired, and she knew why Susan was here.

Susan came and put her purse down on the bed and leaned over Alice and put her cheek to Alice's cheek and pressed against Alice, and Alice tried to find her own arms to hug back. Alice cried. Susan cried.

It was like Susan to know, and when Susan knew, it was final, even in the part of Alice that was still embarrassed by Susan.

Fifteen years ago when Susan, out of the blue, said Vic drank too much, then it was true. And it was true, which was what she was really saying, that Vic would always drink too much.

Eight years ago, she told Vic to his face that he was a failure, and Alice hadn't known that he was, not really. She had hated Susan for telling Vic in his own home, but Vic was already falling apart and Susan had seen it, and Alice had to realize that she wouldn't have time, or a proper home, for Sam anymore.

It was then that Alice and Vic began to plan for boarding school.

And the summer before he was to go off to school, the summer he turned twelve, it was off to camp as well.

For boarding school, they all drove up together on a Saturday in mid-September, with the Scotch cooler for a picnic beside the road. Vic was in a tweed sportcoat and proud to be taking his son to school, and they all laughed and somehow it seemed just as it should have been, and Alice foolishly said that and infuriated Vic.

They stayed at the good motel in Concord, and Alice could pick out the other families that were there to bring their boys to school. And those families could pick them out, she knew. It was hot when they arrived, and Vic wanted to take a nap in his shorts, and Alice suggested Sam do the same. Sam was shy about himself; she would not have made him, but he did take off his clothes and lie down on the motel cot, and he looked thin, and still so little a boy. So much different from Vic, but so different too from her baby. She hardly saw him without his clothes anymore, and suddenly she wanted to hold him to her bosom again. She was ashamed, or would have been ashamed, to tell. He was wearing the new undershorts she'd gotten for him for school, boxer shorts like his father wore instead of the children's jockey underwear. She asked him if he didn't like his new shorts, if they didn't make him feel a little older and more like his father, and he said, "Yes, Mother," and lay with his eyes open until it was time to go to dinner. At dinner Vic had his martinis and was funny and Alice and Sam both laughed, but Alice knew the signs.

The next morning they settled Sam into his alcove at school with thirty other boys on every side, and there was so little settling-in to do that it was done in no time. Alice wanted to shake Sam and make him see her, see his mother before she left, but she might as well have already been gone. At the car, when she hugged him, and kissed him, he stood with his hands at his sides. She held back her own tears, and got into the car and said good-bye to him. As they drove off she watched him stand and wave, and his face wanted to cry and she thought he might, but then he turned away and went into his dormitory among the other boys and she had lost him. And as soon as they got outside the grounds, Vic wanted to have lunch and a drink before they started back.

Three years ago, when Alice had her breast taken off, Susan came to the hospital. To say good-bye, Alice was sure. There was nothing else to be revealed then. Vic was long past the first woman, past the psychiatrists and Payne Whitney and Hartford and the drying-out farms in Vermont. Sam was out of Susan's reach; Sam was a different generation and immune. But Alice was still afraid of dying then. Forty-one. It hadn't seemed possible. Yet there was Susan, and Alice had to be ready, just as she'd had to be ready before.

It was Vic, though, who was dying then.

Susan wasn't a gossip; she simply saw, and was free to say. Susan knew Vic was a drunk because he drank too much not to be. She knew Vic was a failure because her beaux were all successful men. She knew Vic was dying because she was alive herself. Vic's horror by then had taken over Alice's life so much that Alice understood nothing else. It had never occurred to Alice that Vic would not go on forever.

When Alice woke, Susan was gone. There was a doctor at the door, leaving, and Alice said, "Hello." He stopped and looked back and smiled, a tall, fine-looking young man. Even in her drowsiness, his smile made Alice embarrassed of her hair and her appearance. She made herself cheerier and she said, "I'm awake now, ready to be pushed and pulled and pinched and poked."

"Not today," he said. "Doctor Meyers just asked me to look in."

In a couple of years Sam would be a man like that. She smiled and said, "I thought maybe I'd worn out all the other doctors and you were the reinforcements."

"Oh, I was in before, with Doctor Meyers. We just decided to give you a day off today."

"I didn't remember you. I'm sorry. I didn't realize that even the patients got days off."

Sex had been the hardest. She had loved sex. Everything about it, even laughing about it. When they're drinking there isn't much sex. She'd learned that, but it hadn't made her any less jealous, and it hadn't prepared her for never ever having a man in bed again. Doctor Meyers told her that it was necessary to bring in other doctors, so she had to say what the hell and take her shirt off for all those men to see her with half a chest. Young men like this one who smiled and went. She told herself that they were all doctors, but she wanted to say out loud that she'd had big, handsome bosoms, and not so long ago.

In the first year that Sam came home for the whole summer, rather than just for the two weeks before camp, the apartment was filled with sex. He was teaching tennis and he was learning about girls, and she was jealous of him. He would come home sweaty from his teaching, and take showers while she had her cocktail after her own day's work. If it had been a girl, probably Alice would have been more jealous, but it would have been more familiar; she could have nodded at it. With a boy it was so different; she almost could smell it. And he took such long showers. He'd be in the shower for twenty minutes. There would be steam and the noise of the water and simply the sense of him in there.

On one afternoon he called the shop to ask if he could stay late at the club and play tennis after work, so Alice went out for a drink with Martha. It was a Saturday and they had two instead of one, and laughed and snorted like a couple of gals off the second shift at the factory. They pretended to look at the men, but they both knew they were perfectly safe even if it wasn't the Pickwick with their friend George behind the bar. Then when she picked Sam up at the tennis courts, some of his new friends were there and they were laughing and Sam was going to go out with them all later, and all of them were full of life and of each other. Alice tooted the horn and waved to them and tried to look very gay, but they made her gayness from two drinks with Martha a little pale, and the wind was out of her sails. Sam, though, was cute with them. He held his own. Alice was pleased to see that. But when he got in the car and they were driving home, he didn't have anything to say to her, and she had looked forward to his company.

She had told Martha how fun it was to come home and have Sam to talk to, but he sat in the car spinning his tennis racket and she was irritated. When they got home, he went right into the shower to get ready to go out, and she sat with a drink and wanted to talk with him just for a moment. He took so long in the shower that she knew he wouldn't have any time to sit with her.

When he came out, he ran back to his room to get into his clothes. He was still thin, but he was almost a man. He had muscles coming in his arms and his chest. Not like some of them, but he was nice looking. The girls would like him. They would like his curly hair, though he was so shy he wouldn't know it. It dawned on her that he always ran through without any clothes on, as if she was not even there, as if she didn't count. While he was getting dressed, she had another drink, which really was more than she ordinarily had, though she never put any rules on her cooking whiskey or her smoking, no matter what Henry Meyers said.

Then Sam was dressed and ready to go. Alice had said he could have the car. She finished her drink. She asked him if he had to take such long showers, and he shrugged the way they do. She asked him what he was doing when he was in there that long, and he said he was just taking a shower, and shrugged again. She said she'd never known anybody to take showers that long, and she thought he was doing something in there. He asked what she thought he was doing, and she said she thought he was playing with himself.

Oh, God. Then he was horribly offended. He stalked off, and she was horrified herself.

But then it was odd, because once she'd said that, once she'd been a nasty, stinky mother, and thought him a stinky, nasty boy, that seemed to get it out of their systems, and they could be comfortable with each other.

They did dishes together, and there were dirty shirts and underwear and sneakers all over the place, and she let him have beer in the icebox, and it all filled up the little apartment, and Alice, to tell the truth, didn't mind a bit, though she felt she had to nag about things once in a while, and he would tease her about that. He hid a jockstrap above the visor in the car, and the next time she pulled the visor down, the jockstrap fell into her lap, and she screamed. Which pleased him no end.

He came out with Alice and Martha, and didn't mind it when she and Martha would have their two cocktails and get giggly. What was nicest, and maybe hard for him, was that he would listen. Aside from Martha, she really had no one, and she needed to talk just to hear herself go on, which you have to do, especially when you're alone. She didn't tell him the awful things. She let him understand how differently things had turned out from what she had expected. They joked about the wig; they spoke to the wig when it was on its stand. When she got to be friends with their gang, all of them laughed at that damned wig, which was just the right thing to do. She became the sort of den mother to their gang, and got all the inside scoop, once they'd gotten away with whatever they'd been up to.

This past summer, that gang of Sam's threatened Alice with bringing a man and making her come out on a date with them all. The first time they said it, they scared her half to death, and they got a good laugh out of that. Much as she wanted a man, the thought of it now was really more than she could cope with, and it was a relief to recognize that.

Then of course Simon McGruder showed up for a day in the middle of the summer, out of the blue, in the way he was prone to do, and that got the boys going again. They had come in for some strategy, or to steal beer or something, early on Saturday evening, so they were there when Alice got home from the shop. She hadn't gone for her drink with Martha because Simon had called her at the shop and asked her out for dinner. She'd come straight home to get ready. She really didn't think it was a big thing, and she sat for a minute with the boys before taking her shower. She asked them what their plans were, and they made up something or other, and then she said, just so they wouldn't think she had nothing happening at all, that an old friend had called her up and she was going out too.

Well, the way those boys congratulated her was too sincere and too patronizing not to annoy her. Sam even asked who "she" was, this old friend of his mother's. Alice should have known better, but they were all of them so satisfied with themselves that she went ahead and told them that "she" was a quite handsome and prosperous man who had once very much admired Sam's mother, before Sam's time. Alice arose then, and departed in her grand exit for the shower, and they were stunned, even quiet for a change, and Alice felt quite pleased with herself. As she closed the door they began their hooting.

When she came out, all dressed, they still were there. They were slouched down low in their chairs, and they'd been quiet so she would think they'd left. They all looked at her up from under their eyebrows, Sam the worst of them. When she told them to go on their way and mind their own business, they didn't budge. She tried to use her mother's voice with Sam to get him moving, but he put on a hangdog look and rolled out his lower lip, and the others took the cue and did the same thing. So she did exactly what they wanted her to do next, and tried to reason with them. "Oh, it's only Simon McGruder," she said to Sam, and Sam looked at her like a perfect stranger and gasped.

"Simon McGruder?" As if it were Burt Lancaster coming to her on his knees. And all the others piped, "Simon McGruder? Simon McGruder?" and sat up in their chairs and gaped at her, and then howled with laughter and pointed at her so that she couldn't get away with being angry. She would have begun to plead with them, except the doorbell rang with Simon, and so she glared at them and ran down to let him in.

She tried to prepare him. She told him Sam was there with a few of his friends and they were being a little difficult. She tried to tell what was up, with expressions of her face the way you do, but she could see that the expressions on her face made him think she was having a small stroke. It really wasn't fair, since she hadn't seen him for three years. There was no way he could be expected to understand their foolishness.

But the boys were all on their best behavior and all stood up while she introduced them, all very respectful. After she'd introduced them, she said, "Sam and his friends are on their way out for a night on the town. You have a nice night tonight, boys. Drive carefully," and they all smiled as nicely as they possibly could and sat right back down, except Sam, who asked if he could fix Simon something to drink. Alice was appalled. But Simon, as comfortable as you please, just said he'd have a bottle of beer like the boys, and Sam brought it. She'd forgotten what a big man Simon was. Really he was bigger than any of these boys, who thought they were such big shots.

Simon asked them, "Don't you boys have anything going tonight? Can't find any women on a Saturday night?"

The boys squirmed, and Alice said, "Now don't embarrass them, Simon. They're nice boys. They're just a little shy with the girls." Oh, they glared at that.

Sam, of all people, said, "They're shy all right, Mr. Mc-Gruder, but they've been after me for weeks to get them in to talk to Mother. And now you've come along and cut them out." Alice was taken aback by that, but the boys were not; immediately they hung their heads and looked appropriately devastated.

Simon said, "It's rough. There are only so many beautiful women. You guys will have to make do with the dogs tonight." There. Well. Wasn't that nicely put. Alice sat back with complete composure and looked down her nose at the boys, who grinned at one another through their moans and groans.

At which point Simon said, "But I never hang around if they don't put out, so maybe you guys will get another chance."

"Simon," Alice gasped, and blushed like a beet.

And the poor boys didn't know what to do.

Until Alice gave in. She went ahead and laughed like an old horse, just as Simon had known she would, and then the boys roared and roared with Alice, and Simon grinned like far more of a hell-raiser than those boys. And when the boys stood up to go, Alice could tell that they thought her old boyfriend was cool enough. Before they left they shook his hand and slapped him on the shoulder and wished him luck. Ho, ho.

And she and Simon did have fun at dinner. She told him

how pleased she was that he'd handled the boys so well. He said he'd liked Sam and liked his friends, and especially liked how much they all cared for Alice. Then Alice felt rather proud of herself after a second martini, and told Simon just how well she was doing, how much she did enjoy those kids, and that they did enjoy her, and how good it was having Sam home for whole summers, and about her job and being on her own and being pretty tough. She bragged, but Simon didn't mind. He was as glad as she was that she had gotten some spunk and begun to be herself and enjoy herself, after being unhappy so long. Simon was just the same as always. He was always just the same, a little older, strong and good natured, doing whatever it was in the Midwest that had gotten big enough now that he probably had money coming out of his ears. Simon was like her father, though her father had never been rich. Simon had always been like her father, always steady and gentle, which was why she had married Vic, and why she had wished often that she'd married Simon instead.

Here he'd let those boys have it though. He'd done that for her, she knew, and she was touched. And he still had the twinkle in his eye when he told her that this was the first time he'd seen her since she was officially a single woman. He raised his eyebrows and teased her the way he had with the boys, and they both loved it. He asked her about her health, and she had to tell him that she was a wreck. He knew about her bosom, so she didn't have to tell him that. She told him about the radiation and her hair falling out a mile a minute, and they both laughed about the wig, its little stand on the bureau and a name for it and Sam thinking she'd taken leave of her senses when he first heard her talking to it.

When they got home, Alice leaned over and gave Simon a big smack on the lips and thanked him and lay her head on his shoulder for a minute and then opened her door and told him she'd just go up by herself, she was used to it, and he should get started if he had to get into the city. He put his arm around her and hugged her—ooh that felt good—but when she started to get out of the car he said he wanted to come up and have one drink and a cup of coffee before he left. He said it with that grin and that twinkle in his eye, so she raised a lascivious eyebrow herself and grinned right back at him and laughed and led him on up. It was early, long before Sam. It would be quiet, and nice to talk more. She was sorry Sam had to be gone, because she would like for Simon to really talk with him.

She made some coffee to keep Simon's eyes open on the drive back and sat down with him on the sofa. He put his arm around her and she slid over and snuggled against him. He was a big, strong man. It had been so long since she had been held by a man. When she saw he was going to kiss her, she said, "Don't be silly, Simon." He kissed her anyway, on the lips. He kissed her as if he wanted to make love to her, and she kissed him back and turned on the sofa to face him and to press against him. He wrapped his arms around her and she pulled her hands against his back, rubbing them against the cotton of his sportcoat. She twisted her mouth against his. She tasted him and she felt his tongue and rubbed her face in the wetness of his lips. She lost her breath and more than any other thing she needed to be loved. He squeezed her against him, with his hands holding her beside her breasts, and she ran her tongue full into his mouth and began to cry low into his open mouth for her need of him, and then she felt as he squeezed her the hardness against her chest of her own false breast. She turned away from him and pushed herself against the back of the sofa as tightly as she could, and was horrified at herself. The cry she had begun in his mouth, of sex and her need, became sobbing. She cried into her hands and held her front turned away from Simon and against the back of the sofa. She held hard and would not let Simon turn her around, and he kissed her gently on her neck and under the hair of her wig and did not speak to her. He had felt it, that plastic breast against him. He knew about it, now he had felt it. At least he had not touched it with his hands wanting to hold her real breast. She held hard to the sofa until she was too tired to hold any longer and then she begged him, "Please don't, Simon. Please don't turn me around."

He didn't make her turn around. She had known he wouldn't. He didn't say anything. What could he say?

"You go ahead, Simon. I'm fine. Really I am. You go on. You know me. I was always a weeper. The fitter told me I had a handsome breast for a woman my age. Wasn't that nice? And now my wig is all askew." For his sake, so he could escape, she made herself sit up and smile and wipe at her eyes. She put a hand up to the wig to settle it and she laughed for him. He wanted to go. She would make it easy for him. "You see how hard it is to keep myself all in one piece? Isn't it silly? Now you go on. You've got such a long drive."

He kissed her again on the mouth and she let his tongue come into her mouth again, and she tasted him again, and tried to push him away as he leaned against her, and she could not let go of his mouth. He laid her down on the sofa, still with his mouth to hers, and she kept her eyes open and watched his face. He stopped kissing her and opened his eyes, but did not look into her eyes. He looked at the top of her head and took off her wig and put it beside the sofa on the floor and kissed her forehead and then all over her head in her thin hair. She lay very still, and didn't cry any longer, and kept her hands beside her, but she could not keep away her shortness of breath. She closed her eyes and he began to unbutton her blouse and she wanted to make him not. She held her eyes closed. He had to reach under her to unfasten her, and she would not help him, but he was strong enough to hold her up and reach under and loosen it, and as he held her up and she felt it come loose, she could not keep herself from looking at him again. He looked only at her bosom and laid her back down and she closed her eyes again and he kissed her nipple, and she pushed her hands under herself not to hold him there, and then his mouth came away from there and he kissed all over her empty chest. She could not keep herself from touching him, and she hugged his head to her and she moved him to her nipple again and the tears began to come again, but he would not stay there. He ran his face and his wet mouth over her belly. He undid her skirt and brought that down and her pants and stockings and then he stood up. She watched him undress and wanted to be frightened, wanted to hide herself, wondered if her body still could work for him. She wanted him to hurry. He kneeled over her on the sofa and she opened her legs for him and touched his naked waist and pulled him at her and he moved into her and filled her and she lay back and then quivered and shuddered with him in her. He began to move in her and she squeezed her arms and legs around him, and she saw him full of excitement, and full of love for her, full of need for her, need of the sex and everything else. She loved more than she could love. He moved harder in her and she worked with him and she shook and held to him for her life and cried and came to it with him.

"Mrs. Armstrong? Mrs. Armstrong?"

Alice opened her eyes and pushed herself up a little bit. She didn't hurt so much. That was a pleasant surprise. She smiled for the nurse. When she was a girl in the hospital and her father was a doctor she had wanted to be called something older. She had wanted to be called "Miss." She had her father tell all the nurses on the floor, but as soon as he left they all said, "Alice," again, and asked if her father was strict with her. Now when she told them just to call her "Alice," they wouldn't pay attention to that either.

"I'm sorry, Mrs. Armstrong. You have a phone call and we were going to take a message and not disturb you, but it's your son, Sam."

Somebody had told him. He wasn't supposed to know, and somebody had told him. "Who told him?"

"Told him what, Mrs. Armstrong?"

"He wasn't supposed to find out, and you know that very well. That's why he's calling. I want to know how he found out. Is he on the phone now?"

"Yes he is. I'm sorry, Mrs. Armstrong. I don't understand."

"It's not your fault. I don't mean to scream. I suppose I look like hell. All right." Alice picked up the phone.

"Hi, Mother. It's me."

"Who told you?"

"Told me what?"

She couldn't help it. She was livid. "You weren't supposed to know."

"Know what? I just called to say hello and ask how you are. I missed you. I thought you might be lonesome."

That didn't sound like him, but she could tell he didn't know. "You don't know?" She could tell from his voice he didn't, but now she'd worried him. Oh, spit. Why couldn't she keep her mouth shut?

"What is it?"

"Oh well, it's sort of silly, really. You know me."

"I'm not sure. Am I supposed to?"

"That's enough of that, Smarty Pants. What I was going to say was that I've had all sorts of visitors, and I told all of them how much I missed you. And I didn't want any of them to let you know that. I didn't want them to bother you in your first weeks at college. I just told them because I wanted a little sympathy. When people come to visit they're such a bore with being hearty and pretending you're not sick. They all seem to think that if they show some sympathy they'll worry you. Well, I like a little sympathy. And here you knew all by yourself that I was lonely. You see? That's the nicest thing that could have happened to me today. Well, how is it? What's the scoop on that college life? Any pretty girls yet? Terry and Peter came to see me, and Terry was with the girl whose name I always forget. Looks awfully bottom heavy. You're not missing a thing."

"Those guys came in to see you? Did they break anything?"

"No, they were very nice for a change. I teased Terry about a pimple so he wouldn't think I was going soft, and otherwise everything was fine. You know they're always a little subdued when there's a girl around, even a dull one like what's-her-name."

"I don't know why I was worried. I just felt like calling. Everything's okay here. You know, it's kind of new, but there are some nice guys and there's a pool table and stuff down in the basement, and the classes have started. I've been thinking about you."

"Well, there's certainly nothing to worry about here. I'm as comfortable as I can be, and Henry Meyers has his eye on me a couple of times a day. I shouldn't get so upset about the idea of people calling you to tell you I'm lonesome for you, but I know how important these first months are at college. I want you to get a good start and really settle in. You hear me?"

"Uh-huh. Yes, Mother."

"Well, don't 'Yes, Mother' me. What good is it being a mother if you can't nag? You get to those books, you hear me."

"Uh-huh. Yes, Mother." There, that sounded just like him. "What else, while I've got you here? Be careful in the car."

"I don't have a car."

"Well, good."

"I've been thinking maybe I should have one."

"Let's not go overboard, thank you. You can just worry about your schooling a little and forget about a car. Terry and Peter were my only visitors who weren't like company, so I'm delighted you called, and now I want you to get back to your studies before you run up a big telephone bill."

"I charged it to our home phone."

"Then you just get off this minute."

"I'll write you and tell you what's happening, over the weekend."

"Don't hurt yourself. I know pencil and paper can be painful. Bye, bye."

"Bye, Mother. I love you."

She listened to the hesitation and then the click, and bit her lip to keep from calling after him.

"I know who you've been talking to. That was young Samuel himself. Nurses told me. Oh my, you look tired. Is he already asking for the car and the big allowance?"

"Flora. Thank goodness. Let's have a drink. I need one."

"You sure?"

"I'm so tired, Flora. And I hurt."

"I'll call the nurses. They're playing magnetic checkers. They don't know how to play worth beans."

"Make us a drink, Flora. And I want us to have two tonight."

"Okay. Think you're tough enough? Don't look it."

"I wish I were as tough as you, Flora. I was afraid someone told him. He never calls. It's all I can do to get him to write one letter a year, and that sounds like it's coming from a stranger."

"Who's telling what?"

"He was worried that I was lonesome."

"Sounds like a fine boy, Mrs. Armstrong, but I've got some bad news. My niece Michelle went bowling with the halfback last night, and there were stars in her eyes when she came home. I'm afraid there's no hope now, even if Sam was a football player. I've been trying, but after a while they don't listen."

"I thought it was the quarterback?"

"Heavens no. The quarterback is ugly as sin and interested elsewhere."

"That's the last time I'll talk to him. I was good. He didn't know; I'm sure of that."

"You're not drinking your drink."

"The last couple of months it hurt so much sometimes, and then I'd get so dopey with the medicine, but he never knew. I got him off to school and I thought that was it. He left for his college with everything all right and with a real home and that was so important. But there he was on the phone, and I was afraid someone had told him, and then when he said he didn't know, I wished that he did. I wanted him to come and be with me. I wanted to tell him that I needed him. But I'd tried so hard through the end of the summer that I couldn't. I'm so tired. I might have cried. I might have told him how much it hurt. And if he got here he'd see me. I pretended all I could at the end of the summer. I don't want him to have to see. I was good on the phone. I teased him. I said, 'Good-bye,' and he said, 'Bye, Mother. I love you,' and I don't know when he's said that last. They don't say that at his age, not to us, do they. He went off to see some nice guys. I bit my lip to keep from telling him not to hang up. I listened until the line went dead. Will he be all right, Flora?"

"He'll be fine. You let me see that lip. Open up. You've cut it. That's what that foolishness was good for."

"I hurt so much, Flora. Make me another jolt of that cooking whiskey."

"You haven't touched what you've got. You want me to make the next one in the ashtray?"

Alice closed her eyes and listened to the sounds of her house on Hunting Ridge Road, to Flora's footsteps through the rooms and to mice in the walls. It was autumn, and field mice were coming back into the old walls for winter. She began a letter to Sam without pen and paper, and that seemed enough.

I suppose I might as well tell you.

And when she realized what she had forgotten to write, she began again from the beginning.

Dear Sam,

I suppose I might as well tell you, because if you don't already know, then you must think I've lost my mind. No need to comment, thank you. What I have to say is important, and I want you to pay attention.

Though in fact the really important thing doesn't involve my health or sanity one way or the other. What I want you to remember is something different. That's right, and I don't care where you're supposed to be or who's waiting. You can sit up straight and stop jigging. I'm still your mother.

It makes the world go around, and don't you ever forget.

Alice opened her eyes and saw Flora's hand on the bed. She took that hand in her own and said, "Is that all right?"

"Nobody tried to steal it yet, except the cocker spaniel some people had."

"I wish I'd told him, Flora. I wish I had him."

"You'll settle for Flora. It could be worse."

"I need a man. Oh God, I need a man."

"You just squeeze on that hand and we'll get by. I got a tough old hand, and we'll get by."

Alice rolled on her side and tried to curl her legs up and the hurting was so much that she let it go, and snuggled to be near her father and that felt much better. She squeezed against him until she hardly could breathe, and made him hold her to make her feel better, and every time she breathed in she could smell him just come from the hospital. He loved her and held her and he was her father and she was his baby girl and she could do what she pleased but she would stay here for now.

She held her own baby. She held her own baby and felt its naked softness and pressed it so gently against her breasts. She was strong and young and full of love and a baby was such joy. She was a woman and this was her baby and life was a wonder. Each of them would be this much a joy. She knew it was so, and knew nothing could ever be like holding this one, this first naked one, to her nipple until it wasn't hungry and slept the first time in her breasts. She was a mother. She would have more milk than she needed. Her breasts were sore with it.

And she was sore between her legs. And she was full everywhere with life and joy, and she cared nothing for the soreness.

When Vic finished, she was sore. When Simon finished. She
chose Simon. She made him stay with her when they were
done. He would have gotten up, but he didn't mind staying.
She held her arms around his waist and laughed and made
him hold her and put his leg over her to keep her warm, and
he didn't mind. He wrapped her up in his big arms and with
his leg, and laughed at her snuggling to him. She made him
happy. She did that, when he did everything for her she ever
could want. What else was there? It made the world go
around. They made it go around. And it still went, crazy as it
seemed. When she tickled a finger between the cheeks of his
bottom, he growled in fun deep in his throat, and she giggled.

Ralph Lombreglia

SOMEBODY UP THERE
LIKES ME

I logged on and got a Network fortune cookie, followed by E-mail from my distant wife.

Afternoon favorable for romance. Try a single person for a change.

Date: Mon, 12 Apr 99 14:27 GMT
From: Snookie Lee Ludlow <snooks@women.tex.edu>
To: Dante Allegro Annunziata <dante@media.sjcm.edu>
Subject: RE: For your delectation

Dante,

Your last missive was so cold, I thought somebody sent me an Alaskan sockeye salmon. Then I saw on TV where the sockeye's extinct, so now I don't know what your problem is.

Stop hurting people, you monster.

Snooks

I was on the old mainframe terminal in my office at school, surrounded by cinder-block walls and shelves stuffed chaotically with tapes and disks. I hadn't seen a friendly face in a week. Sometimes when I was down, the random-sentence generator cheered me up, so I knocked off a few new ones.

The president's unlikely urchin is tripping.
The awful dogs are howling.
Couldn't robots dine on jurisprudence?
And why shouldn't buildings puzzle over people?

You could feed the generator your own personal glossary of terms.

Vengeful Snookie bubbles San Antone into flames while academic watchmen practice celestial sloth in bed.

In my last mail to Snookie Lee, I had sent some morsels like these—affectionately, to make her smile—and she'd taken them all wrong: the whole story of Snooks and me. She was in San Antonio and I was in San Jose, and some people say that when a woman moves 1,500 miles from her mate to get a Ph.D. in women's studies, it's the beginning of the end, if not the end of the end, and refuting those prophets of woe is not easy. Yes, we had taken some bad falls, Snookie Lee and I. We were edging into the Humpty Dumpty zone. But I thought we could put it together again, and I was doing my best to convince Snookie of that.

<flame on>
MY letter was cold! Ha! You've been like ice! Maybe *my* feelings are hurt! I'm the loyal and true one! I'm the one who acts like he cares! You're the one who's trying to dump the whole thing down the sewer!
<flame off>

I made my computer do anagrams of your sweet name, Snooks—about 100,000 before I pulled the plug. Then I spent a whole day picking my favorites when I was supposed to be grading papers. Do men do this if they're not in love?

Like, elude solo now. Loud, sleek loin woe. Look, we use old line. Woo skill elude one. I use lone lewd look.

Look, Lee, we sin loud. Oil noose well, Duke. Look, Lee,
widen soul. Would Snook Lee lie? Look, slow Lee due
in.

Do lie low, keen soul,

Dante

Besides Snookie's letter I had four from Mary Beth—three
from last week, which I had not read, and a new one posted
early this morning, all bearing the subject line "Your position
here"—and I could have gone on to read them now, but I
wasn't in the mood. Mary Beth was the chair of language and
media studies at San Jose College of the Mind, where I was a
junior professor. She was also out to get me. Indeed, Mary
Beth's machinations were part of the reason that Snookie was
gone. Snooks had wanted to teach too, to chisel those young
minds, and she deserved her chance. Not only did she have
sufficient credentials, but she had more heart than the whole
College of the Mind put together. But Mary Beth wouldn't give
her even a section of Mastering Capitalistic Prose. I volun-
teered to give her a section of mine, and Mary Beth said no.
When they offered me the position, they said I'd come up for
tenure in three or four years; after Snooks applied to teach,
Mary Beth took me off the tenure track.

I met Snooks at a poetry slam in 1995, when I was finishing my
graduate media degree at MIT. She was up from Alabama to
show them a thing or two at Harvard, where she had made it
all the way to her senior year. Somehow we never crossed
paths in Cambridge, though she was all over town and hard to
miss. We slammed, finally, in the bowels of Boston, in a basement bookstore on Newbury Street, where Snookie Lee de-
claimed verses of outrage and indignation while shaking her
spiky hair and waving Simone Weil at the audience. They
loved her. I had to follow her on with my sheaf of technological rhapsodies. They hated me. But the opinion I cared about
was Snookie Lee's. I sidled up to her after the gig and asked
what she thought of my stuff. She hated it, but she loved my
name. On the strength of that, I asked her out. "I've got a date
with Dante!" she said, laughing, to one of her girlfriends.

She was all bluff and flying feathers, and then she was my everything. We graduated and I got the offer from College of the Mind, and since my fellow Ph.D.s seemed ready to slit my throat for the job, I took it. Snookie said she would follow me if I promised it was nice. My best childhood friend, Boyce Hoodington, had lived twenty miles north, in Palo Alto, for years, and he loved it out there. He was a project leader for a company trying to simulate human consciousness with a computer. Many California outfits were trying to do that, without much luck, but Boyce's firm had achieved a few small, sexy triumphs that kept the investors turned on. The firm's computer now recognized specific people when they walked into the room, greeted them, and commented on the clothes they were wearing. It could do other things, Boyce had told me— things he wasn't allowed to talk about.

So I promised Snookie she'd like California, and we lived there for three incredibly crummy years—crummy for me, the indentured professor in the house, thermonuclear for Snooks. Our problems went beyond Mary Beth. We experienced other disillusionments, too, such as the discovery that certain faculty couples masquerading as our friends were doing us dirty behind the scenes. Looking back on it, trying to fix the damage by getting married was not the best idea. Snookie said so at the time. I won't say that in those dark days when she didn't get out of bed till 4:00 P.M., and never took off her robe, and College of the Mind was leaking its acid into my brain, I was Jovian about it. But I still think that in the disappointing run of men I'm a prize.

I told all this to Snookie Lee as we stood on the dead lawn of our rented bungalow, her ancient, eggplant-colored Le Car parked halfway up on the sidewalk, stuffed full of her things. She was going to San Antonio to get her own Ph.D. In the last year of our three Snooks ended up as a night-shift checkout girl at a discount drug superstore, and the worst thing was, she liked it. She stopped blaming me for ruining her life. She now said that I'd inadvertently brought about her rebirth. She'd made a lot of new girlfriends at the store, muscular young women who weren't ever going to College of the Mind or college of the anything, and Snooks would go aerobic dancing and skating with them. She decided that the best thing in life was sisterhood. I hardly ever saw her anymore. On our separation day her friends spun over on their blades to bid Snookie Lee good-bye. They stood wobbling on the brown grass in their colorful tights and kneepads, saying supportive things to Snooks and giving bad looks to me.

I said, "Sisterhood means a lot to me, too, you know." The women had a good guffaw over that. I told Snooks she was breaking my heart.

She said, "You know those plastic ant-farm things? How you buy one, and then later decide you don't really want ants after all, and you empty the whole thing out on the ground? That's heartbreak, Dante. For the ants, I mean. You're not heartbroken. You don't even look sad."

"I'm very goddamn heartbroken," I said. "Don't tell me how heartbroken I am." The girlfriends rolled closer to Snookie Lee. I *was* heartbroken, but Snookie and I had beaten each other down so badly that our parting scene was playing like dinner theater. "And that analogy's no good," I told her. "Those ant-farm ants are an exotic breed that can't live in the wild. Otherwise they wouldn't *be* heartbroken. They'd be happy. They'd be free."

"You're free," Snookie Lee said.

"I never asked to be free! I'm exotic!" I exclaimed, but I got nowhere. Snookie Lee drove away.

I was about to log off when my terminal chirped and said, in its silly voice, *"You have new mail."* I hoped the message was from her. If she was online, maybe I could ping her for a real-time chat. But the letter turned out to be from Boyce. I punched it up.

Date: Mon, 12 Apr 99 20:53 GMT
From: Boyce P. Hoodington <boyce@softbrain.com>
To: Dante Allegro Annunziata <dante@media.sjcm.edu>
Subject: Death and pasta

Would have got back to you sooner, but I died. Have not logged on in days, and now speak to you from the beyond. My #*^!%!* computer went down like the Hindenburg—cellular port hosed, motherboard toasted.

I'm on the dusty laptop now, shades of Orville Wright. It periodically stalls out and drops through the clouds of our thrilling but turbulent present-day network. If I suddenly disappear, that's why.

I must have a new box, Dante! Let's shop for it together! Tonight, after partaking of a momentous baked ziti. Mounds of baby peas, asparagus, and musky salad greens from the garden have turned our kitchen into a Tuscan stone cottage. I may videodisk it, it's so beautiful. But Janet regards me strangely when I videodisk food. And wait till you taste this fresh-faced fumé with overtones of apple and pear. Spanking beverage. Bought a case. Snatched a spicy zinfandel, too. Come on up!—BPH

P.S. I'll tell my sad corporate story. Slithering beast of commerce, it's a snakepit out here. Be thankful you chose the cloistered life.

P.P.S. We must talk about Snookie. You don't sound good, my brother. Janet has thoughts for you. Never mind free enterprise, Dante; women are the great challenge of our lives, the parabolic arena where we Rollerblade like angels at the speed of light, and where, I fear, we are destined to wipe out grotesquely. Yet we skate on blindly into the night. Why? Because of love, that hot transistor smoking within us.

My office hours at College of the Mind had another hour to run, but not a single student had come to see me so far. True, my door was closed and locked, and I was being very quiet. My lights were off. If I left now, I could go home and take a shower, change into my jeans (Mary Beth forbade teaching in jeans), and still make it to Boyce's for happy hour. I blow-gunned my answer into the bitstream—

I Brake for Baked Ziti

—and was yet again on the cusp of logging off when I remembered the text-dissociation software they had on the server. It could sometimes ease the misery inflicted upon people by words. I gave it Snookie's letter to eat.

St. Dante,

I, thou monster. I saw on Sockeye TV where the salmon is cold. Cold, cold, cold. I thought somebody sent me an Alaskan Salmonster, but now I don't know what your last missive was. Your problem's extinct, you hurting salmon.

You, monstero, the Sockeye Salmolast.

Salmonstop,

Snooksego

It didn't kill much pain, but I sent it to her anyway.

I drove my Fuji Chroma up 280 from San Jose to Palo Alto amid contorted oaks on hilltops, like bonsai trees in amber waves of grain, except the waves weren't grain, they were dead meadow grass, two or three feet high and browned-out from drought, emblem of our republic. Also a fire hazard that should have been mowed down. A red-tailed hawk sailed from a knobby tree, plunged to the undulating grass, and flapped back to its branch with mythic pumps of the wings, taking a field mouse on a commuter hop to God.

The foothills reminded me of hobbit-land, furry café-au-lait knolls where Frodo, Gandalf, et al., would have felt at home. Zipping up the artery in my tiny car, I succumbed to a conviction that hobbits were living there now, in burrows beneath the gnomish topography. The old Tolkien books—the interactive laser-disk versions—had lately made a great comeback with students, and I'd been using them in my classes at College of the Mind. For doing that and certain other groovy things, I was considered a cool professor, and my sections never failed to fill up. I got glowing reviews in the campus electronic magazine, to the profound irritation of Mary Beth, whose classes the students routinely panned. And yet educating endless waves of the young had begun to unnerve me. The act of teaching unnerved everyone eventually, but usually because your students were always nineteen while you withered into your grave before their eyes. My problem was different—I remained the same while they mutated into a different species. My students implanted digital watches in the skin of their wrists, tattooed and barbered themselves so as not to appear human, took personalized drugs made from their own DNA, and danced epileptically to industrial noise. I fantasized about taking them on a field trip to the foothills for the semester-wrap picnic and then, in the thick of the hobbit hunt, vanishing—never to be seen again. Perhaps they'd start a religion based on the mystery of my disappearance. Perhaps spirituality would flower on earth once more.

When I pulled up to Boyce's, his front lawn was preternaturally thick and green, like a gigantic flattop haircut for St. Patrick's Day. He and Janet loved landscaping and were always ministering to their lawn. I wished I had a nice house and yard like theirs. Actually, I wished I had anything. It hit me that I should enter the private sector, like Boyce, where your bosses didn't punish you for doing your job. I found him in his modern, shiny kitchen at the back of the house, assembling a fine baked ziti in a big casserole dish. He was a North Carolina Methodist, supposedly, but some Mediterranean blood had got in there somehow. The man could cook. "Romano!" he said in greeting, pointing to a quarter wheel of the stuff.

"I got E-mail from Snookie today," I said, grating the cheese.

"Excellent!" Boyce said. "You're talking! What did she say?"

"That I was a monster."

"All women say that about men, Dante. It's a figure of speech."

"What does it mean?"

"It means we're monsters."

We built the ziti and slid it into the oven. Boyce poured us big goblets of fumé. "To a new life for us all."

We clinked and sipped. "What do you want a new life for?" I asked.

"I meant the new one we're all getting, want it or not."

"What happened?"

"Tell you outside. Where nature can absorb the toxins."

We took our glasses to the verdant back yard. Boyce and Janet had a triple-depth lot—150 feet of Palo Alto crust in which Boyce had laid drip-irrigation lines, so that now it looked like the Garden of Eden back there. Lemons and limes and oranges hung over our heads at the round terrace table. Zippy the hummingbird was doing his air-and-space show, flashing in from nowhere to sip at his feeder, and then buzzing our heads before zinging back to the treetop where he lived. The little nugget of his beelike body stood in relief against the sky, microscopic stud on a eucalyptus branch.

"You can't see the knife?" Boyce said, twisting to show me his back.

I looked around him. "You've got it hidden pretty well."

"I'm out."

"Of what?"

"SoftBrain Technologies."

"What? You were in charge of the whole project. It was your division."

"The division they lopped off in the corporate downsizing."

"They lop off whole divisions?"

"That was the normal part. The stinky part was tricking me into lopping it for them."

And then Boyce told his tale. Nearly a year before, without telling him, his bosses had cut a deal to sell the consciousness-emulation division. The buyers thought they were paying too much and wanted something extra thrown in, something big and sweet. Boyce was assigned a strange and urgent top-secret task, on which he worked his heart out until just the week before—working, though he didn't know it, for his own extinction. I demanded that he tell me this top-secret thing.

"Oh, it was so typical. So depressingly superficial. Nothing. They wanted to see the computer hold a credible conversation."

"But it's been doing that for years."

"Not with its lips."

"*Lips!* It has *lips?* I didn't know it had lips!"

"I just violated my nondisclosure agreement. Don't spread that around."

"Lips!"

Monday of the previous week, at 9:00 A.M., Boyce had demoed the lips for the company brass and some invited guests with English accents. The lips were gorgeous. Everybody loved the lips. The brass congratulated Boyce in a way that implied a promotion and a load of stock. He returned to his office to pop corks with the team, though it was only coffee-break time. He felt the burgeoning glory of his division, soon to be the company jewel. At 3:00 P.M. he got the call to close it down. The British guests were the buyers. They were taking the sucker to England, lips and all.

It took me a minute to absorb this slimy information. "But they *liked* you," I said at last.

"Oh, they still do," Boyce said. "They love me. I'm a great guy."

In the week since his severance he'd been home in seclusion, drinking boutique wine and having his spine realigned by a private masseuse. Only this morning had Boyce awakened with a craving to re-enter the world.

"How's Janet taking it?"

"Overjoyed. She thinks I've been miraculously spared from my own worst tendencies. She thinks I was going corporate—me, of all people."

"Were you?"

"Of course I wasn't! I thought the lips were stupid. Here we were on the trail of consciousness itself, and all the managers cared about was lips."

"Humanity's signal-to-noise ratio isn't so hot, is it?"

"Worst in the animal kingdom. By a mile."

"But we've put out some pretty clean signal, too," I said reflectively. "Over the years. Down through the centuries. It adds up."

Boyce slapped my arm. "That's what I woke up this morning thinking!" he exclaimed. "That's what I've learned from all this!"

"What?"

"That everything we've done with computers until now is totally trivial and wrong! Why have we not yet created a fantastic, free, self-reflective knowledge base of every good thing

humanity has ever thought or dreamed? Not just consciousness, Dante. *Cosmic* consciousness! That's what I want to build
now. The computerized mind of the world!"

"And you say Janet's not worried about you?"

"She doesn't know yet. She'll love it when I explain it. I
kind of got the idea from her, in fact. But since you mention it,
it's you she's worried about."

Fumé went up my nose and fizzed my sinuses. *"Me?"*

"She wants me to watch you very closely. She thinks you
may do some harm to yourself."

One is rarely prepared to meet the shabby figure one actually cuts in the world, even if one already has a pretty clear
mental image of the wretch. "You don't think that, do you,
Boyce?"

"Would it make you feel better or worse if I did?"

"Worse. Definitely worse."

"Then I don't."

My harming myself was a silly idea, but it was nice to have
friends who considered me a walking pipe bomb and yet continued to care. True, that was practically Janet's job: she was a
Jungian therapist, not to mention a splendid woman at whose
sagacious feet I should probably throw myself for guidance.
She was certainly the best thing that ever happened to Boyce,
and her wonderfulness made me wish that I had a wife too.
Then I remembered—I did.

"Can I use your Chokecherry to check my mail?" I asked
Boyce.

"Be my guest, but it might not even get you on. I had a hell
of a time with it today. A few keys are falling off, too."

"I'll nurse it along."

"Try slapping it."

I ducked the pendulous oranges and crossed the back yard
beneath fantastical shapes in the California clouds, smiling at
the idea of Boyce's still using the old Chokecherry 100. The
kitchen was like a lung filled with baked ziti's life-affirming
breath. I walked through it and on into the darkened living
and dining rooms, where the recently restuccoed walls were
already cracked again from tremors. In Boyce's study the big
computer lay dead on its table, the little Chokecherry sleeping

beside it and waking up reluctantly when I touched its wobbly keys. Once, people had thrilled to own this little appliance of the brain. True to its name, it choked when I logged on, but I lashed it forward with repeated jabs of the Escape key. It tried to read me the fortune cookie that appeared on the screen, but the loudspeaker was broken and the latest assessment of my destiny sounded like a faltering Bronx cheer.

It may be that your whole purpose in life is simply to serve as a warning to others.

And then my one new letter flashed onto the gray wafer of screen. It was from Snookie Lee.

Date: Mon, 12 Apr 99 21:09 GMT
From: Snookie Lee Ludlow <snooks@women.tex.edu>
To: Dante Allegro Annunziata <dante@media.sjcm.edu>
Subject: RE: Dissociated Love

Dante,

I'm going nuts and you're helping me do it. You're helping quite nicely.

What was that stuff you sent? "Salmonstop" and all that. "Snooksego." What was that supposed to be? I don't understand your problem anymore. I used to think I did. I'm not studying to be a shrink. I'm studying to be a scholar, which I now realize means I need a shrink myself. Maybe yours would take me on; she's used to people with bullet holes in their feet AND their heads.

Would Snook Lee lie? No, she wouldn't. I'm taking my orals an hour from now. You'll claim you didn't know, though I've told you numerous times. You don't listen when I talk. I'm not nervous. Nerves are not why I feel like barfing. I feel like Polly, the girl who wanted a cracker. They've stuffed me full of their theories, and now they want me to spit them back. But I don't even believe in half that stuff. More than half. My professors

aren't bad people, they just turn their students into apes.
No, they don't do it, this system does it! This rotten
system! I hate it!

But why am I telling you this? You're an ape yourself!

This is what I've been living with. I would've told you
before, but I, for one, don't believe in throwing up on
people. I gotta go.

Snooks

P.S. Get help.

From the time-stamp on Snookie's letter, I figured her orals
were over by now. I clacked out my answer on Boyce's broken
keys.

I'm up at Boyce's for dinner. I'm sorry you're not getting
this before your exams. I would have wished you luck.
You never told me they were today! You didn't! This is
something you're always doing, telling me you told me
things when you didn't tell me.

You were having pre-exam hysteria, Snooks—all that
stuff about spitting back theories and whatnot. Classic
symptoms. Just calm down and be yourself and you'll
do fine. God, what saccharine advice. Fortunately, you
didn't get it. If you're reading this, it's all over, and you
did just fine, didn't you? Academia does this to people,
Snooks. I, for one, am getting out.

When you have your Ph.D., I'll work in the drugstore and
you can teach college! I can't wait!

I am not an ape and you know it.

Love, love, love,

Dante

P.S. Remember Boyce's incredible baked ziti? It's in the
oven right now. And then we're going computer
shopping for him. I'm gonna call you later.

I shot my letter into the colossal web of the Net. When I looked up, Janet was standing in the door. "Fixing Boyce's computer?" she said.

"Hi. No, I was just saying something to Snookie Lee."

Janet looked around. "Snookie's here?"

"I meant I was E-mailing her."

"Oh, E-mail. Not talking on the videophone?" We giggled over that for a second. Janet famously loathed all technology after the fountain pen. "Boyce thought the little computer was broken too," she said.

"It is, Janet. Just because you can answer your mail doesn't mean a computer works. See?" I picked up the Chokecherry and turned it upside down. Five or six keys fell off and a guitar pick dropped out. "He needs a new computer."

"I've heard. Well, you're communicating, at least."

"Of course we're communicating," I said, skeptical that Janet really considered Boyce's layoff a great development. "I'm here, aren't I? But it would be a hell of a lot easier with a better computer."

"Oh, I'm sure a better computer would help immensely. When was the last time you told her you loved her?"

"I thought we were talking about Boyce."

"We were clearly talking about Snookie Lee."

"We were talking about Boyce and computers! You shrinks always do that."

"What?"

"That! Ambush people."

"Have you told Snookie you loved her any time in the past two years?"

"Of course I have."

"She says you haven't."

"Goddamn gossip!" I cried, and threw the Chokecherry onto Boyce's desk. It broke in two pieces. "When did she tell you that? You two have been talking? What else did she say?"

"Plenty."

In Boyce's ziti the asparagus had given itself to the pasta like a submissive lover. The food was so ambrosial that we didn't even need the spicy zin, though we drank it anyway. My own baked ziti never came out nearly this good, and I was the Italian one. In my present frame of mind I could take a thing like that hard, as a comment on my general integrity.

"Did you know that Janet has serious misgivings about us, Dante?" Boyce asked. "About our relentless fascination with technological goods, the way machines work, what's the latest thing." We were having dinner outside, at the round redwood table, where I sat between Boyce and Janet, opposite the empty fourth chair. "Something about it is fishy, she thinks."

"I didn't know that," I said.

"Yes, I may start studying you two," Janet said. "I may write a book on this phenomenon."

Janet had her own private practice full of wealthy clients. She wasn't jumping through flaming tenure hoops under the stony gaze of some Mary Beth, and yet she still had thoughts of writing books. What pluck!

"Why do you know so much about computers?" she asked me. "Him I can understand. But you're supposed to be a humanities guy."

"Fear of death," I said. "Sexual terror."

"Nice try."

"Because he knew I'd need a new one someday," Boyce said, "and he wanted to help me pick it out."

"Good, Boyce," I said. "Right. But follow through. What kind of computer would you like? You haven't told us."

"A Revelation 2000."

This magical product name buzzed past my ear with such an unreal twang that I looked around to see if little Zippy had just gone by again. The Revelation 2000 was the first microcomputer with a holographic screen, 1,000-bit audio/video, three billion instructions per second, and direct wireless uplink to geosynchronous satellites. It was the sexiest hardware you could put on a desk. And though I personally subscribed to the old chestnut about buying computers—get the most iron they'll let you charge on your card, and if you can't use all that power, you're doing something wrong—I couldn't believe Boyce was talking about a Rev 2K. "Revelations cost a fortune," I said.

"I've got one lined up for three thousand bucks."

"Bull, Boyce! They're twenty times that."

"My man has one for three."

"What man?"

"This guy Mickey. I've never met him. He's a friend of Bru-baker's."

"Oh, no, Boyce. No."

"Honey," Janet said, "I don't think 'Brubaker' was the cor-rect magic word."

"You said you were never dealing with Brubaker again."

"It's a *friend* of his, Dante. Plus, I'm a big boy now."

"He's saying I'm being too protective," I said to Janet.

"That seems to be it," she said.

Brubaker was an avatar of free enterprise who'd been in bed at one time or another with almost every breathing being do-ing business in the Valley. Like countless others, Boyce had worked for the mythical Bru. Unlike most, he remained on friendly terms with Brubaker after the experience, but then, Boyce was friends with everybody. Brubaker had seen the high times, and now he was researching the lows. He'd been charged with various white-collar crimes in recent years, wrig-gling off every time except the last, when they popped him for soliciting capital investment without a prospectus. He got a hefty fine and sixty days of community service—which he dis-charged by teaching street youths to set up their own "S" cor-porations.

"Stolen goods," I said to Boyce. "Hijacked tractor-trailer."

"You know I wouldn't do that."

"How does Brubaker meet these people?"

"I don't ask."

"That's the understanding you have?"

"No, I don't ask because he'd tell me."

"Since when is three thousand dollars cheap?" Janet said.

"Last computer I'll ever buy, honey," Boyce told her. "Cross my heart."

"Are you going to use it to change the world?"

"You're reading my mind."

"All right, then, you can have it," she said, sipping her zinfandel and staring into the reddening California sky. "I think I'll call my book *Modern Man in Search of a Dumpster for His Soul.*"

Boyce turned to me. "And you were upset about being called a monster."

I was halfway to the street when I realized that Boyce wasn't behind me. He was standing on his Crayola-green lawn, under the lady's-slipper-colored dome of California sky, staring at my cerulean vehicle parked at the curb in the striated shadow of a mimosa tree. "Do I look like I can ride in a Chroma?" he said. I was forgetting that Boyce, six foot four, couldn't even get into the freeway bubble I drove. I joined him on the lawn leading to his car. The sprinklers popped up and sprayed our legs like mechanical cats. "The downside of homeownership," Boyce called out, as we dashed off his effervescing grass.

"You finally get a pot to pee in, and it pees on you." We made it back to the sidewalk and shook our ankles. "Still, I wouldn't mind. A little pot to pee in with Snookie Lee. But I guess SoftBrain Technologies won't have a gig for me now."

"I guess not, cowboy. You wanted one?"

"I was thinking maybe technical writer."

"Impeccable sense of timing, Dante."

His silver Kodak Image hulked in the transcendental evening light. The automobile was so large it seemed designed to lure Japan into the quicksand with us once and for all—the two rivals going down in a cruise-controlled death embrace. When we approached it, the driver's door slid open, but not mine. "Look at that," I said. "It didn't do my side. A snoutful of microchips and it can't even open the door."

"You have to stand where it can see you, dude."

I walked to the passenger side, and the door retracted with an overdesigned hermetic suck. "My Chroma sees me no matter where I am," I said. When we were gliding through the peaceful streets, pastel homes clicking by like Necco wafers, I said, "So. Mickey."

"Brubaker says the overall impression is of an alienated vet. But in fact Mickey is not a vet. Not of any actual war."

"He's in a private militia?"

"No, just the opposite. Mickey wouldn't join any organized anything. He's a loner. He's this guy who came out the other side of the Valley dream."

"He went in the front?"

"Wrote system code in the glory days, burned out on that, went independent, specialized in lockout software. He's into hardware now."

"Designing it?"

"Testing it, more like."

Offices and malls and taco stands swept by on El Camino. We arrived at the outskirts of Palo Alto, where start-ups roiled in every dingy industrial park, in the bedrooms of brick apartment buildings, at the whittled wooden tables of the old hamburger bars. Nothing could kill the entrepreneurial spirit, not even the nineties in California. Everybody had an angle, everybody had a scheme. It was endless, and now Boyce was one of them. He parked in front of a run-down hacienda with silver Quonset huts on either side. Night had nearly fallen. The air was acrid with the resins of burning electronics.

"You guys seen Mickey?" somebody asked when we got out of the car. A tall black man in rags had stepped out of the bushes.

"No, we haven't," Boyce said.

The guy took a step back into the light, and I saw that his clothes weren't rags. They were expensive designer things with all kinds of shapes and flaps cut into them.

"We just got here," Boyce said. "Where is he?"

"Didn't I clearly imply that I do not know where Mickey is?" the guy said, and went back into the shadows.

Then a white guy dressed in rags approached us from the opposite direction. "You guys seen Mickey?" he said.

"Would you mind stepping into the light?" I said, leading him underneath the lamp at the curb. This guy was really in rags, actual rags.

Boyce said, "What's with all you cats asking if we've seen Mickey?"

"All us cats?" the guy said. "Do I know you guys? Have I ever, like, *seen* you guys?"

"I just told the other dude. No, we have not seen Mickey."

"What other dude?"

I pointed at the bushes. "Over there somewhere. Wearing real fancy clothes. He's looking for Mickey too."

"He didn't actually say he was looking for Mickey," Boyce said. "He wanted to know if *we'd* seen Mickey. Just like you."

"That's true," I said. "Maybe you guys don't want to see Mickey at all."

"I see Mickey all the time," the guy said, and walked off into the darkness.

A small Filipino woman answered the door when we rang the bell. She seemed surprised to see us. "Isn't Mickey expecting us?" Boyce said.

"You're different," the woman said, and led us into her dwelling, where furniture and clothing and plastic media trash tumbled together indistinguishably in every room. We wound up in a wood-paneled den where two children played on shag carpeting in the blue glow of a sexual-hygiene program on the big TV. They looked a lot like their mother—for that was who she had to be. The kids were no more interested in us than in the blurry sex on the tube. I thought of my students, aliens whose human parents paid my bills, and I understood them better now. This was where they'd grown up. The house was from the sixties, when people put wet bars in their recreation rooms. On the dusty surface of a side table lay two handguns and a rifle—not toys, not dusty.

Mrs. Mickey walked us along a breezeway to one of the Quonset huts we'd seen from the street. At the entrance, midway along the metal pod's fuselage, she left us staring inside from the threshold. The shape and corrugation made it feel like an aircraft hangar—one in which had taken place, for some reason, the Battle of Silicon Valley. Mutilated corpses of computers from the past ten years lay in heaps around the cylindrical room, most horribly crushed or burned or melted. At a workbench in the midst of this wreckage, surrounded by banks of test equipment, a large bearded man in sleeveless fatigues was blowing a heat gun at a computer in a plain black box and laughing. Text and a picture were bending like taffy on the screen. A high-pitched squeal was emerging from the thing. An oscilloscope portrayed the computer's demise in ghostly green wiggles—lots of waves, lines with some waves, nothing but lines. Finally the screen crackled violently and then went blank. Blue-black smoke twirled from the computer's vents into an exhaust hood above the bench.

"He's an *abuse tester*," I whispered to Boyce. "You didn't tell me that. He kills computers for a living."

"Don't say 'kills,' " Boyce said. "*Stresses*."

"Piece of crap!" the man barked at the melting computer, and then he looked up and saw us standing there. He stood very still, staring at us, breathing deeply, with the heat gun still in his hand.

"Mickey?" Boyce said. "Are you Mickey? Hi, I'm Boyce. You were expecting us, right? Brubaker said we were coming?"

The man said nothing. Boyce looked worried, and worry was not a Boycean trait. It made me worried myself. But then, staring into this situation, I realized something about Mickey. He had just completed a kill and he wouldn't want to fight. He'd feel unthreatened and kingly. Unless overtly attacked, he'd be docile. He might even let smaller creatures pick at the edges of his prey. I pointed to the smoking prototype on his bench. "Did you drop it on the floor yet? I hear that's the first thing you're supposed to do. Drop it on the floor."

These words revived his inner animal. "You hear that 'cause that's what I do! *I* developed the protocol! *Me!*" He slapped himself on the chest. "Damn right I dropped it on the floor. I dropped it on the floor several times!" And then he laughed uproariously.

We were all right. He was verbalizing. Brubaker had told Boyce to expect a bearlike creature who communicated mainly by snuffling in his sinus passages, scratching himself, and emitting inexplicable giggles or guffaws.

Suddenly Mickey stopped laughing. "Brubaker told me one guy."

"That's me. Boyce. I just brought my friend along. Dante."

"*Dante?*" Mickey said, his face clouding over as he pronounced my name. He stared across the hut at old Fillmore West posters taped to the rippling metal walls. "The tomato family? Don't tell me this is the ketchup heir, the little tomato-paste trust-fund boy."

"Not *Del Monte*," Boyce said. "Dante. He's not from ketchup money."

"They're all related," Mickey said.

"The Del Montes maybe, but he's not a Del Monte."

Mickey cackled again, but he put his heat gun down, and though he didn't explicitly invite us in, he didn't not invite us either, so we picked our way through the technological waste. "The Revelation brothers," Mickey said.

"That's us," Boyce said.

A color TV in Mickey's lair was tuned to a news story about the thousands of people living at Moffett Air Field now that NASA's demise had left the old base free to become a homeless shelter. It was an election year, and a local politician came on to gas a few bites about the looting of taxpayer coffers.

"Bring out the old rockets," Mickey said. "Ship 'em to Mars!"

"What are you saying that for?" I said. "You have homeless friends yourself. We saw a homeless guy right here in front of your house."

Mickey peeped out a small window. "Where?"

"Right out front, man. He was asking for you too. 'You guys seen Mickey?' he said."

"That's no homeless guy!"

"He looked homeless," Boyce said.

"They just dress up like that."

Our deal seemed on the verge of going bad, so I said, "Hey, let's see this great computer."

"Hey, let's see this great computer," Mickey said.

"Well, if you don't mind."

He opened a door in an unpainted plasterboard wall and rolled the Revelation in on a cart. It wasn't burned or smashed or even dented. It maybe had a few scratches on it. He plugged it into the wall and flipped the switch. "Come on, sport," he said to me. "Let's see you do your stuff."

I'd never actually seen a 2000 in person before. Holographic software objects floated in the space between the computer and me, one of them announcing the machine's readiness for telephony in any form. I sat down and logged onto my account, bracing myself for power and speed. Even so I wasn't ready. The thing whomped me onto the Network like a jujitsu flip.

Hanlon's Razor:
Never attribute to malice that which is adequately explained by stupidity.

You have new mail.

from: marybeth@media.sjcm.edu
"Your position here"

from: marybeth@media.sjcm.edu
Re(1) "Your position here"

from: marybeth@media.sjcm.edu
Re(2) "Your position here"

from: marybeth@media.sjcm.edu
Re(3) "Your position here"

from: marybeth@media.sjcm.edu
Re(4) "Your position here"

"You got mail, dude," Mickey said.

"I see that, Mickey."

"Who's marybeth?"

"My boss."

"How come she's writing you so much? You two into something? You got something going with the boss lady, Don?"

"Dante, Mickey. Don Tay." The thought of having something going with Mary Beth was so ludicrous I forgot what I was doing. I sat there like an idiot who didn't know what a computer was for.

"Don't know how to read mail?" Mickey said. "No problem on a Revelation. Just tell it what you want it to do."

"I don't want to read that mail right now. I'll read it some other time."

"But then how are you gonna know how blazing the Revelation is at your daily tasks? *Read the mail,*" he barked at the box.

My first letter from Mary Beth joined us in the room as though we were reading the woman's mind. You couldn't describe the 2000 as "fast"—reality and the Revelation were basically indistinguishable. Everything just *was,* and in 3-D it all seemed almost edible besides. It was an amazing hardware experience. The message content was kind of a downer, though.

Date: Mon, 5 Apr 99 20:23 GMT
From: Mary Beth Hinckley <marybeth@media.sjcm.edu>
To: Dante Allegro Annunziata <dante@media.sjcm.edu>
Subject: Your position here

My dear Dante,

I assume some awareness on your part, however dim, of your contract's impending expiration, and of your ongoing evaluation for renewal in this department.

"What's this 'my dear' crap?" Mickey said.
"Scorn."
"Is she like this in person?" Boyce asked.
"No, she's more relaxed in the mail."

I—all of us, actually—have been reading your student evaluations. They make a most striking collection of documents. Indeed, we've never seen anything quite like it. The students are deliriously uncritical of you, Dante. It seems you can do no wrong. Are you, perhaps, being uncritical of them? There is no learning without criticism, mon cher. We're not here to have the children like us. We're here to teach, to mold, to impart.

More than being peculiar—nay, unprecedented—I'm afraid such student reaction to a professor raises serious questions. We must talk.

MBH

"You poor bastard," Boyce said. "Why didn't you share it with us? You didn't have to bear it alone."
"I've always told you I hated the place."
"That's true, you have."

"You put some major mojo on this chick," Mickey said. "She wants you, Don. She wants you bad."

"I don't think so, Mickey. For one thing, she's not a chick."

"Listen to me, dude. I know, *Next*," he said, and Mary Beth's next letter materialized in our midst, followed by the others in succession as Mickey said *"Next"* again and again, each letter more aggrieved than its predecessor, until finally her last message bodied forth from the screen, dated this afternoon.

Signor Annunziata:

Your silence is rude and mystifying, but I'll say no more about it here. Indeed, I'll say no more here at all, since this is the last mail you'll receive from me.

The formal hearing into your future will be held tomorrow, Tuesday, 13 April, at 9 AM, in the Provost's office. Feel free to join us, in the flesh or via video, though the proceedings will be conducted in absentia in any event. If you're feeling pressed for time, I expect a very brief session.

What happened, Dante? You seemed so promising at first. And with that lovely name. I hoped you'd join our little family. But not as the Prodigal Son.

MBH

"I like how they're doing it in absentia whether you're there or not," Boyce said.

"That captures it, doesn't it? But I'll hack on your Revelation till dawn, shave and shower, drag myself in there, plead for my job. It's all I have. I'll say I've been sick. I'll get some students to claim they don't like me."

"Reply," Mickey said, causing an empty text-window to appear, at which he recited an incantation that scrolled obediently up the screen as he spoke. Mickey was one of those holdovers from the early days of computers, people who type

everything with Caps Lock on, and he must have trained the Revelation to do the same whenever it heard his voice.

STUCK UP BITCH

DON'T MESS WITH DONNY

HE COULD OF BEEN YOURS

BUT YOU WERE HOTTY

NOW SUFFER

"Hotty?" Boyce said.

"Yeah. Stuck up. Superior. *Hotty.*"

"Oh. I see."

"That's great, Mickey," I said. "Thank you for coming to my defense. I'm touched, really I am. Now erase it, please."

"*Send,*" he said, and his voodoo poem-curse to Mary Beth vanished from the screen, sucked away by the Network's solar wind.

Sometimes you don't know how close you are to flaming out till it happens, and this was the case with me. I sat down on a deformed plastic chair in this computer criminal's Quonset hut, and I began to cry. Not big out-and-out boohooing, but there's crying and there's not crying, and I was crying.

"What's he doing?" Mickey asked Boyce, backing away from me.

"He seems to be crying," Boyce said. "You okay, pal?"

"Well, make him stop," Mickey said.

"How am I gonna do that? You just got him fired from his job, man."

"She was messing with his mind. What does he wanna work there for anyway?"

"What does anybody want to work anywhere for, Mickey? Plus, things aren't going real well with his wife right now."

"What's the problem?"

"She left."

My weeping did become out-and-out boohooing at this point.

"He's a total loss, isn't he?" Mickey said, gazing down at me. "But he likes computers, right? Computers make him happy, it seems like."

"They always do seem to cheer him up," Boyce said.

Mickey went into his secret room and wheeled out another cart.

"What's that?" I said, sniffling. "That looks like another Revelation."

"I was gonna keep it for parts, but you seem so sad, dude. I don't like people feeling sad. It makes me feel weird. You want it?"

"How much?"

"Same as for him."

"Three thousand bucks? Where are you getting these?"

"Don't ask questions like that, Don. You want it, I take cash. You don't want it, you never saw it."

I had thirty-five hundred bucks in my savings account, and after that it was the graveyard shift at Drugs 'n' Such. "I'll take it." I turned to Boyce. "Get me to a bank machine."

Mickey put his huge, heavy arm on my shoulder. "Then you're feelin' better about things?"

"Yeah, I am, Mickey, thanks. Can I ask you a question, though? I'm just curious. What's in the other Quonset hut? The one on the other side of the house?"

"What's in it? My in-laws. You want one of them, too? We could work something out. Can't do better than a nice Filipino girl."

We drove out onto the strip to look for an ATM. As the owner of a Revelation 2000, I could network with Boyce's machine and be part of his new venture, the construction of humanity's electronic mind. He offered me a job. I accepted. Then he revealed the identity of his major investor. I worked for Brubaker now.

Alongside a taco stand we found a riotously bright bank machine, its colored panels burning like gas in the California night. It sucked my card and started beeping at me.

Greetings, valued customer Dante Allegro Annunziata!
You have new Network mail! Read it now at your
Mitsubishi ATM!

(Small service charge applies.)

(Reminder: your credit account is past due.)

I pushed the button and they dropped me right into my
mail, no list of letters received, no fortune cookie, no nothing.
They literally didn't give me the time of day. What did I expect? It was a bank. I had only one new letter anyway, from
Snookie Lee.

Date: Tue, 13 Apr 99 02:03 GMT
From: Snookie Lee Ludlow <snooks@women.tex.edu>
To: Dante Allegro Annunziata <dante@media.sjcm.edu>
Subject: I did a wild thing

Dante,

I went kind of crazy. I did a wild thing.

They asked me their parrot questions, like I knew they
would. No big surprise. But when I actually heard it
happen, something inside me plopped. I refused to
answer. I refused to say anything at all. I just sat there
doing a Bartleby in my oral exams. It was so weird. I
couldn't believe it. They couldn't believe it either. Surely
you're going to say something, they said. I'd prefer not
to, I said. This can't be happening, said my adviser. It's
happening, I said. I can't believe you're not finishing this
degree, she said. I'd prefer not to, I said.

There's a blank place after that. Somebody drove me
home. I called Janet. She's picking me up at the airport
in San Jose. I'm flying in at 10 PM. I sold my Le Car
about a month ago. I guess I never told you that. Got
five hundred bucks for it. We have to talk. This does not
mean I'm staying. I'm on my way home to Alabama.
Well, the long way. If I did stay, it would be because I

had seen a Goddamn miracle walking around in your
pants, I'll tell you that.

Oil noose well, you said. Oil well indeed. I slipped out.
But how did you know that? You are one spooky cat.

Snooks

P.S. Lie low, keen soul, you said. Slow Lee due in. How
did you *know* that? I've been having some bourbon. It
reminds me of my lost home in the South. Been looking
at your pictures too. You were always so cute, you
Italian thing.

P.P.S. That doesn't necessarily mean anything.

"This is incredible," Boyce said. He'd been reading over my
shoulder. "She wouldn't speak in her oral exams? She sat there
in silence?"

"Yes, and what a woman she is!" I exclaimed, dropping into
savings for my three thousand bucks, full of hope and dreams
beyond reckoning, even by a Revelation 2000. A gigantic flashing jet was crossing the sky, coming in for a landing at San
Jose. I checked my watch. It was tomorrow morning, Green-
wich Mean Time. "Snookie's on that plane!" I cried, and with
my life's liquid assets wadded up in my hand, I dashed for
Boyce's Kodak Image and the golden future of knowledge and
love.

BIOGRAPHIES
and Some Comments by the Authors

Alice Adams: "I was born in Virginia, and grew up in Chapel Hill, North Carolina. In the course of writing my most recent novel, *A Southern Exposure*, which takes place in a similar town, during the thirties, I was thinking of Chapel Hill. I then read Susan Faludi's excellent piece on The Citadel in *The New Yorker*, and at around that time I heard some gossip about a couple who was reconciling—unwisely, it was generally felt. Thus all these elements came together in my head, and I wrote this story about a Citadel product, a man who would seem to have more than a little trouble with women."

Alison Baker is the author of two story collections, *How I Came West, and Why I Stayed* and *Loving Wanda Beaver*. She lives in southern Oregon.

"I usually work on two or three stories at a time, one of which I consider my main effort; the others are rest and recreation from, or receptacles for ideas and paragraphs that don't fit into, the story I'm paying most attention to.

" 'Convocation' was one of those secondary stories, into which I casually popped characters and situations that I couldn't squeeze into something else: a woman whose daughter is schizophrenic, a very short hairdresser, a bad haircut, a woman who is turning into a priest, and a couple of professors, one boring and one wacky. After spending a lot of time on the *other* story, I turned to this one to find that it had just about written itself. I rearranged some events, added a few connecting paragraphs, and dropped everything into a small college town, and there was 'Convoca-

tion.' It was a real treat; these self-writing stories are few and far between."

Frederick G. Dillen's first novel, *Hero,* was among the finalists for the 1994
National Book Critics Circle Award for Fiction, and is named the best first
novel of 1994 in the current edition of the *Dictionary of Literary Biography.*
As well as in *The Gettysburg Review,* Mr. Dillen has placed fiction and
essays in *The American Voice* and *The Santa Fe Review.* He is also a Past
Fellow of the O'Neill Playwrights Conference, and his screenplay of *Hero*
is under option.

    " 'Alice' is all about my mother in the life of our family, in my life, in
her own life."

Ellen Douglas lives in Jackson, Mississippi. She grew up and has lived all
her life in small towns in Louisiana, Arkansas, and Mississippi. She has
received two NEA fellowships and an award from the Fellowship of
Southern Writers for the body of her work. Her most recent novel, *Can't
Quit You, Baby,* was published by Atheneum and is presently in paper-
back from Viking Penguin. Earlier novels, *The Rock Cried Out* and *A Lifetime Burning,* have recently been reissued by LSU Press; and the University Press of Mississippi has reissued *Apostles of Light* and *Black Cloud,* a
collection of stories. She is presently at work on a group of stories, of
which "Grant" is one, about remembering and forgetting, lying and
truth-telling.

    "I think of a quotation from Robert Stone's 'The Reason for Stories'—
'We are forever cleaning up our act'—as an epigraph for 'Grant,' which is
about how we learn to live with our knowledge not only of our failures
but of our mortality."

Elizabeth Graver's story collection *Have You Seen Me?* (Ecco, 1993), was
awarded the 1991 Drue Heinz Literature Prize. Her stories have been
anthologized in *Prize Stories 1994: The O. Henry Awards* and *Best American
Short Stories 1991.* She teaches at Boston College and has recently completed a novel.

    "I wrote 'Between' after spending some time in Provincetown a few
summers ago. To me, it's partly a story about community—a subject I
think about a lot. The story explores how love and longing exist in blurry,
complex ways in the space between words like 'boyfriend' and 'roommate'; 'straight' and 'gay'; 'family,' 'friend' and 'lover'—words which
often over-define immensely complicated terrain."

Becky Hagenston: "I grew up in Maryland and have spent the past four years in Tucson, where I'm an M.F.A. candidate at the University of Arizona. My fiction has appeared in *The Crescent Review* and *Shenandoah.*

"Several summers ago I attended a wedding in New London, Connecticut. After the reception, everyone in the wedding party—including the Reverend—went down to the beach, stripped to their bathing suits or underwear, and threw themselves into the water. The image of the Reverend out there on the dock made such an impression on me that I decided to write a fictional story describing how these people may have gotten there."

William Hoffman is the author of ten published novels and three collections of stories. His fiction has appeared in *The Atlantic, Sewanee Review, Virginia Quarterly Review, Shenandoah,* and *Best American Short Stories,* as well as other magazines. He's received D.Litt. degrees from Hampden-Sydney College and Washington & Lee University and is a Virginia Cultural Laureate. He's a winner of the Dos Passos and Hillsdale prizes, both awarded for a body of work.

"While hunting birds, I came across a dilapidated mansion in the tangled wilds, the occasion which planted the seed which grew into 'Stones.' "

Lucy Honig: "My short stories have appeared in *Double Take, Glimmer Train, Witness, The Georgia Review,* and many other magazines. After five years as the director of a county human rights commission in upstate New York, I now teach writing in the graduate program in international health in Boston University's School of Public Health.

"I wrote this story after brooding for a long time about two incidents that happened in 1991 in a small city in New York state. A man bicycled around an intersection, warning his neighbors that police were nearby, and, in so doing, drew a small crowd, invoked the name of a well-known civil rights activist, and was arrested on charges of obstructing governmental administration, inciting a riot, unlawful assembly, and disorderly conduct. Four weeks later, the same man was killed in an unrelated fight with a small-time creep, who a grand jury did not indict. A muted ripple of community outrage quickly subsided.

"Something besides outrage kept gnawing at me, and eventually I started a story. 'Citizens Review' is that start."

Stephen King: "I was born in 1947, which now makes me forty-eight; if I were a bottle of port, I'd just be coming to a drinkable age. I've written about forty books—thirty-two or -three novels, one book of criticism, and perhaps six volumes of shorter fiction.

" 'The Man in the Black Suit' comes from a long New England tradition of stories which deal with meeting the devil in the woods ('Young Goodman Brown' by Hawthorne, for instance). Sometimes he's known as Scratch, sometimes as the Old Fella, sometimes as the Man in the Black Suit, but he always comes out of the woods—the uncharted regions—to test the human soul.

"When I write, I hardly ever see the point I was trying to make until I've finished, and that makes the second draft more interesting (to me, at least) than the first. In 'The Man in the Black Suit' I think I was writing about how the fear of evil is persistent, and how triumph over evil is, at best, temporary."

Leonard Kriegel is the author of seven books, the last a collection of personal essays, *Falling Into Life* (North Point, 1991). His essays and fiction have appeared in *Harper's, Partisan Review, Present Tense, Virginia Quarterly,* and *The Sewanee Review.* He has been the recipient of a Guggenheim Fellowship and his work has been included in *Best American Essays.* Recently, he was the recipient of The Kenyon Review Award for the essay. He lives in New York City and spends his winters on the South Carolina Coast.

"In a sense, it was writing the personal essay that sent me back to the short story. I hadn't written a story for more than twenty years and then, in the midst of a burst of writing one personal essay after the other— some of them painful, all of them intimate—a story simply took over my mind. I couldn't get back to writing essays until I could put the story down on paper. I sent that story to *Partisan Review,* where it was published in the fall of 1987. I've been writing stories ever since. For me, writing stories has become a way out of the self. Even autobiographical stories aren't as stressful as the personal essay. I suspect it has to do with the leeway writing fiction allows. 'Players' had its origins in an incident related to me by my friend Ed Quinn, during a semester he spent as a visiting professor at Berkeley. For me, the story is my own guarded tribute to the New York Irish, whom I've also written about in my memoir *Notes for the Two-Dollar Weekend,* as well as in a forthcoming essay in *The Sewanee Review,* 'Homage to Boss Flynn.' But 'Players' is not only a story about the Irish, it's also a story about the limitations of the academic life. I feel a certain sympathy for the way Charlie Dolan gives up an academic chair to return to a plebeian life in New York. And there's a lot more of me in Charlie than I thought there was when I wrote the story. At this point, I'm rather pleased by that."

Ralph Lombreglia is the author of the short story collections *Men Under Water* and *Make Me Work*. His fiction has appeared in *The Atlantic Monthly*, *The New Yorker*, *The Paris Review*, and other magazines.

"I was a fairly early wanderer in 'cyberspace,' and for years I thought about writing fiction that would incorporate E-mail and other bits of network life and lore. But I didn't want to impose digital theater–business on material that didn't require it, so I waited for the right characters and situations to arrive. Meanwhile, scraps of material—found, invented, donated—accumulated on my hard drives, loitering with intent but not much else. In the end, 'Somebody Up There Likes Me' was born when I resorted to the time-honored technique of commandeering the lives and personalities of one's friends. The piece also owes something to Terry Gilliam's film *Brazil*, with its fragile tone of unreality and the set-design and props that went into its portrayal of a future laden with inexplicable anachronisms and technological wrong turns. Finally, the story's anagrams and random sentences really were software-generated (by me), and the on-line 'fortune cookies' really were plucked from the vast smorgasbord of the Internet."

T. M. McNally is the author of *Low Flying Aircraft*, which received the Flannery O'Connor Award for Short Fiction, and a novel, *Until Your Heart Stops* (Villard, 1993). He lives in St. Louis.

"Lacy is the result of a particular moment—a girl with pale yellow hair, dressed in black, dancing wildly by herself—that became the emotional catalyst for my first novel, in which she appears as the girl who had been on 'Star Search.' I had hoped to draw on that energy which conveyed an unconditional love for the physical nature of this life: namely, gravity, and the thrill of resisting it by an act of will. Later, I began a story, and as Lacy's voice emerged, it eventually became clear to me that she was deeply afraid of becoming bad. In the depths, Rilke says, everything becomes law; the source of her fear belonged to her roots, in this case familial; and once I knew why she had been dancing by herself, it then became possible for me to discover precisely what she wanted. To survive, she would have to escape into the unknown. It's the kind of decision I like to think we were born to celebrate, if only because it always hurts to make."

Daniel Menaker worked at *The New Yorker* for twenty-six years, most of them as a senior editor, primarily of fiction. He is now Senior Literary Editor at Random House. His stories, journalism, and humor pieces have appeared in many magazines and newspapers, and he has had two story collections published—*Friends and Relations,* in 1976, and *The Old Left,* in 1986 (the title story of this collection won an O. Henry Award in 1984). He lives in Manhattan with his wife and two children.

" 'Influenza' is the fourth in a series of four stories, all of which have appeared in *The New Yorker.* I'm now at work trying to retrofit them into the first half of a novel whose second half I am also working on. This story and the others—and the book as a whole—are meant to be about how we come to be who we are through the influences of random chances including genetics, upbringing, relations with others, self-construction, etc."

Walter Mosley, whose blues novel *RL's Dream* was published last summer, was born and raised in Los Angeles and presently lives in New York City. He is the author of the popular Los Angeles–based novels starring the reluctant P. I. Easy Rawlins, including the upcoming *A Little Yellow Dog,* the *New York Times* bestseller *Black Betty, White Butterfly, Red Death,* and the first, now a film starring Denzel Washington, *Devil in a Blue Dress.* A two-time nominee for both the Edgar and Golden Globe Awards, Mosley is a member of the Executive Board of the PEN American Center, where he chairs the Open Book Committee, and of the Board of Directors of the National Book Awards.

"Why 'The Thief'? Poverty makes morality a tough issue, when every decision you make is based on day-to-day survival. Those moral decisions become even more difficult when you're hungry and a blind eye means a full belly. This is the motivation for much of Socrates' philosophy; it also motivates my stories concerning him."

Socrates Fortlow, the hero of "The Thief," will have an entire book of his tales published in 1997.

Joyce Carol Oates is the author most recently of the novel *Zombie* (Dutton) and the book-length monograph *George Bellows: American Artist* (Ecco). "Mark of Satan," included in this volume, has been reprinted in her recent collection of stories, *Will You Always Love Me?* Her fiction and essays have appeared in *The New Yorker, The Kenyon Review, Boulevard, The Paris Review,* and elsewhere.

" 'Mark of Satan' began with a vision of a rural setting—the forlorn house, the shimmering heat waves, bamboo growing wild and ragged in a marshy backyard. There's that eerie rustling sound of dried bamboo in the wind. I was thinking of the diminishment of the soul, at the point at which it veers toward extinction; and I wondered if we generate, out of our own desperation and terror of spiritual death, some sign of 'grace' to lead us back to life. In this story, the bearer of grace is a real person. To experience grace, we have to surrender irony; but—is it possible to surrender irony, entirely? What would take its place?

"Out of a mix of these elements, 'Mark of Satan' came quickly to be born."

Tom Paine is a graduate of Princeton University, and is the Ellis Fellow in Columbia University's M.F.A. Program in Creative Writing. His fiction has been published in *The New Yorker, Boston Review,* and elsewhere. He is an editor of *Columbia,* and a former journalist based in the Caribbean.

"There was a desire to drown a Republican. But like a cockroach, Eliot was not easy to kill off. There is a distinct separation between the writing soul and the social self. The writing soul feels, strongly, we are living in a corporate totalitarian state and staring one-eyed down the barrel of a fascist future. The end of communism has mutated into a generalized hatred of humanism, of creativity, of wild nature, of empathy for the unknown other; the worship of a lobotomized and rabid capitalism owned by the Bastards is the only given option. So the story was nurtured in a surprisingly homicidal revulsion and nausea. Some writer better create a new metaphysic soon, cobble together all the schisms of horror, mosaic a new sanity for life on this little old glowing globe.

"There was a desire to step into the ring with Hemingway, Conrad. Nobody can stop you from doing that sort of thing when you are alone at your desk. The goal was to tell an old-fashioned story: one with an unapologetic plot, one with characters identifiable without a telescope, one that didn't rival Sominex as a sleep aid. The story was plucked from the slush by Deb Garrison at *The New Yorker.* It was my first published story; a miracle. Deb polished it: line by line, paragraph by paragraph, hour after hour, fax after fax, day after day. *Merci beaucoup,* Deb."

Julie Schumacher is a graduate of Oberlin College and Cornell University and lives in St. Paul, Minnesota. Her novel, *The Body Is Water* (Soho Press), was published in 1995; her story "The Private Life of Robert Schumann" appeared in the 1990 edition of *Prize Stories: The O. Henry Awards.*

" 'Dummies' was originally a part of *The Body Is Water,* but it didn't quite fit inside the novel so I excised it, moved it to Ohio, and added a mentally retarded brother to give Bea and Alice a sense of doomed responsibility. The story seemed to lack focus until I wrote, 'Generally I have found that the future is useless.' The sentence worked like a bell, so that I suddenly understood what Alice felt: even infinite time and distance can't alter what she is experiencing right *now*—the present moment and its unhappiness will always exist. 'Dummies' is probably the most depressing story I've written.

"Several readers have asked me about Alice's final telephone call: I intended it as a moment of necessary betrayal, Alice overriding Bea's authority and informing her parents about Dan's deterioration. As for the Cornish hens, I have never been able to eat animal products that clearly betray their origins while on the table."

Akhil Sharma: "Between the first draft of 'If You Sing Like That for Me' (three pages long and told from a Jewish woman's point of view) to when it was published there was a full bachelor's degree, part of an M.F.A., and a stint as a screenplay writer. I started writing the story as a freshman in college and finished it in my senior year. Then I gave this and several stories to an agent who sent two of the stories out, once each, and stopped returning my calls. I sent the story out myself after a year in my M.F.A. program when I was getting increasingly depressed by the novel I was writing (which I am still writing) and what I perceived as growing and uncontrollable oddnesses in myself. I had put garbage bags over my windows to create the proper atmosphere and could be found at all hours lying on the strip of packing foam I used to sleep on, eating cupcakes and giggling to myself as I read 'Henry IV, Part Two.' I sent the story to five nationals and got prompt rejections from four and didn't hear from *The Atlantic Monthly.* In my paranoia I assumed that *The Atlantic* had kept the stamps from my SASE and thrown away the story. Bastards!

"Three months after the mass mailing, I got a letter, actually just a contract, saying, Sign at X and return. I called the woman who had agreed to be my agent (to gloat) and left a message with her secretary about the sale. She called back that same afternoon and asked for her commission. I, of course, refused.

"A year and a half after I signed the contract, 'If You Sing Like That for Me' was published. And now here I am, in law school, an O. Henry winner."

Jane Smiley is the author of nine books, including *A Thousand Acres* and *Moo*. Her stories have appeared in *The Atlantic Monthly, Playboy, McCalls,* and a variety of other publications. "The Life of the Body" was first published in a special fine-print edition by the Coffeehouse Press in Minneapolis, and then in *Antaeus.*

"My older daughter fell down the stairs and broke her collarbone when she was three. That close call was the form of this story, which I consider both my best and my strangest story. Usually, I cultivate a style of cool, somewhat humorous irony. This story makes me feel exposed and a little fragmented. I'm glad I was capable of such raw emotion once, but I'm also glad I don't do this sort of thing all the time."

David Wiegand is an arts and entertainment editor at the *San Francisco Chronicle,* where he also writes a weekly column on the Bay Area arts scene and is a frequent book critic.

"I wrote the first drafts of 'Buffalo Safety' a couple of years ago. It sat in a drawer for a while until a friend found it and liked it and I took another look at it. The fact that I didn't hate it entirely prompted me to think it might be worth a revision. I was fortunate to have objective feedback from two real heavyweights, Roger Angell and the guest editor of *Ploughshares,* Ann Beattie, during the writing process. This is my first published story.

"In writing the story, I was disturbed by how many people seem to adopt emotional wariness these days as a kind of survival technique: the unspoken theory of modern life too often seems to be, 'If I don't say hello now, I won't have to say good-bye later.' AIDS is one of the reasons we've perhaps become 'too safe,' but it isn't the only one. Sometimes I think the other reasons are just as sad."

AUTHORS IN
PRIZE STORIES:
THE O. HENRY AWARDS,
1967–1996

1967
Joyce Carol Oates
  (First Prize)
Donald Barthelme
Jonathan Strong
Jesse Hill Ford
Marvin Mudrick
Miriam Goldman
Josephine Jacobsen
James Buechler
John Updike
Ernest J. Finney
Diane Oliver
M. R. Kurtz
Conrad Knickerbocker
Robie Macauley
Allen Wheelis
Richard Yates

1968
Eudora Welty (First Prize)
E. M. Broner
Shlomo Katz
Calvin Kentfield
Nancy Hale
Gwen Gration
F. K. Franklin
Norma Klein
Brock Brower
Jay Neugeboren
James Baker Hall
David Stacton
Eldon Branda
John Updike
Paul Tyner
Marilyn Hattis
Joyce Carol Oates

1969

Bernard Malamud
(First Prize)
Joyce Carol Oates
John Barth
Nancy Huddleston Packer
Leo Litwak
Leonard Michaels
Anne Tyler
Evelyn Shefner
Eunice Luccock Corfman
Peter Taylor
Thomas Sterling
Michael Rubin
Grace Paley
Ben Maddow
Max Steele
H. L. Mountzoures
Susan Engberg

1970

Robert Hemenway
(First Prize)
William Eastlake
Norval Rindfleisch
Perdita Buchan
George Blake
Jonathan Strong
H. E. F. Donohue
James Salter
Bernard Malamud
Patricia Browning Griffith
Tom Cole
John Updike
David Grinstead
Nancy Willard
James Alan McPherson
Joyce Carol Oates

1971

Florence M. Hecht
(First Prize)
Guy A. Caldwell
Alice Adams
Reynolds Price
Julian Mazor
Evelyn Harter
Thomas Parker
Robert Inman
Josephine Jacobsen
Joyce Carol Oates
Eldridge Cleaver
Eleanor Ross Taylor
Philip L. Greene
Stephen Minot
Charles R. Larson
Leonard Michaels
Edward Hoagland

1972

John Batki (First Prize)
Joyce Carol Oates
Judith Rascoe
Mary Clearman
Starkey Flythe, Jr.
Brendan Gill
Anne Tyler
James Salter
Patricia Zelver
Elaine Gottlieb
Jack Matthews
Alice Adams
Rosellen Brown
Charles Edward Eaton
Margery Finn Brown
J. D. McClatchy
Herbert Gold
Donald Barthelme

1973

Joyce Carol Oates
(First Prize)
Bernard Malamud
Rosellen Brown
Patricia Zelver
James Alan McPherson
John Malone
Alice Adams
Judith Rascoe
Raymond Carver
Jane Mayhall
Diane Johnson
John Cheever
Josephine Jacobsen
David Shaber
Curt Johnson
Henry Bromell
Shirley Sikes
Randall Reid

1974

Renata Adler
(First Prize)
Robert Henson
Alice Adams
Richard Hill
Frederick Busch
John J. Clayton
John Gardner
James Alter
Blair Fuller
Robert Hemenway
Rolaine Hochstein
Peter Leach
Norma Klein
Guy Davenport
Raymond Carver

James Alan McPherson
William Eastlake

1975

Harold Brodkey (First Prize)
Cynthia Ozick (First Prize)
Alice Adams
Raymond Carver
Susannah McCorkle
Eve Shelnutt
Ann Arensberg
E. L. Doctorow
William Maxwell
Thomas M. Disch
Patricia Zelver
Linda Arking
James Alan McPherson
Russell Banks
John Updike
Jessie Schell
Ann Bayer
William Kotzwinkle

1976

Harold Brodkey (First Prize)
John Sayles
Alice Adams
Guy Davenport
Josephine Jacobsen
Patricia Griffith
John William Corrington
Helen Hudson
William Goyen
Ira Sadoff
Mark Helprin
Joyce Carol Oates
Jerry Bumpus
Tim O'Brien
Anita Shreve

John Berryman
Anne Halley
Rosellen Brown
H. E. Francis
John Updike

1977
Ella Leffland (First Prize)
Shirley Hazzard (First Prize)
Andrew Fetler
Sheila Ballantyne
Stephen Minot
Paul Theroux
Hollis Summers
Patricia Zelver
Charles Simmons
Mary Hedin
Alice Adams
Joanna Russ
Emily Arnold McCully
Laurie Colwin
John Sayles
Stephen Dixon
Susan Engberg
John Cheever

1978
Woody Allen (First Prize)
Mark Schorer
Robert Henson
Alice Adams
Max Apple
Susan Engberg
Blair Fuller
Joyce Carol Oates
Josephine Jacobsen
Tim O'Brien
Jessie Schell
John J. Clayton

Curt Leviant
Harold Brodkey
James Schevill
Edith Pearlman
Mark Helprin
Susan Fromberg Schaeffer

1979
Gordon Weaver (First Prize)
Henry Bromell
Julie Hecht
Lester Goldberg
Steve Heller
Fred Pfeil
Anne Leaton
Annabel Thomas
Thomas W. Molyneux
Joyce Carol Oates
Jonathan Baumbach
Patricia Zelver
Herbert Gold
Henry Van Dyke
Lee Smith
Anthony Caputi
Lynne Sharon Schwartz
Richard Yates
Mary Peterson
Thomas M. Disch
Alice Adams

1980
Saul Bellow (First Prize)
Nancy Hallinan
Leonard Michaels
Shirley Ann Taggart
Peter Taylor
Marilyn Krysl
Walter Sullivan
Daniel Asa Rose

Jayne Anne Phillips
Robert Dunn
Helen Chasin
T. Gertler
Ann Arensberg
Barry Targan
Stephanie Vaughn
Gail Godwin
Alice Adams
John L'Heureux
Andre Dubus
Ann Beattie
Millicent G. Dillon
Jean Stafford

1981
Cynthia Ozick (First Prize)
John Irving
James Tabor
Kay Boyle
Nancy Huddleston Packer
Lee Smith
Alice Adams
Tobias Wolff
Sandra Hollin Flowers
Alice Walker
Jack Matthews
Marian Novick
W. D. Wetherell
Joyce Carol Oates
Ivy Goodman
Barbara Reid
Annabel Thomas
John L'Heureux
Steve Stern
Annette T. Rottenberg
Paul Theroux

1982
Susan Kenney (First Prize)
Joseph McElroy
Ben Brooks
Jane Smiley
T. E. Holt
Nora Johnson
Kenneth Gewertz
Kate Wheeler
Stephen Dixon
Peter Taylor
Ivy Goodman
Michael Malone
Tim O'Brien
Joyce Carol Oates
Tobias Wolff
Florence Trefethen
David Carkett
Alice Adams

1983
Raymond Carver (First Prize)
Joyce Carol Oates
Wright Morris
Irvin Faust
Elizabeth Spencer
W. D. Wetherell
John Updike
Gloria Norris
Leigh Buchanan Bienen
David Jauss
Mary Gordon
Peter Meinke
William F. Van Wert
Elizabeth Benedict
Steven Schwartz
Linda Svendsen
Lynda Lloyd
Perri Klass

Gloria Whelan
David Plante

1984
Cynthia Ozick (First Prize)
Gloria Norris
Charles Dickinson
David Leavitt
Edith Pearlman
Alice Adams
Daniel Menaker
Lee K. Abbott, Jr.
Melissa Brown Pritchard
Bernard Malamud
Andrew Fetler
James Salter
Willis Johnson
Jonathan Baumbach
Donald Justice
Elizabeth Tallent
Perri Klass
Grace Paley
Helen Norris
Gordon Lish

1985
Jane Smiley (First Prize)
Stuart Dybek (First Prize)
Ann Beattie
Helen Norris
Susan Minot
Claude Koch
Wright Morris
Louise Erdrich
R. C. Hamilton
Joseph McElroy
Steve Heller
Ward Just
Tobias Wolff

Gloria Norris
Peter Cameron
Ilene Raymond
Eric Wilson
Joyce Carol Oates
Rolaine Hochstein
Josephine Jacobsen
John Updike

1986
Alice Walker (First Prize)
Stuart Dybek
Greg Johnson
John L'Heureux
Joyce R. Kornblatt
Ward Just
Peter Meinke
Bobbie Ann Mason
Merrill Joan Gerber
Gordon Lish
Peter Cameron
Alice Adams
Deborah Eisenberg
Anthony DiFranco
Jeanne Wilmot
Elizabeth Spencer
Irvin Faust
Stephanie Vaughn
Joyce Carol Oates

1987
Louise Erdrich (First Prize)
Joyce Johnson (First Prize)
Robert Boswell
Alice Adams
Stuart Dybek
James Lott
Donald Barthelme
Gina Berriault

Jim Pitzen
Richard Bausch
Millicent Dillon
Norman Lavers
Robert Taylor, Jr.
Helen Norris
Grace Paley
Lewis Horne
Warren Wallace
Joyce Carol Oates
Daniel Stern
Mary Robison

1988
Raymond Carver (First Prize)
Alice Adams
Andre Dubus
Elizabeth Spencer
Richard Currey
Shirley Hazzard
Joyce Carol Oates
Peter LaSalle
Joy Williams
Salvatore La Puma
Bobbie Anne Mason
Richard Plant
Ann Beattie
Jay Neugeboren
John Sayles
Sheila Kohler
Jane Smiley
Philip F. Deaver
Jonathan Baumbach
John Updike

1989
Ernest J. Finney (First Prize)
Joyce Carol Oates
Harriet Doerr

Jean Ross
Starkey Flythe, Jr.
Alice Adams
Frances Sherwood
Banning K. Lary
T. Coraghessan Boyle
Catherine Petroski
James Salter
David Foster Wallace
Susan Minot
Millicent Dillon
Charles Simmons
John Casey
Barbara Grizzuti Harrison
Rick Bass
Ellen Herman
Charles Dickinson

1990
Leo E. Litwak (First Prize)
Peter Matthiessen
Lore Segal
Joyce Carol Oates
Carolyn Osborn
James P. Blaylock
Jane Brown Gillette
Julie Schumacher
Joanne Greenberg
Alice Adams
T. Coraghessan Boyle
Marilyn Sides
David Michael Kaplan
Meredith Steinbach
Claudia Smith Brinson
Felicia Ackerman
Reginald McKnight
Bruce Fleming
Devon Jersild
Janice Eidus

1991
John Updike (First Prize)
Joyce Carol Oates
Sharon Sheehe Stark
T. Alan Broughton
Charles Baxter
Ursula K. Le Guin
Patricia Lear
Wayne Johnson
Perri Klass
Dennis McFarland
Helen Norris
Diane Levenberg
Charlotte Zoe Walker
Millicent Dillon
Ronald Sukenick
Alice Adams
Marly Swick
Martha Lacy Hall
Sylvia A. Watanabe
Thomas Fox Averill

1992
Cynthia Ozick (First Prize)
Lucy Honig
Tom McNeal
Amy Herrick
Murray Pomerance
Joyce Carol Oates
Mary Michael Wagner
Yolanda Barnes
David Long
Harriet Doerr
Perri Klass
Daniel Meltzer
Les Myers
Ken Chowder
Alice Adams
Frances Sherwood

Antonya Nelson
Millicent Dillon
Kent Nelson
Ann Packer
Kate Braverman

1993
Thom Jones (First Prize)
Andrea Lee
William F. Van Wert
Joyce Carol Oates
Charles Eastman
Cornelia Nixon
Rilla Askew
Antonya Nelson
John H. Richardson
Diane Levenberg
John Van Kirk
Alice Adams
Stephen Dixon
Lorrie Moore
Kate Wheeler
Peter Weltner
C. E. Poverman
Jennifer Egan
Charles Johnson
Linda Svendsen
Daniel Stern
Josephine Jacobsen
Steven Schwartz

1994
Alison Baker (First Prize)
John Rolfe Gardiner
Lorrie Moore
Stuart Dybek
Marlin Barton
Kelly Cherry
Elizabeth Cox

Terry Bain
Amy Bloom
Michael Fox
David McLean
Elizabeth Graver
Susan Starr Richards
Janice Eidus
Judith Ortiz Cofer
Mary Tannen
Dennis Trudell
Helen Fremont
Elizabeth Oness
Katherine L. Hester
Thomas E. Kennedy

1995
Cornelia Nixon (First Prize)
John J. Clayton
Elizabeth Hardwick
Padgett Powell
Alice Adams
Elliot Krieger
Peter Cameron
Allegra Goodman
Ellen Gilchrist
Joyce Carol Oates
Michael Byers
David Gates
Deborah Eisenberg
Bernard Cooper

Edward J. Delaney
Alison Baker
John Updike
Anne Whitney Pierce
Charles Baxter
Robin Bradford
Perri Klass

1996
Stephen King (First Prize)
Akhil Sharma
William Hoffman
T. M. McNally
Alison Baker
Joyce Carol Oates
Daniel Menaker
Lucy Honig
Alice Adams
Ellen Douglas
David Wiegand
Becky Hagenston
Julie Schumacher
Tom Paine
Jane Smiley
Walter Mosley
Elizabeth Graver
Leonard Kriegel
Frederick G. Dillen
Ralph Lombreglia

MAGAZINES CONSULTED

Agni, Boston University, Creative Writing Program, 236 Bay State Road, Boston, Mass. 02215

Alaska Quarterly Review, College of Arts and Sciences, 3211 Providence Drive, Anchorage, Ak. 99508

American Short Fiction, Parlin 108, Department of English, University of Texas, Austin, Tex. 78712-1164

Antaeus, 100 West Broad Street, Hopewell, N.J. 08525

Antietam Review, 7 West Franklin Street, Hagerstown, Md. 21740

The Antioch Review, P.O. Box 148, Yellow Springs, Oh. 45387

The Apalachee Quarterly, P.O. Box 20106, Tallahassee, Fla. 32316

Arizona Quarterly, University of Arizona, Tucson, Ariz. 85721

Ascent, P.O. Box 967, Urbana, Ill. 61801

The Atlantic Monthly, 745 Boylston Street, Boston, Mass. 02116

Boston Review, Department of Political Science, E53-407, Massachusetts Institute of Technology, Cambridge, Mass. 02139

Boulevard, P.O. Box 30386, Philadelphia, Pa. 19103

Buffalo Spree, 4511 Harlem Road, P.O. Box 38, Buffalo, N.Y. 14226

Buzz, 11835 W. Olympic Boulevard, Los Angeles, Calif. 90064

California Quarterly, 100 Sproul Hall, University of California, Davis, Calif. 95616

Canadian Fiction Magazine, P.O. Box 1061, Kingston, Ontario, Canada K71 4Y5

The Chariton Review, The Division of Language and Literature, Northeast Missouri State University, Kirksville, Mo. 63501

The Chattahoochee Review, DeKalb Community College, North Campus, 2101 Womack Road, Dunwoody, Ga. 30338-4497

Chelsea, P.O. Box 5880, Grand Central Station, New York, N.Y. 10163

Christopher Street, 28 West 25th Street, New York, N.Y. 10010

Cimarron Review, 205 Morill Hall, Oklahoma State University, Stillwater, Okla. 74078-0135

Clockwatch Review, Department of English, Illinois Wesleyan University, Bloomington, Ill. 61702

Colorado Review, 360 Eddy Building, Colorado State University, Fort Collins, Colo. 80523

Columbia, 404 Dodge Hall, Columbia University, New York, N.Y. 10027

Commentary, 165 East 56th Street, New York, N.Y. 10022

Confrontation, Department of English, C.W. Post College of Long Island University, Brookville, N.Y. 11548

The Cream City Review, University of Wisconsin-Milwaukee, P.O. Box 413, Milwaukee, Wis. 53201

Crescent Review, 1445 Old Town Road, Winston-Salem, N.C. 27106-3143

Crosscurrents, 2200 Glastonbury Rd., Westlake Village, Calif. 91361

Denver Quarterly, Department of English, University of Denver, Denver, Colo. 80210

Double Take, Center for Documentary Studies, Duke University, 1317 W. Pettigrew Street, Durham, N.C. 27705

Epoch, 251 Goldwin Smith Hall, Cornell University, Ithaca, N.Y. 14853-3201

Esquire, 1790 Broadway, New York, N.Y. 10019

Farmer's Market, P.O. Box 1272, Galesburg, Ill. 61402

Fiction, Department of English, The City College of New York, N.Y. 10031

Fiction International, Department of English, St. Lawrence University, Canton, N.Y. 13617

The Fiddlehead, UNB, P.O. Box 4400, Fredericton, New Brunswick, Canada, E3B 5A3

The Florida Review, Department of English, University of Central Florida, Orlando, Fla. 32816

Four Quarters, La Salle College, Philadelphia, Pa. 19141

Gentleman's Quarterly, 350 Madison Avenue, New York, N.Y. 10017

The Georgia Review, University of Georgia, Athens, Ga. 30602

The Gettysburg Review, Gettysburg College, Gettysburg, Pa. 17325-1491

Glimmer Train, 812 SW Washington Street, Suite 1205, Portland, Oreg. 97205-3216

Grain, Box 1154, Regina, Saskatchewan, Canada S4P 3B4

Grand Street, 131 Varick Street, #906, New York, N.Y. 10013

The Greensboro Review, Department of English, University of North Carolina, Greensboro, N.C. 27412

Harper's, 666 Broadway, New York, N.Y. 10012

Hawaii Review, Department of English, University of Hawaii, 1733 Donaghho Road, Honolulu, Ha. 96822

High Plains Literary Review, 180 Adams Street, Suite 250, Denver, Colo. 80206

The Hudson Review, 684 Park Avenue, New York, N.Y. 10021

Indiana Review, 316 N. Jordan, Bloomington, Ind. 47405

Iowa Review, 308 EPB, University of Iowa, Iowa City, Ia. 52242

Iowa Woman, P.O. Box 680, Iowa City, Ia. 52244-0680

The Journal, The Ohio State University Department of English, 164 W. 17th Avenue, Columbus, Oh. 43210

Kalliope, a Journal of Women's Art, Florida Community College at Jacksonville, 3939 Roosevelt Boulevard, Jacksonville, Fla. 32205-8989

Kansas Quarterly, Department of English, Denison Hall, Kansas State University, Manhattan, Kan. 66506-0703

The Kenyon Review, Kenyon College, Gambier, Oh. 43022

Kiosk, English Department, 306 Clemens Hall, SUNY at Buffalo, Buffalo, N.Y. 14260

Ladies' Home Journal, 100 Park Avenue, New York, N.Y. 10017

The Literary Review, Fairleigh Dickinson University, 285 Madison Ave., Madison, N.J. 07940

The Los Angeles Times Magazine, Times Mirror Square, Los Angeles, Calif. 90053

Manoa, English Department, University of Hawaii, Honolulu, Ha. 96822

The Massachusetts Review, Memorial Hall, University of Massachusetts, Amherst, Mass. 01002

Matrix, c.p. 100 Ste-Anne-de-Bellevue, Quebec, Canada H9X 3L4

McCall's, 110 Fifth Avenue, New York, N.Y. 10011

Michigan Quarterly Review, 3032 Rackham Building, University of Michigan, Ann Arbor, Mich. 48109

Mid-American Review, 106 Hanna Hall, Bowling Green State University, Bowling Green, Oh. 43403

Midstream, 110 East 59th Street, 4th Floor, New York, N.Y. 10022

The Missouri Review, 1507 Hillcrest Hall, University of Missouri, Columbia, Mo. 65211

Mother Jones, 731 Market Street, San Francisco, Calif. 94103

Nassau Review, Nassau Community College, One Education Drive, Garden City, N.Y. 11530-6793

New Directions, 80 Eighth Avenue, New York, N.Y. 10011

New England Review, Middlebury College, Middlebury, Vt. 05753

New Letters, University of Missouri-Kansas City, 5100 Rockhill Road, Kansas City, Mo. 64110

The New Renaissance, 9 Heath Road, Arlington, Mass. 02174

The New Yorker, 20 West 43rd Street, New York, N.Y. 10036

Nimrod, Arts and Humanities Council of Tulsa, 2210 S. Main Street, Tulsa, Okla. 74114

The North American Review, University of Northern Iowa, 1227 West 27th Street, Cedar Falls, Ia. 50614

North Atlantic Review, 15 Arbutus Lane, Stony Brook, N.Y. 11790-1408

North Dakota Quarterly, University of North Dakota, Grand Forks, N.D. 58202-7209

Northwest Review, 369 PLC, University of Oregon, Eugene, Oreg. 97403

The Ohio Review, Ellis Hall, Ohio University, Athens, Oh. 45701-2979

OMNI, 1965 Broadway, New York, N.Y. 10012

The Ontario Review, 9 Honey Brook Drive, Princeton, N.J. 08540

Other Voices, The University of Illinois at Chicago, Department of English (M/C 162), 601 South Morgan Street, Chicago, Ill. 60680-7120

Pangolin Papers, Box 241, Nordland, Wash. 98358

The Paris Review, Box S, 541 East 72nd Street, New York, N.Y. 10021

The Partisan Review, 236 Bay State Road, Boston, Mass. 02215

Playboy, 680 North Lake Shore Drive, Chicago, Ill. 60611

Ploughshares, Emerson College, 100 Beacon Street, Boston, Mass. 02116

Prairie Schooner, Andrews Hall, University of Nebraska, Lincoln, Neb. 68588

Puerto del Sol, College of Arts & Sciences, Box 3E, New Mexico State University, Las Cruces, N.M. 88003

Raritan, 31 Mine Street, New Brunswick, N.J. 08903

Redbook, 224 West 57th Street, New York, N.Y. 10019

Rio Grande Review, Hudspeth Hall, U.T.–El Paso, El Paso, Tex. 79968

River Oak Review, P.O. Box 3127, Oak Park, Ill. 60303

Sailing, 125 E. Main Street, P.O. Box 248, Port Washington, Wis. 53074

Salmagundi, Skidmore College, Saratoga Springs, N.Y. 12866

Santa Monica Review, Center for the Humanities at Santa Monica College, 1900 Pico Boulevard, Santa Monica, Calif. 90405

Science Fiction Age, P.O. Box 369, Damascus, Md. 20872

Sequoia, Storke Student Publications Building, Stanford, Calif. 94305

Seventeen, 850 Third Avenue, New York, N.Y. 10022

The Sewanee Review, University of the South, Sewanee, Tenn. 37375

Shenandoah, Box 722, Lexington, Va. 24405

Short Fiction by Women, Box 1276, Stuyvesant Station, New York, N.Y. 10009

Snake Nation Review, 110 #2 West Force Street, Valdosta, Ga. 31601

Sonora Review, Department of English, University of Arizona, Tucson, Ariz. 85721

So To Speak: A Feminist Journal of Language and Art, 4400 University Drive, George Mason University, Fairfax, Va. 22030

South Carolina Review, Department of English, Clemson University, Clemson, S.C. 29634-1503

South Dakota Review, Box 111, University Exchange, Vermillion, S.D. 57069

Southern Humanities Review, 9088 Haley Center, Auburn University, Auburn, Ala. 36849

The Southern Review, Drawer D, University Station, Baton Rouge, La. 70803

Southwest Review, Southern Methodist University, Dallas, Tex. 75275

Stories, Box Number 1467, East Arlington, Mass. 02174-0022

Story, 1507 Dana Avenue, Cincinnati, Oh. 45207

Story Quarterly, P.O. Box 1416, Northbrook, Ill. 60065

The Sun, 107 North Robertson Street, Chapel Hill, N.C. 27516

Tampa Review, Box 135F, University of Tampa, Tampa, Fla. 33606

The Threepenny Review, P.O. Box 9131, Berkeley, Calif. 94709

Tikkun, Institute of Labor and Mental Health, 5100 Leona Street, Oakland, Calif. 94619

TriQuarterly 2020 Ridge Avenue, Evanston, Ill. 60208

The Urbanite, Urban Legend Press, P.O. Box 4737, Davenport, Ia. 52808

Urbanus, P.O. Box 192561, San Francisco, Calif. 94119

The Village Voice Literary Supplement, 36 Cooper Square, New York, N.Y. 10003

Virginia, 24N Buckmarsh Street, P.O. Box 798, Berryville, Va. 22611

The Virginia Quarterly Review, University of Virginia, 1 West Range, Charlottesville, Va. 22903

Vogue, 350 Madison Avenue, New York, N.Y. 10017

Washington Review, Box 50132, Washington, D.C. 20091

Webster Review, Webster University, 470 E. Lockwood, Webster Groves, Mo. 63119

West Coast Review, Simon Fraser University, Burnaby, British Columbia, Canada V5A 1S6

Western Humanities Review, University of Utah, Salt Lake City, Ut. 84112

Whetstone, P.O. Box 1266, Barrington, Ill. 60011

Wind, RFD Route 1, Box 809K, Pikeville, Ky. 41501

Witness, Oakland Community College, Orchard Ridge Campus, 27055 Orchard Lake Rd., Farmington Hills, Mich. 48334

Yale Review, P.O. Box 208243, New Haven, Ct. 06520

Yankee, Main Street, Dublin, N.H. 03444

Zyzzyva, 41 Sutter Street, Suite 1400, San Francisco, Calif. 94104